The Terror of Tannery Lane

M.R.C. Kasasian was raised in Lancashire. He has had careers as varied as factory hand, wine waiter, veterinary assistant, fairground worker and dentist. He lives with his wife in Suffolk in the summer and in a village in Malta in the winter. He is the author of two previous historical mystery series, published by Head of Zeus, including the bestselling Gower Street Detective series.

Also by M.R.C. Kasasian

The Violet Thorn Mysteries

The Horror of Haglin House
The Montford Maniac
The Terror of Tannery Lane

M.R.C. KASASIAN

THE TERROR OF TANNERY LANE

CANELO

First published in the United Kingdom in 2026 by

Canelo, an imprint of
Canelo Digital Publishing Limited,
20 Vauxhall Bridge Road,
London SW1V 2SA
United Kingdom

A Penguin Random House Company
The authorised representative in the EEA is Dorling Kindersley Verlag GmbH.
Arnulfstr. 124, 80636 Munich, Germany

Copyright © M.R.C. Kasasian 2026

The moral right of M.R.C. Kasasian to be identified as the creator of this work has been asserted in accordance with the Copyright, Designs and Patents Act, 1988.
All rights reserved. No part of this publication may be reproduced or transmitted in any form or by any means, electronic or mechanical, including photocopy, recording, or any information storage and retrieval system, without permission in writing from the publisher.
No part of this book may be used or reproduced in any manner for the purpose of training artificial intelligence technologies or systems. In accordance with Article 4(3) of the DSM Directive 2019/790, Canelo expressly reserves this work from the text and data mining exception.

A CIP catalogue record for this book is available from the British Library.

Print ISBN 978 1 80436 906 7
Ebook ISBN 978 1 80436 909 8

This book is a work of fiction. Names, characters, businesses, organizations, places and events are either the product of the author's imagination or are used fictitiously. Any resemblance to actual persons, living or dead, events or locales is entirely coincidental.

Cover design by Sarah Whittaker

Printed and bound in Great Britain by Clays Ltd, Elcograf S.p.A.

Look for more great books at
www.canelo.co | www.dk.com

For Tiggy

1

FEAR AND DEATH IN THE NIGHT STORM

IT WAS a dark and stormy night. The teeming rain was lashed into my face by violent gusts of wind. My saturated coat hung heavy. It sagged and clung to my dress, which wrapped around my lower limbs.

I told you to wear your Aquascutum, I scolded myself, but I had never been adept at listening to my own advice.

Another gust and my umbrella blew inside out. 'Botheration.' One glance told me that the spokes had snapped. 'Blimmid thing.' Giving up trying to re-erect it, I rammed the mangled remains into a waterlogged bin of ashes. Doubtless both would be taken for scrap metal and rags. There were few things in that wintery autumn of '98 that somebody would not collect in the hope of scraping enough money together for food and shelter.

Hand on hat, water running down my sleeve, I paused under a lamppost at the kerb. The road that ran around the perimeter of Seraphim Square could have been mapped as a sizeable river and I was not convinced that my short calfskin boots would protect me nor that I would not be swept off my feet.

'May I help you over, little girl?' A man materialised at my side.

I could have corrected him that I was a mature woman and entitled to be addressed as *milady* but that would have been ungracious in the face of his gallantry.

The gaslight flickered wildly, throwing us into grotesque shadows, but the flame was not extinguished. 'That is kind of you.'

'Not at all.' The stranger tipped the brim of his bowler. 'I am going in that direction anyway.'

I hesitated. His face was muffled in a Balaclava helmet, as were many others in this inclement weather. He spoke well, though, and was attired respectably enough with his ebony cane and sodden Ascot coat, but I had nearly met death on more than one occasion at the hands of those who I had previously believed to be gentlemen.

'Do you think it is safe?'

'I have forded swollen rivers in Himalayan gorges.' The stranger raised his voice against a squall. 'This is a mere trickle in comparison.' He projected his elbow as if escorting me to dinner and, thus reassured, I slipped my arm through the triangular gap. 'Take my cane,' he proffered. 'It will give you extra support.' Gratefully I accepted. 'Ready?'

Looking at the dark, rushing stream, I was far from happy with my situation. However, there was not much choice. I had been visiting my friend, Hettie Granger, and stayed much longer than intended in hope that the storm would die down. Unfortunately it had worsened. She had offered me a couch in her studio but, when she was called out to visit a sick niece, I decided to take my chances. Hettie would be away until the morning so I could not return there and the prospect of a night in the open was not an enticing one. Besides which, I was almost home.

A light shone in the sitting room window of Break House on the other side of the road and across a wide pavement.

I took a deep breath. 'Ready.' And off the kerb we stepped. That was our first mistake. We had not taken account of the gutter that ran along the edge of the road and we found ourselves submerged, almost to my knees. 'Dalmatian,' I cursed. My boots filled immediately.

'Steady,' the gentleman said, and I was not sure if he was encouraging me to be careful or reprimanding me for my canine expletive. 'Slippery, these cobblestones.' He skidded a few inches sideways to illustrate the point and I braced myself against us both falling.

'We should get better purchase on the road,' I forecast. 'The stones have been tarred.'

'Good.' He stumbled out of the gutter, clutching my sleeve, and it occurred to me that, so far, it was I who was assisting him.

There had been letters in the *Montford Chronical* about the surface not being properly cambered but the problem was rather more serious now than the puddles about which they had complained. We were still about ankle deep, but the strength of the current was of more concern. Lower Montford would be flooded, and not for the first time, but I had never known the Uppers to be so badly affected.

'All this makes me think...' But I was never to find out what my companion thought, for he teetered and toppled, throwing me aside as he flung out his arms. I sat down, letting go of his cane and barking my knuckles in my efforts to save myself.

'Hell's tonsils,' I cursed and was about to remonstrate with the man for his clumsiness when I saw that he was floundering. He was almost up to his neck in the current and flailing as I watched in bewilderment. The water could not be more than six or eight inches deep or the pavement would have been swamped.

'I can't swim.'

I got to my knees and reached towards him.

'Take my hand.'

'I can't.'

His head submerged and, at last, I understood. A manhole cover must have been lifted off by the flooding and he had fallen into the open drain. I shuffled towards him, almost swept over by the strength of flow, and he bobbed up again, his hat floating rapidly downstream, disappearing as it left the gaslit area of the surface. Having nothing else of which to get hold, I grabbed his collar. His arm emerged and waved about.

'Keep kicking your feet,' I urged as his hand shot out and clutched at my left wrist. If he were to be washed away now, he would probably take me with him.

His other hand appeared and snatched at my hair. It hurt but that was of secondary interest. In his efforts to haul himself out, the stranger was pulling my head down and my face underwater.

I tried to hold my breath but the current was forcing water up my nose and down my throat. Letting go of his coat I tried to prise his fingers out of my hair, but they were tangled around a tress. With my free arm I managed to lift myself just enough for a breath before I was forced under again. Mercifully he released my hair and, choking, I lifted my head.

Up the stranger came again, struggling to heave himself out, pulling on my wrist and thrashing about frantically. Back he fell a second time, only his face above the surface now.

'Fear,' he croaked. 'They must be stopped.' A wave washed over him and he spluttered. 'Kill the prince.' Under he went but bobbed up, wheezing his words out. 'Fear... dressed as a woman. They must...'

He sank, ducking me again. I tried to pull him back, but he was too heavy and I found myself being dragged to the edge of the hole, my arm inside the drain up to my shoulder and the crown of my head hitting the rim. I could not hold my breath any longer. I tried to heave but he was bigger and heavier than I and there was a sharp pain in my hand. In the man's desperation for purchase he was biting me.

Is this it? Am I to die in a sewer?

Simultaneously the clenching on my hand and his grip on my wrist loosened and he let go. Up I went, gasping for breath. After inhaling I submerged once more, finding the curved edge of the manhole and feeling as deeply as I dared into it, but there was nothing solid and I knew that the man must have been swept away.

Edging backwards, I crawled through the torrent towards the far side. The gutter took me by surprise again and I fell, flailing in my attempts to regain my balance, already exhausted by my efforts and the cold. The instant I managed to get back on my knees I was knocked off them again and found myself being carried helplessly towards Angel Street. On this road, being narrower than the square and running downhill, the current, I knew, would be faster and more forceful. I clawed at the ground but there was nothing on which I could gain purchase.

'Come you here,' a familiar voice roared above the tumult and I felt the great hand of Agnust, my maid, gripping my forearm and heaving me up to deposit me on my feet under a gas lamp on the pavement.

'Splashin' about in puddles, makin' a show on yourself,' she scolded. 'What kind of behavin' way is that for a young lady of old breedin'?'

I coughed in an effort to clear my windpipe. 'There was a man.' I retched.

'Int there alway?' she asked grimly. 'And, where there's a man, there's trouble.'

'No, he...' I bent over, fighting for air. 'I can't...' I could not even say *breathe* but Agnust had me up in her arms and was turning me, holding me almost upside down to expel quantities of filthy water. 'He drowned... Fell down a drain.'

'Lord take his soul.' My maid uprighted me but did not put me down. 'You do need come inside before you join him.' With that, Agnust stooped, put her right arm under my legs, carried me to Break House and, like a new bride, over the threshold into the safety of my home.

2

A PIG IN A PIPE AND NEEDLE-BONES

GERRUND, MY MAN, had been about to go to bed but redressed hastily when he heard what had happened and joined us in my sitting room.

'That's a bad bite on your hand,' he informed me though I was all too aware of that. 'Nasty thing a human bite,' he assured me. 'Worse than a mongrel.'

'And near as bad as a dog,' Agnust contributed. 'Never you mind though.'

'I need some iodine,' I told Gerrund but my maid laughed knowingly.

'You dint want none on that. When e'er you have a bite, goose fat will set it right,' she chanted but her remedy held no appeal for me.

More conventionally, Gerrund fetched my medical chest and, under my instructions, cleaned the wound with a wad of gauze before pouring gentian violet onto a fresh pack, spilling hardly any of the dye on my best Persian rug.

I viewed the tooth marks in the back and palm of my hand. They showed quite clearly that the lower teeth were irregular and there was a gap between the upper incisors, and I hoped that I would not be permanently scarred with the pattern.

'Lucky he didn't drag you under,' Gerrund sympathised as he unwrapped a bandage, 'or you'd look even worse than you do now.'

'Dint you goo speakin' to her ladyship like tha'.' Agnust pumped herself up. 'She'll make a lovely corpse, she will.'

Encouraged by their words, I slopped upstairs. While Agnust ran my bath, I got out of my sopping clothes and into a dressing gown. It was a new woollen one and itched like a hair shirt.

Worn a lot of those, have you? Ruby Gibson, heroine of many of my stories and constant inhabitant of my brain, asked. She was good at sarcasm but had been of no use to me during my ordeal. *You have put me through worse.* That much was true. In one of her expeditions she had been attacked by ravenous baboons.

Gerrund had mixed me a hot toddy and left it on a tray in the corridor. It would not do for him to see me in nightwear even though it came to my knees.

'I have telephoned the police, milady,' he called through the door. 'They will search for the body in the morning.' Unsurprisingly I had not made a study of the town's drainage system but assumed that the unfortunate gentleman would have been swept down to the sewage farm on the edge of Lower Montford. The police were not keen to enter that area and then only in squads for the Lowers was a sprawling warren of slums ruled, it was said, by criminal gangs and – having ventured there a few times – I saw no reason to doubt it. 'I told them you would go there in the morning to make a statement – weather permitting.'

The elements did not look likely to oblige but I could do nothing about that. Gerrund heated a bowl of broth, so packed with beef and vegetables that it was almost a stew, but it was hot and comforting and I was glad of it.

It was my habit to end the day with a glass or two of absinthe chilled with iced water dripped through a sugar lump from a glass fountain, but I needed warmth and poured myself a very large Very Old Ben Nevis Malt, drawing my chair close to the flickering fire. Agnust had gone to bed, her prayers reaching me from her room on the first floor.

'Help Lady Violet to be more like me,' she bellowed, for she knew that she was vying with millions of others for God's attention. 'Make her see the error of her weariful wicked ways.'

I liked to think that I was not irredeemably dissolute but, according to my maid, I had been born sinful. Who else would come into the world with one eye blue and the other green? And why had I wilfully refused to grow to what she regarded as a respectable height?

Her prayers for Gerrund, who had a much shadier past than I, were brief, including an exhortation to help him be patient with me. There followed a long list of thanks for all the splendid qualities that God had bestowed upon her, and she bade him farewell, reminding Jesus to clean his teeth and get a good night's sleep.

I finished my drink, slid the guard in front of the fire and went to bed and a fitful sleep. Every time I closed my eyes I saw the terrified face of the drowning gentleman. Could I have done more to save him? If I had not let go of his cane, I might have been able to lay it across the manhole for him to hold. If I had shouted for help, Agnust might have come sooner. My father always told me that regrets are for the flowers that wilt and die. We Thorns are hard and sharp and regret nothing – yet another occasion when I wondered if I had been adopted. 'Who on earth would want to adopt you?' my mother had asked, and I tried to imagine that she meant her question kindly.

—

I woke early, my hand throbbing, propped myself up on my pillows and treated myself to a stick of Beeman's chewing gum, my first of the day. On my side table was a notepad in which I had intended to record any ideas for plots, characters or dialogue. It was filled, however, with random scribblings – *Ask Agnust to clear the cobwebs* – *Do not forget that Millicent Bowers has a club foot* – *What is the population of New Zealand?* – *Do not ask Agnust to clear the cobwebs. TELL her.* – *Ask Rommy if there is an antidote to curare*. Romulus was my second cousin and a doctor, and I had relied on him for information and medical assistance on more occasions than I cared to remember. I had only a hazy idea of who Millicent Bowers might be. Possibly I had planned to murder her in my yet-to-be-written *Death on the Deben/The Mountain of Fear/The Woman in Blue*. I had not even settled on a title, let alone a story.

On this morning, I jotted a few notes about the previous night's events. I did not need to refresh my memory but I was trying to organise my thoughts.

The rain had eased when I drew my curtains, but the clouds looked so heavy that it was a wonder they did not come crashing to the ground.

Gerrund had grilled two Yarmouth bloaters. They were not a favourite of mine. First, I had to search every mouthful to extract the myriad needle-bones which pervade their flesh, making it difficult for me to read over breakfast. Worse still, they had their heads on and I was not comfortable eating them while those white eyes, shrivelled in their sockets, watched my every move.

Crunching on a triangle of buttered toast I perused *The Chronic*, as the *Montford Chronical* was commonly known and uncommonly spelt.

DEADLY PLAGUE STRIKES MONTFORD, it blared. The flooding had led to an outbreak of cholera in the town, confirming my parents' belief that it was a place of pestilence. Many households still relied on public pumps for fresh water and some of these had been contaminated by overflowing sewage.

The hospitals were full and the morgue was filling, an editorial rumbled, and it was all the fault of one Arthur George Riddell, Bishop of the Dioceses of Northampton, which included Suffolk. During the long summer drought, he had prayed for rain but had failed to specify when and how much he wanted.

Our mains supply had been declared safe, but we were not convinced and Gerrund spent a great deal of his time locked in the kitchen, boiling water in his largest pots.

MAN WITH WOODEN LEG FINDS REAL LEG caught my eye. Apparently it was not his old leg, but he had come across one sawn off at the hip in the gutter in Poplar Lane. He had tried to sell it to the cat's meat man, who had rejected it as too decayed and handed it in at the police station. 'You could have knocked me down with an omnibus when it landed on my desk,' Sergeant Webb told their reporter.

Inspector Havelock Hefty, another of my characters, glanced up from his devilled kidneys. *In my experience legs usually come in pairs so what...* He rose to stand in the hearth. *Has happened to the other one? Also...* He rested his elbows on the mantlepiece. *What was the leg doing in the gutter in the first place?*

Rotting. Ruby was pouring herself an advocaat. *Eggs, sugar and brandy,* she explained to Scotland Yard's premier detective. *The perfect nutritional diet. Half a dozen of these should see me through to my champagne elevenses.*

The Suffolk Trumpet, never missing an opportunity to live up to its name and reputation, blared, *WILD MAN OF GORHAM STRIKES AGAIN*. And went on to claim that the bone had been gnawed and that a dentist had certified that the tooth marks were of human origin. I read on, 'This ogre roams the countryside, slaughtering innocent women and children at will and yet the police have made no attempt to capture him. A reliable source told our reporter that the Wild Man is in fact the idiot son of a member of our royal family who escaped from incarceration in Windsor Castle.'

Legend had it that the Wild Man lived in the fens, emerging to feast on human flesh. He had been sighted crawling out of bogs and creeping out of ditches by a number of reliable witnesses including an unnamed bishop, a party of schoolgirls from an anonymous school and Freda, the bearded lady, who lived off charity and gin on the pavement outside my front door.

I topped up my coffee. The silver pot had been a present from my parents and was nicely made, fluted and engraved all around with foliage, but I would rather have used a pottery jug which would retain the heat better. Agnust was insistent, though, that the daughter of an earl should only use the finest of tableware. Besides which, polishing it was one of the few chores that she enjoyed, probably because it was a task she could perform while seated.

The first post was propped in a brass rack, cast in complicated whirls of tangled weeds interspersed with the heads of animals, possibly hyenas. I had purchased it from pity in much the same way as one might take in an ugly puppy.

'Nothing obviously untoward,' Gerrund said as he brought it in. He had taken it upon himself to check the envelopes after I had received a number of threatening letters.

A number does not mean anything, Miss Kidd, my old governess, pointed out. I thought I had shut her out of my thoughts a long time ago, but, *My door is always open*, my brain declared and I resolved to consult a cranial locksmith.

As usual there were accounts from shops, mainly clothing. At Ruby's urging I had purchased a saffron gown. It was lovely on her but made me look jaundiced and I felt it as I perused the bill. I pushed the circulars aside, ignoring the opportunities offered for a correspondence course on how to amaze and entertain my friends with conjuring tricks or to build up my biceps.

The doorbell did not so much ring as make a raucous shriek – *loud enough to kill the dead*, as Agnust once described it. A few months ago, a man, bristling with screwdrivers, hammers and those scissor-plier things from a dozen pockets in a paint-splattered blue overall, had promised to replace it with one more sonorous. I had given him a small deposit which, in hindsight, was not very small at all. Needless to say he had yet to return.

Agnust, grumbling as usual, opened the door. 'Oh, it's you,' she said in much the same way as she might greet the cat's meat man, who had taken to calling weekly in the hope that I had acquired a pet.

'We'll make a detective of you yet.' I recognised the voice immediately, forsook the mangled corpse of my fish and went into the hall.

Alfred Stanbury, an old friend and an inspector in the Central Suffolk force, stood on the mat, wiping his feet vigorously. He had been scolded before for leaving a muddy footprint on what my maid referred to as her floor.

'Violet.' He shook his raincoat vigorously out of the doorway. 'I hear you had a narrow escape last night.'

'The gentleman with me was not so fortunate.' Since Agnust gave no sign of doing so, I hung his coat on a hook on the stand where it dripped onto the cast iron base. 'Will you take coffee?'

'Thank you.'

'Agnust,' I began.

'I'm not deaf,' she said, though she was when she wanted to be, which was often.

My visitor and I went into the sitting room and settled into my two William Morris armchairs overlooking the square.

'No body has emerged yet,' he told me when I had finished my account of the previous night's events.

We looked out over Seraphim Square, deserted except for a young couple splashing through the great medieval gate towards the monastery gardens. The rain had slowed to a drizzle and the river had quietened to a stream. Usually there were stalls selling models of the ruins or the shrine of Montford's patron saint, Aegbald. For those not tempted by religious mementoes, there were miniature blocks with *Marvellous Farthingale* engraved upon them. The escapologist had allowed himself to be manacled, shackled, blindfolded and encased in a block of concrete. More than a decade later he had still to emerge.

Agnust brought a tray.

'No feet on the table,' she told Alfred, though he was not in the habit of mistreating my furniture. She had known us both since we were children and, I suspected, still thought of us in those terms.

'I won't,' he promised, 'and I shan't stub my cigar out on it or spit on the floor.'

'Be sure you dint.' She lumbered out of the room.

'If my men could hear that I would never live it down,' Alfred chuckled before his face became more serious. 'How are you feeling now, Violet?'

'My hand is sore and my body a bit battered, but I am sure I will recover.' I did not mention that I had vomited twice in the night. It was not a ladylike activity and I had not engaged in it since losing track of the number of glasses of Liqueur des Pères Chartreux that Hettie and I had consumed after Sir Visto won the Derby by three quarters of a length. I poured our coffees. 'Before he was swept away, the man said something very odd.'

Alfred helped himself to milk. 'Which was?'

'He said that fear would kill the prince.'

The inspector's brow furrowed. 'He could have meant FEAR, the Free East Anglia Revolutionaries, but they are a few harmless cranks. The most anarchistic act they have committed so far was to pour vinegar into the mayor's milk bottles.' He took two lumps of sugar.

'He said that Fear would be dressed as a woman.'

Alfred snorted dismissively. 'In which case we just need to look for a lady with whiskers.'

'The man thought it was serious enough that he had to tell me when he was fighting for his life.'

Workmen arrived to replace two circular manhole covers in the road and Alfred stirred his coffee. 'I'll instruct my men to keep an eye out when His Highness comes next week, but I won't lose any sleep over it, and neither should you.'

I did lose sleep over the problem though. If the gentleman had used his last breaths to give me the information, I could not sit back and wait.

'There is nothing more you can do, milady,' Gerrund sought to reassure me.

'Typical man,' Agnust sniffed. 'There int nothin' milady can't do.' But, before I could bask in the sunshine of her praise, she added, 'if I set my mind to it.'

'You?' I queried.

'I find a solution to where your missin' shoe is when nobody else can,' she pointed out, omitting to mention that she had been using it as a doorstop. She clapped her hands together. 'If you stick a hatpin in his chest and he dint scream then you know he's a man.'

'But I can't go round stabbing everybody,' I objected.

'If you are determined to find him,' Gerrund said. 'There is one thing men have that women don't.'

'Conceit,' Agnust suggested and Gerrund rolled his eyes.

'I am talking about a physical thing.'

Steady on. Havelock Hefty rose into my consciousness but sank immediately below it.

It's the only way you can be sure, Ruby glided by, rather lovely in cerise.

That is my new dress, I objected.

Yes, she confirmed, *but it is wasted on you.* And, as she swept away, leaving a trail of cigarette smoke in her wake, I found myself unable to refute her claim.

My good friend Anthony Appleton came that evening, protected by a long oilskin coat and with a sou'wester tied in a large bow under his chin.

'Come you in,' Agnust was greeting him.

Anthony stepped out of his galoshes in rather a natty pair of white-topped half-brogues and slipped off his coat to reveal a bottle green jacket, canary yellow waistcoat and a blue polka dot cravat.

Agnust held out her hands for his outerwear with a fond smile. She had saved his life once and cradled his unconscious form.

I took his hand and turned my head for him to peck my cheek. Such louche behaviour with any other man to whom I was not related would have earned me a scolding from Agnust but Anthony, who could do little right in Alfred Stanbury's eyes, could do almost no wrong in hers.

'I came to see if you were all right.' He released my hand, unaware that Inspector Hefty was scrutinising a clue that he had found in Anthony's jacket pocket.

Clearly a hair from the beard of a wild Tibetan yak. He slipped his find into a brown pocket envelope, though it looked more like a strand of Whiskey Flake pipe tobacco to me.

'I am quite recovered, thank you.'

Anthony viewed me in concern. 'Recovered from what?'

'I assumed that you had heard.'

'I just came to check if your house had suffered any damage in the flood.' His eyes narrowed. 'What should I have heard?' His eyes widened. 'And what happened to your hand?'

'Come through.' I ushered him into my sitting room and, over a whisky and soda, explained everything.

'Oh my dear.' For a splinter of a moment I thought that this was an expression of affection, but he concluded with, 'Lord.'

For pity's sake, Thorn. Ruby swished in, a glass of pink Plymouth gin in one hand, a silver serpent cigarette holder in the other. *Just tell him how you feel.* But in truth I was not certain how I felt, or even if I felt anything. I had loved a man and he had betrayed me, returning only to betray me again. *Anthony is not like that.*

'How can I be sure?' I asked unintentionally aloud, and Anthony tugged an earlobe.

'Sure of what?'

'Anything,' I floundered.

'Who is?' He put down his glass. 'When I was young…'

'You still are.'

'Younger. I took an interest in philosophy until I came to the conclusion that it questioned everything but answered nothing.' He twisted the lobe clockwise. 'But thank heavens and Agnust you are all right.'

'I was very lucky.'

'To nearly drown?'

'To not drown.' I sampled my drink.

'Hallows Square.' Anthony twisted the lobe counter-clockwise.

'Now who is being enigmatic?' I squirted more soda into my malt.

'Sorry. I was just thinking.' He released the lobe, apparently satisfied that it was securely attached. 'When I came to Montford as a child, visiting my Aunt Perpetua, a pig managed to fall into a drain where the workmen were digging up the road.'

'I remember reading about that, but what of it?'

'It didn't get very far but it blocked the channel and the flow diverted it into…'

'Hallows Square,' I put in.

'Exactly.' Anthony tucked one hand into his trouser pocket, an act that would have put him firmly into my mother's NAG – Not a Gentleman – list. 'There was an old cesspit which had been connected to the sewage system and, as far as I know, there still is.'

'So you think the gentleman's body might have been washed into it?'

'It's a possibility.'

'I will tell the police.' I detected a slight frown. 'Sorry. Am I stealing your thunder?'

He shook his head. 'Not in the least. Inspector Stanbury would probably ignore the suggestion if I made it. Also…' He rotated a signet ring on his little finger. I had not seen that before.

The finger? Havelock Hefty puzzled. *He has always had it.*

The ring.

Anthony was still talking. 'I was just thinking, I believe part of the roof had caved in and so they concreted over it. My aunt will not be very happy if they have to dig up the square, so the suggestion is probably best coming from you.' He smiled wryly. 'You don't rely on her for an allowance.'

'When your play is a success, you will not need to depend on anyone,' I told him.

'Don't tell my aunt that,' Anthony said in mock alarm, for I had never even met the woman. 'She might believe you.'

We both knew that Anthony would not make his fortune with this production. *The Three Daggers Mystery* had not done well when it was first produced, and I was not convinced that it would fare any better now. The plot was tortuous and had been described by one reviewer as *a Gordian knot never satisfactorily untied* and another as *a splendid opportunity to catch up on lost sleep*. The pity of it was that my friend had been given the leading role, that of Jarvis De Hivernale, a detective who arrived at most of his solutions in dreams.

'How are the rehearsals going?'

'Half the cast are struggling to understand the plot.' He scratched his brow. 'The other half have given up.'

'And in which half are you?'

'I have moved effortlessly from the first to the second.' He drained his drink. 'I can only hope the dramatic scenes will carry it through.'

'If they do not, you will,' I strove to reassure him guiltily.

Guiltily, Hefty echoed. *Is that a confession, Lady Violet?*

Yes, I admitted, *I gave him the lead role in* The Devil Stalks the Strand.

And what an unqualified success that was, Ruby sarcasmed but I did not need reminding that the play had closed during its first performance.

'Anyway.' Anthony put his glass on the mantlepiece. 'I must be on my way. Final dress rehearsal today then Norwich tomorrow.'

'Are you sure you do not want me to come to the opening night?' I asked, secure in the knowledge that there were a great many seats still unsold.

'It would be too distracting.' He patted down his neatly macassared black hair. 'I would be looking for your reaction all the time.'

We went back into the hall. 'If you are sure…'

'I am.'

Agnust, who often failed to hear my bell, must have heard our quiet conversation for she came hurrying to take Anthony's coat from the hook.

'Had enough of her already?' she asked. 'Dint blame you. I have enough when she is born and she int improved since.'

'Unlike you,' he responded gallantly to my maid but ungallantly to me but, after a squeeze of my hand and a slightly lingering kiss on my cheek, I forgave him. I could never be angry with Anthony. Apart from anything else, he had fought to save my life twice and it was not his fault that he had not been very good at it.

3

MEPHISTOPHELES AND THE GREAT HEATHEN ARMY

THERE WAS BLOOD everywhere – I wrote, not the best of opening lines but it would have to do for now. – 'What do you make of that?' Inspector Havelock Hefty quizzed Miss Ruby Gibson.

One moment, Lady Violet. Hefty clambered out of a sulcus in my forebrain. *What in the name of all that is holy is that woman doing in my story?* He pronounced *woman* as if it were a species of vermin.

My story. Ruby floated off my limbic lobe. Heaven only knew what she had been doing there.

It is quite simple. I put down my Aikin, Lambert and Co Magic Pencil. *Ruby's admirers will buy the book because she is in it and Hefty's admirers…*

Of which there is only one – himself. Ruby poured herself a coupe of Veuve Clicquot. *Whereas mine are more numerous than the flaws in his investigations.* She put the bottle back in the ice bucket. *Besides which, I am a glamourous adventuress and do not play second fiddle to any man, especially a flatfooted blockhead like him.*

How dare you? Havelock Hefty jutted his full square jaw. *You, Miss Gibson, are a frivolous amateur whereas I am Scotland Yard's premier detective.* He tucked his thumbs into his waistcoat pockets. *Women are all very well for being rescued or selflessly sacrificing their lives to save mine, but I would never ask the advice of any feather-brained female.*

The only advice I will give you is to take a swim in the sea at Sackwater, where you will be dragged under the waves by the weight of your colossal ego.

'Stop squabbling,' I said aloud. 'Or I shall kill you both off at the end.'

Even I was shocked by that threat but, for one wonderful moment, they fell silent and peace reigned throughout my head – until I picked up my pencil again.

'I hardly know what to make of it, Inspector,' Ruby admitted.

'But you are such an intelligent woman.'

What? Two voices bayed. And the clamour of my characters choking in indignation was only silenced by the ripping of a page from my moss green notebook, the crumpling of unlined paper and the soft sounds of it bouncing off the edge of my blue metal wastepaper basket and onto my Armenian rug.

This was hopeless. I had written nothing for months and, to heap despondency onto my melancholia, neither my agent nor my publishers had pressed me to produce anything.

All that aside, it was difficult to compete with *The Chronic*'s account that morning of more sightings of the Wild Man, this time in Stolham St Ernest where he had been seen, glowering in through a widow's window, clawing at the glass, salivating and frothing horribly, only driven away by the bulldog her son had bought for her protection.

There was a tap on the door. Servants do not knock as a rule but both of mine knew that I did not care to be disturbed while I was trying to work. Only fifty per cent of them paid any attention to that rule though and, in response to my response, he entered my study.

'It is nearly half past, milady,' Gerrund announced.

What is nearly half what past what? Hefty, unheard by my man, interrogated him. *I must caution you that I find your silence on the matter highly suspicious.*

'Thank you Gerrund.' I closed my notebook, having written minus two hundred and thirty words that morning.

There is a real-life murder to prevent, I told my characters.

Ruby polished off her champagne. *It cannot be any more real than my life.*

Hefty sprang into action. *I shall fetch my revolver.*

You will both stay here, I told them. *A man's life may be at stake and I do not need any distractions.*

In which case I shall open another bottle. Ruby Gibson vanished.

And I have a more pressing case to attend. Inspector Hefty evaporated and I wished that I could do that. It was much quicker than using the stairs.

-

The rain had stopped three days ago and the drains had carried most of the water away, but there was still no trace of the man who I had seen drown. Many of our sewers were old, some dating back to the medieval monastery that once dominated our town. Newer channels had been constructed on an ad hoc basis, I was informed, so it was possible that his body had lodged in an ancient cul-de-sac.

'I expect she imagined him,' I had heard Inspector Goodman say as I was quitting Montford police station.

I will have you know, Lady Violet has no imagination, Hefty had defended me staunchly though some fickleness might have been less insulting.

It was a bright but chilly morning as we stepped out into Seraphim Square and, unusually for a Monday – because Wednesday is market day – the whole town was bustling. Half the gigs, growlers and hansoms of East Anglia were jostling for space where there was none to be had. This was the first visit to our town by a royal personage since King Edmund had passed through on his way to meet two things – the Great Heathen Army and his death.

The main thoroughfares had been closed to allow the prince's carriage easy access, but the side lanes and alleys were not designed for the flow of the traffic that they were experiencing that day.

Like most people we went on foot. Gerrund – very smart in his Prussian blue suit, bowler and Ascot overcoat – was using his bulk to open a channel but it was hard going to follow in his wake. Always looking for something to liven his humdrum existence, he had taken no persuasion to join us. Agnust – shorter than he but of greater circumference – was bringing up the rear. She was in her half-day charcoal. The Pre-Markian sect, of which she was a devoted member, did not approve of colours, especially the scarlet I had donned that morning. Agnust had insisted on coming with us, reminding me how I would have met a fate worse than death and then death itself had it not been for her intervention three years previously.

'Someone do need keep an eye on you,' she had told me, 'and, when it's a man, it's alway for the wrong reason.'

I had not seen so many pedestrians since Professor Caver Badfield had launched himself and his trusty stallion in a giant rocket bound for the moon. There had been an enormous explosion, creating a crater which had yet to be uncreated in the Priory Gardens. The coroner had adjudged that the occupants had been splattered over much of the town but *The Chronic* published reliable sightings – complete with an artist's impressions – of Badfield galloping over the lunar surface in pursuit of those gazelle-like creatures who inhabit the extinct volcanoes. I had inherited a telescope from a previous occupant of Break House, but it cannot have been powerful enough for I had never spotted the professor.

'People are not going to like it,' I mithered but, ignoring my concerns, Agnust began to pull me through the melee.

'They will like it a great deal less if we fail, milady,' Gerrund reasoned as we battled through to Market Square, hanging on to each other to avoid being separated.

At twenty-eight I was too old to be holding my maid's hand but old enough for holding my man's hand to create a scandal in most eyes.

'This is so undignified.' My hat had been knocked forward over my eyes.

'You have plenty of times to be dignityed in your grave,' Agnust forecast cheerfully.

Believe me you will not, Ruby assured me, for I had locked her in a coffin in one of her escapades and she had not found it to be a decorous experience.

'Move.' Agnust jabbed a plump gentleman in the ribs with her black umbrella and he stepped aside.

'Do you think you will be needing that?' I had asked when we set off, for there was not a cloud in the sky.

'Could turn coarse,' – which in Suffolk meant *stormy* – she had forecast.

There was only a light breeze and hardly a cloud in the sky, but I suspected that I knew what Agnust had meant.

'I shall feel foolish,' I predicted.

'You do worse,' my maid reminded me, and I was only grateful that she had not mentioned the time that I met Princess Beatrice. 'Like the time you meet Princess...'

'Do not remind me,' I squirmed. 'I only hope that you are right.'

'Do I ever be wrong?' she demanded.

Well... Inspector Hefty brought out his notebook. 'On August the fourteenth...' but Agnust was never one to listen, especially to what only I could hear.

We came to a halt. The square had been roped off to avoid a crush, thereby creating one in all the approaches. A brawny policeman guarded the entrance.

'Goh a pass?' he demanded, and I recognised him as Constable Collins.

Gerrund brought out his wallet.

'There you are, officer.' He slipped the constable a ten-shilling note and I had no doubt that I would be held liable for that expenditure.

'Well thank you very much.' Collins beamed but did not budge.

'Here,' Gerrund said indignantly. 'That's not how it works.'

'It is today, brod,' the policeman assured him serenely, a *brod* being a good old Suffolk boy, which Gerrund was certainly not.

'This lady's father is Lord Thetbury,' Gerrund tried but the constable shrugged and said, 'Should've get you a pass then.' He slipped the note into a pocketbook.

Why didn't he give you one? Ruby enquired, blowing smoke in Collins's eyes and, somewhat to my surprise, he blinked.

My father is not supposed to know we are here, I explained before remembering that she was not supposed to be there either.

Agnust sidled up. 'Surely you can make an exception, officer.' And she fluttered her eyelashes, reminding me – and probably him – of an Aberdeen Angus with grit in its eyes.

'Course I can,' he agreed amiably, 'but I wint.'

Let them through this instant, constable, Inspector Hefty barked, but he had no jurisdiction off the printed page.

I squeezed through.

'Good morning, Constable Collins,' I greeted him cheerfully.

'Marnin' Lady Violet.' He nodded amiably. 'Int allowed to let nobody else in now I do be afeared.'

'Oh, but Constable Collins.' I smiled what I hoped was sweetly. 'We all do things that are not allowed.' I lowered my voice. 'As I am confident you can vouch.'

'Wha'?' He scratched at a miniature cauliflower growing on the tip of his nose.

'But do not worry,' I reassured him. 'Your secret is safe with me.'

I knew little about the officer and certainly nothing that could harm his career, but his cheek muscles bunched briefly before he muttered, 'Be sure it is,' and stepped aside.

'Hang on,' a young man in rather a flashy red-and-yellow-striped blazer objected. 'Why are they allowed in?'

'Do you have a pass?' I enquired sternly as the three of us went through.

'No, but I didn't see yours.'

'It is not you who needs to see it,' I told him, and Collins closed the gap.

The crowd stood six or seven deep on the pavement surrounding Market Square, soon to be renamed Victoria Square in honour of our podgy monarch. Suffolk was usually at least a decade behind London in fashion and twice that in public works, as the cholera outbreak had demonstrated. In having this ceremony, however, we were a mere seventeen months late for the diamond jubilee. This, my father had explained, was because the royal diary was chockablock with appointments for loyal subjects anxious to express their devotion to the queen empress. Montford was not a large town and probably only received a visit at all because it was en route for Newmarket, a favourite venue of the prince's even though the racing season had ended.

From where we stood, we had a splendid view of backs, bobbing bonnets and towering toppers.

'We need to get to the front,' I reminded my companions.

'Easier said than done.' Gerrund grimaced for, being fifteen inches taller than I, he had a much better view of the obstructions.

'I will take this side,' I continued. 'You, Gerrund, can go to the left and you, Agnust, to the right.'

'That way,' Gerrund goaded her because she had got confused when we planned it on a map.

I'll come with you, Lady Violet, Hefty assured me loyally.

I wonder if Millie's Milliners is open, Ruby mused, disloyally.

Go away, I told them both.

'Good luck,' I said, and we were off, Agnust and Gerrund using their bulks and leaving me facing a wall of people's backs. 'Excuse me,' I tried.

'Crod off,' an unkindly old gentleman snapped. 'I queued for an hour to get here.'

'Let her through,' a woman who was presumably fortunate enough to be his wife scolded. 'She's only a child.'

I bridled at this but did not correct her. There had to be some advantages to being small and fresh-faced and I could do with a bit of cooperation if I wasn't going to be stranded.

'Thank you so much,' I said as he shuffled a few reluctant inches to one side. 'That could not have been easy, burdened as you are with your odious manner.'

'I am odious,' he agreed in tragic tones. 'The trouble is soap doesn't work on me.'

Sadly I had not the time to recommend an effective toiletry nor a good dictionary and went about my way.

Gerrund, despite his size, was lost from view but I caught sight of Agnust trawling through the human ocean while I struggled not to drown in it. I squeezed through another gap between two caped nurses, hoping that we would not be needing their assistance in the near future.

By the time I made it to the barrier Agnust was thirty feet away, brushing people and their objections aside and scrutinising them through hands held to her eyes like binoculars.

I turned left and a middle-aged woman brayed with excitement. The royal carriage was approaching at a stately glide from what was soon to be Prince Albert Street. It was a landau drawn by two white horses, the top folded back so that we might be granted sight of HOM, His Obese Majesty, as Ruby had dubbed him. The Prince of Wales bulged inside a colonel's uniform bedecked with medals and ribbons all, doubtless, earned on the battlefield. His lazy, puffy eyes hardly troubled to survey his surroundings but the tall man in a grey frock coat beside him was scrutinising the crowds intently. Unusually a board had been affixed at the back of the carriage and two other men stood upon it, equally alert. It would appear that they too had received some kind of warning.

Our future king had a reputation for keeping people waiting. It was said that a band had had to play the national anthem fifteen times while waiting for Edward to disembark from the royal train at Aberdeen once. Today, however, unless the town clock was fast, he was eighteen minutes early.

'Blimmit,' I breathed and twisted my neck to look at the woman's.

There was no problem there. She was right against the rope, though, and obviously not intending to give up her prime position, so I worked my way behind her.

A young couple were next.

Look out! Inspector Hefty yelled. *She has a bomb in that blanket.*

It is a baby, I told him to Ruby's derision.

The woman was holding her child up as if he would appreciate the honour that was being disposed on us. She too looked genuine.

It was easier to pass between two women, I discovered for, unsurprisingly, a flowing dress had much more give than a pair of trousers. Also, women were more likely to make way, if only to avoid having their finery damaged, whereas some men moved closer, pressing themselves against me as I tried to brush past.

Three men in crumpled gaberdine coats came next and I recognised one as a clerk at the Fynce and Drove Bank. The next woman looked decidedly dodgy. Unlike everybody else I had seen, her face did not exude happy anticipation. If anything, she looked bored to tears. She was tall and heavily built. It would have caused a stir if she had tried to force her way in front of the others, so she had probably waited a long time to claim a ringside spot and I had a suspicion that I knew why. I edged next to her. Unfortunately, she was well wrapped up but Ruby Gibson, Extraordinary Investigator, would not have worried about being embarrassed and neither would I. I went up and tugged at her raincoat collar.

'Here!' she cried, suddenly animated. 'What's your game?'

'Golf,' I said brightly, though I had never been on a course except to caddy once for my father when he gave me thruppence for treading his opponent's ball into the mud.

I hurried on.

There was a group of girls next, and I worked my way through them quickly. They were much too young for me to worry about and the two women teachers with them were mercifully scarfless with open coats.

'Get out of their way, you big bully,' one scolded me and I treasured the word *big*.

'I am sorry,' I fought my way through, 'but I have lost my...' Would they believe *daughter*? 'Little sister,' I hit upon, my anxiety all too obvious.

'Oh dear. I do hope you find her.'

'So do I,' I shuddered. 'She is blind.'

I did not know why I added that last detail. Ruby had warned me about my tendency to overegg my stories.

Keep it simple, she had advised after I had told a journalist that my mother had been eaten by Fijian cannibals four years ago and then had to explain why I had said that the pendant I was wearing was a present from her last Christmas.

The next woman appeared to be on her own. She was waving a Union Jack enthusiastically on a stick in her left hand – was that to leave the right hand free? I decided on a different approach.

'Excuse me.' I took hold of the middle of her tartan woollen scarf. 'I think I saw a wasp.' I pulled it down and was just about to say *My mistake* when she screamed, 'A vasp!' Then something like, 'Highly Ger hod and sack.' So much for my German lessons.

'My mistake,' I tried to reassure her, but she was hurriedly unbuttoning her long brown coat.

'It goo down your bodice,' the farming boy next to her in his Sunday best leered.

I did not wait to see whether she believed him or not but hurried on, working my way to and round the corner.

The carriage stopped in the centre of the square beside the flag-draped statue of his mummy that Prince Edward was there to unveil.

Bother-bother-botheration.

A dozen yards away I spotted Agnust, making steady progress, and just past her on the other side of the rope were the tiered seats occupied by those too great and good to mingle with the hoi polloi but not quite great or good enough to greet His Royal Corpulence. Squire Crow sat at the front with his unnecessarily large family. Having appeared before him, I recognised Mr Wellowes, the magistrate, but not the round-headed man behind him, and there was a sprinkling of clergymen, some of whom I knew at least by sight. I was not sure how Mr Tomlins, the ironmonger, had inveigled his way into the group but perhaps he was there because his young wife was constructed in a way that might appeal to our illustrious visitor's discerning eye.

My father, Lord Thetbury, stood to attention near the sandstone pedestal, looking very smart in his colonel of the old West Suffolk Militia uniform. He had actually earned the medals proudly pinned to his chest – well some of them at any rate.

I was only about a third of the way along my side when I caught sight of Gerrund making stately progress while Agnust appeared to be wrestling with Daisy Dixon, the Diamond Queen, who often played the ukulele and sang in Seraphim Square.

A cheer swelled up from all around and I glanced over to see that the two men had got down from their perches and were approaching the doors of the landau. This was hopeless. Agnust had reached an old lady in a pastel coat, skipping excitedly on the spot, and I was just edging on when I saw my maid brandishing her umbrella like a sabre and smashing it down onto the lady's floral bonnet.

I couldn't hear the impact above the brass band that had started up on the central platform and the 'God save our Royal Queen,' roaring from thousands of loyal throats but the old lady crumpled, falling forward onto the rope and slumping on the cobbles, her bonnet coming adrift. A police sergeant had his back to them, facing his monarch, but he must have heard or seen something because he turned. A bear of a man was trying to pinion Agnust's arms but my maid shrugged him off as if he were a toddler. She was even stronger than you would expect from her muscular build. Gerrund had beaten her when, indignant at some jibe of his, she had challenged him to an arm-wrestling contest, but I noted that he had declined her offer of a return match.

The attendant waiting to help the prince out must have seen the commotion too because he spoke urgently to His Royal Highness and smartly closed the door. His right hand went under his jacket and I did not think that he was reaching for his cigarette case. It stayed there while he scanned the scene. The other two men rushed to guard the vehicle and there was a confused buzz all around.

Agnust ducked under the rope and stood straight, a revolver in her hand. The bodyguards whipped out theirs and I had no doubt who would come off worse in a shooting contest, but my father had got into their line of fire as he raced over, ceremonial sword at the ready. My heart filled with pride. No longer a young man and with a battle-damaged shoulder, my father did not hesitate to tackle what could have been a professional assassin for he was not wearing his eyeglasses, believing them to be unmilitary.

Amidst the yells and screams, most of the public were trying to back off. A scrawny vicar cried, 'Get out of my way, idiot child,' and pushed a little girl over in his panic.

'It is all right,' Agnust shouted, and I saw that she was holding the gun by its barrel and bending to place it on the ground.

'You?' my father called in confusion.

I broke through and ran across to them.

'What the blazes are you doing?' my father challenged the maid he had foisted upon me.

'She kill this lady,' a woman shrieked.

'Murdered,' her neighbour corrected her, presumably because *killed* did not sound dramatic enough.

'She's still alive,' Agnust asserted – regretfully, I thought – and plonked her massive fists on her even more massive hips.

'What in the name of Mephostipheles?' my father demanded and I was quite impressed that, in all the confusion, he got most of that demon's syllables in the correct order.

One of the men appeared behind us and put his gun to the back of my maid's head.

'Get on your knees,' he commanded.

'Kneel not upon the ground,' my maid recited from, I suspected, one of her religious meetings, 'for serpents crawl upon it and demons dwell below.'

'But you attacked this lady,' he reasoned, clearly rattled by her serenity.

'A lady do as a lady do,' she declared and, though her statement baffled him, I almost quarter-knew what she meant.

'What?' my father demanded, having had more than enough of her at the family seat of Thetbury Hall.

It must have taken him an age to wax those moustaches so symmetrically. Normally he let them droop, but a nobleman should try to look his best for his future monarch.

'I'll show you,' Agnust promised but three guns defied her to take another step.

'If you dint believe me, believe your daughter,' she urged.

'Violetta?' my father watched in confusion as I moved towards the unconscious figure.

'Are you sure?' I checked.

'Sure as six pennies is sevenpence halfpenny,' she asserted.

'Stop right there.' One of the bodyguards with short ginger hair stepped towards me, gun aimed warningly as I crouched.

'I'm not armed.' I showed him my empty hands.

'What in heaven's name is going on?' my father demanded.

'This person is a member of FEAR,' I announced.

'We had heard there were threats,' the ginger man admitted. 'Did you spot her gun?'

'No I dint,' Agnust admitted unwisely. 'It do be my revolver.'

'So how did you know it was her?' he puzzled.

'Her?' my maid chuckled and tipped her head towards me. 'Kindly make an explanation, Lady Violet.'

A title often comes in handy when people in authority are pointing guns at one, for everybody knows that a lady is above suspicion. It was said that a certain countess had been apprehended, splattered in gore, in Whitechapel in the midst of Jack the Ripper's fourteen murders but released the moment that she had proved her identity.

'Let me ask you something,' I said to my father as if I, and not Gerrund, had come up with the method. 'Have you ever seen an Adam's apple like that on a woman?'

Where is Gerrund? Ruby appeared at my side in an ermine hat and I hoped that she had not charged it to my account.

My father leaned over the crumpled form.

'Well...' he began uncertainly.

'How on earth did you knock her out with that?' a hook-nosed bodyguard asked, and Agnust handed him her umbrella. 'By Jove, it's heavy.'

He returned it.

'Filled with lead,' she explained.

'Good Lord!' the man with the gun lowered his weapon.

'Still looks like a woman to me,' my father marvelled.

'Escept he wear a wig.' Agnust poked the ferrule of her umbrella under the crushed bonnet, which fell aside, but the hair remained firmly attached to the lady. 'Oh,' Agnust breathed in dismay.

The unconscious form stirred.

'Oh indeed,' my father said grimly as the woman struggled to get onto her elbows.

'Let me help you.' Agnust crouched at the woman's side and I could not catch what my maid said next, partly because she was speaking in a low voice but mainly because at that moment there was a bang and, whatever Grantham Hogarth might write in his awful Hydrangea Devine stories, shots are not bells. They do not ring out. They explode and, sometimes, they ricochet, and this was one of those occasions.

4

FINDING FINGERS AND PICKING UP TOES

UNLIKE MOST officers I had come across, Inspector Stanbury did not confuse good policework with disorganisation. His colleagues' offices were usually strewn with documents waiting to be read, filled in or disposed of or filed, remnants of snacks or apparently random pieces of evidence. I had once found a mechanic's finger looking like it had been stubbed out with all the cigarette butts in an ashtray in Sergeant Gorbals's room. He had tried to pretend that he was using the ash as a preservative, but his excuse was even less convincing when my attention was drawn by Havelock Hefty to a severed toe in the coal skuttle.

Despite the sunshine the gas mantles were fully on for the only natural light came through a skylight and was filtered by fallen horse chestnut leaves glued to the glass with bird droppings. The side window had been boarded over following a suspect's attempt to escape through it.

'I am surprised at you, Agnust.' Alfred folded his arms sternly.

I had not realised that he held my maid in such high esteem or, indeed, in any esteem at all. After all, it was Agnust who had forced him to drink a jug of lemonade after he had substituted salt for sugar on April Fool's Day, though that was over twenty years ago.

Alfred lowered his head to peer at me over his half-rimmed wire-framed reading glasses. My maid and I had not been offered chairs and so the three of us stood in the middle of the room.

'Lady Violet have reliable information,' she protested.

'So reliable that you beat an innocent old lady unconscious,' he pointed out and his finger at her.

'It do sound bad when you say it,' she admitted.

'It would sound very bad when anybody said it.' His sandy hair fell loosely over his forehead. 'Especially when that person is a reporter on *The Suffolk Evening Post*, *The Chronical* or the *Trumpet*.'

I had seen the articles too. ARISTOCRATIC AUTHORESS SETS SERVANTS ON ELDERLY WOMAN, being one of the more restrained headlines.

'And who gave this information?' Alfred raised a hand to forestall any reply. 'A drowning and, doubtless, confused stranger.'

'But the information was essentially correct,' I argued. 'A woman did shoot at the Prince of Wales.'

'No, she did not,' the inspector corrected me, somewhat to my surprise.

'But Gerrund disarmed her.'

'The *Preußische Geheimpolizei*...' Alfred began.

Good pronunciation, Ruby approved.

'The Prussian Secret Police,' he translated for our benefit, 'also had a warning – only theirs was a reliable one – that a terrorist organisation in Düsseldorf was planning to assassinate the Prince of Wales and so they sent one of their best officers, Lena Schneider, posing as a German tourist, to foil the attempt.'

Blimey, Ruby said admiringly. *He said all that without drawing breath.*

Stanbury flicked his head to propel the hair backwards as if he too were proud of his achievement. 'The Kaiser is anxious to avoid a war with England.'

For the time being, Hefty chipped in.

'From what I can gather, an unidentified girl alarmed the *Polizeioberkommissar*…'

Now he's just showing off. Ruby lit a Little Queen cigarette.

'By putting a hornet down her dress…' Alfred poked his thumbs into his waistcoat pockets. He had been warned by the superintendent that his habit of waving his hands about was so unsavoury that some of the men had dubbed him *Frenchy*, which was almost as bad as being a Londoner. 'So that, in her anxiety to eject the insect, she revealed her weapon. A plain-clothed man from the royal bodyguard spotted it and, as they struggled to take possession of the gun, it went off, damaging the statue of the queen.'

I had heard that her bustle was chipped. Ruby pealed with laughter at this announcement but, aware that Stanbury was watching me closely, I adopted the blank face that had lost me an entire box of buttons playing poker with my brothers.

'Modern children,' I tutted. 'I wonder where she got a hornet from at this time of year.'

Alfred hmmmed. 'I went to see Mrs Greaves this morning.' His voice was gravelly from too many hours shut in his office with only his cigars for company.

'The woman who…' Agnust began.

'You attacked,' he jumped in. 'Luckily nothing was broken.'

'My umbrella get dented.' Agnust bridled at the woman's unreasonable behaviour, but Stanbury shrugged unsympathetically.

'Mrs Greaves is confused,' he continued, 'probably because of her head striking the pavement.'

'Cobbles,' Agnust insisted, doubtless fully aware that all men, especially police officers, like nothing better than to be corrected by women, particularly on trivial matters.

Alfred rolled his eyes, twisting round to pick up his notes from the desk, unaware that his colleague and rival, Havelock Hefty, was peering over his shoulder.

'She has a compelling case for battery against you…' He indicated to my maid with a chewed wooden pencil. 'And a case, though less strong, against you for being an accessory, Lady Violet.'

'She make me do it,' Agnust protested untruthfully and disloyally. 'I deny havin' said that in court,' she assured me from the corner of her mouth.

'Does your maid believe I am hard of hearing?' Alfred asked incredulously and she flushed in indignation.

'That is a private conversation,' she told him haughtily.

Alfred took a breath and let it out slowly.

'There is no such species in this office,' he told her, though he and I had had many a confidential chat in that room.

'Tha's the last time I let you lick out the puddin' basin,' Agnust threatened a fifth of a century too late to achieve the desired effect.

'However…' Stanbury touched his ruby tie pin self-consciously. It had been a present, but he would never divulge who had given it to him. 'Mrs Greaves is still undecided if she will press charges against either of you. Apparently she believes she is eligible for a medal.'

'Whowhatever gave her that idea?' Agnust wondered, but I had not forgotten how she had spoken in the woman's ear.

'And if she does not press charges?' I asked before my maid made things any worse.

I was not sure what the penalties might be, but I had seen enough of Her Majesty's Prison, Montford not to regard it as a desirable residence.

'Then I shall not,' Stanbury assured me. 'The Prince of Wales has no interest in pursuing the matter.' He tossed the statement back onto his desk, but it fluttered, fledgling-like, onto his chair behind. 'It appears that His Royal Highness thought the incident enlivened what would otherwise have been a tedious occasion. The suggestion that there might be an accomplice at large gave him an excuse to skip all the speeches in favour of meeting a friend in Newmarket.'

The whole county knew of Prince Edward's friend, the actress Lillie Langtry, but it would be a foolhardy officer who spoke her name.

I never listen to scandal, Hefty said primly.

Neither do I, Ruby concurred. *I create it*.

'And he was amused to see that his mother had been shot in the...' Alfred paused to think of a proper way to speak of an unspeakable part of our monarch's anatomy without molesting our delicate feminine ears.

Arse, Ruby prompted and Hefty flinched at her coarseness, but she had learned a great deal worse while working disguised as a Cistercian nun in Tunbridge Wells.

'In the square,' I suggested and was treated to an unsuccessfully suppressed smile.

'I shall pay Mrs Greaves a visit,' I decided.

'You will not,' he informed me firmly.

'But surely…'

'I thought you might suggest it and asked if she would give you an opportunity to apologise but she was adamant that she did not want to see either of you.'

'Not even me?' Agnust, the innocent bystander, checked.

'Especially not you,' he replied, and she flinched. The thought that Agnust might not be welcome anywhere rarely occurred to her.

'Well, we must not detain you, Inspector,' I said before he changed his mind and detained us.

Alfred lodged the pencil behind his ear, reminding me of a builder assessing how much a job and, more importantly, a customer was worth.

'No you must not,' he agreed as Agnust picked up her handbag from the chair where she had deposited it.

'Still think it's you who steal those biscuits,' she grunted and he stiffened.

'Good day,' I put in hastily. 'Thank you,' I mouthed.

'Good day, Lady Violet,' Alfred Stanbury said with a nod to me and a hint of a wink, which I thought rather impertinent. There had been far more than a hint in the one that I had given him.

-

I was just about to extricate Havelock Hefty from drowning in the fenland marshes in his pursuit of the one-headed doberman when the telegram came. Agnust had been taught by my mother to deliver such communications on a salver and so she delved into her apron pocket and presented me with a crumpled paper ball.

'What happened to the silver tray?' I gave her a withering look.

'Dint you worry 'bout tha',' she reassured me, completely unwithered. 'It can prob'ly be repaired.'

I flattened the telegram on my desk. TO THE WOMAN WHAT ATTACK ME STOP CALL ON ME AT NOON TODAY STOP YOUR VICTIM MRS GREAVES STOP

Very fishy, Ruby commented. *She could have had another two words for her sixpence.*

Excuse me, Hefty called out.

I looked at my watch. 'I suppose we had better check with Inspector Stanbury.'

'We?' Agnust queried.

'Yes, both of us,' I said in a manner that brooked no argument after the first ten minutes.

I'm still drowning, Hefty spluttered as he went under for the third time.

—

Alfred Stanbury took one look at the telegram and two looks at us.

'You can visit her.' He pointed at me and then Agnust. 'But you cannot.'

'Told you it was nothin' to do with me,' Agnust gloated.

'It has everything to do with you,' Alfred told her, 'but I don't trust you not to attack Mrs Greaves again.' He turned his attention to me. 'I assume you will go unarmed.'

'Probably,' I agreed as we left, though I rarely carried anything more lethal than my charm bracelet and a box of Beeman's.

Hello, Hefty gurgled faintly, but it was high time that Scotland Yard's premier detective learned how to look after himself.

5

THE GREAT FIRE AND TEASPOONS

FRIENDLESS, OUR CABBY, was waiting for us on the high perch of his seat at the rear of his hansom as we emerged into the drizzle. He was well protected in a long rabbit-skin coat, broad-brimmed leather hat and patchworked scarf almost big enough to be a blanket.

Old Queeny stood patiently in her harness. Many drivers did not regard their horses as anything other than machines for hauling carriages, but Old Queeny was the love of her master's life. She was a small animal, dappled grey with a black patch around her eye giving her a buccaneering air at odds with her placid character.

Agnust boarded first, the carriage tilting under her mass, and I scrambled up, squeezing into the narrow space beside her.

'Give me room to breathe.' She expanded herself until I felt my bones creak.

'Home,' I called through the open hatch overhead.

'Tint,' Friendless argued.

It will be if we stay here much longer. Ruby slipped her hands into the sleeves of her mink coat, a present from a Bragislanian prince, she had told me, but I still resolved to look out for an account from the furriers.

'Take us to Seraphim Square.'

Friendless double-clicked his tongue and flicked the reins and off we trundled.

'Seraphim Square,' he began. 'There do be a terble fire there.'

'In what part of the square!' I asked in alarm.

'Start right up in that corner where your house stand as I hear told,' he said brightly.

'My bible,' Agnust cried. The sect to which she belonged had been created by St Ethel of Ickworth, who believed that the Gospel of St Mark was the work of the devil in AD 666 and that it was her duty to destroy it, but only at the rate of one word a day. 'My rocking chair.' It was actually my rocking chair but not high on the list of things I treasured most. 'My love letters,' she ended in alarm.

That Agnust had an admirer was a revelation to me. The very idea was bizarre but I had other concerns. 'Was anybody hurt?'

'Twenty-eight people and women burnt to death.'

'Oh dear God!' I cried and Friendless piffed.

'Int no use to get all fizzed over it,' he told me placidly.

'I told the plumber that my geyser was not safe.'

'I never even know you have a husband,' Friendless told me in such wounded tones that an observer might have concluded that he had expectations of his own.

'Geyser, not geezer,' I explained, then, realising that did not explain anything, re-explained, 'I was talking about my gas geyser. Is Gerrund all right?'

'Far as I know.' Friendless shrugged, or at least I imagined he did for, being above and behind me, I only had glimpses of him when I cricked my neck back and he leaned forward.

'When did the fire start?'

'Around and about 1130 if I remember aright.'

'How did it start?' I asked, returning to my immediate concerns.

'I do believe they do believe it start with a small fire that grow into a big one and then a bigger one.'

'You surprise me,' I muttered.

'Tha's how fires goo,' he informed me, turning into Mathew Street with as much caution as he might if he were expecting a salvo of bullets. 'Then they get smaller again. Then...' He took a deep breath. 'They do die.'

'Lord rest their souls,' Agnust commiserated while Friendless concentrated on his manoeuvre. Relaxing when he had completed it, he burst into a snatch of song. 'I accidently eat my motherrrrr and now I'll never have anotherrrrr,' he warbled more cheerfully than the subject of his song merited.

Hefty banged the table though I was not at all sure how he and the furniture got into our cab.

And how did you dispose of her skeleton? he demanded.

'What else can I dooooo but boil her bones for stewwwww?' Friendless continued obligingly if tunelessly, unaware that Scotland Yard's premier detective was summoning a black maria to take him away.

'My collection of borrowed teaspoon,' Agnust muttered.

A small boy ran up and took Old Queeny's bridle, but she shook him off.

'Wash your horse for thruppence,' he offered. 'Geroff!' he yelled as Old Queeny snatched his rag, devouring it with greater relish than she had demonstrated for the toffee that I had given her on the way there. He raised a hand to smack her nose.

'Touch my horse and you'll feel my lash on your grovel,' Friendless threatened puzzlingly.

I had seen what our cabby could do with his whip but could not imagine him using it on a child.

'It do eat my cloth,' the boy protested.

'And if it stick in her liver you do pay to have it unstuck,' Friendless warned, but the situation was resolved by Old Queeny lowering her head, coughing violently and depositing the saliva-sodden rag into the gutter.

Ignoring the boy's protests we continued on our way.

'Street slugs,' Friendless grumbled, an unkind local term for what most of the population referred to as *urchins*. 'Wha's the point on 'em? They int even real slugs.'

'I cannot smell any smoke,' I commented when we were only two streets away.

'What? Never?' Friendless tried to pluck a long hair from his chin but it slipped through his fingers. 'Hope your house dint never catch fire then.'

'But you told me it did,' I objected with a glance at Agnust. She was uncharacteristically quiet.

'In 1130,' Friendless confirmed.

'IN 1130?' I budgerigared.

Budgeri-what? Miss Kidd picked up a stick of chalk. To the best of my knowledge she was still alive, so I never understood how she could have access to my brain.

Parroted is such a cliché, I explained uneasily.

'Or maybe 1150 and 7.' Like every workman I have ever come across, Friendless upwardly revised his estimate.

'The great fire of Montford,' I realised. 'In 1326.'

'Tha's the one,' he agreed, but I was still relieved to see Seraphim Square in general – and Break House in particular – looking unscathed.

My great aunt, the Dowager Herbena Lady Strainge, had intended to leave the property to my second cousin, but poor Dorissa died suddenly of a seizure when she was a child and the inheritance had passed to me. It was chastening to consider how much of my fortune had been acquired from premature deaths in the family but not even my characters were insensitive enough to cast any suspicion on me.

Of course your house didn't burn down, Ruby told me. *I would have been chained in the attic if it had.*

Ruby was forever carping about the ordeals through which I put her, but she was the first to complain if I wrote an entire chapter without imperilling her.

Friendless lowered an empty tin, labelled *Fray Bentos Corned Beef*, through the hatch on a string and I dropped his fare into it.

Agnust seemed to have expanded during our trip and I struggled to extricate myself.

'Mind my hat.' She elbowed mine, wounding the rim, probably terminally.

'Oh, and Old Queeny ask me to tell you,' Friendless called after me. 'She appreciate tha' toffee but it do stick stuck to her tooth.'

'I shall bring her an apple next time,' I promised as I disembarked.

'I dint mind the toffees though,' he cadged and, with a hearty, 'She make such a tasty stewww I cook my grandmamother toooo,' set off on his way.

6

CRACKLE-HEADS AND THE TRANSPORT OF DISEASES

THE TENNYSON nursing home had been built on the outskirts of town so that patients might enjoy the fresh country air. With the boom in house building, though, it found itself on the in-skirts, its vistas of the not especially glorious Suffolk countryside being replaced by a splendid view of the Suffolk Coal Gas Company's factory with its tall – but not tall enough – chimney. With the wind in the right direction, the fumes blew out over the fens. On a still day, such as this, they hung over the hospital and surrounding homes in our very own miniature peasouper.

A porter in a fetching cranberry-coloured uniform admitted me, took me to a long high desk where I was interrogated by a maggot-faced receptionist in a sour-cream coloured dress, and thence along a white-painted hallway.

Looks expensive, Ruby commented with a glance at the oak-panelled doors and the chandeliers.

Quite so, I agreed uneasily, for Mrs Greaves had not looked especially affluent and I had a suspicion who might be called upon to foot the bill.

Through an open door I spotted a bedroom, carpeted, curtained and furnished in a manner that the Imperial

Suite at the Splendid Hotel would be hard-pressed to match.

'Mrs Greaves must be very comfortable in here,' I observed and the porter sniggered.

'She int in here.' He snuffled like an asthmatic pug. 'She's in the tepee.'

'The tepee?' I queried.

'TP,' he said slowly enough for even a woman to understand that he meant the letters of the alphabet.

'Short for…' I prompted as we came to a green door.

'TPTWA, of course,' he scoffed at my silliness.

'Short for…' I reprompted.

'Too Poor To Worry About,' he explained impatiently and pulled open the door. 'It's a medical term.'

I could not remember coming across it in my conversations with Romulus and I did not believe that he would have applied that description to anybody. It was by no means uncommon for him to tend a farmworker's family knowing that they had no hope of remunerating him. 'It is people like you who bring the profession into repute,' he once told me a colleague had complained.

I followed the porter through into a whitewashed corridor with frayed burnt-ochre oilskin flooring. The cabbage green door was not even painted on the other side, I noted as he closed it behind us, and those along the right side were iron studded and had observation hatches in them. This was more reminiscent of a prison than a hospital.

'Used to be where we keep the crackle-heads,' my guide told me, ' 'til someone say they need be treated kindly.' He made a hawking noise but, fortunately, did not follow it up. 'What use is that? They only understand cruelty. Spare the rod and spoil the loon, I say.'

He stopped at a door and peered through the peephole.

'Looks safe,' he said.

'Why wouldn't it be?'

'Because it's only gone from treatin' crackle-heads to cracked heads.' He opened the door. 'And many's the time there int much difference what I can see.' He stood aside to let me through.

'Thank you,' I said. 'I can find my own way back.' Yet still he hovered.

'Are you expecting a tip?' I wondered and he perked up. 'I am afraid you are THTDO,' I told him, and he perked down.

Perked down? Miss Kidd despaired.

'THTDO,' the porter pondered. 'Too Horrible To Deserve One,' he translated to my astonishment before nodding in agreement and heading away.

Mrs Greaves lay on top of an iron-framed bed in a spartan room with no aspirations to rise above being a cell. The walls were plain red brick and the small high window barred. Apart from a battered pine table and chair there was no other furniture.

Her arms were crossed over her bosom and, as I drew close, I saw that her eyes were closed.

This is your lucky day, Thorn. Ruby assessed the situation unhesitatingly. *She's dead.*

'Who's dead?' Mrs Greaves opened her eyes. It was a bad habit of mine, thinking aloud.

Never mind, milady, Hefty consoled me. *What with you being a woman it's a wonder that you can think at all.*

'That fly,' I waved a hand vaguely to encompass most of our surroundings.

'You call it *she*.'

53

'It's a female,' I flailed. 'You can tell by the markings on the thorax.'

'Sore axe,' she cogitated before renewing her interrogation. 'Why's it a lucky day then?'

'They carry diseases,' I informed her and she piffed dismissively.

'Flies?' She scoffed. 'They int hardly not big enough to carry half a crumb let alone a whole disease.'

I had learned a smidgeon of bacteriology while helping Romulus with his medical studies and I was almost sure that bacilli are much smaller than crumbs but, never having seen one, I let her comment pass.

'How are you feeling…' I began.

I am a trifle attenuated, Hefty replied, for he had been up all night investigating *The Mystery of the Mexican Cufflink*, a tale that I had no intention of writing.

'…Mrs Greaves,' I finished.

'Who are you?' she demanded.

'Lady Violet Thorn,' I replied, and she squinted at me.

'Oh yes,' she said grimly. 'The 'spector mention you.' She raised a crooked finger poised to tap an invisible Morse key. 'The girl who attack me.'

'Well actually my maid…'

'Under your 'struction,' she insisted.

'Your telegram said that you wished to see me.'

She nodded slowly. 'I want to know what you have to say 'bout my…' She searched for the bon mot, but it was too well camouflaged. 'Grievingous injuries.'

'I am very sorry that you were hurt.'

'Anyone can say tha'.' She waved a work-worn hand. ''cept a dumb mute.'

Try a different tack, Ruby advised, so I tried a different tack.

'You must be very proud.'

'Pride is a deadly sin,' Mrs Greaves declaimed then, after a pause for reflection, 'Why?'

'For creating the diversion that saved the life of our noble Prince of Wales.'

'Oh,' she grinned – gappily, I noticed, wondering if I had just made up that adverb and if she had lost any of those teeth as a result of her fall.

Could be in line for a medal, Hefty prompted, mainly to remind Ruby that he had more than she.

'His majesty wanted to visit you in person, but he had an urgent appointment in… Hartlepool.' I had no idea why I selected that town. 'He asked me to express his gratitude.'

'Gratitude.' Mrs Greaves chewed the word over, relishing the flavour before she swallowed it.

Medal. Hefty had pinned his to his coat.

'He did mention that you could be in for a medal,' I promised recklessly and she sat up, primping her hair and simpering.

'Medal?'

'Medal,' I confirmed. 'But, if you make a complaint against us, people will think that you were just an innocent bystander and had not done anything brave or clever at all.'

Zum Donnerwetter but you're ruthless, Ruby said admiringly, but mainly to prove that Inspector Stanbury was not the only one who could speak a few words of German.

'All right,' Mrs Greaves decided. 'I say no more about it.'

'A wise decision,' I assured her.

'If…'

Here we go, Ruby sighed, *she wants five hundred guineas and a villa in Anglethorpe.*

'You sing me to sleep.'

'But of course,' I agreed, as if it were something that strangers asked me to do every day.

Ruby rooted about in her crocodile-skin handbag. *Need my hip flask to get me through this ordeal*, she muttered unkindly, though I had been told that my voice was not unpleasant for a baritone.

It took two renditions of Brahms's 'Lullaby', one of 'Polly of Petticoat Lane' and two of 'My Mother Was a Mermaid in the Sea' before she closed her eyes.

Thank heavens for that, Ruby unblocked her ears as I crept across the room.

But I was more interested in the sounds that greeted me as I opened the door.

7

THIEVES, MURDERERS AND CHRYSANTHEMUMS

VOICES WERE RAISED in another room – two women – one young and the other less so, I judged – and then a man joining in.

'Very well then,' he was saying, and I assumed their door had been opened for his voice was becoming clearer.

'You leave us with no choice,' the woman asserted. I have rarely found that statement to be true. It is usually an excuse for being nasty and I expect the Stolham Slasher believed that he had no option other than to lacerate men who parted their hair in the middle.

'You can't just…' the younger woman protested but the older butted in with a mirthless laugh.

'Oh Miss Bite,' she sneered, 'I think you will find that we already have.'

Ten guineas says she has thin lips and a scrawny neck, Ruby forecast but I did not accept the wager for, though I knew it was not possible, I could not quell a suspicion that she had been out to take a look.

'If you know what's good for you,' the man said, 'you will keep well away from Tannery Lane.'

I opened the door a fraction wider.

Tannery Lane. Hefty brought out his notebook. *Well away,* he printed thoughtfully.

I had been along that road many times and it had always seemed quite safe and salubrious though the old tannery still stood at the far end of it.

Saloob... How do you spell that? Hefty licked the graphite tip of his Faber-Castell wooden pencil.

I-G-N-O-R-A-N-T, Ruby mocked.

'I shall call the police,' the younger woman was threatening.

'We don't have to listen to this,' the man told one or both of them, his voice reedy enough to thatch a small cottage. 'Come along, my dear.'

There was some rustling and, after a dozen or so pairs of footfalls, I glimpsed them, a tall, stooped man in a hard felt hat, his skin greying and his whiskers tawny. He walked quite stiffly as if his legs were mechanical and in need of lubrication.

The woman with her billhook nose was almost as tall and even more ashen than her companion. She wore an odd clamshell-shaped mobcap held onto the back of her head by a ribbon under her sharp, upturned chin. Both were clad in dark brown with light brown coats flapping as they strode past.

As I predicted. Ruby was wearing a narrow-rimmed crimson hat with a pink feather and I touched the brim of mine to make sure that I was still wearing it.

'She is quite clearly deranged,' the man said.

'Oh good,' I breathed, for one could never have too many mad women in one's life. I had been trapped in the attic of Haglin House with one once and it was not an experience that I yearned to reprise.

'Pity I didn't kill her,' the woman muttered and I stepped to one side for it is rarely, if ever, a good idea to be discovered by a couple with womanicide on their minds.

An interesting word, Ruby commented sarcastically.

Indeed, Hefty concurred. *Couple comes from the Latin copula, if I remember aright.*

'Thieves,' the girl was yelling after them.

'You ought to be more careful,' the man called back as they walked away. 'That's slander.'

'How about this then?' the girl challenged, and her voice sank to an accusatory hiss. '*Murderers.*'

The couple were leaving through the door into the Rich Enough To Pamper wing of the hospital and, putting my head out, I saw the profile of a young woman standing on the opposite side of the corridor two doors up. She wore a long grey nightgown with *ESCAPE FRO ONT ORD LUNAT SYLU* printed in faded red, some of the letters hidden by its folds. Her face was largely obscured by two curtains of frizzy ginger hair reaching to her bosom.

Steady on, Hefty blushed as the object of our discussion turned towards us, drawing the drapes apart to reveal her face poking out like an inquisitive rodent.

'Are you all right?' I called, though clearly she was not.

'Those people,' she answered tremulously, her hand raised to point in their wake. 'They have murdered my parents and stolen their house.'

'Would you like me to call a nurse?' I decided against approaching her. 'She might give you something to calm you.'

'I am not mad.' She trembled. 'Am I?'

Mad as a chrysanthemum. Ruby opened a bottle of surgical spirit.

AS A *C-R-I-S*... Hefty started to print and she laughed.

C-R-Y-S... She stopped uncertainly.

'I just thought you might be feeling unwell,' I explained.

'Unwell?' she wondered. 'Perhaps I am.'

Ruby swigged from the bottle, wiping her mouth with the back of her hand.

'Who was that couple?' I was not so foolish as to suggest that they might be friends. 'Are they acquaintances of yours?'

Her breath sissed out. 'I became acquainted with them the other night in my home. They are the Brutons, though the Brutals would be a more apt name. On top of everything else, they tried to kill me.'

Her claims seemed so patently absurd that I almost rejected them, but Mrs Bruton's words sounded again in my mind, so clearly that Ruby and Hefty both looked over their shoulders.

'*A pity I didn't kill her.*'

8

FRENCH MUSTARD, THE MOUSE, THE SLUG AND THE HERMIT

THE GIRL stumbled unsteadily back into her cell and, heedless of my decision not to approach her, I followed to find her wrenching open the drawers of a plain pine dresser.

'Where are they?' She looked about hopelessly.

'They went out into the main hospital,' I said, re-evaluating my sanity diagnosis.

'No.' She patted the thin misshapen stuffed sack languidly posing as a mattress. 'I mean my clothes.'

I scanned the room, not a long process since it was as bare as the one occupied by Mrs Greaves.

'I cannot go out like this.' The girl plucked at her nightgown. 'I do not even have any shoes.' She hugged herself and I saw that she had a gold watch on her wrist, a practice that my father abhorred as being the sure sign of a rascal. 'For my feet,' she explained.

'Are you well enough to leave?' I was not sure that she looked it.

'The doctor said I am.'

I touched her arm, surprised at how thin it was inside her nightdress sleeve, and she shivered. She had a lean, freckly face as if she had raced a lady's safety bicycle through a muddy puddle. Large powder blue eyes darted nervously from side to side. Her chin was dimpled and she had a tiny, upturned nose. Something about her reminded me fleetingly of Isabella, a horrid little girl who used to come to Break House to play with Dorissa. Much as I disliked Isabella, I could not help but feel sorry for her. She had witnessed Dorissa's apoplectic fit and been unable to summon help in time to save her.

'There is a suitcase under your bed,' I told her.

'What is it doing there?'

Nothing much. Ruby had done something different to her hair. It was pinned up in curls. *The Gibson Girl look,* she explained. *Clearly named after me. I saw it in your American magazine.*

'*Harper's Bazaar,*' I said aloud.

'Is he?' the girl asked distractedly as she dragged her suitcase out. 'Goodness, this is even heavier than I remembered.'

'Would you like me to put it on the bed?' I offered.

Are you mad? my spine protested. *What do you think you are, a stevedore?*

We won that weight-lifting contest, I reminded it.

You were five and your sister was three.

And you cheated, my arms reminded me.

'Oh, could you?' the girl was enquiring.

No she cannot, several body parts chorused.

'Of course,' my larynx said, blithely aware that it would have no part to play in the exercise except for fabricating all the appropriate grunts at the appropriate times. I heaved.

Oh for pity's sake, my joints protested as my nerves sprang into life.

'Uff,' I uffed, and dumped it on the mattress.

'Goodness but you are strong,' the girl said admiringly and my muscles preened.

We like to keep in shape. They flexed modestly.

'I have not introduced myself,' I remembered and held out my hand. 'Lady Violet Thorn. Please call me Violet.'

She took my hand. Hers was chilly enough to cool my nightly absinthe.

'Cherry,' she said. 'Cherry Bite, spelt B-I-G-H-T.'

'I live locally, in Seraphim Square,' I told her. 'If you are sure you are well enough, why not come with me? I expect you would like something to eat.'

And so would I, having missed my elevenses that morning. *Not to mention lunch*, I mentioned to myself.

'I couldn't impose,' Cherry said, though I was confident that she could.

'I shall wait in the corridor while you get dressed.'

The porter came by, pushing a heavily laden laundry trolley, and I stood to one side.

'Goh a dead body in here,' he chuckled and Hefty spun around.

He was joking, I assured my detective.

Then how do you explain this? He whipped a dirty sheet back to reveal another one. *Or this,* he pulled that away and uncovered two pillowcases. *Or this,* he mumbled disheartenedly but the trolley was disappearing through the double back doors.

A mouse was scurrying along the oilcloth, keeping close to the skirting board, its fur bedraggled and whiskers drooping. It reached my left foot and stopped. One hears stories about mice running up people's trousers or dresses and I was not sure that I believed them, but I had no wish to have my scepticism demolished.

The mouse got up on its hind legs and I prepared myself to swat it down, but it was looking up at me looking down at it.

'Go around,' I said, and it raised what would have been its eyebrows if mice were equipped with such devices. 'Oh, very well.'

I stepped away from the wall and it strolled behind me.

'You are not a gentleman,' I called after it.

How do you know it is not a female? Hefty asked.

No girl would be seen alive in a coat like that, Ruby explained on my behalf.

I looked side to side, then, having nothing else to do, up and down then up again. I stifled a yawn but, realising there were no disapproving males within eyeshot, unstifled it.

Cherry Bight appeared in something...

Slug brown, Ruby identified the colour unkindly. *But accurately,* she said.

'It's all a bit creased,' Cherry told me.

Oh, I wouldn't say that. Ruby sprayed a cloud of my Fleurs de Bulgarie perfume around Cherry's head. *I would say it was extremely creased.*

'They just rolled my clothes into a ball and crammed them in.' Cherry sniffed. 'That's a nice perfume.'

'The porter said we can get out this way,' I indicated to the doors and Cherry set off towards them.

'What about your suitcase?' I called, for it lay open on her bed.

'Oh yes please,' she called back. 'I'll wait for you outside.'

What a sauce, Ruby fumed. *She didn't even notice my amethyst earrings.*

Whose amethyst earrings? I put my fingers up, relieved to find my own still screwed firmly, if uncomfortably, in place. When I thought about it, my earlobes had been whinging ever since I put them on.

You put your earlobes on? Ruby checked but we both knew what I meant.

I would send for the case, I decided, rather than end up with my right arm longer than my left like a hermit…

A hermit? Hefty echoed incredulously.

Crab, Ruby completed my sentence for me.

'Are you coming?' Cherry called in much the same tone that my father would use when we were going to church.

Ruby had changed into my Wilber-Lowe cranberry shoes. *Quick question, Thorn. Why are you doing this?* And it occurred to me, as I trotted obediently after Cherry Bight, that I had absolutely no idea.

9

RUSSIAN CARAVANS AND WHITE TIGERS

ALTHOUGH the floodwater had mostly drained, some of the gutters were still flowing with murky streams and the pavements were slippery with mud and so, of course, there was not a cab to be had. At least the weather had driven the hurdy-gurdy man away, I consoled myself. I felt sorry for the traders though. Most of them had given up trying to keep their goods dry and to attract customers from the people scurrying home. Only the coffee stand, the hot pie stall and the chestnut man were doing any trade. Nobody was interested in postcards of their own town or models of the priory gate in the stiff breeze that was getting up.

'Oh,' said Cherry when we arrived at Break House. 'You live in the corner. I've often wondered how it was built.'

'It is wedge shaped,' I explained and fumbled with cold wet hands for my keys but I need not have bothered for the door was flung open by Agnust.

'Boots off and coats on the hooks.' We obeyed meekly. 'How is Mrs Greaves?'

'Bruised, but I do not think that she will put in a complaint,' I assured her.

'Should think not,' my maid sniffed. 'Personating an assassin. If that int a crime I dint know what is.'

Being an assassin is somewhat more serious, Hefty told her. *Did I ever tell you how I foiled an attempt on the life of Archduke Franz Ferdinand of Austria?*

Eight hundred and forty-three times. Ruby yawned theatrically. *And nobody would care if he were killed anyway.*

'This is Miss Bight,' I announced, and Agnust snorted in amusement.

'And is your bar...' she chortled.

'Yes, it is much worse,' Cherry interrupted and Agnust pouted sulkily.

'I dint finish.'

'I think Miss Bight knew what you were going to say.'

'I was goo say, *Is your bar-ometer forecastin' more rain?*' Agnust lied utterly unconvincingly but quite quick-wittedly, I thought.

'One should always be wary of signs of intelligence in servants,' my father once told me. 'They will start to believe that we are not their betters after all.' I rather thought that many of them had reached that conclusion long ago.

'Would you like a coffee?' I offered my guest.

'I would rather have a tea,' she said to my irritation, for I am not fond of the beverage.

'Tea the great healer,' Agnust misquoted approvingly.

'Then we shall have a pot of each,' I told her, and she scowled.

'As if I dint have enough to do without workin'.'

I took Cherry through to my front sitting room.

I was very proud of my two modern high-railed William Morris armchairs upholstered to match the latticed wallpaper, but Cherry did not appear to notice as she slumped into the one I indicated. I sat to her right, both of us angled towards each other and the window overlooking the square.

'Who were those people?' I asked. 'And what did you mean when you called them murderers?'

Inspector Hefty brought out a blue cardboard-covered notebook and a juniper wood pencil, the graphite freshly sharpened and the vulcanised rubber eraser in pristine condition.

'Exactly what I said,' Cherry replied, looking over her shoulder as if expecting them to spring out of my sideboard where Ruby stood, mixing herself a white tiger milk cocktail. 'They mur...' Her voice fractured but she quickly reassembled it into working order. 'Murdered my parents and stole their house.'

'But how?'

'I don't know, but I do know that they did.'

'Have you seen your parents' bodies?'

Cherry started, as if the idea that her dead parents might now be corpses came as a shocking revelation. 'No, of course not.'

Why 'of course'? Hefty prompted.

'But how do you know they are dead?' I asked, struggling and failing to put an indelicate question delicately.

Cherry flushed. 'They must be. Why else would they disappear? They would never have sold our home and moved away without consulting me.'

Agnust appeared bearing a tray laden with all the paraphernalia that two different beverages require except, I noticed as she deposited it clatteringly on the low table between me and my guest, for any cups.

'Have we forgotten something?' I asked.

'Yes,' Agnust told me. 'To say thank you.'

My father had also taught me that one does not thank servants, at least not very often. They might start to believe that you are obligated to them rather than vice versa.

'Cups,' I reminded her and, having nothing to say on the matter, my maid grunted but, to judge by the grumbling sounds that came from the hall as she left, she had plenty to say on the matter after all.

'What are your parents like?' I probed gently and tears sprang into Cherry's eyes.

The only place they can spring into, Ruby pointed out but realising how insensitive she was being, turned her attention back to my sideboard.

'They were lovely people, kind and gentle. I was rarely scolded as a child and never smacked.' Just as I was going to offer her my handkerchief, she found her own in her handbag. 'They never quarrelled, not once in all my life.'

Inspector Hefty stood in the hearth, his elbows on the mantlepiece but not disturbing the clock and photographs that adorned it.

In my experience if people are too good to be true, they are too good to be true, he opined. *The woman is either a liar or a lunatic.*

Ruby bristled. *You think that of all women.*

Tis the voice of experience, he declared as if that were a quotation.

Cherry blew her nose and Agnust reappeared with the crockery.

'Dint you let her upset you.' She put the cups and saucers down but, oddly, the advice seemed to be aimed at me.

'They were devoted to each other,' Cherry wept when we were alone again, 'and to me.'

69

I reached out and touched her shoulder and she looked at me gratefully.

'You are the only person who has tried to help me.'

'Why were you in hospital?'

She reached up and took my hand into her lap, forcing me to twist sideways over the tray.

'I was attacked and beaten unconscious in my own home.' She tightened her grip, pulling my arm onto the coffee pot which, after all the times it had been tepid at best, was now of course steaming hot. I took a sharp breath and she glanced over in surprised realisation. 'Oh my goodness. I'm so sorry.'

'There is no harm done,' I assured her and, waving away my arm's indignant, *Speak for yourself*, rubbed my sleeve. 'Did they break into your parents' house?'

'They must have.' For all her troubles Cherry eyed me with concern. 'Either that or they tricked their way in.' She dabbed her eyes. 'My parents were very trusting. On more than one occasion they admitted beggars with tales of woe.'

'Had you ever seen them before?'

'The beggars?'

'The Brutons.'

Cherry shook her head vigorously, her orange hair flailing side to side. 'No,' she said, though she hardly needed to after such an emphatic denial. 'Never,' she added, though her *no* had already avowed that. 'Not once,' she insisted redundantly.

Ruby was pouring herself a Russian caravan tea from a heavily ornamented brass samovar, a memento of her visit to the court of Tsar Alexander III. *The lady doth protest too much methinks*, she-thinked, and that actually was a quotation, to my surprise, for she detested Shakespeare with no hope of a vengeance.

'Did they both attack you?'

Her hair only swayed this time. 'Just her with an iron cooking pot.'

'Were you in the kitchen?'

'The hallway,' Cherry replied. 'She was hiding it behind her back.'

Inspector Hefty had eschewed his usual briar for a long churchwarden clay pipe and he pointed the stem in her direction. *So we are to believe that Mrs Bruton hides cauldrons about her person on the off chance that Miss Bight will make an appearance.* He puffed thoughtfully. *Sounds reasonable to me,* he decided.

Cherry's face had almost disappeared again. Why did all that trichological drapery not irritate her? It certainly irritated me.

'Would you like a ribbon?' I asked and she parted her tresses to peer out like an armadillo I had seen in the first volume of *Fortescue's Natural History of South America*.

'What for?'

It was not my place to tell her what to do about her appearance, so I did. 'To tie your hair back.' The suggestion seemed to confuse her. 'So that it does not annoy you.' *As much as it annoys me.*

And me. Ruby stood at the ready with a pair of shears.

'Yes please.'

As I went upstairs to fetch a length of ribbon – I only had red – I had a quick think. Cherry Bight could be a case for Dewbury Hall asylum. The director was a relative of mine and I knew that they treated their inmates humanely.

Cherry was standing in the hall when I descended. 'I wonder if I might use your…' She hesitated. Few things divide society or cause more embarrassment than our inability to come to a consensus over what to call what I was raised to refer to as the water closet if indoors or the privy if outside.

'It is just up the stairs and the third door on the left.' I reached the bottom step. 'Would you like me to show you?'

'I'm sure I shall find it.'

I returned to my sitting room, ribbon still in hand, and went to stand by the window. The muffin man came by, tray on head and a canvas sheet over his wares in an attempt to keep them dry. His handbell clanged unheeded by the scurrying pedestrians.

'Black death returns to Montford,' the paperboy bawled. 'Buy a *Chronic* to see if I'm lyin'.' Were the rampages of cholera insufficient to stimulate public interest?

A faint, transparent figure appeared behind him, the reflection of Cherry returning to the room, by which time I had made my mind up. However it was presented, a hospital for the insane was a prison without trial or right of appeal. We would take recourse to another institution before I played any part in incarcerating my guest.

10

MOLLUSCS AND THE NEANDERTHAL MAN

IN MORE favourable conditions I might have been tempted to take the fifteen minutes' walk to Montford police station but Agnust was of the opinion that ladies who walked the streets were little better than women who walked the streets. I was not afraid of my maid but I rarely defied her, at least not openly.

Grousing that his oyster pie preparation would be ruined if he left it, Gerrund went out to summon a cab. As far as I was concerned the pie would be ruined the moment he slipped slimy molluscs into it, but I reassured him that it was bound to be delicious anyway.

He had redressed my hand earlier, which still looked nasty and felt even nastier. The bite marks were scabbing over and a bruise had spread across my palm, yellowing in an attractive contrast to the gentian stain.

'Do you think your man should come with us for protection?' Cherry asked.

'You will be perfectly safe,' I sought to reassure her.

'And I have her ladyship's dinner to prepare,' he added.

I could only whistle by using the silver charm that hung from my bracelet but, with a thumb and forefinger in his mouth, Gerrund could put a referee's Acme Thunderer to shame. While my man went out to summon a hansom,

Cherry and I donned our coats. I glanced at her headwear, brown and limp with what looked like a trampled flower garden. If it were not damaged it might have been acceptable a decade ago when such floral millinery creations were more fashionable.

It would not have been and they never were. Ruby pinned a crimson teardrop to her golden tresses.

'Would you care to borrow one of my hats?' I offered and she ran an eye over the selection on my table.

'Goodness no thank you.' She patted a faded hellebore. 'Mine is much nicer,' she told me with no apparent malice.

Pay no attention, Hefty advised. *Her hat is only a little bit nicer than yours.*

We both bobbed and had hardly enough time to lace up our outside boots before Gerrund had a hansom waiting on the road that ringed Seraphim Square. As we quit the house I noticed the new manhole cover in the middle of the road and shuddered to recall what had occurred on that night. That poor man's body must still be trapped in a filthy drain somewhere.

'Oh, for heaven's sake.' I felt a thump in my back as Cherry stumbled into me, her handbag flying down the steps.

'Let me help, deary.' Freda bent over the spillage on the pavement.

'Do not touch anything,' Cherry told her sharply and Freda backed away with a scowl. There might have been good pickings in the scattered contents that Cherry gathered together, but I had not seen any and had never known Freda to resort to theft anyway.

There was something not quite right, but I could not put my finger on it.

'I think that's everything.' Cherry straightened up.

Our driver was wearing smoked-glass spectacles.

Blind, Hefty diagnosed.

No more so than the average policeman, Ruby quipped.

'Been in Break House have you?'

'Yes,' Cherry answered.

'Lucky to get out alive.' He flicked the reins and we set off.

'But why?' she enquired.

'There's a mad writing woman what live there.'

'I hear she is very nice,' I protested to a knowing snigger.

'Dint let tha' fool you.' The cabby brought his whip with unnecessary vigour onto his horse's flank. A good driver would rarely take his whip from its cradle and then only to crack it in the air. Friendless used his most often to swat flies from around Old Queeny's head. 'I work the square sometime and I see people goo in what never come out.'

'What do you think happens to them?' Cherry asked, and for the first time I saw a twinkle in her eye.

'She eat 'em,' he asserted with such confidence that I wondered momentarily if he were right. 'Though she int growed much on it,' he ruminated just when I thought he dropped the topic. 'In fact – geroutovit,' he yelled at a tabby cat that shot across the road. 'A regular dop-a-low maukin, she is.' *Dop-a-low* meant short in stature and was not necessarily insulting but a *maukin* was a scarecrow and I may have been slender but I was rarely ragged.

I sucked a deep breath. Though I was petite, I was – or so my fiancé had assured me – perfectly proportioned.

He also said he loved you, Ruby pointed out cruelly, for I did not need reminding how I had been jilted.

'Rather that than a neanderthal man like you,' I called up.

'Nanderthorpe?' It was our driver's turn to feel insulted. 'I int from Nanderthorpe.' To the best of my knowledge nobody was, there being no such place. 'Montford man bred and borned, I am.' He flicked his head to spit sideways. 'Hate those Nanderthorpian scrope-bags, I do.' He counterflicked his head to spit otherside-ways. 'Comin' here leavin' us to do our jobs and lettin' our women alone.'

Time to change the subject, Thorn, Ruby advised.

'Why do you wear darkened spectacles?'

The cabby tapped a lens. 'What else can I do with them?' he reasoned, leaning back to heave on his reins as violently as if we were stampeding towards a precipice. 'Woah,' he yelled as an afterthought, flinging us back in our seats and forcing his unfortunate horse's head back at an angle for which neither God nor nature had designed it. 'Woah,' he repeated, although we already had, and his horse shuffled backwards.

'What an unpleasant man,' Cherry said, loud enough for the subject to hear, when we had safely disembarked.

'May be unpleasant,' he called after us, 'but least I int a woman.'

Make a crushing retort, Ruby urged, and I would, the very moment that I thought of one.

The lobby was quiet, with only the occasional clack of a typewriting machine coming from the back room where, doubtless, a constable was struggling with the apparently random sequence of keys.

A ragged man sprawled on one of the benches, his trousers heavily repaired, the soles hanging off his boots. His heavy grey stubble was patchy, reminding me of Rodrigo, my kitten, when he caught mange.

One of my officers working in disguise, Hefty claimed.

And a great deal more smartly attired than most of your men, Ruby declared.

Sergeant Webb was behind the desk, his massive head lowered in concentration, I thought, until I heard a snore escape from him.

'Good morning,' I boomed, but his only response was a wheezing exhalation.

I leaned over the desk, picked up the weighty charge book, raised it high and let it fall beside him.

'Goff.' Webb jumped, looked behind and then about and focused his eyes on me, focusing my eyes on him. His nose always reminded me of an old parsnip with its rough mottled skin.

'Lady Violet,' he greeted me warily, for I rarely brought him anything but headaches.

'Good morning, Sergeant. We have an appointment to see Inspector Stanbury.'

'In that case you'll be glad to know you've come to the right place,' he reassured me in apparent sincerity, though I had been there many times over the years. 'Down the hall and third door…'

'On the right,' I broke in.

'On the right,' he concluded as if I had not spoken.

Smarten up man, Hefty snapped, and Webb fastened the top button of his jacket. *His own jacket,* I put in before Miss Kidd, hovering behind my eyes, had a chance to enquire.

Alfred Stanbury installed himself behind his desk, unaware that the chair was already occupied, but Hefty just managed to slip aside before he was sat upon.

'If it is all right with you, Miss Bight,' Alfred continued, 'I should like to conduct an interview so that we have all the facts in a regular order.'

'I'll try,' Cherry promised, 'but parts of it were quite confusing.'

'Very well.' Alfred picked up his pencil, the wooden casing had teeth marks in it. *Made by a Canadian Otterhound,* Hefty judged as Alfred continued, 'Let's start with a few details. Your name, age and address?'

My new acquaintance took a breath. 'Bight.'

'B-I-G-H-T,' I clarified.

'I know,' Cherry said crankily.

'T,' Alfred murmured as he made a note.

Yes please. Hefty brightened. *Milk and two sugars.*

'Your Christian name or names?'

'Cherry Blossom.' She puffed her cheeks. 'So silly, but I didn't choose them.'

'Few of us do.'

He recorded the details.

I did, Ruby Gibson claimed and, in truth, I could not remember why I had called her that.

'I was born on the ninth of July seventy-nine.'

Which makes her... Hefty calculated ...*twenty-nine. She doesn't look it.*

Nineteen, I corrected him as Cherry continued.

'I reside – or at least I always have – in my parents' home, Maccabee House, Number Nine, Tannery Lane.'

Hefty licked his lead and made a note.

'And their names are?' Stanbury enquired.

'Arthur Richard and Jean Victoria Bight,' Cherry replied with a glance at me though I could neither confirm nor contradict her statement. 'My father is – or was – a civil engineer.'

Alfred leaned forward. 'Why do you say "was"?'

Cherry swallowed.

'I believe they are dead,' she said in hushed tones and then, more fiercely, 'They have been murdered. They murdered them.'

'Who murdered them and how?'

'Roger and Joan Bruton,' Cherry continued. 'I don't know how but I know they did.' She stopped. 'Might I have a glass of water?'

'By all means.' Stanbury poured one from the carafe on his desk and slid it towards Cherry, her hands shaking as she took it in them both like a child with a big tumbler of milk and raised it to her lips.

'Whenever you are ready,' Stanbury pressed gently and Cherry lowered the glass into her lap.

'I should say that I have been away. I am studying at the Institute of Chemistry.'

'An unusual subject for a lady,' the inspector commented.

'You think we lack the mental acuity?' Cherry bridled and Alfred raised his hands pacifyingly. He had long thick fingers, the nails chewed to the quick though I had never caught him nibbling them.

'I merely meant that I imagine few women study the subject.' Alfred rubbed his jaw. 'I have never come across one before.'

'That is true,' she conceded. 'There are only two of us in a class of forty-five men.'

'I presume you live in London during term time,' he said, for one could hardly commute daily from Montford.

'I have been lodging with a Mrs Forrester in Camden,' Cherry confirmed and took another sip of water, managing a steadier hand this time. 'I came home yesterday — at least that's what I supposed I was doing. I took the train from Liverpool Street to Cambridge and then another to Bury St Edmunds and then a third to Montford. For once the journey went well. The connections are not guaranteed and, on previous occasions, I have spent many an hour nursing cups of stewed tea in cold buffets, but on that day I arrived on the dot of three o'clock in the afternoon. The station clock was striking as I handed my ticket to the porter. It can be difficult getting a cab there and so my father always booked a gig and came with it to collect me. This time, however, there was no sign of him. At first, I told myself that he had assumed I would be late and so I waited, but by four o'clock he had still not arrived and so I decided to make my own way back.'

Men are so unreliable. Ruby blew playfully in Alfred's ear and I thought that he shivered. *They spend a fortune on clocks and watches, but they never consult them.*

I am invariably punctual, Hefty protested.

You are, she concurred. *Always just in time to see the murderers abscond or for the victims to die before they can reveal the identity of their killers.*

'Did your parents have a telephone?' Alfred twiddled his pencil and Cherry jumped.

'Why did you say "did"? Is there something you are not telling me?'

Alfred shook his pencil as if it were a mercury thermometer.

'I used the past tense because you have already told me that they are no longer resident there.'

Cherry touched her temple with her fingertips.

'No, they do not have a telephone. My mother is frightened it will electrocute her.'

Note that the suspect has reverted to referring to her parents in the present tense, Hefty commented, though I was not aware that she was suspected of anything. *Everyone is suspected of everything,* he declaimed, *until they can be positively excluded.* I did not trouble to point out the impracticality of such an approach.

'I could have walked to the house,' Cherry said. 'It is only about twenty minutes, but I had my suitcase, which was quite heavy.'

I could certainly corroborate that statement.

'And it was starting to get dark,' Cherry drained her glass. 'I managed to take a hansom, arriving at about a quarter past four. Maccabee House was in darkness. My mother always put the outside light on when they were expecting me or any visitors, for the street lighting leaves the driveway in the shadows.'

'Does the house have gas or electrical lighting?' Stanbury enquired.

'Both,' Cherry replied, 'but the outside light is electrical.'

'Your mother is not worried about that?'

'She doesn't have to hold it to her head.' Cherry spoke quite sharply. 'The lamp is high from the ground and would be a nuisance to turn up and down if it were gas. Why do you ask?'

Stanbury picked up the rule again, holding it by one end as if about to perform a magic trick.

'In my experience electrical light bulbs frequently fail,' he explained, 'which is why they will remain an expensive novelty.'

'I could see just enough to judge that the gravel was badly rutted, which surprised me,' Cherry told him. 'It was not like Clopton, my father's gardener, to let it get so uneven. He came twice a week and raked it. I put down my case, found my key and unlocked the front door.'

'You did not knock or ring the bell?' he checked.

'No,' Cherry said. 'Apart from a live-out cook, my parents only keep one general maid, Addie, and, if she were engaged in another task, she would have to change her hat and apron to answer the door.'

'That was considerate of you.' Alfred picked up his reading glasses but did not put them on.

'I acted in my own interests as well,' Cherry told him. 'I was cold.'

'And so you let yourself in,' he said, and she nodded.

'Was there anything unusual about the hallway?' I asked, and Stanbury tutted. This was his interview and I had no right to interfere.

'No.' Cherry wrinkled her brow. 'Everything was the same – the elephant's foot umbrella stand, the long table and the floral wallpaper.'

'Were there any lights on?' Stanbury asked.

'The gas mantle was lit low, but enough to see my surroundings,' she replied. 'It had not been visible from the outside because the curtain had been drawn over the door and side-windows. I forgot to say that annoyed me as well because it was a struggle to get in.'

'Could you hear any voices or activity in the house?' he asked and she shook her head, her long hair swishing side to side.

'Nothing, but I could see a light from under the sitting room door to my left and they would never waste gas if they were not occupying the room.' She touched the crown of her head and winced. 'I didn't want to startle them by bursting in – my mother is, or was, of a nervous disposition – and so I called out, *Hello. I'm home.*'

'Did anyone respond?' Stanbury scribbled a note.

'There was a murmur coming from the breakfast room at the back of the house on the right-hand side,' Cherry told him. 'I had not seen any light from that because the hallway is L-shaped. The door opened and a tall scrawny woman came out. She was silhouetted against the light, but it was obvious at once that she was not my mother. She is thin as well but much shorter.'

Heavy footsteps approached and Cherry looked to the door apprehensively, but they faded again and she continued.

'I greeted her amiably but she stopped dead in her tracks...'

Dead? Hefty repeated. *What caused her death? Also what tracks were laid in your parents' hallway and how?*

'Opened her mouth,' Cherry mimicked the action, 'and screamed.'

11

UNARMED COMBAT AND THE GIRL NEXT DOOR

ALFRED INTERLOCKED his fingers and cracked them rather as I had seen pugilists do in preparation for a bareknuckle fight. 'What next?'

Cherry picked abstractedly at a loop of yarn snagged from the sleeve of her coat. 'I apologised for startling her though she was the stranger and she had startled me.' She worked her third finger through the loop. If ever I did that, my finger would get snared.

Alfred scratched at his slightly bedraggled moustaches. 'And then?'

Cherry struggled to release her finger. It had gone purple at the tip.

'The woman called out.' Cherry's voice rose to resemble that of a pantomime witch. '*Roger. Roger.*' Her voice fell. 'But nobody came. I asked if she were a friend of my mother's and she asked if I had escaped from Dewbury asylum. I explained that I lived there – in the house I mean – and...' Cherry did the old crone's voice again, even clawing her hands this time. '*Roger!* she shouted. *Come quickly.*

'There were sounds of movement in the sitting room and I heard a muffled grumble. *Oh for goodness' sake, Joan, what is it now?*'

Cherry cleared her throat. 'An even taller but not very sturdy-looking man poked his head out a few feet away from me. *Please don't tell me you've seen that ghost again.*'

Cherry coughed with the strain of trying to recreate the gruffer, deeper voice of a man.

'It is not necessary to imitate their tones, Miss Bight,' Alfred said, and she nodded gratefully, though I was not sure why she had thought mimicry might be an official requirement.

'*It's her.* Joan pointed at me, but Roger smiled and said, *Good evening. Who are you?*

'He was dressed in a smoking jacket and carpet slippers. I don't know if that is important.'

'It is unlikely to be,' Alfred told her.

Good heavens, man. Hefty prompted his colleague. *You have not even asked if the carpet slippers were tartan.*

'But, whenever I read Miss March Middleton's engrossing accounts of the cases of Mr Sidney Grice, he always insists that the most trivial detail is often the most important.'

'Perhaps you had better consult him then,' Alfred said sourly, for *The Suffolk Trumpet* had compared him unfavourably to the Gower Street Detective when the front door was stolen from a spinster's house and he was unable to apprehend the culprit.

'Perhaps I should,' Cherry said in all seriousness before returning to her narrative. 'I told him my name. *Are you the girl from next door?* he asked. *If so could you please close the window next time you practise scales on your alpine horn?*

'*She is an intruder,* Joan pointed at me.

'*There has obviously been a misunderstanding,* I said. *This is my home.*

'The couple exchanged glances. *Do you think she's escaped from Dewbury Hall?* he whispered, though I was closer to him than she was.

'*I asked her, but she says not,* she whispered back.

'*We seem to be talking at cross purposes.* I tried to smile pleasantly but they were starting to annoy me, behaving as if they owned the place. *I'm Mr and Mrs Bight's daughter.*

'They glanced at each other and the woman shrugged.

'*The Bights?* Roger checked.

'*Yes,* I said. *I live here.*

'*No you don't,* Roger told me.

'*You most certainly don't,* Joan insisted. Any chance of a cup of tea?'

Stanbury wrinkled his brow. 'Who said that?'

'I did.' Cherry poked a finger through a buttonhole in her coat. 'To you just now.'

'I see,' he said and, to be fair to him, it had not been clear.

Alfred rose and strode to the door.

'Three teas required here,' he called. Somebody grunted and Alfred returned to his chair, glancing at the clock on the wall pointedly even though it had not worked since an intoxicated farmer had thrown it at his head.

'I've nearly finished,' Cherry assured him, and he shrugged.

'Take your time,' he said unconvincingly.

'I didn't know what was going on,' Cherry obliged, 'but, whatever it was, it had gone far enough.

'*Where are my parents?* I demanded, and Joan took another step backwards.

'*Here Jasper*, she called.

'*Who's Jasper?* Roger asked, and she laughed nervously.

'*Jasper*, she said. *You know... Jasper... Jasper, our... bloodhound, Jasper.*'

Hefty was taking copious notes. *Rather reminiscent of my pursuit of the one-headed doberman of Grisly Green.*

'I assume no dog appeared.' Stanbury stood his rule on one end.

'You assume correctly,' Cherry confirmed. 'And I was so distracted by Roger telling me that even if I didn't like the hospital, it was for my own good that I hardly noticed his wife reversing into the breakfast room. I was too busy telling him I had never been to St Aubrey's and that I had lived in Maccabee House with my parents for most of my life. I was even born there, upstairs.

'*That doesn't give you the right to break in,* Joan said as she reappeared with her hands behind her back.

'*I didn't break in,* I said. *I don't need to. I have a key.* It was still in my hand, I realised, and I held it up as proof of my claim. *See?*

'*I told you we should have changed the locks*, Joan scolded her husband.

'*No you didn't*, he protested. *You said it wasn't worth the expense.*

'*No, you said it would cost too much*, she argued. *And now look what's happened. She could be a murderess for all we know.*'

Alfred drummed his fingers on his blotting pad, but Cherry hardly paused. 'I was turning back to reassure her that I was not a homicidal maniac when I saw that she was holding an iron pot high over her head like a sporting trophy, and I was just wondering why she was showing it to me when she smashed it down onto my skull.' Cherry winced at the memory. 'And the next thing I knew I was in hospital with a splitting headache.' She touched her scalp. 'Ow.'

'Would you like an analgesic?' Inspector Stanbury asked solicitously but she waved his offer aside.

'I feel befuddled enough as it is without taking laudanum,' she explained but he was pulling open a top drawer in the front of his desk.

'I have some tonic that I take for toothaches.' He brought out a brown bottle. 'I find it very effective and, because it is made of pure cocaine in alcohol, unlike laudanum it's completely non-addictive.'

'I suppose I could try some,' Cherry announced as if she were making a great concession and he rooted through for a conical ounce glass.

'It's quite clean,' he assured her as she screwed up her nose.

Only quite? Ruby queried. *Still, I suppose that's better than the water dripping down a slimy dungeon wall that you made me lap up.*

If you think that's bad, I once had to consume China tea from a China cup with a chipped handle, Hefty countered.

Oh you poor little goose, she said and he smiled bravely, not realising that she was being sarcastic.

Cherry sniffed the drink suspiciously, sipped and rolled it around her mouth.

Dr Wiseman's Coca Elixir, Hefty read from the label as Cherry polished off her medicine.

'When you…' Stanbury began but Cherry closed her eyes and put a finger to her lips to shush him.

'Well really,' he bristled.

'I know a good dentist,' I said to distract him before he decided to evict her, and he looked at me blankly. 'For your tooth,' I explained.

'Oh that,' he remembered as if the conversation had taken place months previously.

The next time you get annoyed at men not listening to you... Ruby reclined on a buttoned moss green chaise longue. I had never seen that in the office before. *Just remember that they never listen to themselves either.*

'I have no need of dentistry since I discovered this.' Stanbury tapped the neck of the bottle with the side of his pencil.

'I say!' Cherry exclaimed with a lopsided smile. 'That tonic is rather good.'

'I take two ounces every morning and every evening,' the inspector told her, and she licked her lips as he refilled her medicine glass. 'When were you last in communication with your parents?'

'I saw them on the eighteenth of September,' she replied, 'on the day I went back to university.'

'That's an early term start is it not?' he checked, and Hefty brought out his notebook.

Sardines, he jotted enigmatically.

'I had an experiment to finish.'

'And did you have any contact with them after that?' He peered at her, his eyebrows raised.

'I sent them a card from Brighton on the twenty-fifth.'

'You had time to take a holiday?'

'It was a day trip on a Sunday.'

'And since then?'

'I wrote to them once saying I was short of cash,' she replied, dreamily.

'And did they give you any?'

'My father sent me...' She closed her eyes for so long I thought that she must have nodded off. 'Four pounds.'

'That was generous of him,' I commented to Alfred's evident annoyance.

'He was a generous man.' She opened her eyes, reluctantly, it seemed. 'The next time I wrote to inform them that I was coming home the following week for my mother's birthday.'

'Not much communication in all that time,' he remarked and Cherry shifted uncomfortably.

'It wasn't very long.'

'Three months,' he reminded her.

'I was busy,' she snapped, but he looked as unconvinced as I was.

'Too busy to write more than one postcard and one letter?' he pressed, and she scowled.

'Since when,' she demanded, 'have the police cross-examined people on how often they correspond with their parents?'

'Since that person claimed that she knows a crime has been committed because her parents would have kept her informed.' He folded his arms.

'Well they would have,' she insisted. 'In the meantime the Brutons – if indeed that is their name – can move into my home without fear of prosecution. For all we know they could be holding my parents prisoner and torturing them in the cellar. You could at the very least search the house.'

Alfred pinched the bridge of his nose. 'I would need more than speculation before a magistrate would issue a search warrant.'

Cherry took a fistful of her hair. 'I don't understand why I am being interrogated when you…'

Alfred flicked his fringe back. 'I did not ask you to come here, Miss Bight. In point of fact…'

'…Should be arresting them,' she talked over him.

Alfred upturned his palms. 'It is not that simple, Miss Bight.'

'Why is it not?' Cherry gripped the edge of the desk with her free hand. 'Have they gone on the run? I can give you a good description of them.'

'To the best of my knowledge they have not absconded, nor do they have any reason to do so.' Alfred gazed at her cooly. 'Besides, as I have already explained, I know what they look like.' He rested his forearms on his desk. 'The thing is, Miss Bight, they want me to arrest you.'

Two pink circles appeared on Cherry's pale cheeks as suddenly as if she had been slapped. 'Me?'

Alfred puffed out his cheeks. 'According to Mr and Mrs Bruton you broke into their house.'

'It is not their house.'

'They assured me that it is.'

'Did they show you the deeds?'

'I cannot go marching into people's homes demanding that the residents give me proof of ownership.' A fly landed on the back of Alfred's hand and he brushed it away.

'They are not the owners.' Cherry slapped the desk partly, I suspected, in frustration but also in an attempt to swat the fly, which dodged aside and circled before finding refuge in my hair.

'I did not break in. As I told you, I used my key.'

'And where is that key now?'

While I sought the fugitive insect, Cherry unclipped her handbag and, after a prolonged fruitless rummage, upended it to spill the contents over the desk. A large white cotton handkerchief with the initials CBB sewn erratically into one corner, a packet of Gold Plate cigarettes bearing the portrait of a woman with bushels of auburn hair and exposing enough shoulder to cause a breach of the peace. A miniature bottle of Mrs Collins's lavender water. A box of Swan White Pine Vestas. A silver powder compact, a wrinkled leather purse, which she opened to reveal a few coins including a silver sixpence.

'I haven't got it,' she admitted reluctantly. 'They must have taken it after they attacked me.'

Alfred motioned for her to clear her things away. 'They claim that you attacked Mrs Bruton and that they were obliged to evict you.'

'Then they are liars on top of being murderers and thieves.' Cherry's voice portrayed weariness now rather than outrage. She looked towards the door. 'That tea is taking a long time.'

'Sergeant Webb is probably busy.' Alfred put down his pencil.

Cherry put her fingertips to her temples. 'I have such a throbbing headache.'

She eyed the tonic, brightening a little as Stanbury took a hold of the bottle but dimming a great deal as he put it back in the drawer.

'You need to rest,' he told her. 'We can talk more when you're recovered. Where are you staying?'

'I don't know,' she realised.

'Have you a friend you can stay with?'

With whom you can stay, Miss Kidd corrected him.

'I can't think.' Cherry massaged her brow.

'Miss Bight is staying with me,' I announced to my surprise but not, apparently, to hers.

'That's right,' she agreed.

Doubtless the effusive expressions of gratitude will follow shortly, Ruby sarcasmed and Miss Kidd slapped the desktop.

Sarcasmed is not a recognised word.

I recognised it, I replied cheekily, secure in the knowledge that, being confined to my brain, she could not rap my knuckles anymore. *Ow.* She rapped a crinkly bit of a gyrus instead.

Cherry rose, holding onto the desktop unsteadily, and I readied myself to catch her.

'Do you require any assistance?' Stanbury enquired. 'I can get a constable to drive you home.'

'No,' she said abruptly but to my mild relief.

I have never been overly concerned with what the neighbours would think, but my being brought home by a burly policeman would not do my reputation much good. It was already tarnished by my being a single woman who conversed freely and unchaperoned with men.

Cherry made it to the door. 'Seventy-two.'

'Seventy-two what?' Stanbury puzzled.

'Days since I wrote to my parents,' she explained. 'Not three months.'

'Does it matter?' he asked irritably.

'I don't know. You're supposed to be the detective.'

'There is no supposing about it,' Stanbury bridled. 'I am a police inspector, but I have my doubts about how reliable a source of information you are.'

Cherry hung onto the doorpost, swaying as if we were in a storm-tossed ship.

'What beautiful eyes you have,' she told him. 'Almost… smoky,' she decided as she staggered into the corridor.

'Is it too late to accept your offer?' I asked and Alfred Stanbury snorted in amusement.

'Your black maria awaits you, milady.' He dashed forward to catch Cherry as she crumpled against the opposite wall.

12

THE SILENCE OF HANDBAGS AND THE WILD MAN OF GORHAM

POLICE VANS were built to hold criminals and suspects securely but not luxuriously. The seating consisted of two parallel wooden benches and the only light came through a small grilled window in the rear door.

When the guard opens the door distract him by pretending to swoon and, when he turns towards you, I will garotte him with my pearls strung on cheese wire, Ruby instructed Inspector Hefty and he jutted his square chin.

Scotland Yard's premier detective neither swoons nor pretends to swoon, he told her stiffly. *I will knock him cold with a manly blow to his jaw.*

I left them to their schemes.

'How are you feeling?' I asked Cherry who, even in the gloom, looked decidedly queasy.

'Queasy.' She put a handkerchief over her mouth and nose. 'My head is splitting and it stinks in here.'

Probably a decomposing corpse under the false floor, Hefty speculated, unfolding his folding penknife in an attempt to lever up a loose board.

More likely the stench of corruption that permeates the police force, Ruby suggested.

We are in England, he reminded her indignantly. *You will not find any dishonest officers in this country.*

I waited for Ruby to list all the corrupt policemen that she had exposed but she was screwing the ferrule off her umbrella to reveal a miniature circular saw.

Powered by clockwork. She twisted the handle to wind it up.

We were travelling at quite a speed, every bump and pothole slamming the benches into us. Ruby stood steadily, however, her blade spinning against one of the two bars, sparks flying like fireworks all around her. Havelock Hefty watched with interest.

At this rate we should be free within the month, he calculated as we swung around a corner so violently that Cherry flew off her bench, stumbling into my arms.

'Be careful,' she scolded me, and I was half-regretting catching her when I remembered that she had been concussed and how confused I had been after a hay waggon had rolled over my head when I was eight. I still had the dent in my skull, which a phrenologist once told me indicated an acquisitive and deceitful nature.

Perhaps if I push hard the dent might pop out, my cerebral cortex suggested, but my brain was strained enough already in struggling to devise escapades for my characters.

As Ruby paused to rewind her saw, we came to an abrupt halt, Cherry and I sliding to collide with the front of our portable cell.

There was a great deal of clumping and muttering and a fair amount of thudding and clattering and the door swung open to reveal Constable Wilson, even ruddier faced than he had been when we started out, for he would have been fully exposed to the winter air on his high perch.

'Here we are, ladies,' he announced, and glanced up at the bars.

Ruby and I held our breaths, but he did not notice that she had almost sliced through one and, as I disembarked inelegantly, I could not see any damage either.

'Crumbs,' a paperboy exclaimed – *A boy made out of paper?* Inspector Hefty queried – 'they've arrested that straculiar woman from the cornered house.'

'I alway know she's a wrongun,' a ragged woman announced. 'Pretendin' to be a child when she's a adult with bone too bone idle to grew.'

Excuse me, my spine spluttered indignantly. *I work hard to earn my keep.*

And us, one hundred and seventy of my other bones chorused. My left knee was sulking since I had knocked it on a table leg and had refused to apologise.

'We have not been arrested,' I explained.

I had seen the woman collecting cigar butts from the pavement, never cigarette ends for she was a specialist and proud of it. They were soggy and split but, dried out, she could sell them to a man in the Lowers for sixpence a pound.

'Well you should be,' she insisted, 'havin' tha' hurly burly gurly man scritch every hour outside your house.'

I battled with the hurdy-gurdy player almost every day as he set up his scratchy-whining grinding machine outside my sitting room window. Did he not realise that I murdered people for a living?

Not what I would call a living. Ruby had acquired a rather fine diamond necklace.

'The policeman was kindly giving us a lift,' Cherry sought to explain, and the woman folded her arms – her own arms, I clarified before Hefty asked me why the woman would be folding Cherry's arms for her.

'Small wonder our streets are littered with the corpse of starvin' cabbies,' the woman said accusingly, though she must have had better eyesight or more imagination than I for I had not spotted one yet.

'Come inside,' I said to Cherry.

'Don't mind if I do.' The woman fished a grey globule out of her mouth, looked at it and popped it back in.

'I was talking to this lady,' I explained, half-distracted with trying to work out if what was oozing out of the woman's left ear was the same as what was discharging from her left eye.

'Then why you look at me?'

'I did not.'

'Difficult to tell with you bein' wall-eyed.' Some of the effluent drew up her nose like a snail sliding back into its shell.

I could have denied it indignantly but, if truth be told, I had been trying to keep one eye on her at the same time. I did not like the way that she was looking at my handbag.

She is probably wondering if it is one of hers, Ruby theorised, for it was a favourite of mine and long overdue replacement.

I waited for my handbag to react but, unlike my characters or body parts, handbags never talk. *Never,* I insisted as it cleared its non-existent throat.

Freda, the bearded lady, was sitting by the steps on a rough-hewn box, about the size of a beer crate. It probably contained everything she owned.

'Spare a bottle o' gin for a poor widda woman,' she beseeched as always but, as usual, I did my best to ignore her. Gerrund sometimes took her food and I gave her a blanket one snowy day, but Agnust often threatened to throw a bucket of water over her, though I knew that my maid would do no such thing.

Agnust stood in the open doorway, her massive arms folded under her even more massive bosom and, from her expression, I was in trouble. Had she observed the vehicle in which we had arrived? Had she found my cache of Butterworth's Chocolate Delights? After I had been sick while eating four bars of chocolate when I was three, my mother had forbidden me to eat any more and Agnust had taken this as a lifetime proscription to be rigorously enforced. Had she read in my journal the unspeakable fate that I had plotted for her for ripping my autographed etching of John Martin-Harvey, a minor but beautiful young actor with whom I had fallen in love for a whole month after seeing him in the Lyceum Theatre when I was sixteen?

'Brought her back here again.' She sniffed.

'I know.'

'If my presence is inconvenient…' Cherry hesitated.

If it is inconvenient, what? Ruby hated unfinished sentences.

'Tint for me to say,' Agnust said in a way that suggested it was.

'Of course it is not,' I hastened to reassure my guest.

'You say tha'.' Agnust shifted her arms, dragging her bosom sideways. 'But you dint know what lie in store.'

A rabid baboon disguised as a nurse, Havelock Hefty guessed.

'Then perhaps you would be so good as to enlighten me,' I prompted.

'You wint like it,' she warned as I drew near and hope sprang, though not eternal, in my breast.

'Are you leaving?' I gasped with such feigned anxiety that I almost deceived myself.

Agnust chortled and sniggered simultaneously.

Chiggered, I coined, *or chortered*. They were both good words and I would send them to the *Oxford English Dictionary* though they had already rejected my suggestions of *aroundipity* and *tripupsteps*.

'Oh Lady Violet,' she snorted.

For heaven's sake girl, Miss Kidd scolded. *Not satisfied with massacring the so-called characters in your trashy stories, must you also murder the English language?*

'I wint never ever leave your service,' Agnust vowed, though I often wondered when she was going to enter it.

'Thank heavens,' I said with an insincerity so deep that had I fallen down it I might never have been able to clamber out.

And you call yourself an author, Ruby said derisively. I did not bother to rejoin that I had created her for she was convinced that she had created herself.

'You never do guess wha',' Agnust said in the way that people do when they want you to have a go so that they can ridicule your attempts.

'In that case I shall not try,' I resolved, and she deflated visibly.

I never guess, Hefty declared loftily. *Guessing is for so-called lady adventuresses.*

'What has happened?' I asked before Ruby could retaliate.

'We only get broke into,' my maid informed me grimly, 'annnnd...' she paused for dramatic effect for so long that, had our sizes been reversed, I would have been tempted to pick her up and shake her. 'Only by...' Another pause while I debated whether or not I could pretend to tripupsteps and dobbin her in the abdomen. 'Theeeee…' A shorter pause this time while I decided that I would probably just bounce off her and tripdownsteps. 'The Wild Man of Gorham,' Agnust concluded with a shiver.

13

BLOOD ON THE BLADE AND THE DEAD WALK

I LOOKED at Agnust. It was quite a novelty to see my mountainous maid in such a state. The Agnust that I knew was not afraid of anything. After all it was she who had confronted an unarmed murderer from a safe distance with nothing but a loaded revolver to protect her.

'Oh my goodness.' Cherry put a hand to her mouth. 'Is he still in there?'

'The Wild Man of Gorham does not exist,' I told them both. 'He is just a fictional character.'

Just? Inspector Hefty repeated indignantly. *It was just a fictional character who murdered my beloved...* He put a fist to his brow. *What the deuce was her name?*

Buffoon, Ruby brushed him aside. *You were only attached to one foolish girl. I have had sixteen amoureux and I remember everything about them all.* With that she swept into the house impossibly past Agnust doubtless to smoke a cigarette in my sitting room, a habit that I abhorred.

'Fictional, is he?' Agnust plunked her six-fingered fists on her considerable hips. 'Character?' She rolled her eyes and piffed. 'Frictional?' she developed her theme, though neither far nor rationally. 'Then tell me this, Lady Violet Elizabeth Antoinette Cordelia Thorn...' Agnust had a knack of saying my names as if they and I were foolish things. 'Do frictional charactures burglar houses?'

'Of course not,' I conceded, 'but how do you know it was him?'

'Who else do it be?' she enquired, as if nobody other than a crazed cannibal would dream of breaking into my home.

'Oh dear,' Cherry contributed as a terrible thought struck me.

'Has anyone been killed?' I asked, not sure why I said 'anyone', because only Agnust and Gerrund would be in the house and she was certainly alive.

She could be a zombie, Ruby – miraculously at my shoulder – suggested, for she had been attacked by one in *The Dead Walk Sideways* and, looking at my maid's glassy stare, I could not fully discount that theory.

'In a manner of speaking,' Agnust said, 'no, but, in another manner of speaking, yes.'

Is that blood on her hand? Hefty stood well back. He was wary of my maid at the best of times for she never hesitated to walk straight through him.

It is a birthmark, I told him and set my foot upon the lower step.

'Shall I ask the policeman to wait?' Cherry proposed, but the black maria was already trundling away.

'You wint like it,' Agnust warned, as if I were expecting something delightful but I had had enough of that game.

'Let me in,' I commanded, and Agnust contracted her vitreous oculi but expanded her muscular thorax, narrowing the already narrow gap between her and the doorpost.

I had a theory that it was her job to do as she was bidden but I had yet to be in a position to prove that hypothesis to my complete satisfaction.

'Dint say I dint warn you.'

Hefty took out his warrant card. *Step aside*. But Agnust did not even glance in his direction.

'What has been taken?'

'Tint what's taken,' my maid corrected me, though I rather thought that it should be. 'It's what's added.'

What on earth is she talking about? I asked my brain.

Do not ask me, my brain replied with a shrug of its corpus callosum. *And stop showing off with anatomical terms. You only helped Romulus swot for his exams for six weeks – though admittedly more than some qualified doctors appear to have studied.*

'Perhaps I should go.' Cherry made as if to do so.

'Please do not,' I urged. 'I am sure that we are not in any danger.'

'Danger?' Agnust unplonked her fists but kept them clenched. 'I laugh in the face of danger.' But not so much as a hint of a snigger emerged, reinforcing my belief that there was no danger about which to guffaw.

'What on earth are you talking about?' I asked my maid.

'Dint ask me.' She shrugged her right shoulder, her left being occupied with supporting whatever the vertical part of the frame is called.

The jamb. Hefty plucked a hair from Freda's beard and she twitched.

'You wint like it,' Agnust started again and, had I been carrying my Lady Derringer, I might have been tempted to fire a warning shot in the air, if I could remember how to load the gun and operate the safety catch. I had had enough of her gnomic declarations the first time around.

'Let us in,' I commanded, drawing myself up to my full four foot ten and one eighth inches. At my height every fraction matters.

'Perhaps I will wait outside.' Cherry backstepped nervously, showing that there was no *perhaps* about it.

'It might be better for a moment.' I reverse-backstepped.

'On your head be it,' Agnust cautioned, sidestepping into the hall for me to tripupsteps after her.

'Dear God.' I struggled to shut the door behind me, look ahead and regain my balance simultaneously.

'Told you you wint like it,' Agnust reminded me because, of course, I would have forgotten in the many seconds that had passed since she had done so. 'Dint I?' she asked with great satisfaction, though she would never be graced with a reply.

The figure of a woman in a pale blue floral-printed dress sat in one of my dining room chairs in the middle of the hall. She had a dark blue hat on with a gauze veil, her long black hair dangling untidily. Her white-gloved hands gripped the arms. What alarmed me most, though, was the curved handle of my Arabian dagger protruding from the middle of her chest. A dark stain surrounded it.

'What in heaven's name is happening?' I whispered as the sound of heavy feet approached from the back of the hall.

Look out. Hefty fiddled with the catch on his swordstick as Gerrund, wild-eyed, his usually immaculate clothing dishevelled with his checkered waistcoat hanging open and his usually meticulously brushed-back hair dangling over his face, came hurtling towards me, wielding a cleaver large enough to serve for slaughtering an ox, and, still more alarmingly, there was blood on the blade and on the hand of the man who clutched it.

14

SCREENS, TUMBRILS AND CARDIAC ICICLES

I TOOK a step towards Gerrund. My father had taught me a great many things, including how to deal from the bottom of the pack, play billiards, open a bottle of wine with a sabre or, in the absence of one, a pencil but, more relevantly, he had impressed upon me that we should never let the servants know we are all frightened of them. Society would collapse if one's alleged inferiors knew how we trembled at accounts of the French Revolution.

'What on earth are you up to, Gerrund?' I demanded, having carefully added his name to remind him who he was and, more importantly, to avoid concluding my sentence with a preposition.

'Fetch a screen,' Gerrund commanded, and I heard the rumble of tumbrils in the square.

More likely the coal merchant's waggon, Inspector Hefty reassured me as the noise faded, and I realised that Gerrund was addressing my maid.

Almost incredibly, she meekly obeyed, bustling off into the music room more readily than she ever complied with any of my instructions. I had acquired several screens with the house. Most of them were flimsy affairs but Agnust returned carrying a solid oak construction as lightly as if it were bamboo and paper, dumping it to lean against the wall as heavily as if it were a heavy wooden screen.

'Right then.' Gerrund put his cleaver on the hall table, having first spread out a large green handkerchief to protect the varnish. The blood was still fresh on the blade. 'Help me put the screen up around it.'

His use of the word *it* grated disturbingly. He was, after all, referring to a human being.

'Is she dead?' I asked, though there was no reasonable doubt that she was, and Gerrund chuckled. It was not like him to be so stony-hearted.

'Oh no, milady,' he assured me. 'It's a man.'

'Really?' I stepped towards the figure. 'She looks like a woman to me.'

'No, milady, it's a man eh.'

'Are you sure?'

'Yes, milady.' He patted the figure's shoulder. 'It's a mannequin.'

'Oh,' I said sagely, still loath to think of the model as an *it*. She was much smaller than I had judged on first viewing. I crouched to lift the veil. Her face had been constructed from papier mâché and was surrounded by black woollen hair. Her complexion had been painted white as white lead. She had a tiny nose and a dimple in her chin. She was quite nicely made but I believe I actually jumped when I looked at her eyes. The left one was green and the right blue.

'Me,' I whispered. 'It is meant to be me.'

It will be you, a man said huskily, *next time.*

I looked up but there was only Agnust and Gerrund peering over my shoulders and it had been neither of their voices. It was darker and more menacing than any that I had heard before.

Have a care, Thorn, Ruby cried. *He is here, lurking in your mind.*

I never gave much credence to talk about living people's blood chilling and Romulus had confirmed that it cannot, but I had icicles in my heart for I had never heard Ruby Gibson, my intrepid lady adventuress and heroine, sound frightened before.

15

THE MAD AXEMAN

I STRUGGLED to organise my thoughts.

Good luck with that project, Ruby spoke, all at once nonchalant again and nibbling a marasca cherry on a stalk.

'How did it get in here?'

'I don't know.' Gerrund wiped his bloodstained hands on a cloth tucked into the pocket of his blue-and-white-striped apron. 'The back door was locked this morning – I know it was – but just after I heard Agnust scream…'

'I dint scream.' Agnust took up a vaguely pugilistic stance. 'I hollered to make sure you hear me with your big gushy ears.'

'My ears are not big,' he bridled. They were a bit, but I had no idea that he was sensitive about them.

'Big as a Scotch elephant,' she asserted, though that was not a breed with which I was familiar.

'Talking of elephants…'

'What happened?' I asked before this escalated into a bare-knuckle brawl.

Gerrund gave Agnust a just-you-wait glare. 'I was in the kitchen with the door closed, chopping up a lovely rack of goat…'

I shall dine out tonight, Hefty announced.

Do their faces remind you too much of your sweetheart? Ruby asked cruelly.

'I heard footsteps hurry by and they were too light to be hers.' Gerrund jerked a thumb towards Agnust. 'So I went to investigate and saw the back door open.'

'Did you see anyone?'

His apron was splattered with shreds of the unfortunate creature.

'A tall well-built man in a long blue cloak and a floppy-brimmed hat. I ran after him into the alley but he had a good start on me. Thought I caught sight of him heading down Matins Street, but it was a parson and I'm almost sure his cloak was shorter.'

'Had you seen him before?' I asked, prompted by Havelock Hefty.

'Never.' Gerrund went to scratch his jaw but, doubtless remembering what he had been handling, left his itch to prosper undisturbed a while longer. 'But I don't socialise much with the clergy.'

'You must have created quite a stir racing through the town with a bloodstained cleaver,' I conjectured, and he grinned.

'Wonder what *The Chronic* will make of it.'

'Mad Axeman Rampages Through Montford,' I speculated as he and Agnust went back to the screen.

The noise from the square grew louder and it was only then that I became aware of a fourth person in the house.

'What on earth is happening?'

I had almost forgotten about Cherry. She was just inside the threshold with the door wide open. I must not have shut it properly when I tripped. Standing on her box behind Cherry was Freda, clutching the iron rail and trembling not with fear, I suspected, but with her craving for alcohol.

'Come in, Cherry,' I urged, but she shook her head.

'Can you see her too?' Freda tugged at her goatee. 'Thank the scrise for tha'. Thought was gettin' hallucgin-ations.'

The last was an unintentionally clever amalgam of words, I thought, before remembering that Freda used to be a teacher until she gave up her profession for the love of a man and the bottle, neither of whom returned her affection.

'Has everyone in this town gone mad?' Cherry pushed her flaming hair back from her face.

'It is just a practical joke.' I sought to reassure myself as much as her.

'You're quite safe here.' Gerrund sought to reassure me as much as her, I thought.

'Your friends have a distorted sense of humour.' Cherry was backing away, feeling the steps with her feet and not taking her eyes off any of us.

'They are not my friends.'

'Who are they then?' She reached the pavement.

'I do not know... yet. But come in, Cherry. It is quite safe.'

'I cannot stay here.' She waved a hand to encompass most of the square.

'But where will you go?' I asked in concern.

'I have a friend in Gallows Lane. I will stay with her.'

'Gallows Lane?' Agnust cracked her knuckles, all thirty-two of them. 'You dint want to hang around there.'

I wondered if my maid was making a joke and decided that she was not before I glimpsed a smirk and redecided that she was.

'Let me fetch you a cab, miss,' Gerrund volunteered. 'It's quite a walk even without your luggage.'

Cherry's brow wrinkled. 'I'm not sure I have enough money.'

'Dint you worry over tha',' Agnust said breezily. 'Lady Violet will pay.'

'And…' Gerrund looked me in the eye. *Which eye?* Hefty enquired while my man continued, 'She will give you a few pounds to tide you over until all this is sorted out.'

My generosity, it often appeared, knew few bounds while others were making the offers on my behalf.

'How?' Cherry stared at us all hopelessly. 'My parents have…' The rest of her sentence was drowned out by a cry of 'Any rag bone?' from the driver of a cart pulling up nearby.

You, Ruby scoffed, for he was clad in rags and his horse's bones were all too discernible through its calloused and ulcerated skin.

'Any rag bone?'

'I will get to the bottom of this,' I vowed as Gerrund went out into the square.

Agnust tutted at my use of the word beginning with B but *I will get to the sit-upon of this* made little sense.

'How?' Cherry repeated, flapping her arms like a lost child.

Gerrund put his wiped fingers to his lips and blew an almost eardrum-shredding whistle.

'Any rag bone?' The sacks behind him were almost empty. By the end of the day, he would hope to fill them with scraps of fabrics, rugs, bones, bottles, pots and broken metal. Legend had it that there was good money in the trade but I had never come across a street collector yet who reeked of prosperity.

Constable, move that man along, Hefty commanded, but only he could see the officer who was doubtless marching forward to obey his order.

'Dint you fret on tha',' Agnust called. 'When Lady Violet say she do somethin', she do it.' And I was touched by her loyalty until she added, 'or she have me to answer to.'

Mistresses do not answer to their servants for anything, I declared haughtily in my mind. 'Yes I will,' I confirmed lamely.

A four-wheeler clattered by carrying a family with three boys dressed in sailor suits and I felt a dull ache in my heart. My brother Decimus ran away to sea when he was twelve and was never heard from again.

'I hope so.' Cherry's voice barely reached me above the general hubbub of the street and my thoughts. 'Or I do not know who I can turn to.'

In response to my man's wave, a cab pulled up. Cherry clambered in and Gerrund lifted her suitcase, depositing it on its end beside her. Hansoms had no luggage racks and anything put in the footwell could easily slide off.

'Be careful.' Cherry watched anxiously as if her case were filled with Ming porcelain.

Check your China cabinet, Hefty advised.

'Gallows Lane,' Gerrund instructed the driver.

'Gallows Lane?' the cabby bared his blackened dentition in mirth. 'You dint want to...'

'Any rag bone?' came bellowed over his doubtless amusing and original banter.

'What number?' The driver's head was hatless and bald. 'It's a longly wearisomish road.'

'I'm not sure, but I'll recognise the house when we get there.' As the hansom set off Cherry turned and gave me an imploring look. She mouthed something.

Good riddance, you scrivelled sowpig, Ruby suggested, boarding a sporty-looking high-flyer phaeton driven by a rather dashing man in black, but I rather thought that Cherry had said, 'Help me, please.'

'Any rag...'

'Feed your horse,' I told him in disgust for, to judge by his girth, he certainly fed himself while his unfortunate animal was barely able to stand.

'I do.'

'Feed it with food next time.' I spun on my heel and managed the full about-turn without catching my heel or losing my balance.

Well done Violet, I congratulated myself just before I stumbled on an uneven paving slab and it was only Gerrund's rapid reactions that saved me from making a public exhibition of myself.

'Tottering about the square in the morning.' Mr Bran-Breamish, the man from next door, shouldered his horn-handled cane. 'And making a public exhibition of yourself. What must the neighbours think?'

'I doubt that they do,' I retorted as Gerrund let go of my arm and the three of us re-entered Break House.

Unmiraculously the mannequin was still impaled in the chair, and I saw that its gloved wrists had been tied to the arms with white threads.

'Exactly what happened?' I asked Agnust.

'Somebody put it there,' Agnust explained.

'Yes, but...'

'Then you come home.'

'I know that, but...'

'With that awkwish girl.' It was quite a feat to stem Agnust in full flow and I had rarely mistressed it. 'What do I tell you time and time 'gain 'bout lettin' people you dint know in the house?'

I could have asserted that it was not Agnust's place to instruct me on who I might entertain in my own home but, whenever I tried to stand on my dignity, Agnust always managed to kick it out from under my feet.

Besides which she is right. Ruby was loading caviar onto a slice of hot buttered toast with a mother-of-pearl spoon.

She did not need to list the strangers who I had admitted and who had come close to destroying my reputation, my life or both. Hefty, it transpired, did need to list them. He produced a black-cloth-covered notebook and licked his finger to turn the pages.

On the first Thursday of March in the year of our Lord eighteen ninety-four... he began.

'Mr Appleton has never caused me any trouble,' I said, knowing I was on strong ground there, for she did not know how he had colluded in my surveillance of Haglin House.

''part from encouragin' you to spy on Haglin House.' Agnust stroked the furry mole on her upper lip as if to pacify it. 'And we all know what horridable things happened there.'

Comprehensively defeated, I withdrew from the combat and returned to the more pressing topic. 'What happened to your hand, Gerrund?' There was more blood on it than could be explained by his preparations of the goat.

'When Agnust found the mannequin,' Gerrund, ever the voice of reason, informed me, 'she screeched so loudly that I missed the meat and cut myself.'

'I 'sumed he put it there for a joke,' she explained.

He wiped his hand on a cloth dangling from the waist cord of his apron, but his left index finger was still bleeding freely.

I unclipped my handbag and took out my handkerchief.

A clean one, I hope. Miss Kidd was checking through my latest manuscript for speling misteaks.

Ignoring my governess's remarks and my man's protests, I wrapped it around the digit.

'It is quite a deep wound.' I tied a knot in my already sodden makeshift bandage. 'It might need stitching.'

Gerrund, who had fearlessly accompanied me on a nocturnal trip through the squalid alleys of Lower Montford and into the bowels of the January sales at Hickman's Department Store, defended me without hesitation from a panther and once picked up a hairy spider with his bare hands, blanched. 'I'm sure it will heal itself, milady.'

All bleeding stops, Hefty pronounced the surgeons' maxim, *one way or another.*

'And where were you, Agnust, while somebody was stabbing mannequins in my hallway?'

'Puttin' your laundry away.'

'How long did that take?'

Agnust gritted her teeth. I had seen her crack walnuts between them on both sides simultaneously. 'I dint have a stopping-watch.'

'You were up there about half an hour.' Gerrund found a handkerchief of his own and bound that tightly around my binding.

'Give or take two and thirty minutes,' she conceded, and I tried to imagine what minus two minutes might look like.

'And neither of you heard anything?'

'Nothing.' Gerrund placed his knife on the floor and wrapped his right hand around the haemorrhage.

'I hear a pigeon on the windowsill,' Agnust contributed.

Ask her what species of pigeon, Hefty urged, but I ignored them both.

'How did this person get in?'

Agnust groaned. 'She never listen, even as a baby,' she told Gerrund and turned back to me. 'It... int... a... person,' she explained slowly. 'It's a man-O'Kin.'

'How did the person who sat it there get into the house?' I asked with nearly all the patience of the patron saint of patience.

'Now you're askin',' she told me helpfully.

'Would you like me to telephone the police?' Gerrund offered and I scratched my temple, an exercise I have yet to find useful for encouraging thought or, indeed, anything other than dealing with an itch.

'I suppose I had better do it,' I opposite-of-enthused. 'Inspector Stanbury will be sick of the sight of me.'

I wouldn't say that, Ruby waved her amber silver-ringed holder loaded with an Egyptian Kyriazi Frères cigarette. *I would say he is sick of the sight of you already.*

My morale thus fortified, I went to the sideboard in my sitting room where my candlestick telephone stood beside an ambrotype of my mother with my youngest brother Marcus perched on her knee, a memento of his sixth birthday. I remembered she had great difficulty in persuading him to sit still even for the twenty seconds it took to expose the glass plate. He was a loveable mischievous child, but he was never to have another birthday. The Klebs–Löffler bacillus saw to that. It ravaged him with diphtheria.

The earpiece clicked as I lifted it from the cradle.

'Hello Violet,' Mrs Corncroft greeted me, but I soon put her in her place.

'I do not remember giving you permission to address me by my Christian name.'

'Course you dint pipkin,' she giggled, clearly unput in her place after all. ' 'cause you never did.' There were a few crackles. 'Puttin' you through now, pumpkin.'

'Through to whom?'

'S'prised you need ask me tha', petal. Good job I know how many beans make six.'

'Five,' I corrected her.

'No, poppet, six beans make six.'

'To whom are you connecting me?' I looked at the mouthpiece as if that had the answer.

'Why the catch-rogues of course, sweet pea.'

'But I did not ask for the police.' I had an itch in my right ear but could not take the appliance away to scratch myself.

'Dint have to, flower.' There was a series of clicks. 'You dint never want anybody else.'

'Yes I do,' I protested. 'I call Thetbury Hall and Suthy Hall.' These were the homes of my parents and Romulus respectively.

'Yes, chicken, but tha's in the past and there's no point livin' in tha',' Mrs Corncroft expounded. 'Puttin' you through now, kitten.'

I almost insisted that she connected me to another number but then I would have had to concoct a reason for my call with the telephonist listening to every word.

'Montford police station.'

I recognised the voice immediately. 'Good afternoon, Sergeant Webb, this is Lady Violet Thorn.'

'Tsk,' he tsked. 'I could've guessed tha'.'

I was unaware that we were supposed to be playing a game. 'I wish to speak to Inspector Stanbury.'

Webb piffed. 'Well you can't,' he told me with what sounded like considerable satisfaction. 'He's away and out.'

'When will he be back?'

Webb puffed as if trying to blow a midge away. 'Your guess int as good as mine and I have no idea.'

'None at all?'

'Tha's what *no idea* mean.' There was a long pause. ''Spector Goodman is 'vailable.'

If there were a contest for the least aptly named person, Goodman was a strong candidate for the championship, though it would probably be won by the Honourable Morel Ethics, our undistinguished member of parliament.

'I had better speak to him then,' I said in resignation.

'I'll see if he's 'vailable. Just goin' to cover the earpiece to stop you listenin'.' Obviously Webb had not fully grasped the technical details of their device yet. ''Spector Goodman,' he bellowed. 'There's Lady Vi'let wants to speak.'

'What, that crackle-headed interfering midget?' came back from close by. 'Tell her I'm not here.'

'Hello, Lady Violet. He int here.'

'Then perhaps you could inform him that whilst I may be mad and I am certainly petite, I am also Superintendent Padmore's...' The line was crackling. 'Goddaughter.'

That last claim was a lie, though I knew Paddy Padmore quite well as he was a friend of my father's.

'She says she's a lunatic and she's petty but to remind you she's Super-nintendent Padmore's daughter.'

'Goddaughter,' I repeated over a whistling noise.

'She says she's God.'

'Told you she's a crackle-head.'

'I am Superintendent Padmore's goddaughter,' I yelled.

'Blink my crittels,' Mrs Corncroft cursed. 'Near blow my drums you do, scritchin' like a barncat with one tail.' She paused. 'Not tha' I'm listenin', ducklin'.'

While she was talking, I missed the conversation between Sergeant Webb and his superior but the next voice I heard was Inspector Goodman's. 'A'noon, Miss Lady Vi-let, how might I be of assistance?'

In common with all police officers, Goodman had risen from the ranks but in his case I suspected his promotion was more the result of outliving his predecessors than from personal merit. Alfred tried not to criticise fellow members of the force in my presence, but the expression dunt-head had escaped his lips on one occasion.

'Somebody entered my house and put a mannequin in my hall.'

'A manny-what?'

'Mannequin.'

'Is that a fish?'

'Dummy.' I heard a sharp intake of breath and hastened to explain. 'A mannequin is a dummy.'

'Right then,' Goodman said decisively. 'We'll soon get to the bottom of this one.' This was fighting talk indeed for the man who had insisted that his own muddy footprints were those of a burglar.

'I hope so.'

'Sergeant Webb,' Goodman bellowed, 'do you put dummies in Lady Vi-let's house? Out with it man.'

'No, 'Spector.'

'Smith, do you hang dummies in Lady Vi-let's house? Tell the truth and ashame the devil.'

'Not me, 'Spector. I swear it on my mother's gravy.'

'Cooper?'

'Dint think so, 'Spector. Sure I 'member if I do.'

'Hear tha'? Lady Vi-let?' Goodman came back on the telephone. 'Wint none on us.'

'No, I...'

'Anthin' else I can help you with? Only we're busy as a bean pole here.'

'I cannot imagine that you can possibly be of any further assistance,' I told the inspector, and I could almost hear him preening.

'Glad to be of help, milady miss,' he said as he put his receiver down.

'Men,' Mrs Corncroft interjected just as I was about to return my earpiece to its cradle. 'They're as useless as a four-legged horse. I tell you who leave models in your hallway, lamb.'

'Please do,' I said resignedly.

'Why it's as plain as your face,' she told me. 'Must be the Montford Maniac.'

'Goodbye.' I ended the call. If there was one thing of which I was certain, it was not him. That murderer had been murdered.

The ghost of the Montford Maniac, Hefty hissed.

I know I promised not to kill you. I took the stopper off a decanter without so much as a glance at the silver tag hanging from its neck. It was alcohol and I wanted it. *But,* I returned to Scotland Yard's premier detective, *I never promised not to put you back on the beat.*

Must go, Hefty mumbled. *There's a strangled steeplejack in Lower Downhill Up.* And he was off, but not before he had downed my tumbler of neat gin. Well, somebody had, I realised guiltily, and was relieved to see that it was Ruby in an ivory charvet dress who was putting the glass back down onto my cabinet.

16

THE SERPENT AND THE VAMPIRE BAT

I PICKED up my pencil and nibbled it absentmindedly before remembering that while it was made of metal my teeth were not.

'*You filthy fiend!*' Ruby Gibson cried defiantly and Count Zugravescu laughed maniacally.

For the love of laudanum, Ruby flicked ash onto my pituitary gland, *pay attention, Thorn. I have called him that twice already and he laughed maniacally in the last paragraph.*

'What the devil does it matter?'

Hefty, who had no part in this chapter anyway, flinched at my coarse language. I retracted the lead and put the pencil down. For too long I had sought solace in the company of my characters but even they brought me no comfort now.

Would you like a cup of coffee? he asked, possibly solicitously but probably more to keep in my good books or even my bad ones.

I would rather you cooperated in creating a readable story.

Havelock Hefty tapped a dottle from his pipe into my precentral sulcus. Small wonder I was having trouble concentrating. *We can only do what you tell us to.*

Ruby would rather wear mauve than admit such a thing. *Don't listen to him,* she yawned histrionically. *Listen to me. Just because your heart was broken by your fiancé doesn't mean it can't be repaired.*

Miss Gibson is right. Hefty stood on the hearth with his back to the fire.

Stop agreeing with each other.

I was distraught at the death of my beloved what-was-her-name? He leaned with one elbow on the mantlepiece. *But I shall find true love in this book.*

No you will not, I told him.

And so will you, he asserted.

She has found it already. Ruby played a scale idly on a grand piano. How had she got that up the stairs and into my study?

No I have not. I unwrapped a stick of Beeman's to the sound of the front doorbell caterwauling like a… I chewed on my gum meditatively… like a cat, I decided.

Congratulations Violet, Miss Kidd towered over me, a trick I never really understood because she was not very much taller than I. *You have invented the circular simile.* She chalked on the blackboard. *Caterwaul, to shriek like a cat.* I knew that really. *Write it out two hundred times and neatly.*

The bell shrilled like a shrill bell.

'Ouch.' The blackboard duster hit me just below the eye.

Gerrund was out, I remembered, having given him permission to go to Drimpkin's to view their latest range of silk handkerchiefs. Agnust would be at her mid-morning prayers and even God dared not interrupt those. Many was the time I had heard her scolding him for his manners. If this was the soap-seller, Agnust had told the man already that I never used it, omitting to mention that I did use other products.

Down the stairs I went – a much less dangerous exercise since dresses had shortened sluttishly to above the ankle – and along the hall.

'Make her grow to a respectable height,' I heard, and I did not need to wonder to whom she was referring.

Alfred Stanbury stood on the doorstep, his moustaches drooping in the mizzle that enveloped him.

'Come in.' I stood back.

Alfred marched on the spot, feet sliding over the mat to clean his boots. We did not kiss – that would have been too forward for him – nor did we shake hands – too formal for both of us.

'Forgive her, Lord, for her ingratitudes to me.' There was another pause while, doubtless, Agnust awaited a response.

'I hope this is not inconvenient.'

'It certainly is. You have distracted me from twiddling my thumbs.'

I helped him out of his damp coat and hung it on the stand. His jacket always bulged with odds and ends – cigar case, boxes of matches, notebook, pen and pencil, penknife, magnifying glass, spare handkerchief, ball of string and Lord knew what other bric-a-brac. Small wonder that his pockets sagged and the linings tore. Today his right flap pocket looked as if it had a half brick in it.

Agnust was still bawling her invocations. Did she think God needed an ear trumpet? 'And make her see sense for once in her buffleheaded life and wed that nice Mr...'

'Come into the sitting room,' I urged loudly but we both knew who she thought I should marry. 'I cannot offer you coffee, I fear. Agnust is busy lamenting my shamelessness.'

'So I heard.' He wiped the rain from his face with a large polka dot handkerchief. 'I wouldn't say no to a small whisky though.'

In my experience people who ask for a small drink are consistently miffed if you give them one. I poured us both a very large Very Old Ben Nevis. Nobody should have to drink alone.

You do. Ruby was mixing a fluorescent green drink for herself, *a cockatiel cocktail,* she informed me.

Only because Lady Violet has no friends, Hefty defended me stoutly. He had a pint glass of bitter, not a drink that I stocked.

'Good health,' I toasted my friend and we clinked glasses. 'Shall we sit?'

We settled in my William Morris armchairs overlooking the square.

The newspaper vendor passed my window, paused and turned to look straight at me. 'Montford man misses train and has to wait for next train,' he blared and I held up my copy of *The Chronic* to show that I already had one. 'Miserybald Montford mowther refuses to buy paper from starvin' seller,' he shouted and moved on.

Alfred laughed and sipped his whisky. 'Have you heard any more from Miss Bight?'

'Nothing. I only know that she went to stay with a friend in Gallows Lane.'

He swirled the glass. 'Obviously the poor girl is mentally disturbed.'

I absently watched a gentleman in a silk hat wave his cane only to be ignored by a cabby outside the Splendid Hotel across the square. 'Probably.'

'You have your doubts?'

'Possibly.'

'I did not care for the Brutons, but I am convinced that they are the rightful owners of that house.' Alfred watched me thoughtfully. 'You won't get embroiled in anything?'

'Why did you not like them?' I skilfully dodged the question.

'They seemed rather cold fish to me.' He swirled his drink. 'You won't get embroiled in anything?' he repeated, demonstrating that I had no interrogation evasion skills whatsoever.

'I will not take any risks,' I promised.

'That is not the same thing.'

'Did Inspector Goodman tell you that I spoke to him on the telephone?'

'I gather you accused the police of putting a dummy in your house.' Alfred cocked his head quizzically.

'It was not quite like that.' I took a bigger drink than I had intended and coughed, waving away his concerned enquiry. 'Somebody got into the house,' I wheezed, resisting the urge to pat myself on the chest in company. 'And left a mannequin in my hall with a dagger in its breast.'

'How horrible.' Alfred grimaced. 'And outlandish.'

'You were not there and I wanted him to look into the matter, but he misunderstood.'

'Must have been a bad telephone connection.' Alfred eyed the world through his malt.

'It was a bit crackly,' I agreed as a lady wobbled by on her unsafe safety bicycle.

'And you have no idea who did it?'

'I only know that it was not one of your men.'

Alfred smiled ruefully. 'Have you still got the mannequin?'

I placed my tumbler on the table between us. 'Would you like to see it?'

'Might as well while I'm here.' We went into the hall.

'It was in a chair.' I indicated the area as we crossed into the music room. Here the shutters were closed and the only time I had ever opened them was when Agnust had screamed that a gigantic vampire bat had flown in. Gerrund, who had tackled all sorts of unsavoury people and wild animals on a number of occasions, was wary of confronting the creature. I was frightened too but, the longer I lived, the more noblesse obliged me and the fewer privileges it granted so I steeled myself to confront the animal, only to discover nothing more ferocious than a privet hawkmoth.

My Great Aunt Herbena, Lady Strainge, a gifted cellist, often played there, once accompanied by the snores of a crown prince of Württemberg. Having few instrumental skills I rarely used the room and, doubtless inspired by my example, Agnust did not appear to have entered it either. I turned the light on, concerned as always by the heat emanating from the switch, to find the grand piano draped rather like Miss Havisham's wedding cake by cobwebs heavy with dust.

Gerrund had laid the mannequin on a chaise longue in the corner, hands folded in her lap, dress pulled decorously down her legs which, we had discovered, were stockings stuffed with balls of pages from *The Suffolk Trumpet*.

Alfred approached. 'Looks…' he hesitated.

'Like me,' I contributed.

'A bit,' he conceded. 'How did they get into the house?'

'I only know that whoever it was got out through the back door.'

'Could the door have been left unbolted?'

'No. Gerrund and Agnust are both scrupulous about keeping it locked.'

'Any footprints in the garden or house?'

'There were some muddy smudges in the hall but nothing that could help determine boot size.'

Alfred blew out through closed teeth. 'What about the clothes?'

'They are not mine.'

Nor mine. Ruby unkinked his watchchain. *I wouldn't be seen in a dress like that, not even when I was disguised as a Hungarian beggarwoman in Rottingdean.*

'Was Miss Bight here at the time?'

'She stood in the doorway but would not come in.'

He held the figure's wrist as if checking for a pulse but really, I presumed, to see how it was constructed – long white gloves, filled in the same way as the legs. 'But she was here before that?'

'I brought her to see you from here.'

Alfred ran his fingers through the dummy's hair and it slid over her eye, looking rather like I did after a sleepless night.

'Could she have unbolted the back door?' Alfred refolded the arms.

'No,' I replied without thinking, but then I thought about it. 'She did use my water closet on the first floor.' I thought about it a little longer. 'I suppose that she could have before then or on the way back. But one of us would have noticed. And why would she anyway?'

'She is certainly an unusual young lady.' He pushed the wig back, but it was still askew. 'Who knows what goes on it that head?'

For a moment I thought he was referring to the mannequin.

'Shall we finish our drinks?' I suggested and we returned to our armchairs.

Alfred inhaled the fumes from his tumbler.

Should I be recording that information? Hefty produced his notebook.

No.

Then why did you?

Because I can.

Fair enough. He slipped his notebook back into his inside breast pocket.

Alfred looked at me and then the floor.

'There is something else,' I said, for I had known him since I was a little girl and he was a big boy.

'I was going to ask you to do something,' Alfred admitted, 'but I don't think I can.'

In my experience, Ruby spiked an olive on a silver stick, *married men are only after one kind of favour.*

Does he want her to launder his socks? Hefty asked innocently.

'His wife does his laundry for him,' I heard myself saying.

Alfred frowned in puzzlement. 'Who are you talking about?'

'Sorry.' I slapped my cheek. 'My mind was on my story and I have just thought of an important clue.' Before Scotland Yard's premier detective could tell me that all clues were important and to remember the significance of the hard-boiled eggs floating in the custard, I added hastily, 'What do you not think you can ask me?'

'We found a body,' Alfred grimaced.

'Where?' Could Anthony have been correct that it would be Hallows Square?

'An old sewer collapsed in Orchard Lane.'

'I heard about that, but surely it is upstream of here.'

'A lot of debris was flushed into the drains. Amongst other things they found an old bicycle and a new pram. With all the blockages the water could have flowed backwards.'

'And you want me to identify him?'

Alfred puffed out his cheeks. 'Not exactly him. His own mother wouldn't recognise him after all those days in sewage.' He paused, then, probably recalling that I was not a delicate flower who swooned at the slightest indelicacy, added, 'And the rats, of course.'

'I can imagine.' I suppressed a shudder. One of the labourers at Thetbury Hall Farm had gone missing and I had seen him fished out of a slurry pit weeks later. 'What can I do then?'

'Possibly nothing.' Alfred put a hand into his right flap pocket and I was surprised not to hear the sound of ripping fabric. 'But did you see his teeth?'

They were in his mouth, Havelock Hefty informed me helpfully.

Surely the police had not extracted the dead man's incisors to show me?

'I suppose so,' I responded doubtfully.

He had an eighth of an inch diastema between his upper left central and lateral incisors, Inspector Hefty reminded me, but that would not be useful information if the teeth were rattling round an old tobacco tin.

'There was a small gap on the top left,' I translated for the man who could not have heard his fictional colleague anyway.

'He had false teeth.' Alfred brought out a cardboard box. 'There were a few gaps where they had been badly repaired and one tooth was out of line. That's why I hoped you might recognise them'

'Possibly,' I concurred doubtfully. 'Now that I think of it, the lateral incisor was slightly rotated.'

I knew it was a denture, Hefty put in quickly but unconvincingly as Alfred took the lid off.

'It's been washed in antiseptic.' Alfred tilted the box to let me see.

I was about to observe as much, Hefty put in more quickly but even less convincingly.

'You can see for yourself,' I realised, and unwrapped the bandage. The tooth marks were healing well but the pattern was still clearly visible and obviously different.

Alfred clicked his tongue in disappointment and I rewrapped my hand. I was becoming quite adept at that.

'I am sorry.' I did not know why, but I felt that I had let him down. He had told me more than once that witnesses were sometimes so anxious to be of help to the police that they would confidently identify people that they had never seen before, and I began to understand how they felt. 'But these are not the gentleman's teeth.'

Alfred put the lid on and stuffed the box back in his pocket with a faint but distinct ripping sound.

'So now we have one unidentified man missing and one unidentified man found dead.'

'Would you like another?'

'Unidentified man?' He forced a wry smile.

'Drink.'

'Just a small one.'

I took the stopper off a decanter. 'So the body did not have a leg missing?'

'The one that was found in Poplar Lane?' Alfred slid his glass towards me.

'If the press is to be believed it was the work of the Wild Man of Gorham.' I topped his drink with less than I intended then far more on my second attempt.

'As Romulus will vouch, the most common cause of missing limbs round here is agricultural accidents.' Alfred watched me without complaint. 'With traditional scythes and modern equipment, farms can be almost as dangerous as battlefields and these cases rarely get reported. Most farmworkers would rather rely on each other than go to hospital. They probably cauterised it themselves.'

I winced. It had been painful enough when a doctor had burnt a wart off my shoulder with the tip of a red-hot knife sharpener. It did the trick, but the resultant scar was far more unsightly than the growth ever was. 'I remember Shillidge, the pigman at Thetbury, sealing his daughter's stump with pitch when she lost a hand.'

'As if she didn't have enough misfortunes with him as a father.' Alfred stretched wearily.

Ruby was perched on an American high pressed back chair languidly flicking through that month's copy of *Vogue*, showing the very latest American fashions. She whipped off her reading spectacles when she spotted me. Like most women she hated to be seen wearing them. They were a reminder that she had human frailties though, unlike me, she had yet to reach the grand old age of twenty-eight.

The door flew open and Gerrund, apron on and hair wild as a tom cat's, charged in.

'Stay in there, milady,' he gasped. 'It's on the loose.' It was then that I saw that he was gripping his cleaver, and I hoped that this was not going to become a frequent habit.

'What is?' I asked in alarm, but the door slammed shut.
It could hardly slam open, Miss Kidd pointed out.

'What's going on?' Alfred hurried up to me, sending Ruby's magazine flying out of her hands.

'I do not know.'

'Stand back.' Alfred brought out a life-preserver from his inner pocket and, with his free hand, opened the door.

'Don't let it in,' Gerrund panted as Alfred stepped into the hall.

The door closed again, leaving me alone and bewildered.

'There,' I heard Gerrund shout.

'Hell's teeth. It's a monster,' Alfred cried in alarm.

It was so obvious there was something appalling and dangerous in my hallway that I hesitated for almost one tenth of a second before I flung open my door.

'No,' both men cried in unison and, before I could jump away, it came straight towards me. Alfred had not exaggerated in his description. A great fat brown snake at least eight feet long wriggled around my shoes. Its head reared up, horrid, yellow-rimmed black eyes staring at me malevolently. Its wicked thin-lipped mouth gaped as it hissed to reveal clusters of needle-sharp teeth.

'Crikey,' I exclaimed weakly.

'I'll get it, milady.' Gerrund sprang, chopping wildly with his cleaver, narrowly missing me, to bury the blade in an oak floorboard.

'Leave it to me.' As Gerrund extracted his weapon with a splintering sound, Alfred leapt to my defence, wielding his life-preserver with a wild swing to bring it crashing down on my soft indoor shoe.

'Blimmid hell,' I cursed, the impact coursing through my soft in-and-outdoor foot. 'Broggit.' I hopped on my uninjured foot.

Unscathed, the serpent completed its circuit of my leg and slithered off back into and down the hall towards the back door. Gerrund flung himself after it, flailing with his cleaver to take a chunk out of my wainscoting while Alfred missed its tail with his weighted club and hit a tile with such force that I was surprised one or the other did not shatter.

Onwards the snake shot, past Agnust, who was standing in her doorway, arms folded to watch the fun.

There was an oak chest to the side at the end of the hall, just below the rack of keys, many so ancient that nobody knew what, if anything, they fitted. I had inherited the chest with the house and did not like it with its grotesque carved faces, but it was useful for storing things that I did not and never would need. The chest was raised on four legs about four inches high and it was under this that the creature slipped.

Gerrund and Alfred hesitated. Doubtless, having seen its fangs, they were wary of reaching for it.

'Men.' Agnust trundled towards them. 'Useless as a hen's beak.' Her massive fist was closed on a thick blackthorn stick. I had no idea from where that came. Up to the chest she strode and banged her stick on the lid, giving its time-battered surface another dent. 'Get you out, serpent.' And, much to our surprise and my alarm, out it came, rearing up, teeth bared. 'None of tha' nonsense.' With a swish of her stick, knobbed handle downwards, she bludgeoned the creature on its head whereupon it fell twitching on the floor. One more blow and it lay lifeless, or so I assumed. It did not occur to me to check its breathing.

Scotland Yard's premier detective was standing on a kitchen chair, trousers tucked inside his argyle socks to prevent the serpent from climbing up his legs.

Fear not, Lady Violet. He jutted his jaw. *Thanks to my carefully coordinated plan of attack, the filthy beast has been destroyed.*

On close inspection, it was not a snake after all. It had gills and a slimy mucous coating in place of scales. As happens with spiders, which never look anything like as big when you have trapped them in a jam jar, I saw that far from eight feet it was about thirty inches long. The teeth, though, were still as alarming, the whole mouth being filled with horrendous spikes, any one of which could have been lethal.

It's an eel, Ruby pointed out, *and, by the way, they do not hiss.*

It looked like it was hissing. Why did I feel the need to justify myself to my characters?

'How on earth did that get in here?' I wondered and heard Gerrund clear his throat.

'It was going to be a surprise.'

'It most certainly was,' I agreed.

'You thought her ladyship would be pleased to have an eel careering around her house?' Alfred checked.

'I was going to make a stew.' Gerrund pulled his cleaver out of the woodwork. I had not seen him strike that blow. 'It's one of her ladyship's favourite meals.'

I did not recollect ever having eaten eels in his presence or expressing a preference for them. To me eels were best chopped up, boiled in water and vinegar with nutmeg and lemon juice, cooled into a jelly and buried in a deep hole.

'I had it in a pan of cold water.' Gerrund inspected his blade. 'But it jumped up, sent the lid flying and leapt out onto the floor. Did no end of damage to the oilcloth.'

'The eel did?' I checked in surprise, for it was a hard-wearing floor covering.

'My carving knife did,' he admitted shamefacedly. 'I was trying to impale it.'

'Somebody has lost a penknife.' Alfred went down on his haunches, just beating Inspector Hefty, to pick it up. It had a carved horn handle and was sheathed in cobwebs. The blade was rusty.

Various other items had emerged with the eel – a cotton bobbin with a few strands of grey thread, a William IV farthing, a lopsided creamy ivory button with three holes in a row.

'Can I borrow that stick?' Alfred indicated an ebony cane, the property of a previous resident, upright in the corner. I passed it to him and with it he swept out more lost treasures – a triangle of white China – probably from the edge of a saucer – the cast-off skin of a preternaturally large spider, the stub of a wooden pencil, a corkscrew, an unidentifiable lump of something mouldy.

A vital clue. Hefty pounced, sniffed it and held it up to the light. *The gall bladder of a strangled Tibetan polo player.*

A potato, Ruby said.

'When did you last clean under there?' Gerrund asked, which was just as well because I was afraid to do so.

'Tha's a knobble-headed question.' Agnust flicked through the debris with the end of her stick. 'I int never cleaned under it at all.' She uncovered a dead earwig. 'How can I?'

'You could bend over and run a duster under it,' Alfred, suddenly an expert on domestic chores, advised.

'I int bowing down to tha'.' Agnust insisted. 'It's full of craven images.'

'Graven images,' I said automatically and Agnust folded her arms.

'Correct not thy maid,' she said so confidently that I almost believed I had committed a mortal sin.

The only kind worth committing. Ruby lay on a divan sofa puffing on an opium pipe.

As Gerrund swept all of our finds, except for the putative potato, into a tarnished brass pot, Alfred pulled out his half-hunter. 'I must go.'

Why not join me? Ruby patted a cushion enticingly but, being unaware of her charms, Alfred was ever immune to them.

Gerrund brought my fountain, a silver-lidded glass bowl atop a silver stand and filled with water chilled with ice shipped over from Thetbury Hall and stored in a deep dry well in my cellar.

My absinthe was in a decanter, etched with flowers and foliage and equipped with a handle and a small spout. It was designed for claret, I believed, but served tolerably for dispensing the liquor into a torsade lead crystal glass. Jack, my fiancé, had given me a set of six but I had smashed five after I had discovered the full extent of his betrayal. One I kept originally for drinking to his damnation but later to give me the strength to pray for his forgiveness. I was not strong enough for that yet.

I've been thinking, Hefty said, and we both waited for a sarcastic remark from Ruby but none was forthcoming. *What,* he pondered, *if the mannequin were not a mannequin?*

Talk sense man, Ruby said, *if such a thing is possible.*

What… He leaned against the mantlepiece. *If it were not a mannequin but something else.*

Such as? She struck a match on his temple.

A kipper, he postulated, *of a crimson persuasion.*

Are you alright? Ruby put a hand to his brow. *You seem to be talking sense.*

Have the pair of you gone mad? I asked to pitying looks from the both of them before turning my attention back to the job in hand.

Resting a slotted silver spoon on my glass, I placed a pure white cube of sugar on top. A fractional turn of one of the taps at the base of the fountain and the water dripped down, dissolving the sugar into a miniature cratered knoll, the solution clouding the spirit into which it fell. The deep emerald liquor slowly swirled in and out of blurred shapes. Was that the figure of the Green Fairy or of a man? If the latter, was he drowning? He melted into a cloud, which, in turn, dissipating and vanishing as it mingled with the water, transfigured into a pale green opalescence.

I rolled it around my mouth before I swallowed. The sugariness faded fast but the bitterness never quite disappeared.

17

WOOL OF BAT, TONGUE OF DOG AND THE HIGHLY SUSPICIOUS ABSENCE OF AN ASPIDISTRA

'*THE ONLY way out is through that skylight,*' *Inspector Havelock Hefty said grimly.*

'*But the roof is forty foot from the ground,*' *Marjorie Hazeldene cried in despair, for the flames were already licking at the window.*

I unwrapped a fresh stick of Beeman's pepsin gum and slid it into my mouth rather as one might slip a coin into a slot machine. It was my third that morning for I was addicted to the *delicious natural and artificial flavors*, as the American wrapper proclaimed.

'What now?' I wondered aloud. 'Why on earth do I do this, tangling myself into impossible situations?'

I could jump off, using my specially adapted cloak as a parachute, Hefty proposed and the doorbell sounded.

Or you could fall onto the spiked railings, Ruby suggested sourly, for she resented not being included in anything that I was writing.

Anthony Appleton was waiting in the hall. I had asked him to dress more sombrely than was his habit and he'd done his best to oblige. The colour of his suit was subdued, being a lightly checked tan with a grey polka-dot Ascot tie but, somehow, he made even this outfit look flamboyant. Agnust was hanging his coat on the stand and depositing his walking cane in the base.

'Good morning, Violet.' He took my hand. 'How are you?'

'I am very well.' I went on my tiptoes to peck his cheek. 'Especially since I saw an excellent review of your play in *The Suffolk Times*.'

'Watchable,' Anthony quoted. 'Hardly a ringing endorsement.'

'By their standards it is.' I did not like to remind him that their previous review of a drama in which he had appeared had said *unwatchable*. 'And the *East Anglian Guardian* said that you brought some much-needed light relief into the production.'

'Ah yes.' Anthony rubbed the back of his neck. 'I accidently fell over a footstool and got such a good laugh from the audience that we kept it in what was an otherwise dreary scene. Odd how a simple trip saved the day.' He looked at me in a way I found pleasingly unsettling. 'How is your hand now?'

'Still sore but much improved. Come through.' I ushered my friend into my sitting room and glanced at the clock. 'We should have time for a coffee.'

I went to the bell rope but had not even tugged it before Agnust, much to my surprise, kicked the door open and marched in, bearing a tray. Normally I had to cajole her or sometimes beg for a beverage.

Keep an eye on Agnust, Lady Violet, Havelock Hefty cautioned. *Remember how Miss Gibson's beau was seduced by her parlour maid?*

The maid was a siren, I reminded them. *Agnust is more like a harpy.*

'Hello.' Anthony waved a hand like a mesmerist checking if his subject was in a trance.

'Sorry, I was in a daydream.'

'That must be a new record. You normally wait for me to regale you with theatrical anecdotes before you drift away.'

'Oh,' I protested. 'But I always love your accounts.' *Except that they always end in disasters,* I thought regretfully.

Anthony settled with a rueful smile in the left-hand chair, watching in puzzlement as I shooed Ruby out of mine. 'Have you heard any more from your guest?' he enquired.

'Not a whisper.' I poured our coffees, leaving him to add his own milk and sugar.

'But you are still going ahead with your plan?'

'*We* are still going ahead,' I corrected him.

'All right,' he said dubiously.

'I promised Cherry that I would try to help,' I explained.

'Then you must.' He stirred his drink. 'And so must I.'

Don't do it, Ruby urged, for she had developed a fondness for my friend that matched my maid's. *You know her hairbrained schemes always end with you being hurt.*

'It is not dangerous.' Only she was supposed to hear me say that, but my larynx had decided to join in the conversation.

'I did not think it would be.' Anthony's bemusement evolved into bafflement.

'Sorry.' I waved a hand. 'I was talking to…' I stopped, aware how absurd my claim would sound.

'Ruby?' he guessed, and I nodded and waited for the mockery that surely would follow, but I should have known him better than that.

'I would love to be able to join in one of those conversations.' He stirred his coffee. 'I have an imaginary friend.'

'Have? Not had?' I checked.

'I speak to her every night.'

'Her?' An irrational jealousy sprang up inside me.

Anthony's lips twitched in amusement. Was I really so transparent?

A human window. Hefty ran his finger down my latticed wallpaper and sniffed it. *Potassium cyanide,* he diagnosed implausibly.

'Her name is Daisy.' Anthony folded his arms. 'I was not allowed a puppy as a child and so I created one in my mind. As I grew older, I did not have the heart to put her down. She sleeps at the foot of my bed. The odd thing is…' He rubbed the back of his neck. 'She never gets any bigger.'

'Rather like me,' I quipped.

'But better behaved,' he counter-quipped.

The diamonds on Ruby's necklace coruscated in the electrical lighting. *It will have to sleep downstairs when you are married.*

'We are not going to get m—' I stopped myself just in time. 'More rain I hope.'

'Indeed.' Anthony rested his right ankle on his left knee and, not for the first time, I envied the freedoms enjoyed by men. They were not forced to sit demurely with their knees together or brush their hair a hundred times a night though, admittedly, I had never troubled to do that, nor had Agnust ever done more than wrench some of the knots out.

We glanced at the clock.

'I suppose...' we said simultaneously and stood in perfect synchronisation, for we both knew what we had supposed. It was time to get going.

—

Gerrund had booked our hansom earlier that morning.

'Friendless was having breakfast with Old Queeny when I arrived,' he had told me. 'And I swear...'

Not in her ladyship's presence, Hefty had reprimanded him.

'He had hay in his porridge.'

'And why not?' I had laughed. 'She has a piece of his cheese for supper.'

'He is here now.'

Friendless, high in his cabby's seat, pulled the cord with great ceremony to unbolt the flaps.

I produced a parsnip for Old Queeny, who could be more aptly dubbed *Very Old Queeny* by now. She sniffed my offering suspiciously, perhaps remembering the occasion when a street boy had dropped a rat into her nosebag. She still had a scar from the wound on her upper lip. Romulus, more accustomed to treating human patients, had sutured it for her. She nibbled the end of my offering, rolled it meditatively around her tongue and spat it out.

'She like them dirty white carrots,' Friendless informed me as I boarded.

'Then why did she spit it out.'

'Int no other way.' He scratched his jaw. 'She can't spit it in.'

'No, but...'

'Thought you'd knew tha'.'

'Wild Man of Gorham writes letter in blood,' the newspaper seller shouted. '*You'll never take me alive*, he says. Read it here. Extrusive to *The Chronic*.'

Anthony had climbed up first and turned to offer me his hand. The ladylike method of boarding a hansom is to place one foot on the iron step and then the other on the platform. The Violet Thorn way is to place one foot on the iron step then skid off it while in the process of raising the other foot and crack her knee on the edge of the running board.

'Ow.'

'Got you.' Anthony grasped me around the waist and half-hauled me as I scrambled into the cabin, plonking myself indecorously beside him.

'Best not to slip,' Friendless advised through the hatch over our heads. 'Another thing I thought you'd knew.'

'Thank heavens I have men to explain these things,' I snapped.

'Dint sound very grateful,' he ruminated as Anthony leaned forward to close the flaps, then called up through the hatch, 'Ready when you are, Friendless.'

The two men were not exactly chums – they never dined together nor played Old Maid, our cabby's favourite card game – but they had a mutual respect, having united in rescuing me once.

Ruby appeared in my frontal lobe, shimmering in a long ballgown, an odd choice of attire for the middle of the morning, I thought. *I have never needed a man to come to my aid.*

What man would want to? Hefty attempted to pick a strand of tinsel from her hair, but she whisked out of reach and he set off to investigate suspicious activities in the shadows of my thalamus.

It was time, I decided, to test Anthony. 'How long have we been married?' I kept my voice low.

'Six months on Tuesday,' he replied.

'Where did we get married?'

'In your family chapel at Thetbury Hall.'

'Who was your best man?'

'My cousin Barthomolew.'

'Is that really his name?'

'I fear so. The registrar misspelt it.' We grabbed the straps in preparation for turning a sharp left, but Old Queeny's pace was so stately that we hardly felt the manoeuvre at all, though Anthony slid to press against me. 'Your bridesmaid was your sister Rose. He is not going to ask us any of this anyway.'

'Probably not,' I conceded. 'But, if one is telling a story, one should always know more than one reveals.'

A pity you do not adhere to that rule when you are describing my adventures, Ruby said. *You don't even know the name of my sister.*

Until that moment I was not aware that she had one. *Emerald,* I bluffed, and she did not contradict me.

We turned right but, for some reason, Anthony did not slide away. 'We had our honeymoon on the Isle of Wight,' he told me.

'Not the south of France?'

'Cowes.'

'They're horses,' Friendless corrected him, but at least he did not say that he thought we would *knew tha'*. He was too occupied with meditatively chewing something. 'They are,' he insisted, as if I had contradicted him, and spat that something at a lamppost, always favourite targets of his. 'Thought you'd knew tha'.'

An omnibus came towards us, swaying and clattering on the cobbles with a few hardy souls on the open top deck. Without any instruction, Old Queeny pulled over to the side.

'Give her one for me, brod,' a youth in a battered bowler yelled.

'I'll give you one,' Anthony threatened. 'That didn't come out quite as I meant it,' he admitted quietly but the omnibus had passed us by.

We were nearing the edge of town now, the terraces giving way to semi-detached houses.

Friendless cleared his throat, a long and noisy process. 'Thinkin' on changin' my name.' He spat again, hitting another apparently blameless lamppost where its midriff would be, if it had one. *It hasn't,* Ruby assured me, and I had to admire the way she quaffed her gin and Indian without spilling a drop as we crashed into and surged out of a pothole.

'That's a good idea.' I accidently placed my hand on Anthony's.

'Never like it.' Friendless spat at a third lamppost but missed. 'It dodge,' he defended his uncharacteristically poor marksmanship before returning to the topic. 'Stupid name... Green.'

'Oh,' I said wisely. It had never occurred to me that he was even in possession of a surname before.

'What will you change it to?' Anthony accidently intertwined his fingers with mine.

'Int Green.'

'What then?' I pressed, not sure if I should care but confident that I did not.

'Tha's it,' he explained patiently. 'Friendless Intgreen, so people know I int green.'

The houses became more commonly detached and more widely separated as we progressed, the streets broadening and growing leafier. Tannery Lane was only about a mile from the town centre as the arrow flies but one might almost be in the countryside by the time we turned into it.

Here the road rose, even the gentle incline troubling Old Queeny as she toiled up it. I almost offered to get out and walk, but I knew that our driver would be gravely offended by any such suggestion. Straight ahead on the brow of the hill stood the old tannery.

I had seen a Prestwood once.

A pressed wood what? Using his folding penknife, Inspector Hefty scraped a sample of paint from the roof into a manilla envelope.

Thomas Prestwood was a Suffolk artist who produced paintings of industrial sites – factories, foundries, gasworks…

I think we all know what the term means. With no regard to the rules of manners or even possibilities, Ruby slipped between us.

Prestwood was a good painter, in my opinion – Miss Kidd snorted in derision of the idea that I might have any views on art – but he was not commercially successful. Few people would want an image of such lowly architecture on their sitting room wall but several of his works hung in a public gallery in Bury St Edmunds.

Prestwood painted a picture of the tannery while it was still a thriving business. It was a long rectangular building with two tall chimneys rising from between the three slate roofs. The cheesy-yellow brick façade was punctured by a triple layer of arched and barred windows and centrally by a massive planked double door. Presumably this was made wide enough for carts to enter piled high with fresh cow and pig skins. Any unwanted remains were probably incinerated there. The stench of this must have added to the stink of the tanning process. Hides were soaked in pures – dog droppings brought from the streets by those unfortunates whose livelihood depended upon collecting buckets of them.

Doubtless to the relief of local residents, the tannery closed. I had been told that this was before I was born but Hettie Granger, who knew a great deal more about local history than I, informed me that the factory was still operational when I was a child.

The tannery still stood at the top of the lane though a sad relic of its heyday.

A relic can no more be unhappy than you can be articulate. Miss Kidd had her Sunday best on even though it was a Thursday, which could only mean that she was en route to meet a young man. It was many years before I discovered the identity of one of them.

As I recalled, there used to be a red brick water tower behind the factory but there was no sign of it now and I was surprised that it had been pulled down. Large areas of Suffolk being flat, raised storage tanks were valuable assets.

I had never understood why the factory had not been demolished when the houses were built some two decades previously. It was not an attractive sight. The doors were boarded up and the glass of many windows smashed. A sycamore had fallen, possibly in the recent storms, and broken through the right-hand roof. Doubtless the ingress of rain would accelerate the building's decline.

Above the door, picked out in orange bricks, was the title SCROFF'S TANNERY 1813.

'Just think,' Anthony said, 'when that was built we were still at war with the French.'

'Pity we int still.' Friendless flung one end of his scarf over his shoulder. 'My greatfather have a flint pit out Branfrod way. Just start diggin' it when old Bonypart goo get hisself lost at Waterloo Station.'

While Friendless's grasp of military history may have been sketchy I could not help but sympathise with the loss of his family's fortune. Flints were essential for muskets and Suffolk flints, being of high quality, were much in demand until the war ended.

'So what did your grandfather do?' Anthony asked and Friendless raised his eyes incredulously.

'He have a flint pit,' he re-explained patiently, 'out Branfrod way.'

'No, I meant...'

I squeezed his hand. 'It is not worth the trouble.'

'Not since old Bonypart goo get hisself lost at Waterloo Station,' Friendless agreed.

'Here it is,' I called and we came to a halt.

The lane was lined by well-appointed villas of individual designs. Cherry's home stood on the left marked by a number nine cut into the stone gate post.

'Why's it called *ix*?' Friendless wondered.

'They are Roman numerals,' Anthony explained.

'Get a lots of Romans here, do they?' Friendless asked.

'*Veni Vidi Vici*,' Anthony quoted.

'Plutarch's *Life of Caesar*.' Friendless identified the source to our astonishment.

There was one more house higher up, after which the habitations were bordered by shrubs on either side, quickly giving way to woodland.

Behind a high, straggly privet hedge only the roof was visible – slate with a chimney stack rising at either end of it, each crowned with three pots.

'You have a rest now old gal,' Friendless told his steed. 'Even Lady Vi wint begrudge you tha'.'

I was rather wounded by his use of the word *even* as I had always been fond of Old Queeny, but I held my tongue as he pulled the cord to unlock the flaps. Anthony and I disembarked, he accidently squeezing my waist as he helped me down.

For the love of money, Ruby said in exasperation, for there were few things of which she was fonder. *You're a clumsy person, Thorn. Slip on your way down and fall into his arms.*

I have my pride. I straightened my hat.

And so little of which to be proud, Miss Kidd, never one to avoid an opportunity to deprecate me, deprecated me.

We all went forward to look at Old Queeny. She was wheezing heavily and seemed unsteady on her feet.

'Why do you not unharness her and walk her home?' I stroked Old Queeny's flank and found it wet with perspiration. 'You can leave your hansom here and I will arrange for it to be collected.'

'And how do I explain tha' to her?' he demanded. 'She goh her pride.' He went to his horse's head, put his arms around her neck and murmured in her ear, 'Dint you listen to her darlin'. She mean well 'cept when she dint.'

I noted that none of my characters said that Old Queeny had little of which to be proud.

'Shall I send for a vet?' Anthony offered in concern.

'A vet?' Friendless expostulated. 'Why they int no better than animal doctors.'

Romulus had come to help in the past, but I could hardly call him away from tending to sick humans for an exhausted creature. 'When we get home I shall telephone to ask Dr Thorn if he can recommend a tonic,' I promised and Friendless appeared to be slightly heartened by the idea.

'He's a good man and person,' he told either Old Queeny or me. It was difficult to tell with his eyes darting side to side in near panic. 'You best goo in now.'

I fairly confidently assumed that his suggestion was aimed at us rather than her.

'Have a good rest, Old Queeny,' I advised, and she turned her weary eyes towards me. Friendless did not.

Anthony offered me his arm and I took it – we were supposed to be a married couple after all – and we passed through a low iron gate onto the wide gravelled though unweeded driveway.

Here we found ourselves facing a pleasant-looking red brick property. Two storeys high, it had double-fronted bays with floor-to-ceiling sash windows. A storm porch protected the front door painted if not Oxford blue then one of its suburbs. Temple Cowley, I decided irrelevantly. There was no sign of a cellar but the raised, though untenanted, flowerbeds in front of the bays and the four wide steps curving clockwise to the door between them, led me to assume that there would be a basement.

There was only a tarnished brass plate below the letterbox to inform the visitor that this was Maccabee House.

What visitor? Hefty asked suspiciously.

Any visitor, in this case us.

I see. He fingered his moustaches even more suspiciously.

'Do I look all right?' I asked Anthony, who was eyeing me enquiringly.

I never fish for compliments. Ruby twirled the holly green parasol, which complemented her flamingo pink silk dress, cut low to show off her décolletage. Why was she not cold in such light attire?

'A stunner,' Anthony decided. I had only sought reassurance that I had not become too dishevelled during our journey, but his response was more satisfactory.

'I was referring to my hat,' I informed him haughtily.

'So was I,' he informed me utterly convincingly and tugged on the iron stirrup at the end of a barley twist pole attached to a chain that ran through the wall. A bell tinkled. 'You look every inch the respectable wife.'

There was something about those words that warmed and chilled me simultaneously.

Impossible, Miss Kidd unbuttoned her gloves at the wrists. I knew that she was correct in her assertion, but emotions are rarely, if ever, governed by logic.

A small figure appeared through the red- and green-coloured glass panes and the door was opened by a child in a maid's outfit.

You know you're middle-aged when the maids look young, Ruby told me.

She is young, I insisted.

'Can I help you?' Her voice was weary and her face white with dark arcs under her watery blue eyes.

Anthony handed her his card. Mine would have given us more status and nobody is more conscious of unearned privilege than those who have none, but I would lose my courtesy title the moment that I married.

Rank does not influence me. Havelock Hefty puffed on his briar pipe. *I have sent two dukes and a countess to the gallows.*

One of whom may well have been guilty, Ruby gibed.

'Mr and Mrs Anthony Appleton,' my friend declared, for we both knew that, despite the worthy intentions of the Education Act, even those who attended school until they were eleven often left it barely literate. 'To see Mr Bruton.'

The girl took his card and stood back to admit us into a long narrow hall, the right-hand side constricted even more by a rising staircase.

'I shall see if he is at home,' she recited, placed the card on a silver tray from the walnut sideboard and trudged to a door on our left. It was only a few feet away but even that effort seemed to fatigue her. Unless the present occupiers had taken on additional staff, she had probably been up since five or six o'clock at the latest. It was a big house to clean in addition to tending to her employers' whims.

You don't worry about your own maid. Ruby slotted her parasol into an elegant papier mâché stand.

I worry a great deal about Agnust. I dropped my umbrella into a hideous elephant's foot. *But for different reasons.*

The maid reappeared.

'The master will see you now,' she whispered wearily.

'Thank you,' I said, and I thought Anthony was trying to hold her hand until I saw him slip half a crown into it, probably more than a fortnight's pay to her.

She eyed him warily, for many a man might think that such a sum entitled him to take liberties. 'I'm a good girl,' she insisted.

'I am sure you are,' Anthony hastened, but she still looked at him askance.

'And he's a good man,' I contributed.

'All wive think tha'.' She took my coat. 'But I int met one yet.'

'You have today,' I assured her to a low cynical laugh, and we passed into a sitting room.

Mr Bruton was seated in a heavy oak armchair by a lethargic fire. His complexion was, as I remembered, slate grey but his tawny mutton chops were bushier than I had recollected. His thin upper lip and weak chin were close-shaven.

With his upright pose, unnaturally straight back and legs raised from the floor as if supported by an invisible footrest, he looked more like a mannequin than the one that had been deposited in my house. His head rotated towards us with an expression more neutral than Switzerland. He blinked as slowly as a lizard and I could not help but feel that I was being surveyed by a puppet.

Bruton closed his newspaper with all the lack of skill that men frequently accuse women of exercising, letting it fall crumpled onto an occasional table, and hinged himself off his seat.

'Good morning,' he rasped, as if his voice box was in need of an oilcan.

'What a charming room.' I smiled coquettishly.

Smirked croquettishly. Ruby looked in vain for a drinks cabinet.

'What is your business?' Bruton's cold cod eyes swam up and down me, with only a glance at my face, settling on an area approximately six inches below my neck.

Hefty produced his Roe Electric Reel Tape Measure but, catching my expression, slipped it back into his jacket pocket where it made not the slightest of bulges.

'I have tendered an offer on a house on this delightful road,' Anthony continued breezily.

'I do not inhabit a road,' Mr Bruton told him as if such a thing were not appreciably superior to a dung heap. 'I live on a lane.' Bruton was transfixed by my bodice.

'Delightful lane,' Anthony corrected himself.

Hefty was examining a bookcase. *Take a look at this, milady.* And I followed his gaze. On the top shelf was a skull grinning in that mirthless way that seems to be a requirement for anyone wishing to play the part of a cranial skeleton. On either side of it were four clear glass jars all containing what looked like human organs, though I could not identify them from twenty feet away.

'Which house?' Mr Bruton's jaws snapped up and down. Some lubrication might help there as well. 'No others were on the market when we moved into the area.' He ran his thumb over the signet ring on his right hand.

'Have you been here long?' I enquired and he scowled, for this was masculine talk in a masculine world. I put my fingers to my top button and he unscowled, drifting into an arid drool.

'Have you been here long?' I re-enquired, as if the topic were a fresh one, and Roger Bruton shot out a hand as if to slap my face but hinged it backwards in three jerky movements to touch one of his shirt buttons.

'Since September.' He twiddled with his button as if daring me to do the same and, rarely one to decline an unchallenging challenge, I followed suit.

'Excellent.' From Anthony's glances it was obvious that he was fully aware of this repulsive flirtation. 'Then you will have employed the services of a solicitor recently.'

'What if I have?' Bruton's hard voice annealed.

'My husband only wants a recommendation,' I explained and Bruton scowled again at my impertinence but returned to a no-longer-dry drool as my hand slid sideways to brush an invisible speck from my dress.

'I am unable to give one.' Unnoticed by him, I assumed, his button came adrift. 'The man was hopeless.'

'Then perhaps you could tell us his name so that we might avoid him,' Anthony suggested.

'A gentleman does not enquire into another gentleman's business.' Bruton's tone was stiffer than his joints.

'Yes, but, if we are to be neighbours…' I took a step towards him, ignoring Hefty's expression of disgust. 'And, I hope, good friends, then surely you could make an…' My voice fell to a husky whisper. 'Exception.'

This is a new Thorn, Ruby said admiringly. *You might have had more success than I in seducing Prince Felix Erhard of Borsvogladden.* This was high praise indeed from the woman who rarely failed to capture any man's heart, though she was usually more interested in capturing their fortunes.

'Wink,' Bruton leered.

Don't lower yourself, milady, Hefty urged, for it would do his promotion prospects no good at all if it emerged that his creator was a slattern.

'Wink, Finbow and Motte?' Anthony guessed, just in time to stop me. 'They are next door to Drimpkin's, my cravat-maker's shop.'

This was also where Gerrund bought his own neckwear, though how he managed on the salary I bestowed on him was one of the many mysteries surrounding my man. I was never even certain from where he came, except that it was in the boreal regions. I knew little about his past, though he did once claim to have been a wing half for Blackburn Rovers and to have sailed the Sargasso Sea in search of HMS *Atalanta*, which had gone missing with all hands.

Pay attention girl. Miss Kidd rapped her blackboard pointer on a cherrywood sideboard, and I found that our lascivious host was agreeing with my friend that he had indeed dealt with Wink, Finbow and Motte and adding that he had regretted it.

'I was even charged for dropping a vase which I was not to know was fragile and should not have been placed within my reach.'

'It is so hot,' I said, though I had been in warmer icehouses, strolled towards the window overlooking the driveway and took three deep breaths.

'My wife always complains that the house is cold. Indeed...' Bruton fleered. 'She rather amusingly compares it to an icehouse.'

'How witty.' I peered at his specimens. 'Is your wife at home?' I folded my hands demurely and his expression grew sullen.

'Mrs Bruton is out collecting money for the distressed manufacturers of toothpicks.'

'Are there many of those?' Anthony unkinked his watchchain.

Bruton stroked his chin in a way that people never do. 'About a hundred a box, I should say.'

'What a fascinating display.' I picked up a jar. Whatever was in it had been badly preserved for it had a fuzzy outline and the liquid was cloudy.

'Indeed.' Bruton clapped his hands. 'That one is the aborted foetus of a Barbary ape.' He rubbed his palms in the manner of an unusually conscientious doctor washing before performing surgery. 'The one beside it is a pug, the next is, of course, a horseshoe bat and the last a jar of pickled leeches.'

Wool of bat and tongue of dog. Ruby looked at a lower shelf. *Eye of newt and toe of frog.*

'Well.' I looked about for things to gather but I had my handbag on my wrist. 'You must not detain us any longer. Kindly summon your maid to see us out.'

'But surely we can...' Anthony began, clearly not wishing to add to the poor girl's labours.

'No, we cannot.' I reached over and tugged the bellpull, a severe breach of etiquette but not as severe as I would have liked.

After a short delay – *Fourteen seconds.* Hefty clicked the lid on his half-hunter – the door opened, the maid came in and bobbed. I have never liked men who make their maids curtsy. A servant who respects her master or mistress should not have to make demonstrations of obeisance.

'Show my visitors to the door,' her master commanded with as much grandiosity as Genghis Khan might have used when ordering his armies into battle. She dipped again and, bidding our host fond farewells, we followed her into the hall.

'Are you Addie?' I looked at the unfortunate creature. She was in desperate need of good food and a long sleep. *And a blood transfusion,* Ruby suggested, though we both knew what a perilous procedure that was.

'Yes miss,' the maid admitted warily.

'And you were employed by Mr and Mrs Bight?' Anthony asked, and I felt an irritation probably similar to that demonstrated by Alfred Stanbury when I joined in his interrogations, though, in his case, the reaction was rational.

'Did you know that they were selling the house?' I asked hurriedly, having seen Anthony's lips part.

I did not think it possible but her face fell further. 'No miss.' She noticed a stain on her apron and wiped her hand over it to no avail. 'They were always very kind to me.'

'Are the Brutons not?' Anthony beat me to it this time and I found that I did not really mind at all.

She glanced about. Walls may not have ears, but Bruton had two of them. 'They cut my pay the moment they come.' She undid the bow in her apron, a sure sign that she felt able to trust us not to complain about her. 'They get me up earlier and they keep me up later.'

'Can you not apply for a better position?' he suggested, but I knew of the hold that employers can exert upon their servants.

'They say if I go they give me no character.' Unlike those in my books, a maid's *character* was a reference, and few would employ her without one.

'You told us earlier that you were a good girl.' I watched her struggle with her bow.

'And so I am miss,' Addie insisted. 'My mum bring me up proper.'

'Does Mr Bruton ever try to make you do anything improper?' I buttoned up my coat.

For the first time some colour came into her cheeks. 'Not really.' She tangled her fingers in the bow.

'But there is something he does that you do not like.'

'It's just the way he look at me.' Her hat was askew and I reached out to re-pin it for her.

'Do you know where Seraphim Square is?'

'The one with the big old stone gate?'

'I live in the corner in Break House. Can you remember that?'

'Break House in the corner,' she recited.

'If Mr Bruton ever tries to force himself upon you.' I retrieved my umbrella from the stand. 'Come to see me.' I was not sure what I could do for her for I had no need of another maid and knew nobody who did, but I could not desert her.

'Thank you, miss.'

'How do you know I am not a Mrs?'

For the first time an inkling of a smile flickered over Addie's face. 'You int wearin' no ring.'

One of the three hundred and eight reasons you will never be a lady adventuress. Ruby's handbag was open to reveal a short-barrelled silver revolver compared to which the Lady Derringer I had at home was hardly more than a toy.

'I might be having it repaired.'

'You int goh no white mark on your finger,' she pointed out to Hefty's annoyance. In his eyes women had no detection skills.

'How careless of me,' I admitted, and the flicker died.

'Ladies dint have to be virtued,' she observed. 'They do as they please but expect us to do as they should.'

I was raised in the belief that we were honour-bound to be examples to our alleged inferiors, but she probably had a point.

'It is not what it seems,' I began, but knew that she was thinking what she dared not say, *It never is.* 'And I meant what I said.'

'Break House, Seraphim Square.' She nodded, and as I put a hand to the door handle, a thought struck me.

'Where were you when Miss Cherry came to the house?'

'Ill in bed,' she answered warily. Servants, like the rest of us, do not care to be questioned. Interrogation can imply that they are under suspicion of wrongdoing. She patted her stomach. 'I had a sick chill in my liver.' A bell sounded from the back of the house, presumably the kitchen. 'Best see what he want.' She bobbed again and opened the door.

Note the highly suspicious absence of an aspidistra. Hefty ran his finger under the dado rail. *And the lack of wet paint is exceedingly significant.*

It is, Ruby concurred, and I shivered. This newfound amiability was quite unsettling. If my characters united, what chance would I have to resist them?

None at all, Ruby told me, though she was not supposed to be listening to that thought.

Less than none, Hefty chipped in.

That makes less than no sense, Ruby scoffed as we stepped outside and left them to their squabble.

18

BLACK MAGIC AND THE BLACK SHUCK

OUR CAB was largely hidden behind the hedge, but as we passed through the gate we saw that Old Queeny was still in harness, her head down to syphon water from the canvas bag Friendless kept hanging from the side of his cab. There were no pumps in view, so I did not know how he filled it.

'Kitchen maid next door bring us out a bucketful,' he answered my unasked question.

'That was kind of her.'

'Tis,' he agreed. 'And she put a drop of cookin' sherry in it.' He patted his horse's withers. ' 'vigorate you up no end, dint it darlin'?'

Old Queeny raised her head and I had to admit that she looked a great deal livelier.

'Would you like me to fetch another cab?' Anthony offered, though where he would find one so far from the town centre I had no idea.

'Lord bless you mister,' Friendless laughed. 'She can't pull two cab at once.'

'I was just thinking we might be a bit heavy for her.'

Friendless appraised us. 'She might be…' He tipped his head in my direction. 'But Old Queeny take offence if she walk home.'

I had not actually planned on walking but had been thinking of other ways that we could find transport. However, when Old Queeny had finished her drink and Friendless had wiped her muzzle with his sleeve, we clambered gingerly aboard and set off at a sub-funereal pace.

'What a creepy man.' Anthony shivered.

'Did you notice his books?' I asked and Anthony shrugged his left shoulder, the side of his arm brushing against mine. 'I saw them, but not their titles.'

'Books on spells, runes and curses.' I strove to remember their titles. '*The World Bewitched* by Balthasar Bekker... *A Sorcerer's Guide* by somebody calling himself Dr Lucifer Warlock. One on ancient burial rites, I think, but I did not want to make it too obvious that I was interested. Something about human sacrifice.'

'Who in the name of God reads books like that?'

'I doubt that God's name comes into it.'

'A creepy man,' Anthony iterated.

Old Queeny produced an odd groan and her ears drooped.

'She's in the dulldrums,' Friendless explained, and I wished that I had coined that word.

'Poor old girl,' Anthony sympathised.

'Old horse,' Friendless corrected him, though he often addressed her as *girl* himself.

Old Queeny sighed.

'Sing her a song, Lady Vi'let,' he urged. 'Somethin' that will make her laugh.'

I had never actually sung to a horse before and some of the few comic songs I knew were not fit for a lady to voice.

I cleared my throat and began. 'You can't take your donkey on a bus...'

'Course you can't,' Friendless agreed, and I battled on. 'You can't take your donkey on a bus. Everyone will make a blooming fuss. It will put its blinking hoof straight through the blinking roof, so you can't...'

'Nuff,' Friendless butted in. 'Bloomin' and blinkin' like a low common coarse vulgar washingwoman. What kind of speakin' language is that for a respectable horse?'

'I am sorry,' I mumbled.

'You are sorry who?' he demanded, and Anthony lowered his head to hide his grin.

'I am sorry, Old Queeny.'

'I should frebbin' well think so,' Friendless muttered, and slammed the hatch shut.

'Creepiness apart, what did you make of Mr Bruton?' I asked Anthony.

'A cold cove.' He squeezed my hand. 'Until you warmed him up with your lascivious display.'

'Was I very disgraceful?' I asked, keeping an eye on Old Queeny. She had picked up her pace and even managed a toss of her head as the road levelled.

'Very.' Anthony tapped with his cane on the hatch, and it shot open to reveal our driver bending so low over the hole that I feared he might fall through it and onto us.

'I have a fancy,' Anthony said, 'to see the monument. Do you think we could pass that way?'

Friendless chewed, and for a moment I thought that he was going to spit on us, but he swallowed and said, 'It's another half twice a half and more mile on the journey.'

'I will happily pay for the extra distance.'

Friendless mulled that over. 'Dint matter to me if you pay cheerful or not cheerful so long as you pay and no bad coins.' He clicked his tongue and we pulled right.

My first and fleeting thought was that Anthony had never shown any curiosity about the monument before. He had no interest in it of which I was aware. My second and dismayed thought was that it was so unlike the Anthony I knew to make an exhausted horse pull us for the extra distance, but then I realised that we would go around Sacrifice Hill, thereby cutting out the steep incline up and the steeper one down. If Anthony had suggested an easier route for Old Queeny, Friendless would have been insulted on her behalf.

'She has had enough,' he said in a low voice. Stopping work meant the knacker's yard for most horses. I was resolved to find a sanctuary for Old Queeny when she retired but we both knew how Friendless would pine for her. Retirement for him was also a grim prospect. With no family, the workhouse or starvation might be his only options.

We had a good view of the town as we rounded the corner. The tower of St Aegbald's Church lay below to our left just off Seraphim Square but the sight of Break House was obstructed by the monastery gate. Above us to our right was the tannery, though I could only just make out the roof through the trees of Grooberry Wood. Almost straight ahead stood the wide sprawling gothic structure of Dewbury Hall asylum.

Three of the most terrible buildings in East Anglia, Ruby said grimly, for she was not nearly so insensitive as she liked to pretend. I had witnessed a woman horribly murdered in St Aegbald's; there would have been countless hides of slaughtered animals in the tannery; and, despite the humane regime, there must be unimaginable suffering in Dewbury Hall.

'What a world,' Anthony sighed, clearly entertaining similar thoughts to mine.

The monument stood in a clearing to our right. The ten-foot-tall plinth was constructed, as were many Suffolk houses, from flints held together by lime mortar and it was topped by a gigantic limestone egg. There was no plaque, and nobody knew who had built the monument or what it commemorated. Some said that it was a mystical symbol of the Warreners, a secret society, possibly affiliated to the Freemasons, probably just a men's club. Others opined that the monument was the work of a mad sculptor in the asylum, a theory that I favoured.

'Shall we take a closer look?' Anthony suggested, and I silently blessed him, for there was not much of interest to see but it would give Old Queeny a longer breather.

'My dear old mumby tell me it's laid by a huge, 'normous, big stone hen,' Friendless informed us in all seriousness. 'She's very wise when she's alive but not so wise when she's not.'

We disembarked but our driver stayed aloft. If nothing else, the way a hansom was designed meant that he lifted the weight from his horse.

'Mind your footing.' Anthony took my arm though the ground was fairly level, if somewhat overgrown with dead brackens.

For the love of Bollinger, Ruby said in exasperation, *how many times do I have to tell you, Thorn? Fall into... what is that noise?*

'Can you hear that?' I asked Anthony, though he would have to have been deafer than the egg not to have. There was a crashing in the undergrowth.

The Black Shuck. Hefty shrank back. The Shuck was a hellhound that frequented graveyards, and it was said that to see it portended death.

'Sounds like a deer.' From the way Anthony's arm tightened over mine, I felt that his words were as much to reassure himself as me.

Not only could we hear the snapping of twigs and cracking of branches now, but also a grunting. A dense thicket of holly, laurels and dogwood overgrown with ivy blocked our vision.

'It must be distressed,' I said, because we both knew that deer go to great lengths to avoid drawing attention to themselves.

A Bengal tiger, Hefty drew his revolver because they were, of course, an indigenous species in Suffolk.

'Probably frightened by a dog.' Anthony tried to disengage himself and stand in front of me but I held on tight, not because I was frightened – which I was – but from self-respect. I may have been a little woman, but I refused to be *the* little woman. 'I am trying to protect you.'

I wanted to say that I knew and that was one of the reasons that I loved him – a revelation that came as something of a shock to me.

'And I am trying to protect you.' I let go and attempted to step in front of him.

The crashing grew closer and there was a high snarling sound. Anthony stepped towards it.

'Have a care,' Friendless yelled and I looked around. 'The Wild Man of Gorham come this way.' Friendless drew his whip out of its sheath. Old Queeny was pawing at the verge nervously. Perhaps she had heard that the creature was also partial to horseflesh.

'What the hell,' Anthony breathed then, more sharply, 'Scrise.'

The bushes shook violently. Anthony adjusted his grasp on his cane. 'Stand back.'

I stepped forward and he shot out an arm to stop me so suddenly that I sat with a bump on a confusion of bracken and brambles.

'Stop right there.' Anthony wielded his stick like a rapier. 'We are fully armed.'

I was not convinced that whatever creature was coming our way would understand but Friendless, who had a better view than us, shouted, 'Come near my horse and she crack your head-bone 'til your spleen bust out your ear.'

I scrambled to my feet, struggling to disentangle my dress and coat from the thorns and putting my hand down in the midst of them in the process.

'Blimit.' I ripped my sleeve free but did not have time to inspect my clothes for damage because the bushes parted with a final rush and a wild animal emerged into the clearing. At first glance it resembled some kind of ape, staggering towards us, bent almost double, snorting fiercely, but it was unlike any monkey I had come across before. The whole creature was raw and bleeding and splattered with mud. It was then that I realised it was completely hairless and, as it raised its blood-caked head, I saw that the wildly staring eyes had no lids.

Anthony raised his stick warningly, but it was a slender affair more suited to resting jauntily on his shoulder than cudgelling any attacker. 'Stay where you are. I won't warn you again.' I touched his arm and he leapt sideways in alarm.

'He is human,' I gasped and, in confirmation, the bloodied figure croaked, 'Help me.' And fell, writhing and twitching to the ground.

We hurried over and it was only then that it occurred to me that he was wearing trousers.

'What has happened to you?' I asked in horror. His whole head was caked in clots with no sign of any hair. His right ear, I noticed, was hanging backwards into the weeds. In a kind of trance I reached behind it and hinged it up again but, the moment I let go, it fell away.

The man whimpered and put his hand up, but Anthony grasped his wrist and pushed it firmly away.

'We are trying to help you.' With his free hand my friend untied his cravat. 'Hold it up again, Violet.'

I did so and, together, we wrapped Anthony's neckwear around the back of the man's head, tying it over his forehead to hold the ear in place. I wiped my hand on the grass, leaving a red smear, but my palm and fingers were still caked and sticky.

'Mind he dint bite you,' Friendless warned.

'He is a wounded man.' I looked over my shoulder. 'And needs our help.'

Friendless pulled his hat low over his brow. 'He can't get in my cab.'

I assumed that he was worried about making a mess and I nearly retorted angrily he was lucky to have a cab at all. He did not know that I had paid for a new one to replace his old after it had been wrecked. But then I realised that it was more a matter of practicality. The man would not be able to sit upright and the bench seat was not big enough for him to lie upon.

'You could go for help,' Anthony suggested.

Friendless pushed his hat back and tugged at a stray tuft of hair. 'I goo get help,' he decided as if it were his own idea.

Anthony let go of the man's arm and it fell limply across the bloodied chest.

'There will be a doctor at Dewbury Hall,' I suggested.

'The madhouse?' Friendless swivelled nervously as if expecting an imminent attack by a horde of maniacs.

'You don't have to go in.' I looked at the man staring up at me with lidless eyes and wondered if he might be unconscious. 'Just ring the bell and explain what has happened.'

'What has happened?' he asked, and the truth was I did not know. I was not even certain that it was not too late to help the unfortunate man lying between Anthony and me. I waved my hands from side to side before his eyes, but they did not follow my movements.

'Is he breathing?' Anthony put a hand on the man's chest. 'I can't see any movement.' He raised his voice. 'Hello.' But there was no response. After a momentary hesitation he bent low and put his ear over the man's heart. 'It is beating, racing in fact.'

Friendless was still dithering. 'Can be crackle-heads roamin' in the grounds.' He indicated towards the asylum. 'Must be one of them do this.'

Looking at the mutilated man before me, his injuries certainly had the hallmark of the work of a madman.

'Can you look after him?' I asked.

'I don't think there's much I can do, but I'll stay with him.' Anthony straightened the man's arm, which was twisted oddly. 'And if whoever did this to him appears, I have my walking cane.' It lay a yard or so away on the ground. 'But is it safe for you to go up there?' He tipped his head towards the asylum.

'The director is a relative of mine.' In truth I could not recollect how we were linked, but it was by a complication of marriages rather than birth. 'He told me the idea that all lunatics are homicidal is a myth born of bad novels. Most of his patients are gentle, troubled souls more in need of kindness than the straitjacket.'

'Well he should know,' Anthony, who had played Mad Silvester in *The Murder of Malachi Turner*, said doubtfully. 'But be careful.' His character had jabbered and frothed at the mouth so convincingly that some of the scant audience had fled the auditorium.

'I will be.' I put a hand on Anthony's shoulder to steady myself and got to my feet. He put a hand on mine and squeezed it in farewell.

I reboarded the hansom. The bench seat was wider than I remembered and I felt lonely occupying it without Anthony. He seemed smaller and more vulnerable than usual and jumped when a bush rustled, but it was only a dunnock rising from its perch.

'I look after her,' Friendless vowed for, though he was obviously afraid, our cabby was no coward.

'And I will look after Friendless.' I raised my chin defiantly.

'I know you will,' Anthony called up, though I was not sure which of us he was addressing.

Old Queeny was cropping a tussock of wilted grass and her owner waited. We might be setting off to seek urgent help for a severely injured man, but it would be impolite to interrupt her snack. I clicked my tongue in impatience but Old Queeny, taking it as a signal, raised her head and set off.

'Here,' Friendless cried indignantly. 'I dint do tha' to your horse if you have one.'

'I did not mean to.'

'Where'd we be...' He turned her head with a gentle shortening of the rein. '...if everyone do things they dint mean to?'

'In Great Bardham,' I hazarded as we slowly but unsteadily climbed the hill, Old Queeny straining on the gentle slope.

'Tha' proves my point,' he crowed. I had hitherto been unaware that our conversation actually had a point. 'If everyone goo Great Bardham they all get dretful squashed.'

I had not realised that my careless tongue movement could result in countless deaths, but I was more interested in our destination.

Dewbury Hall rose dark and forbidding from behind the trees, a jumble of turrets and towers as if the architect himself were in need of treatment there. A high red brick wall topped by crisscrossing iron spikes guarded the perimeter of the grounds with a spear-topped gate between two lodges.

I pulled on a chain and from behind one of the lodges emerged a man in dark grey clothing. He wore a peaked cap resembling that of...

A railway porter, Hefty suggested.

A zookeeper, Miss Kidd opined.

A drum major of the Coldstream Guards, Ruby, who knew a thing or two about uniforms, decided.

The man might have looked very smart had the shirt, jacket and trousers not been so baggy. In my childhood it was still quite common for employers to deck maids and valets in their employers' cast-off clothing. It saved money but also led to confusion at social gatherings, with guests trying to order drinks from each other. It was an inconsiderate or penurious employer who expected their gatekeeper to wear such ill-fitting attire though and I had an idea that Dewbury Hall was well-endowed with funds from its founder's estate. The hat was so large that it wobbled aslant, with the man's long grey hair poking out like stuffing from a torn cushion.

'Good afternoon.' He smiled more crookedly than his headgear, but his voice was warm in the cold damp air.

'There is an injured man down the lane.' I returned his open gaze.

'Oh my goodness.' He polished the toe of a highly polished shoe on the back of his trousers as if about to be inspected on parade. 'Does he need a doctor?'

'As soon as possible.'

Somewhere a man's voice was raised. It was muffled, but he sounded distressed.

'Is he all right?'

'No, miss. He needs a doctor.' His voice was surprisingly refined for a man in such a lowly position.

He took advantage of the charity for teaching menials to speak proper, Miss Kidd explained. Was that a joke? If so, it was her first.

'I meant the man who is calling.'

There was a crashing nearby, but I could not see the cause.

'Young Thesperus?' The gatekeeper chuckled. 'Don't you worry about him, miss. He sounds distressed but he's happy as a sandwich.' He raised his voice. 'Hush now, Young Thesperus. You'll distress the other patients.'

The damp air was turning to a drizzle and, down the road, there was a man lying in the cold and wet and possibly dying.

'Could you summon a doctor?'

'That could be tricksome, miss.' He rubbed the back of his neck. 'I am not supposed to leave my post.'

'Then kindly admit me.'

He tugged an earlobe. 'One moment while I fetch the keys.' He walked backwards from my presence as if I were his monarch until he reached the lodge where he turned to enter. The moment he opened the door, the shouting and clattering increased in volume.

'Shut that buller or I fill your munge with my fist,' my previously amiable companion's voice came out to me. 'Blimmid looney.' There was a loud crash. 'Nothin' but bunch of crackle-heads the lot of you. Give that to me. Give it or I smash your grinders down your gulley.'

There were sounds of a struggle. I glanced back at Friendless, who had dismounted and was hand-feeding Old Queeny a bunch of hay and, when I looked back, I saw that the porter was wrestling with a bigger man who was dressed only in what Agnust would have referred to as his under-mentionables. The two men fell to the ground, the porter's hat flying into the grass.

'Friendless.' I was not sure what, if anything, he could do, but very sure that there was nothing I could contribute to terminate the fray. 'Bring your whip,' I called, deciding that there might be something that he could do after all.

'I always bring it,' he told me sulkily.

'That was not a question. I meant bring it here please.'

Friendless muttered something about it being his whip and I was not going to be allowed to play with it.

The men were trying to throttle each other and, as far as I could judge, the larger man, who was kneeling astride the porter, was making a better job of it.

Friendless arrived and assessed the situation. 'Never get the man on the ground without hurtin' the man on top.'

'But the man on top is the lunatic,' I explained frustratedly.

'No he int.' Friendless looped his whip. 'Look at their hairs.'

Exasperated, I glanced over and saw that he may well have been right, for the top man's hair, though exceedingly ruffled, was neatly trimmed at the back, whereas the other's resembled Old Queeny's fodder.

'Which is why the uniform is too big for hi—' I realised, my last word cut short by the crack of Friendless's whip, and both men looked towards the source of the sound.

The larger man's appearance was familiar, and the memory of a medical dinner I had attended with Romulus when Jane was too ill flicked through my mental photograph album, rejecting the pictures of Dr Lensworthy, who was old and infirm, Dr Cronshaw, who had blown his brains out, and Dr Hubbard, who, to the disgust of many, was a woman.

'Dr Boatswain,' I remembered, and the man on top grinned sheepishly as if he were a schoolboy caught scrapping in the quadrangle.

'Oh hello, Lady Violet,' he croaked. 'Please excuse my lack of attire.'

In his long-sleeved woollen vest and long-legged combinations, the doctor was more decently attired than his opponent, whose ill-fitting shirt had risen and trousers fallen.

'Please do not concern yourself,' I replied, more worried about the man who was trying to claw at the doctor's eyes, but Boatswain broke an arm free, raised his fist and swung it down in a right hook that connected with his patient's jaw in a thwack that must have rattled the teeth embedded in it.

The recipient of the blow slumped in an instant, and Dr Boatswain got up unsteadily, grasped the unconscious man and, dragging him by the collar, staggered towards the gatehouse.

'Excuse us while I retrieve my clothes.' He rubbed his, doubtless, bruised throat. 'He was going to try to walk out in my clothes, but he grabbed the hat when he heard you at the gate. Won't be a tick,' he assured me as they both disappeared.

19

THE SUBMARINE AND THE STRAITJACKET

ABOUT TWENTY minutes later we set off back down the lane, Dr Boatswain holding the strap to avoid indecorously sliding into me as the hansom tilted on the uneven track. Having no ambulance available, he had instructed a waggon to be readied to follow us.

'That was Sir Walter Pendergrass,' he told me, rubbing his reddened throat. 'I saw the door of the lodge had been forced but he struck me from behind. Knocked me clean out. Always causing trouble, he is. Last year, in an escape bid, he built a submarine. It was remarkably well constructed and might even have worked.'

'But we are nowhere near the sea,' I objected, and Dr Boatswain chuckled.

'You have spotted the flaw in his plan.'

'Have any of your inmates absconded recently?' I struggled to avoid slipping to the middle and he brought out his half-hunter.

'It is possible that somebody did today. We count our patients first thing every morning and last thing at night, so it is seven hours since we last checked.' He slipped his watch back into his waistcoat pocket. 'But escapes are rare. Most of our patients are content with their life here but those who are less controllable are kept in a secure wing with, I regret to say, cells.'

'Regret?' I gripped the edge of the seat and hauled myself back to the side.

'We try to treat them as human beings,' he explained, 'not animals to be locked in cages.'

Old Queeny snorted.

'Dint you worry, darlin',' Friendless called. 'He dint mean you.'

Dr Boatswain leaned his head back. 'Do you always listen to your customers' conversations?'

Friendless considered the question. 'Yes,' he decided eventually.

'He does,' I confirmed, and, with a sigh, Old Queeny came to a halt at the monument.

Anthony was kneeling by the supine man.

'Still breathing,' he informed us and the doctor knelt on the other side, laying his gladstone bag on the ground and grasping the man's wrist. 'But he has not spoken apart from a few grunts.'

'Pulse thready,' Boatswain announced. 'Oh Lord, I see what you meant about his eyelids.'

The staring eyes turned towards the source of the voice.

'And conscious,' Dr Boatswain declared. 'Can you hear me?' he asked loudly. 'Can you speak?'

The man's lips quivered and parted but no more than a weak groan issued from them.

'Shinking,' he managed at last.

'He is delirious,' the doctor said.

The man's eyes flickered side to side before fixing themselves on me standing at his head.

'What is your name?' I asked, for people generally remember that no matter how confused they are.

'Shink.' He raised his head an inch or two from the ground. 'Shinks impure.'

There was something else, but it was too indistinct for any of us to make out.

'Do not overtax yourself,' Dr Boatswain instructed. 'I am going to give you a tot of brandy and then we shall take you to the hospital. A vehicle will arrive soon.'

The man's feet drummed the ground and he writhed. 'It was hell.' He half rose. 'Hell.'

The doctor put both hands on his shoulders and pressed him down. 'Stop struggling, man.'

The man's fingers clawed at Boatswain's, trying to heave them away, but the doctor adjusted his grip to restrain him.

'Up, up,' the man gasped.

'Perhaps he needs to sit up,' I suggested, 'to breathe.'

'Perhaps,' the doctor relented, and released his hold. The man shot up, his arms thrashing.

'It's hell,' he cried and, with one last gasp, sank back onto the ground.

Boatswain tried his pulse and then dug his fingertips into the man's neck.

'We are too late,' he said.

'God rest your soul.' How many more times, I wondered, would I be uttering those words before somebody spoke them over me? Stupidly I put my hand out intending to close those staring eyes.

'Amen.' As Anthony crossed himself there was a creaking and bumping and the sound of hooves on the track. A waggon pulled up, hauled by a dappled mare.

Old Queeny and Friendless eyed the new arrival with sniffs as if comparing their splendid hansom to the clumsy cart while the other driver and his mare tossed their heads at the puniness of their rivals.

The driver and his mate swung themselves off their wooden bench.

'Take him to the asylum,' Dr Boatswain commanded, and they approached warily.

Dead men, unless they carry a highly contagious disease, are not dangerous, but I have often noted people's reluctance to touch them.

'One moment.' I leaned over. 'What has happened to his wrists?'

The doctor glanced. 'They are scratched like the rest of him.'

'Those look to me like rope marks.'

'Nonsense.' The doctor piffed.

'They do to me too.' Anthony got to his feet. 'And, unless I am mistaken, those are the same marks on his leg.'

The lower legs were caked with mud, but an angry red indentation was visible on the left ankle.

'How do you restrain your patients?' I asked, and Dr Boatswain rounded on me angrily.

'In extreme cases we will use a straitjacket until the patient quietens. We most certainly do not manacle anybody.'

'I am sure Lady Violet did not suppose you did,' Anthony said diplomatically.

'I only wanted to exclude that possibility,' I confirmed. 'Do you recognise him?'

'No,' Boatswain responded sulkily.

'So he is not a patient of yours?' Anthony sought to clarify.

'I have already said as much.' The doctor waved an impatient hand. 'Take it away.' He gestured and the two hospital workers stooped with expressions of distaste to grip an arm and a leg each.

I had not disliked him until he used the word *it*.

I never trusted him. Ruby wore a glittering gown of sequins, I thought, until I recognised them as diamonds. *His jacket buttons are mother of pearl.*

The attendants dumped the dead man unceremoniously in the back of the cart where he lay, one arm twisted under his back.

Inspector Hefty was examining the blurred imprints of flattened grass and trampled mud. Perhaps he could come up with a useful observation.

I certainly can. He tucked his thumbs into his waistcoat pockets. *By the angle and altitude of the sun I deduce that it is time for a cup of tea.*

The two men raised the tailgate of the cart and set off back up the lane.

'It comes to us all.' Anthony drew close. 'We can only hope for a better death than that.'

It was hell, I remembered the man saying, and prayed that he was in heaven now.

20

THE EYE OF BRAHMA AND THE HEART OF A LION

I HAD plucked up the courage to ask Gerrund for something other than the mounds of meats or fish that he usually prepared for me to start the day. In my experience cooks take the slightest suggestion as an unpardonable affront. When my mother requested that her curry be a touch spicier we were served with a dish almost volcanic in heat. When my father complained that his lamb chop was underdone it came back in cinders. Gerrund, however, had taken up the idea with enthusiasm and made me porridge. Agnust brought it in a gargantuan bowl and deposited it in front of me. I waited in vain for her to slide it away and fetch a breakfast bowl but none was forthcoming.

'There's more when tha's finished.' She wiped a spillage off her apron with my napkin.

'I cannot possibly eat all that.'

'Well you can't do nothin' else with it.' My maid refolded the napkin and slipped it back into its ring, seemingly unaware of the ooze oozing out of it.

Alone with my oats I dipped a spoon in. Admittedly it was delicious, sweetened as it was with honey, but I was loath to admit even to myself that I was suffering from what I believed our American cousins called a *hangover*. The green goddess may have seduced me, but she was punishing me cruelly for falling for her charms.

I fail to see why you cannot eat all that. Hefty knocked out his briar on the leg of his chair. *You made me eat a zebra.*

A zebra fish.

What? He banged his pipe so hard that the stem snapped. *The book said zebra.*

You should have turned the page, Ruby laughed as I took another spoonful.

While I ate, I flicked through the post. There were three bills which I put to one side and the usual advertising leaflets. Hair seemed to be the topic of the day, with irons for straightening my hair and irons for curling it, lotions to remove my facial hair and lotions to make my dundrearies bushier. There was also a letter from a builder who had spotted that we had cracked slates and would replace them for a minimal fee because he felt sorry for me. This was a remarkably kind offer especially as I did not have any slates. My roof was flat, with an observatory upon it.

Ruby was perched at the opposite end of the table. She was having scrambled eggs with shavings of white truffle all washed down with Jose Cuervo Mezcal de Tequila straight from the bottle.

I was filling up but gamely downed four more spoonfuls of porridge.

The *Montford Chronical* had some fascinating articles. An elderly man was taking up knitting and had already made half a sock. A blind cat was found not to be blind at all. *He just wanted sympathy,* a neighbour said. The bells of St Aegbald's Church did not need any maintenance work doing on them.

The front page, though, was dominated by an account of a human lower arm that had been found in the gutter outside the Capricorn Brewery in Canticle Square. Obviously, the editor wrote, the remains of the Wild Man of Gorham's dinner.

Or somebody who misunderstood what is involved in offering his hand in marriage. Ruby had a cavalry twill hacking jacket on. It would have looked manly on me but was somehow graceful and feminine on her. *I can no more help being beautiful than you can help having a stutter.*

I do not have a st-st-stutter, I told her and was wondering if I had when the doorbell cacophonied.

I glanced at my breakfast. Despite my heroinic exertions it did not appear to have diminished. Indeed, this was rather like a torture devised by the Greek gods. The more the object of their displeasure consumed, the greater the volume increased.

Agnust was tramping up the hall, grumbling about being treated like a servant but, as she opened the door, her tone mellowed. Was it Anthony? I hurried to the looking glass to check my hair and wished that I had not. Once my crowning glory, it was still thick and black, but it had grown wild of late.

Now your clowning glory. Ruby shook her golden coiffure so that it glistened in the sunlight which shone on her but not on me.

'Come in, my lord,' I heard Agnust say with such relish that, had her build allowed it, I could imagine her curtsying.

I knew a few lords – Baron Ballcock, who was a plumber and, I suspected, not really a peer of the realm at all – my father, who was an earl but rarely ventured into Suffolk, believing it to be populated by radicals and savages, who were much the same thing in his eyes – my Uncle Tiberius, who was a marquis and owned a zoo – and...

'Romulus, Viscount Thorn of Thetbury,' Agnust announced as if he were Nicholas, Czar of all the Russias, King of the Congress of Poland and Grand Duke of Finland.

'Rommy.' I ran into the hall to give him a kiss and help him off with his coat. 'Come through.' We went into the sitting room. 'Would you like a coffee or a whisky?'

'A large brandy would do the trick.'

'If his lordness want to do tricks, let him.' Agnust bent her knees as if to perform that curtsy but then thought better of it. 'You can always buy new furniture.'

She reversed from the room and Rommy laughed but his face was grey and his sapphire eyes had dulled. I poured him a very large Hennessy but only a soda water for myself.

'You look exhausted.' I settled beside him on the sofa. 'How is Jane?' His wife had been ill for a long time now and he had often expected to lose her.

'Still fighting.' He rubbed his chin and, unusually for him, it rasped. 'She has the build of a mouse but the heart of a lion.'

'She's a strong woman.' Jane and I had been good friends even before she married my cousin. 'And she has a brilliant doctor to tend her.'

Rommy swirled his brandy around the snifter and stared glumly down. 'There is little I can do except try to relieve her pain, but it makes her very drowsy and she doesn't care for that.' He pinched the bridge of his long, hooked nose. 'She doesn't want to sleep her life away.'

'Oh Rommy.' I took his hand but there was nothing I could say that would not be a platitude or a lie.

He raised my hand and kissed the back of it. 'Thank you for not telling me about somebody you've heard of who was even worse and made a complete recovery.'

'We know each other too well for that.' I swallowed. 'Is she able to have visitors?'

Rommy took a drink and I began to wish, early as it was, that I had poured myself something stronger. 'She says that she does not want you to see her as she is but to remember her as she was. She thinks it will be too distressing for you.'

'Is she able to get to the telephone?'

'She cannot leave her bed.'

'I shall write to her,' I decided. 'In the meantime, perhaps you could tell her that I will be far more distressed not to be able…'

'To say goodbye.' Rommy filled in the words for me. 'I shall try. Here.' He handed me his glass. 'I know you don't care for brandy but it will fortify you. You're trembling.'

'Am I?' I saw the waves on the surface of the cognac. 'I suppose I must be.' I took a sip and found I did quite like it after all, so I took another. 'What brings you to Montford so early?' I took a third and handed it back.

'Alfred called me out to look at that man you and Anthony came across at the monument. It must have been awful for you, Violet. You should have told me.'

'I thought you had enough to worry about.' I got up to refresh his glass and pour myself a small one.

'As you said, we know each other better than that.' He raised his glass and clinked mine. 'Alfred tried to get Brigand Ball to do it, but Brig is recovering from taking a shortcut across Calder's pond and falling through the ice.

He was dragged out all but dead. I took a look yesterday evening.'

'Where did you stay?'

'Not on your spare bed. I have slept on softer rocks.' He forced the ghost of a smile.

I have often wondered what happens to smiles when they die, Hefty pondered. *What did he force it to do?*

'I spent a comfortable night at the Splendid,' Rommy spoke over him. He brought out his silver cigarette case questioningly and I nodded in permission. The case had a dent in it caused, he once vowed with a twinkle, by stopping a Burmese bullet, but I was almost sure I had seen the damage before he went away.

'Did your post-mortem examination come up with anything?'

Rommy flicked open the lid to select a Virginian. 'As I am sure you observed, his eyelids had been cut off. You would need a very sharp knife to do that so neatly – so probably a scalpel – and a degree of skill to avoid even scratching the eyeballs, especially on a living patient.'

'Do you think he was anaesthetised?'

'I hope so, but who can say?' He put the cigarette between his lips and struck a vesta.

Assaulted a vesta, Hefty noted.

Rommy lit his cigarette, snapped the matchstick and deposited it in my nasty Limoges ashtray. 'When I had washed him down, I found that he had been scalped. That was neatly done as well.'

'I thought that he was bald,' I admitted.

'So did I at first.' He inhaled deeply. 'And, oddly, the skin had been taken off his left foot, peeled away like a sock.'

I had come across a great deal of cruelty in my life, but it never ceased to shock me.

'Why would anybody do that?'

Rommy exhaled through his nostrils. 'Do you remember the Hadling Heath Torturer?' He handed me his glass again.

'How could I forget? It filled the papers for weeks.'

The tip of Rommy's Virginian glowed as he drew on it. 'He was never caught, but all his victims had an ear missing. It's believed that he took them as trophies.'

'Sometimes…' I took another drink and returned his glass. The effects were already going to my head. 'I almost lose my faith in human nature.'

'As I do.' Rommy flicked the ash off his cigarette. 'But last Monday I went to see an old woman who was starving to death. Her son couldn't understand it because he made sure she had food and milk delivered every day. I spoke to the neighbours and found out that she was giving it all to a twelve-year-old orphan girl up the lane who was trying to look after her three younger sisters.' Rommy pulled out a white cotton handkerchief. 'The woman and the girl give me hope for humanity.' He blew his nose. 'It is God's nature I find myself doubting these days.'

Ruby sat on the other side of Rommy and kissed his cheek.

Hefty cleared his throat but had no observations to make and all Ruby had to say was *Hay fever*, as she dabbed her eyes.

For a long time we sat in silence, hand-in-hand, until Rommy fetched the medical box and untied the ends of my bandage. 'Gerrund made a neat job of that.' He unwrapped it and whistled. 'Nasty,' was his professional opinion.

'The poor man was desperate. I don't suppose he even realised what he was biting. He was hanging on for life.'

'Lucky he didn't take a chunk out then.' Rommy wiped it with a ball of cotton wool. 'It's nice and clean so it should heal uneventfully, though you may have scarring.'

I greeted that news with dismay. It was not so much a question of vanity as the thought that I could carry a physical reminder of that horrible night for the rest of my life.

'Did you hear about the leg that was found in Poplar Lane?' I asked.

'Sergeant Webb showed it to me. It was too decomposed to make much of it.'

'I wondered...' I had an itch in my left earhole but did not want to let go of Rommy to scratch it.

Ladies do not scratch, Hefty asserted.

You have no idea what ladies get up to, Ruby told him, *while the men are busy feeling important.*

'Much as I love Ruby, she does have a tendency to distract you.' Rommy chided me gently. 'You wondered what?'

'If it might possibly have been taken by the Torturer.'

'It could be.' Rommy took one more drag and stubbed out his cigarette in a prissy shepherdess's face. 'Quite a large keepsake though. It could also be an amputation from the infirmary. They are not always scrupulous about how they dispose of their waste.' He released my hand. 'Sorry, I have an itchy ear that's driving me to...'

Colchester, Hefty guessed. 'Distraction.' Rommy puggled about with his forefinger and I followed suit. 'Sorry I haven't finished my drink, but I must be off if I am to catch the express.'

We went into the hall.

'Give Jane my love and remember what I said.'

'I will.' We hugged and, holding my cousin by his right hand in both of mine, I looked him in the eyes. 'There is something you are not telling me.'

'Am I that transparent?'

A human window. Hefty ran his finger down the curtain and I shooed him away but Rommy was not waiting for my response. 'I don't like to suggest this, but I feel I would be letting you down if I did not.' He shifted uneasily. 'Have you ever heard of voodoo?'

'Yes, of course. I mentioned it in *The Dead Walk Sideways.*'

'Yes, of course.' Rommy examined his left fingertips, proving what I had long suspected, that he had not read the book. 'It's just that I was reminded of it by what you told me about that mannequin.' He forced a shrug. 'But it's probably nothing.'

'I am sure of it.'

'Must have been very quiet tricks,' Agnust commented as she loomed up to hand Rommy his hat and help him on with his coat.

'The best tricks always are,' he told her.

'I shall remember tha', your holiness,' Agnust vowed as if he had dispensed sacred text.

Rommy opened the door and I watched him cross the square. He was hunched and his walk was flat.

'Oh Rommy,' I breathed.

Love, Ruby clasped her hands to her cheek in a girlish and very unGibsonesque manner. *If only I had had a man like that, I would not have settled for Anthony.*

What are you talking about?

No time to discuss that now. Ruby took off her white silk glove to reveal an engagement ring, mounted with a diamond to rival the Eye of Brahma, and off she skipped, little considering how treacherous her plans were or how I would always be Lady Violet Thorn, a spinster of the parish.

Alone in my sitting room I thought about our brief discussion. Was I really the target of a voodoo spell?

Yes, Scotland Yard's premier detective assured me.

And who do we know who has books on Satanism and other black practices? Ruby asked.

Anthony? Havelock Hefty guessed.

Roger Bruton, you fool. Ruby Gibson flicked cigarette ash into his hair.

To be fair to me I was in Leamington Spa at the time in hot pursuit of... But Hefty's voice tailed away. He could not remember his arch-enemy's name.

In voodoo, I had read, the malefactors stick pins in dolls to injure that part of their victim. In this case somebody had plunged a dagger deep into my heart.

21

THE HANDS OF A STRANGLER

GERRUND LOOKED very distinguished with his herringbone tweed ulster over a Prussian blue woollen jacket with a moss green waistcoat and matching bowler. Compared to him I verged on the dowdy in my claret ensemble.

Makes you look like a beetroot. Ruby was all in black and heavily veiled for, since I had failed to provide her with an adventure, she was off on one of her own.

More like a radish. Hefty came nobly to my defence.

Anthony was still in Norwich playing, according to his letters, to uncongested houses.

Gerrund had arranged for Friendless to pick us up at noon, in part because it was one of the few times that our cabby was confident of reading from a clock.

'Old Queeny looks livelier,' I commented after she had munched contentedly on a carrot that I had taken out for her and attempted to nibble at my sleeve.

'She was just a touch liverish.' Friendless hardly waited for me to be seated before we set off. 'But I mash a pair of pickled onion in her chicken broth, give her an extra pillow and she's happy as a bat.'

I had not thought of bats as anything other than leathery-winged vermin but perhaps he knew them more intimately than I.

'I am very glad to hear it,' I called up.

'Why?' He leaned forward. 'You got blocked ears? When I have tha' my old mumby drip beef drippin' in them.'

'Good for her,' Gerrund sarcasmed while I watched a nanny with a pram overtake us.

'Int good for her,' Friendless corrected him. 'It's good for me.'

'Crabs,' a barrow boy hollered so loudly that, had my ears indeed been clogged, he would have cleared them. 'Fresh crabs, crunchy-meaty-juicy-fishy craaaaaabs.' His last word rose and fell like a roller in a stormy sea.

'Int no song about cabbies,' Friendless remarked after we had moved on. 'So I write one.'

'Perhaps...' I tried to think of a way of asking him to keep it to himself without giving offence.

'Int no perhaps on it,' Friendless insisted. 'I do.' I had witnessed crashed waggons being cleared with less of a performance than when he cleared his throat. 'Oh I am a Montford cabby. I drive a Montford cab and every night I eat my dinner off a slab and so does my horrrrrse of course. Tha's it,' he announced with great satisfaction.

'Short and...' Gerrund paused, 'short,' he concluded.

Friendless steered us around a puddle. 'Dint want her gettin' a chill on her hoof,' he explained and we came to a halt. 'Tha's it.' He pushed his hat back to mop his brow as if the winter weather were insufferably hot.

'But we are not here,' I complained and Friendless treated us to a hollow raspy laugh.

'Can't never be anywhere else but here,' he reasoned, 'for when we go there, there become here.'

'Descartes has a rival,' Gerrund murmured.

'Yes, but this is not where we want to be,' I argued.

'Tint where we gooin' to goo,' Friendless explained patiently, 'but Old Queeny like to stop here a while and remember.'

'Do not encourage him,' I whispered.

'Remember what?' Gerrund encouraged him.

'She fall in love here,' Friendless explained, 'with a chestnut stallion but he pass by, nose in the air and never give her a third glance.' He flicked the reins gently. 'Come on, darlin'. He int worth it.'

Old Queeny snorted as if in agreement and plodded on around another twenty yards before, with no instruction from her owner that I could discern, she came to a halt.

'Told you there become here,' our cabby announced triumphantly, though neither of us had gainsaid him.

'Wink, Finbow and Motte, Solicitors and Commissioners for Oaths,' Gerrund read, though I was not yet myopic.

'Wha's a missioner on noaths?' Friendless enquired.

'They help people who wish to swear...' I began.

'Dint need no one to do tha' for me.' Friendless fingered his stubbly chin. 'Goh many-plenty on noaths myself.'

'Actually...'

'Thah tint a noath,' Friendless scorned. 'Liver salts is.'

'Liver salts?' I queried.

'My old mumby swear by them.' For a moment I thought that he was jesting but his tone was serious and Friendless would never joke about his mother. She was sacred in his memory. He did not seem to mind her naming of him nor that he had *cockled*, or shrivelled, his hand as a child when she let him pick up a hot coal. He would smile fondly as he related how she had tried to pull out all his hair to save the cost of having it cut. 'It never grow back proper.' He once showed me the bare patches of scalp with as much pride as a man might display his war wounds.

'Good old mumby.' I pushed the flaps. 'Will you wait for us?'

'We dint find tha' funny any no more,' Friendless informed me, and Gerrund looked nonplussed, as well he might. Our driver had told me once that he and Old Queeny thought the way that I said those words was hilarious but now he made me feel like a stale comedian in need of a fresh script.

'It was not intended to be amusing.'

'Tha's better.' Friendless slapped his thigh in unbridled merriment and I was quarter convinced that Old Queeny was sniggering along, tapping the cobbles with a front hoof to emphasise her gaiety.

'We shouldn't be very long.' Gerrund joined me on the pavement and Friendless frowned.

'You int got her comical face,' he critiqued.

The solicitors' offices were situated up a narrow, steep flight of stairs above Bowstrain's, the butcher's shop with its gruesome exhibition of split corpses dangling on hooks in the window. Inspector Hefty lingered to ensure that none of the cadavers were human. *Only one,* he noted with satisfaction.

We found ourselves on a dusty uncarpeted corridor, light seeping through an open doorway straight ahead. There a man slumped behind an enormous desk, outsized head drooping over an undersized chest. Behind him to his left, lurking in the shade, was a large potted aspidistra, its blade-shaped leaves drooping.

'Sleeping,' Gerrund diagnosed, though I could have reached that conclusion unaided.

Dead, Ruby diagnosed, but I had fallen for that with Mrs Greaves.

Dead as a flamingo, Hefty – anxious to prove himself at least her equal – confirmed, but even I knew that dead men do not open their eyes and blink.

'Good morning,' he greeted us without rising. 'Wink, Finbow and Motte at your service.'

In the absence of an invitation, we perched on the hard wooden chairs in front of his desk.

'Which one are you?' Gerrund enquired and the man's brow wrinkled.

'Which one of what?'

'Wink or Finbow or Motte?'

The man laughed airily. 'Your mistake, though stupidus in extremis, is simplicus to explain. Wink, Finbow and Motte is my company. Messrs Finbow and Motte do not nor have ever existed in worldus actualis.'

Gerrund, not a man to take being insulted in cod Latin lightly, jutted his square jaw. 'Then why have their names on your plate?'

Mr Wink rubbed his hands. There was something odd about them.

One is right and the other is not, Hefty explained, but there was more to it than that.

Dexter and... Ruby paused dramatically, *sinister.*

'Nobody is impressed by a company run by hominus solo, as my vile pater antiquus used to say.' He dipped his head mournfully. 'Indeed still does say when he comes to me in the dead of night as a member of the dead of night.'

'I am Mr Ackerby.' Gerrund straightened a crease in his trouser leg.

'Ackerby,' Wink mused. 'What a beautiful name, redolent with the perfumes of fried bacon and coal dust.'

'I fail to see why,' I admitted, and wondered why my man had chosen that surname, though it was as good as any.

'All names emit an aroma.' Wink sniffed the air between us. 'And your daughter's first name is?'

'We are without child.' Gerrund said so mournfully that, for a moment, I was saddened to hear it. 'As yet.' He eyed me with unnerving fondness.

'Then this is?'

'Mrs Ackerby, my wife.' Though we had discussed this at length, it still took me aback to be referred to by my manservant in such a manner.

Wink raised an eyebrow, not an especially noteworthy act as a rule but he raised it with his second finger and the arch collapsed the moment that he released it. 'And her Christian nominus is?'

I was fairly convinced that I could have had a stab at the answer to that one, but the excellent Mr W was probably anxious not to overtax me.

'Violet,' Gerrund told him.

'Let me see.' Wink leaned towards me and snuffled. 'Oddly, the name has a peculiar floral fragrance to it.' He pinched the bridge of his nose so hard with both hands that the tip blanched. 'How on earth does one account for that?'

'Inexplicable,' I murmured.

'Omnibus inexplicabilis,' he concurred, releasing his nose as if he expected it to scamper away.

Gerrund cleared his throat.

Whose throat? Hefty enquired.

His own.

'We are considering the purchase of a property on Tannery Lane,' my man spoke over them.

'Tannery,' Mr Wink inhaled through his dilated nostrils but did not enlighten us upon what scents the name evoked. I had my own theory about that.

'Indeed,' I contributed before remembering that we had agreed that my *husband* should do all the talking.

'Maccabee House,' Gerrund said.

'Maccabee.' If nothing else Mr Wink proved that he was skilled in the art of repetition. 'Maccabus, Maccabum.' If nothing else he proved himself unskilled in the art of declension. 'Surely not?'

'Why?' I asked, brushing my promise aside like crumbs of toast off a dress and throwing up my arms to leave him in no doubt that my alarm was completely genuine. 'Is there something untoward with the property? Dry rot? Wet rot? Subsidence?' I let my arms drop, accidently clipping Gerrund on the ear. 'Is it haunted? Not all four, surely to goodness?'

'Oh you ladies,' Wink – I decided to cease giving him the courtesy of a title – snuckled.

Snuckled? Miss Kidd eyed me sideways.

It is a composite of chuckled and snorted, coined since you were dismissed from service at Thetbury Hall.

Miss Kidd puffed herself up and was about to reply, but I shook my head and she fell headlong down the great longitudinal fissure between the two halves of my brain.

'Do you have an earwig in your ear?' Wink put his peculiar fingertips together. 'Have a care that it does not burrow into your head, though what it would find there…' He chortled. 'Heaven only knows.'

Homicidal intent, I thought, but gave him my second-best smile and said sweetly, 'Why nothing at all, I should think, if women were capable of such a process.'

'Indeed,' he sniggled, unable to recognise sarcasm if it came with a letter of introduction from the Ministry of Mordancy. 'But to return to the matterum in handus, there is nihil whatsoever erratum with the house,' Wink was saying. 'I am replete with mystification that it should be offered for sale so soon after it was purchased.'

'By whom?' Gerrund rubbed his ear gingerly. I had quite forgotten that I had struck it but, obviously, he had not.

'Surely you have had intercourse with him?' Wink rubbed his own ear.

'I have dealt with an agent so far.' Gerrund fished a meerschaum from his outer breast pocket though I had never known him to smoke.

'An agent?' Wink sharpened his skill.

'An agent.'

'Surely you have looked around le property?'

I was fairly confident that *le* was not latin but, when I was eight, I had been very confident that I could walk over the conservatory roof and I still bore scars on my legs which proved that I could not.

Steady on. Hefty blushed, for women's lower limbs were unmentionable in male company.

Gerrund produced a puckered leather pouch from a side pocket and, as Wink watched impatiently, raised the flap and dipped his pipe inside to load the bowl with tobacco.

'We have not.' He buttoned up the pouch.

'But surely…'

'My wife,' Gerrund indicated so violently that he knocked my hat skewwhiff. 'I am so sorry, my dear,' he apologised with insincerity deeper than the Mariana Trench, for revenge is a dish best served and enjoyed as soon as possible. Clearly the role was going to his head. 'Whilst admirable in many respects, my old Dutch is of an impulsive and intractable nature and becomes besotted with every property that we view.'

I was not sure how to react to that assertion. On one hand I admired my man's presence of mind, on the other I fermented indignantly. *Old Dutch?*

'Oh Aloysius,' I simpered, in the hope that he would hate being called that.

'Women are so silly,' Wink sympathised. 'Which is why I have never taken a wife.'

I suspected there were other reasons he remained unattached.

'They cannot help being scatterbrained,' Gerrund defended me in five words while betraying me in nine syllables but, to give him credit, he only emitted the tiniest of yelps when I gave his shin a sharp sideways kick. 'How did you know it had been sold recently?'

'Why...' Wink clasped his hands, and it was only then that I realised all his fingers were of equal length.

A rare heredity condition and invariably a sign of criminality, Hefty declared. *Digitos aequales longitude, the hands of a strangler.*

How could my character's Latin be better than mine?

I went to school, he reminded me, for I had only been governessed at home.

Pay attention, I scolded myself, for Wink was still explicating. 'It was I who expedited the transaction.'

'On whose behalf?' Gerrund clamped on his pipe but did not light it.

As a smoker myself I can confidently inform you, Inspector Hefty confidently informed me, *that one does not light a pipe. One ignites its contents.*

'I'm afraid...' Wink scratched his cheek. 'I have a duty of confidentiality to my clients.'

'I suppose so,' Gerrund conceded. 'But surely just this once...'

Ruby opened Wink's cigar box and helped herself to a fistful, stuffing all but one into her dainty blue handbag.

'To whom do you owe the greater loyalty?' I broke my silence. 'The man whose money you have already misappropriated or the man of whose money you so rapaciously anticipate procurement?'

Spurning the use of a cutter, Ruby chewed off the end of the cigar and spat it onto the floor. Not for the first time I regretted sending her to the slums of Cuba in *Our Woman in Havana*.

'Mr Roger Richard Russel Rueben Clerihew Bruton,' Wink said after four and a half seconds, as timed by Scotland Yard's premier detective. Clearly the ethics of the matter did not require a great deal of consideration.

Ruby struck a sulphurous lucifer on a no-longer-white whitewashed wall and lit her Hoyo de Monterrey.

'What kind of a man was he?' My hat was sliding forward.

'How many kinds are there?'

'Eighty-six,' I bluffed.

Two, Ruby corrected me. *Rich or not rich*. She snapped the matchstick beside the solicitor's ear and he glanced in that direction.

'Why do you need to know?'

'I like to know with whom we are dealing.'

'We?' Wink digitally elevated his eyebrow again.

'My wife is a modern woman,' Gerrund explained and Wink recoiled.

'I have heard of such creatures.'

'What was he like?' I prompted while Ruby blew smokily into Wink's face.

'Tall.' Wink coughed and rubbed his eyes. 'But not as tall as he might have been.'

Gerrund frowned. He disliked riddles almost as much as I.

'Was he stooped?' I suggested.

'Stooped is the word, madam.' He pronounced that word as if he had heard that I ran a house of ill-repute, a rumour started by a malicious neighbour and which – rather like Topsy – *just growed*.

'What about the way he walked?'

'Very stiff.'

'Like a mechanical doll?'

'Not in the least,' Wink fleered. 'His movements resembled those of a clockwork soldier.'

'Annisoice,' I prompted through clenched teeth before parting them sufficiently to rearticulate, 'And his voice?'

'Oh yes.' Wink smirkled. Even I was dissatisfied with that verb. 'Of course he had a voice, little lady.'

Gerrund elevated his hackles. 'I will have you know, sir, that my wife is not…' he hesitated, for he could neither claim that I was not little nor a lady, 'to be addressed in such a condescending manner.'

'Indeed she is not,' Wink agreed fervently, as if a third party were responsible for his impertinence.

'His voice,' I prompted.

'Hoarse. No, that is not the word I am looking for.' He raised the edge of a stack of papers as if he believed that the adjective might be hiding beneath it.

'Dry,' I suggested, 'like the rustling of autumnal leaves.'

'You have it exactly.' Wink let his blotter go, twitching at the faint sound of it landing. 'Hornbeam leaves. But how could you know that?'

'Feminine intuition,' I replied. 'Who acted for Mr Bight?'

'Why I did.' His eyes swivelled to the left.

'Is that usual?' I had a vague idea that it was not legal, or perhaps solicitors gave people that impression to make them think they needed their services.

'I doubt it.' Wink's eyes flicked to the right, like a man planning his escape. 'But I have never claimed to be usual.'

'I suppose it made the sale more straightforward,' Gerrund speculated.

'It would have,' Wink agreed, 'were it not for the unusual stipulation inserted by Mr Bight without consulting meum.'

'Unusual?' Gerrund leaned forward.

'Yes.' Wink put a finger over his mouth to show that his bloodless lips were sealed.

'What did Mr Bight look like?' I asked and Wink pushed both eyebrows down into a glower.

'Why do you need to know that?'

'I think I may have met him once.' Gerrund pointed the stem of his meerschaum at the solicitor.

'He looked ordinary.' Wink deliberated further before adding with great gravitas, 'One might almost say, if one were minded to, that he was nondescript.'

'What about his build?' my man asked.

'Average.'

'His hair?' I tried.

'An ordinary shade, as I recall.'

'His eyes?' Gerrund prompted.

'Two of them. Sky blue... or moss green... or possibly hazel.'

'Did you notice nothing distinguishing about his appearance?' I made no attempt to hide my frustration.

'Nothing at all.' He shrugged. 'Except...' He touched his temples.

'Yes?' Gerrund and I urged.

'His nose,' Wink pondered. 'It was a perfectly normal nose except...'

'Yes?' we chorused.

'That it bent to the left – his left – and then back to the right, his right, of course.'

'Did Mr Bight seem happy to sell?' I made a half-hearted attempt to unskewwhiff my hat.

'I wouldn't say happy.' Wink's chair creaked as he leaned back. 'But then I wouldn't say unhappy. I would say...' He snatched at the desk to stop himself toppling over. 'He was eager to sell.'

'Did he say why?' Gerrund probed.

'We did not discuss his motivae.' Wink blinked. 'But to return to the topicus of your purchase.'

I got to my feet and Gerrund looked at me quizzically but rose also.

'You are going?' Wink remained seated.

'Indeed,' I replied.

'But why?' Wink digitally elevated both eyebrows with one hand and depressed his chin with the other to gape in startlement.

'Clearly a house which comes onto the market so quickly but does not have dry rot, wet rot, subsidence or a ghost must have something abominably wrong with it.' I caught a glimpse of my hat in a looking glass. It was a sight for making eyes sore.

'Indeed,' Gerrund contributed as he followed me out of the office onto the landing.

I trust you observed that the aspidistra was wilting, Hefty counselled, though I had hardly noticed the plant, *contralaterally.* He tapped the oilcloth floor-covering with his silver-handled cane. *That detail may be of the greatest significance yet.*

Greatest significance? Ruby ground out her cigar on the already business-scarred leather desktop while Hefty and I awaited her withering scorn. *Yes, it probably is.*

Inspector Hefty stared at his rival. *Well blow me down.*

'Who do I send my account to?' Wink called.

'To whom do I send my account?' I corrected him from most-way down the stairs.

'Why would you be sending an account to anyone?' reached us faintly as Gerrund opened the door.

Friendless rubbed his eyes and opened the flaps. He looked almost as weary as Old Queeny.

Gerrund swung comfortably back into the role for which I employed him and easily into the cabin.

'Allow me, milady.' I took the proffered hand.

'Surely you mean *Old Dutch*?'

For the first time since I had met Gerrund, he flushed slightly. 'Please don't remind me, milady,' he begged, though I already had. 'You could see what class of man he was and I spoke to you like that to try to get him on my side. As it turned out, I got nowhere.' He slid aside to give me more room on the leather bench. 'Your approach succeeded,' he admitted before I had the opportunity to point that out.

'Seraphim Square please, Friendless,' I called up when we were settled.

Down the road, turning up Thistle Street, Old Queeny plodded. She had slowed so markedly of late that customers were beginning to avoid her.

'It would appear that Miss Bight's father did sell the house without her knowledge,' Gerrund ventured.

'Assuming that she confirms the description of her father's nose.'

Ruby was up aloft beside our cabby though there was only room for one person. *Reminds me of the time I rode shotgun on a stagecoach through Gopher Head Gulch.* She blew a smoke triangle. How on earth was that possible? I wondered before reminding myself that she was not really on earth anyway.

'When I'm a young boy I never live on a hill. Now I'm an old boy and I dint live there still,' our driver belted out what was doubtless another of his compositions. He had a voice that I could only describe as falsetto bass. 'And I dint suppose I never ever never ever will.'

How clever, Ruby commented. *He changed key five times in three lines.*

'When I'm a young boy I never live by the sea,' Friendless continued. 'Now I'm an old boy fiddle-diddle-fiddle-dee.' His voice trailed off. 'Needs a bit o' work,' he admitted modestly. 'Trouble is.' He appeared to have taken a sudden lack of interest in the topic before asserting, 'There int no word who rhyme with *sea*.'

'What about...' Gerrund stopped when I coughed. 'No, actually I can't think of one either.'

'No, actually I can't think of one either?' Friendless mused as we entered Seraphim Square. 'That dint rhyme.'

Daisy Dixon the Diamond Queen was tuning up her ukulele by the massive monastery gate. The hundreds of glass beads sewn to her dress did not glitter in the weak light seeping through the heavy sky but, even on a bright day, she had lost much of her sparkle since her husband had been murdered.

The figure of a woman was seated in my window. I could not see her clearly through the glass – wet on the outside and steamed up on the inside – but, from the build of her and the colour of her dress I could make an educated guess as to who it was.

Only the educated can make educated guesses. Miss Kidd was shooing small children aside with her whalebone walking cane.

Beware the woman in brown, Hefty counselled. *She brings danger.*

Danger and death. Ruby Gibson was descending from her high perch. *A horrible slow lingering death.*

Somewhat tautologous, my old governess chalked the word on a blackboard, *since a lingering death must per se be slow.*

Ruby sprang down. *Tautologise that,* she challenged and pushed Miss Kidd so hard that I felt her crashing into the side of my temple.

'Are you all right, milady?' Gerrund was at my side.

'Yes, thank you. Just a slight headache.'

You have no idea with whom or what you are dealing. Miss Kidd struggled to straighten her bustle, but I was unsure if she was threatening Ruby or, more likely, warning me.

22

SATANIC RITUALS AND HUMAN SACRIFICE

THE RAIN was falling afresh by the time we had crossed the pavement. Gerrund did not wait for my maid to open the door for us but unlocked it himself and stood back to admit me.

'Umbrellas in the umbrella stand.' Agnust came out of her parlour. 'Coats on the hooks. Outdoor boots off and inside shoes on.'

'I see we have a visitor.' I unhooked my cape, shook it dry and stepped inside.

'Miss so-called Cherry Bight.'

I genuflected to untie my bootlace. 'Why so-called?' I put on my soft calfskin shoe.

'You have to ask her parents why they so-called her.'

'How long has she been here?'

'She finish all a whole teapot of tea.'

I changed knees to untie the other boot.

Forty-eight minutes, Hefty calculated, *and nine seconds.* Which sounded a reasonable estimate to me.

'I thought you did not approve of my admitting strangers to the house.'

'And so I daint.' She ran a finger under the long table, tutting at the dust she had discovered. 'But you dint admit her. I do.'

I rose unsteadily to my feet. 'I shall have coffee,' I tried but, as usual, failed to sound imperious. My voice came out as wheedling as if I were a child begging to lick the cake-mixing spoon.

'What?' Agnust recoiled in horror. 'Now?'

'Yes.' I could not stop the 'please' making a break for it from my lips.

Agnust shook her great head in disbelief. 'I suppose that's my job?'

'It is,' I confirmed, succeeding in converting the *sorry* that was tickling my vocal cords into a cough.

'Tell you not to go out without your chest protector.' She had made me wear one of those when I was five – a hideous and hideously uncomfortable item made of canvas lined with asbestos wool, making it itchier than any saint's hairshirt. 'Dint I?'

'Coffee,' I said firmly and was congratulating myself on my unyielding and courtly stance when I tripped over the threshold and stumbled flying into my sitting room.

'Goodness.' Cherry sprang to her feet and spun round to face me. 'Are you all right?'

'Quite, thank you.' I struggled to regain my dignity, but it had been dead and buried so long that lichen was growing over its headstone.

Odd how a simple trip saved the day, I remembered Anthony saying, though it hardly seemed relevant as I struggled to regain my dignity.

One cannot regain what one has never possessed. Ruby was pinching a sample from my grandfather's snuffbox.

Cherry came towards me.

'I tripped over it myself.' She smiled.

'Yes, but I should have been aware by now that it is there.' I took her hand. She had long, quite thick fingers and a grip strong enough to be uncomfortable for me. There was a brown birthmark on the back of her hand which I had not noticed before.

It was the first thing I spotted. Hefty plucked a hair from her eyebrow with tweezers from his evidence bag and I was half-convinced that she winced.

'How are you, Cherry?'

Her freckled face fell. 'At my wits' end.'

'Shall we sit down?'

We settled by the window. The rain was steady now and the few stallholders who had ventured into the square were scrambling to pack away their wares and fold up their stalls before everything was saturated. A rained-off day meant no money and most of them, I suspected, lived hand-to-mouth existences.

'I have been to see Mr Bruton in Maccabee House,' I began.

'When?'

'Three days ago.'

'And what did you discover?'

'He is a strange man,' I began. 'His tastes appear to centre on the macabre and the occult.'

'The occult?' Cherry sat forward. 'Witchcraft?'

'Amongst other things.'

'This is horrible.' She put her fingertips to her temples. 'They could have immolated my parents in some gruesome satanic ritual.'

'I doubt it.' I raised my hands and lowered them slowly, palms down. It was supposed to pacify her, but the action never worked on me and, from her glare, it was not working for me either. 'Mr Bruton gave us the name of the solicitor who handled the conveyancing of the property. Mr Wink of Wink, Finbow and Motte, and he confirmed that this was the case.'

Cherry opened the saggy leather sack that served her as a handbag.

'Then he was lying.'

I reached for her hand, but she snatched it away. 'I do not think so. I did not like him, but I think he was telling the truth.'

'Then he was in league with the Brutons.' She rooted about in her bag. 'He must be one of them. Was he wearing a black signet ring with a pentagram on it?'

'He was not,' I replied confidently, for I had particularly noticed his fingers.

'And who acted for my father?'

I was starting to feel as if I were in the witness box. 'He did. It is unusual but I believe it is allowed if there is no conflict of interest.'

'How do you know that it was my father who signed the contract?' She was still ferreting about, half-taking things out of her bag before dropping them back in.

'Was there anything unusual about your father's nose?'

'His nose? No, of course not.' Cherry laughed humourlessly. 'It was a perfectly normal nose except…'

'Yes?' I leaned towards her.

'That it bent to the left and then to the right.'

'That is exactly how Mr Wink described him.'

Cherry shrugged and produced a tattered black address book, putting it beside her on the chair. 'I want to see his signature.' A silver cigarette case followed.

'I believe you would have to get a magistrate to order that, but I am not an expert in these matters.'

'You think I am?' She produced a lorgnette and unfolded it to view me briefly, doubly squid-eyed through the lenses, adding that to her trove. 'I am sorry, Violet. That was churlish of me. I know you are trying to help me and I am very grateful.' She found a scent bottle to increase her collection. 'But I am so frightened for my parents.'

'Of course you are.' We were both distracted by a rearing stallion on the street. I could not see what had startled it but was impressed by the way the young man riding it stayed in his saddle and brought it under control. He had long flowing blond hair that rivalled his steed's mane in luxuriousness. Ruby rode behind him, her arms around his waist. 'Do you think it possible...' I began tentatively.

'That my parents sold their house and moved away without telling me?' Her eyes shone with tears. 'No, I honestly do not.'

She produced a white paper cone, the sort in which you might be sold a quarter of pear drops, but redeposited it without offering me any of the contents. Sympathetic though I was to her distress, Cherry was beginning to annoy me. She was turning my armchair into a repository for her clutter.

'Are you looking for something?' I hoped that my irritation was not revealed in my expression.

Of course it wasn't, Hefty reassured me. *It was revealed in the harshness of your voice.*

Cherry stopped rummaging and tilted her head like a blackbird listening for a worm. 'Actually I don't know,' she admitted and, for a bisected moment, treated me to a rueful smile. 'I probably wanted something when I started but I've forgotten what. You must think me quite mad.'

Not 'quite', completely. Ruby, undishevelled from her ride, was sampling a cucumber ice-cream.

'You have been under a great deal of stress,' I reassured her. 'If your parents did sell Maccabee House…'

'They did not.'

'Perhaps you could put an advertisement in *The Suffolk News* personal column.' I ploughed on. 'To say that you are concerned about them. They or somebody who knows them might see it and reply.'

'Is that paper delivered in heaven then?'

'I do not imagine so. But if your parents are alive…'

'If they are, they are being held prisoner.' She started scooping her things back into her bag, which must have shrunk because there was not enough space for her address book and two knitting needles skewering a ball of brown wool. 'And,' she tried to push them in, but they sprang up again and a box of matches fell into her lap, 'they are probably being tortured or prepared for human sacrifice.'

Undoubtedly both. Hefty rubbed his hands with relish.

The pleasure or the condiment? Miss Kidd wrote in green ink.

Massacre at Maccabee House, an Inspector Havelock Hefty mystery, he proposed, and he had had worse ideas in the past.

The only Hefty mystery is why people read him. Ruby scraped out the bowl.

'Did you hear me?' Cherry prodded my shoulder.

'Yes. Sorry. I was thinking.' I brushed my characters under my meninges. 'It seems unlikely that the Brutons would do such a thing.'

'They stole the house,' she pointed out.

'We do not know that,' I unpointed out. 'Mr Wink told me that your father seemed eager to sell.'

'I don't believe it. My father loved that house.' She rammed the box of matches into her bag. 'If he did sign the contract he must have been forced to. They must have been holding my mother hostage and torturing her.' Cherry rattled her bag vigorously and everything fell inside. 'And what's more I can prove it.'

'But how?'

She buttoned up the bag. 'I am going to get into my home and search for them.' She stood.

'Do you think that is wise?' I tried.

Everybody knows that is a polite way of telling somebody not to do something stupid or at least asking them to explain their proposal, but Cherry simply said, 'Yes.'

'But how will you get in?'

'Maccabee House has been my home all my life. I will have no trouble entering it.'

'Cherry.' I touched her arm, but she brushed past me. 'If you are caught in the house you could be arrested.'

'For entering my own home?' She puffed in disbelief.

'Have you considered even for one moment that you may be wrong?' I hurried after her into the hall.

'I was rather hoping for your help.' She took her coat off its hook. 'I shall be outside the house at ten o'clock.' Cherry struggled with the latch though it was not a complicated one. 'And I shall wait five minutes, not a moment longer.' She wrenched open the door.

'But Cherry...'

'Coffee,' Agnust announced as she trundled towards us.

Freda was on the front step. 'Spare a bottle o' gin for a poor old...'

Agnust slammed the door on them both.

'I am not going,' I insisted to Agnust, though she could have had no idea to what I was referring, but mainly for the benefit of my characters.

Much better to stay in and help me to escape from the burning house. Hefty was distilling a flask of green liquid on a Bunsen burner.

But I was having second thoughts already. Perhaps I should go to try to dissuade her.

Ruby Gibson's green liquid had already been distilled for her and she was mixing it with a London dry gin. *Wear something spectacular,* she advised, *and don't forget your Lady Derringer.*

23

THE WALL OF DEATH

FRIENDLESS ARRIVED at eight thirty. I had drawn him a picture of a clock to show the time, and he was so impressed by my rough sketch that he vowed to hang it, as if it were a work of art, in the mews where he slept with Old Queeny.

'Pictures who tell the time,' he had marvelled as he showed it to her that afternoon. 'Whoever do they think on next?'

I had told Gerrund that I was going to see my friend Hettie, but he smelled a rat. *Rotting behind the wainscoting.* Hefty rapped the woodwork with his knuckles. *And poisoned with an alkaloid peculiar to the upper Amazon basin.*

I selected a maroon umbrella and stepped out into the drizzle.

'Crosby Street,' Gerrund told Friendless, who sniffed.

'I know tha'. I might be dunt-headed but I int stupid.'

If there was a distinction between those two descriptions of his intellect, it was too subtle for me. I settled back on the bench.

'Fooled him,' Friendless cackled, and I rather wished he had reserved his triumph for when we were out of earshot.

'Milady,' Gerrund called after us.

'How about a song?' I made a grab at my umbrella, but it fell to the floor.

'Yes please.' Friendless put a hand behind his ear.

'No, I meant...'

'Tha's not much of a malady.'

Why not? I asked myself.

Because you will frighten Old Queeny. Ruby ostentatiously inserted her earplugs.

Undeterred, I cleared my throat and sang out, 'When I was a girl my mother said, Marry a sailor if you can. You'll never want for meat or bread. So I married a sailor man. Yes I married a sailor man. The very first...'

'I never know tha',' Friendless wondered. 'Alway think you're a dried old spinster.'

'I was singing.'

He leaned right over to scrutinise me. 'Singin' is s'posed to have tunes.'

This was rich, coming as it did from a pioneer of atonality.

A Daimler motorised carriage approached, chugging and banging, but Old Queeny paid scant attention. There were four motor cars in the town now and hardly a day went by when one did not see or hear at least one of them.

'Can't get manure out of them.' Friendless dismissed it and I found myself unable to refute his point. Rommy had a Thetbury Type 2, one of only eight built, but he rarely ventured far in it, preferring to rely on one of his horses for local visits or the train for longer journeys. Ruby owned a Gibson Special capable of racing along at forty-five miles an hour. She could have won the Paris–Bordeaux–Paris race were it not for an ox cart that pulled out in front of her.

The town was generally quiet. The weather did not encourage people to venture far for frivolous purposes and, as if to underline that point, a wet gust tore at my hat, almost wrenching it from my head.

We turned left at Mystery Crossroads, the origin of the name being a mystery in itself.

'All right for you all tea-cosy down there,' Friendless shouted over the squall, though the upper half of my body was almost as exposed as his and my woollen coat was not nearly so protective as his rabbit skin.

I thought about inviting him down but knew that he would take the offer seriously and expatiate at length why that was not feasible. There must be a word to describe the male sex's penchant for explaining everything – male elucidation – 'malucidation'. I rather liked the sound of that.

'My Lucy ate shun?' Friendless leaned back and out of view. 'Wha's shun then?'

'It is a French dish, and quite delicious,' I extemporised nonsensically.

'French.' Friendless spat sideways rather like Two-Eyed Jake, a gunfighter in one of my Wild West stories. That genre was very popular at the moment. Unfortunately Two-Eyed Jake was not. 'French.' He spat from the other corner of his mouth. 'Wha's the point on them? Why, they int hardly English.'

'Well actually...'

But my driver was in full flow, not even pausing to curse a stray dog that shot past behind Old Queeny and almost under our wheels. 'And you can't eat a dish. It'll break your tooths. Thought you'd have knew tha'.'

So intent was I on our engrossing conversation that I hardly noticed we were turning left and starting up the steeper slope of Tannery Lane.

The derelict tannery was silhouetted against the three-quarters moon.

A waning gibbon, Havelock Hefty informed me.

Stupid man. Ruby waved her twenty-inch jade cigarette holder. *Waning gibbon my eye. It's a waxing gibbon.*

I had a feeling they were both wrong, but I was more interested in the dark, forbidding shapes of the old factory. It would make an excellent murder scene, I pondered.

Death by pures? Ruby lit a Balkan Sobranie. *You can give that one to Hefty. It stinks.*

Nearly as much as your... Hefty hesitated. As a pipe smoker he could hardly complain about her cigarettes. He could not mock her perfume since it was mine. *Feet,* he concluded lamely, since the crown prince of Bragislania had drunk champagne from her shoe.

And ruined it, she recalled. *It was like trying to dance with one foot in a blancmange.*

'Woah, darlin'.' Friendless's needless yell brought me back to the real world. The slightest tug on the reins would have brought us to a halt.

'Old Queeny seems much livelier today.' I bent to retrieve my umbrella. The rain had paused, doubtless so that the clouds could be filled to capacity again.

'She do,' he concurred. 'For I give her a double tot of rum in her breakfast bran.'

'I do not suppose that does much harm,' I said, apparently unheard.

'And her mid-marnin' bran and her midday bran...'

While Friendless ran through the litany of the dozen or so occasions every day when his horse needed a tot, I disembarked.

Maccabee House stood, the top half visible, the lower half hidden by the ragged hedge.

'Will you wait here?' I asked and Friendless threw back his head, in a way I never really believed that people did, in mirth.

'Hear tha' darlin'?' He slapped his thigh pantomimically. 'Just as funny as ever.'

And I could have sworn, though not before a jury of sane men, that Old Queeny trembled in merriment.

'Dwivaaah weel yooo hwait fowr mih?' Friendless chortled and Old Queeny's withers quivered. 'Yaaaas I weel.'

Not daring to thank him for fear of further ridicule. I turned away and set my face towards the house. The front was dark, but some light seeped from the left-hand side of the property, probably through a gap in the curtains in the room where Anthony and I had met Roger Bruton.

I wish Anthony was here now.

So do I, Ruby struck a match, the flame not even wavering in the breeze.

I'm with you, milady. Hefty produced his revolver, but I knew he would be no more than a distraction.

You must go now, I told them both.

But... Hefty managed before he disappeared.

Good. Ruby looked stunning in my saffron gown. Her diamond tiara, necklace and bracelet sparkled in the moonlight augmented by one of the sparsely planted lampposts. *I have a liaison to keep in the Winter Palace.*

Off she glided towards her golden carriage but, when I glanced back, there was only Friendless feeding Old Queeny what looked like a slice of pork pie.

There was no sign of Cherry as I walked across the driveway. Cautiously as I tried to progress, the noise the stones made every time I put a foot down was loud enough to rouse a regiment.

It was probably better, I decided, to make my way around the right-hand side of the house. I would be less likely to be heard or seen there, I hoped. Here was a narrow drive with a shrubbery along its right-hand side.

Rommy had told me that he had attended a lecture in London in which was demonstrated a hand-held lantern. It was powered by a tube of chemicals that produced an electrical charge. This sounded quite dangerous to me, but I would have appreciated some extra lighting as I moved further from the gaslight. To make matters worse, a cloud drifted over the face of the moon.

'Go away,' I whispered and was gratified to find that it did.

'Do you have to bellow like a buffalo?' Cherry appeared from the darkness.

I performed a standing jump that might have qualified me for the Olympic Games, if the action were part of the event. 'Oh Cherry, you made me...'

'Jump,' she laughed lightly and took the cover off a safety lantern to light up the area. Under my shielding hand, a tumbledown stable was visible at the end of the drive and, to judge by the lack of a door, it was unoccupied. 'I'm sorry, Violet.' She touched my hand. 'Thank you for coming. I knew you wouldn't let me down.'

'I came to talk you out of it.'

Her expression fell. 'Then you have had a wasted journey.'

'But what if you are caught?'

'Before I went to university, I sometimes sneaked out to visit a friend my parents didn't approve of.' The lantern swayed in her hands, throwing demented shadows around and over us. 'I would re-enter the house late at night. My mother was a very light sleeper, but she never stirred. I will not be caught.'

'But why do you need me?'

'Since I hurt my knee last summer, I am not as agile as I was.' She pointed to her left leg. 'I need some help, and I would appreciate some moral support and a witness.'

I was not aware that Cherry had a knee injury and had never noticed her limping.

'We could be arrested for trespass,' I told Cherry, though I knew that it was not a criminal offence.

'I cannot trespass in my own home,' she argued, 'besides which trespass is not a criminal offence.'

Why is everyone a lawyer? I asked myself but received no reply.

'How do you intend to get in?'

Cherry cocked her head towards a ground-floor sash window. 'Unless they have repaired it, there is a faulty catch.' She put a hand into her coat pocket, came out with a handle, fiddled with a catch on the side and a blade sprang out, eight or nine inches long coming to an alarmingly sharp point. 'I bought this in London to protect myself when I am out late.'

'And have you ever used it?' I did not care for the way she brandished that knife.

Cherry walked around me to the house. 'Not yet.' She put the lantern on the ground, reached up and slid the blade, blunt edge first, into the slit between the upper and lower halves of the window. Halfway along it came to a stop. 'It was always a bit stiff.' She pushed and there was a grating sound. 'Come on, you awkward cuss.' She strained harder. 'Got you.' She clenched a fist triumphantly, folded the knife and put it away. 'As I recall one of the weights in the frame has come adrift.' She put the heels of her hands under one of the wooden strips holding the panes.

It is called a muntin. Miss Kidd was gone as quickly as she had arrived.

'There was always a bit of a knack to this.' Cherry pushed and the lower window rose. She grasped the underside of the frame, heaved, and up the window slid. 'Hooray,' she yelled.

'Cherry, I do not think you should be doing this,' I said quietly.

'Keep your voice down,' she scolded. 'Now.' She took up the lantern again. 'There used to be a flowerpot in here somewhere. Hold that.' She thrust the lantern at me so abruptly that I nearly burnt my hand in taking it from her. 'Here it is.'

She tipped a large empty pot over and began to push it. Being tapered the pot rolled in a curve but Cherry was obviously an old hand at this for she pushed it out of line so that its path arced towards the house, crouching to upright it in exactly the right place.

'If you go first, I can give you a leg up,' she offered, but I stepped back.

'I am not going to break into anybody's house.'

Cherry glowered. 'Very well. I shall just have to do this alone.'

'What if the police and solicitor are right and Mr Bruton did purchase it legally?'

Cherry stood, unsteadily, on the pot. 'What if I am right and my parents are being held prisoner?'

'It does not seem very likely.'

'The conversion of tertiary amines into quaternary ammonium salts didn't seem very likely until Nikolai Menshutkin demonstrated the process,' she argued unanswerably since I had no idea what any of that meant. 'At least hold the lantern up while I climb in.'

'All right, but then I am going.'

'As you wish,' she said tartly, reached through to grasp the window ledge and pulled herself up and in, struggling over the sill, a flailing arm catching something and knocking it over with a crash. 'Now look what you've made me do, distracting me with your chatter.'

'They will have heard that,' I whispered.

'Stop shouting,' she shouted to the accompaniment of an even louder crash. 'Botheration. Who put that saucepan there?'

'Cherry, you must get away while you still can.'

'Hand me the lantern.' She leaned out and took it from me, and almost immediately jumped in shock. 'Hell's teeth.'

'What?'

She was looking past me. 'Next door's guard dog. How the blazes did that get out?'

I glanced behind me and there it was. Hefty's fearsome one-headed doberman was a loveable puppy compared to this creature. It stood perhaps fifteen feet away, almost as tall as me, broad and muscular, red eyes blazing as it bared its jagged fangs.

'Oh my Lord.'

The hound snarled.

'Take my hand.' Cherry reached down and I grasped it. 'Quickly.' I clambered onto the pot and, as she heaved, scrambled upwards, feet desperately seeking purchase on the brickwork. 'Hurry. It's coming.' The animal's great paws were crunching on the gravel as I threw myself through the opening, barging headlong into Cherry and knocking her over. Just as I was pulling myself through, the hound's jaws clamped on my left boot. Frantically I kicked out with my right, heard a yelp and felt its grip slacken just enough for me to wrench my foot free and hurl myself into the room.

'Are you all right?' Cherry was getting to her feet and helped me to mine.

'A little bruised and battered.' My dress was ripped, but that had been the result of most of my escapades since childhood. 'How about you?'

'Battered and bruised,' she told me as if there were a difference and I supposed, on reflection, that there might be.

The hound's head appeared through the open window. It must have jumped up and had its paws on the window ledge. I could hear its back claws scraping in its attempt to climb in.

'Save me.' Cherry clutched my arm.

'Let go of me.' I shook her off and snatched the first thing I could see that might serve as a weapon. My fingers closed on a heavy wooden rolling pin. I brought it back over my shoulder and swung as if I were playing rounders and trying to propel the ball out of the field. It struck the dog's muzzle with such a heavy whack that I jarred my wrist. The creature gasped and fell back, landing heavily on the ground. 'Help me.' I struggled on tiptoes to close the window but it was askew, and Cherry rammed the other side down so forcefully that a pane cracked. 'Thank God.'

I leaned back against a pine cupboard and saw that we were in a kitchen. My boots, I noticed, were badly scuffed and the left had been chewed beyond repair.

'They must have heard that,' I whispered, though it was rather late to worry about the noise.

'Quickly.' Cherry picked up her lantern, strode to the door and opened it to peer out cautiously. 'Come with me.'

Having no options I did as she bade and found myself in a small dining area with a square table and four chairs.

'The breakfast room,' she told me. 'We used to have breakfast here.' Before I could thank her for that explanation, she had opened the far door. 'Come on. Stop dawdling.'

Uneasily I followed her into what I judged, from her earlier account, to be the short dogleg of the main hall. I peeked around the corner and could see a light escaping under the door of the sitting room, but the door was still closed. Were they deaf? From the way they spoke to each other in the hospital and he spoke to Anthony and me, I did not believe that they were, but it was almost inconceivable that they could not have heard at least some of the commotion.

Also, it occurred to me, there was no sign of Addie. She probably slept, as most lower servants did, in the attic and, if that were the case, she would be less likely to hear any commotion. She would only be in her room, though, if she had been excused for the day, and from what little I knew of the Brutons, they did not strike me as considerate employers.

Cherry turned the key in the door to our left and I saw a flight of stairs running underneath the main staircase. 'You go first.'

While I hesitated, Cherry peered along the hall.

'Damn it,' she breathed. 'I think they are coming.'

In I went, almost stumbling on the wooden stairs and pausing halfway down to look back. Cherry followed, the key in her hand, and locked the door from the inside.

'They'll never get us in here,' she told me as we made our way to the bottom.

The cellar was cluttered – a rusted tin bath hanging from the ceiling, a rocking chair beneath it draped with a dustsheet, a sewing machine, bundles of newspapers. Some gardening tools – a spade and fork, a pickaxe and a sledgehammer caked in dry earth.

There was a window at the far side and I went over to inspect it. It led into a small below-ground moat topped by an iron grid, which was chained to the floor and padlocked.

'How do we get out?'

'Years ago I hid a key in that fishing basket.' Cherry indicated to where it lay on its side on top of a low table.

I tried to see out but the moon was clouded over again.

'What if the dog is still there?'

'I think you have shown you can best that beast.' Cherry grinned. 'It's getting old now anyway. My bedroom is directly above here and, when I was eleven or twelve, I used to hear it howling. It terrified the tonsils out of me.'

Despite my concerns I laughed at her turn of phrase but then I shivered. 'Thank heavens it was not a fraction quicker. Given half a chance it would have torn me to pieces.'

'It was a narrow escape.' Cherry shrugged as she could quite easily, for she was not the one who had been attacked.

I jumped at a knocking sound, but it was only her bumping into an upturned tea chest.

'At least we know that your parents are not being kept prisoner here.'

'Not in this room,' Cherry conceded.

'What on earth are the Brutons up to?' My ears strained for the sound of footfalls, voices, the handle being tried or knocking on the door but there was nothing. 'Perhaps they are summoning the police.'

'They have more to fear than we do.'

'But Cherry, we have no proof of any wrongdoing.'

I could see as I spoke that she was not listening to a word I said. She seemed to be intent on staring over my shoulder.

'What the devil?' Cherry brushed past me. 'There was another room under the stairs there.' She held out her lantern. 'The entrance has been bricked up.' She strode towards it. 'Why would anyone do that?'

'Perhaps it was subject to flooding.' I could see even in the fluctuating light that the wall was built of different bricks. They were darker than the normal Suffolk red.

'There used to be a stack of those bricks here.' Cherry prodded a pile of perhaps a dozen on the floor. 'We had to have a chimney rebuilt and my father saved the spares.' She broke a cobweb with a wave of her hand. 'He never liked throwing anything away.'

I joined her, tripping as I did so on an old boot poking out from the dustsheet and almost careering into her again. There was something odd about that boot.

Cherry was sorting through the tools and selected the sledgehammer. 'Stand back, Violet.'

I did so reluctantly for, if they had not heard us already, they would surely hear her demolishing a wall and I would be an accomplice to her crime. Cherry put down the lantern and, in its light, I was afforded a better look at the sledgehammer. There was something odd about the earth on its head. I picked up the lantern.

'One moment, Cherry.' Holding the light closer I saw that what had looked like soil was granular and flaking. I peered more closely. 'That looks like blood to me, and I think those are hairs.'

Cherry put a hand to her face. 'I believe you're right. My God, what have they done to them?' She raised the hammer high. 'I'll soon get this down.'

'No, Cherry.' I grabbed her arm. 'If that is human we will need to show that to the police.' She frowned and lowered the tool carefully to the ground and I went to the wall. 'This has been very badly done. The bricks are awkwardly laid and there is no mortar.'

'What of it?' she enquired testily. 'We will not give the builders a testimonial.'

'There are spaces between them.' I handed her the lantern. 'It should be quite easy to pull some bricks out.' I inserted my fingers into a gap and pulled. The brick was wedged more tightly than I expected but slowly – and painfully for me – it came grating out. I put it down and reached through again. This time I could bend my fingers around the back of the brick below and it came out much more easily. The third resisted my efforts more determinedly though and the rough surface rasped my skin when I lost my grip.

'Let me have a go.' Cherry gave me the lantern back and put her hand through the hole I had made. 'Come on, you blimmid thing.' She strained at it.

'Try the brick above,' I suggested, and she gripped it.

'It's coming.'

A section of the wall bulged. 'Look out.' I pulled her back as it came crashing down, one brick striking my knee, but most falling inwards. 'Are you all right?'

'I think so.' Cherry patted herself while I rubbed the offended knee.

There was a raggedly circular hole in the wall, about two feet in diameter, and I put the lantern through it. 'Oh dear God.'

'What?' Cherry leaned forward. 'Oh dear God.' She put a hand over her mouth.

There were two people side by side and supine on the floor of the other room, a man and a woman to judge by their clothes. I forced myself to look again and my worst fears were realised. Their heads had been battered into black shapeless pulps.

'Daddy.' Cherry cried. 'Mummy.' Her breath came in short broken gasps. 'My God, what have they done to you?'

She clawed at another brick.

'No, Cherry. If the bricks fall inwards you will destroy evidence.'

'But they are my parents.'

'I know.' I took her hand. 'But there is nothing you can do for them.'

She looked around wildly and fixed her eyes on the stairs. 'I will kill them both.' She grabbed a garden fork.

'You do not know if they are armed. They could have a gun and they must be prepared for us by now.'

Tossing the fork aside she buried her face in her dust-coated hands. 'What then?'

'We need to get out of here.' I went to the fishing basket and lifted the wicker lid.

'But...' Cherry's expression was that of a lost child. 'I can't...' She shook her head as if trying to wake herself up. 'I can't just leave them here.'

'They will not come to any further harm.' I found two keys on a loop of string and went to the window. It opened easily though the hinges squeaked. 'Which key is it?'

'The smaller.'

There were two upright wooden chairs to one side. I dragged one over and glanced back at Cherry. She looked lost. A shoe was still projecting from under the dustsheet and it was then I realised what I should have realised immediately. The shoe had not flown across the room when I tripped over it. It must be attached to something or – I gazed at it in dread. Had we not seen enough horrors for one night?

I was sorely tempted to leave ill alone, but what if there were somebody under that dust sheet, and what if he or she needed our help?

'What are you staring at?' Cherry must have followed my gaze.

'It may be nothing.' I walked to the side of the rocking chair and took hold of the sheet. I had intended to gradually expose as little as we needed to see but, as I pulled it aside, the whole cloth fell away.

A girl was slumped back in the chair, head hanging down. She was dressed exactly as she had been when Anthony and I met her, in a black cotton dress. Her apron was stained dark black, and the handle of a knife projected through that stain on the left-hand side of her breast.

Neither of us said anything at first. There seemed no point, to me, in calling on our creator again. Steeling myself I put a hand under the girl's forehead – it was as chilly as the room – and tipped her head back. As I had been dreading, I recognised the face at once.

'Addie,' Cherry croaked.

'You poor child,' I whispered. 'May you rest in peace.' From Addie's expression you might have thought that she was sleeping.

The lantern shook in Cherry's hand. 'She was just a child.' It would have been petty to have pointed out that I had already said as much, and I felt ashamed that the thought of doing so had even crossed my mind. Cherry tugged hard at a fistful of her own hair. 'They are wicked wicked people.' Her voice rose. 'By God you will suffer for what you have done,' she yelled at the ceiling.

'We must go,' I urged again and went back to the window. The moonlight was streaming through it now. I stood on the chair and unfastened the padlock. There was a length of twine hanging from it, I noticed as I climbed to crouch on the mossy floor of the sunken rectangular shaft. The grill over my head was heavy but it was not, as I expected, cemented in place by dirt and moss. Cherry must have used it fairly recently, but I would have thought at nineteen she was rather too old for schoolgirl pranks. I lowered my head, put my shoulders to the grating and heaved. With a scraping sound I felt it lift. One final effort and I was able to stand. The ironwork tilted and fell clattering onto the gravel. Nervously I straightened up and scanned my surroundings. The hound was nowhere to be seen and neither, I was relieved to find, were the Brutons.

The well was about three-foot deep so that, even with my diminutive stature, I could rest my elbows over the edge to heave and scrabble my way up to the ground. Something scuttled straight towards my face, and I nearly dropped back into the hole before I realised it was just a sycamore leaf in the stiff breeze.

Turning towards the house I called softly for Cherry and she clambered into the space, standing higher out of it than I had but still requiring my assistance to climb out.

'Can you help me put the grating back?' she took hold of one end and I the other, clattering it into place. Cherry had the twine in her hand and used it to draw the padlock up, kneeling to clamp it to the grid. 'They will not be able to get in there now.'

We were both short of breath, probably more through shock and fear than our physical efforts.

'Come with me,' I whispered though, to judge by the commotions we had made earlier, I could have bellowed my words through a megaphone without eliciting a response from the occupants.

'Where?'

'I have a cab waiting.'

'He has waited for you all that time out here?' She checked incredulously. It was difficult to persuade some cabbies to pause while one delivered a gift to a house.

'He has known me for a long time.' I did not add that he had saved my life once, when I had been attacked by the Montford Maniac.

We made our way to the gate and, sure enough, Friendless was still there. He had turned his cab around and was standing murmuring in Old Queeny's ear.

'She worry on you,' he declared on spotting me. 'Not you,' he told Cherry. 'For she dint know you are in there.'

'Thank you,' I said, 'but, as you can see, I am all right.'

He inspected me as if I were on parade. 'Call that all right?' He waved a grubby mottled hand to encompass my entire being. 'Not wha' we call all right.' He leaned backwards to survey me further. 'See mawkins in muddy ditch more all right than you.' A mawkin was a scarecrow and I drew my breath to reprimand him, but I strongly suspected that he was right and, besides, he had not finished. 'See throwed out rubbish wha' the rubbish sorter dint even want look more all right than you.'

'Thank you Friendless.'

'See a stray mongrel come out of a stray mongrel fight look more all right than you.'

I clambered aboard, while being compared unfavourably to a stoat in a drain, and turned to give Cherry a hand which she relied on so heavily that, as I struggled to pull her up, she nearly hauled me off my seat.

'You look all right,' Friendless told her though she was almost as bedraggled as I.

'We need to go to the police station,' I told him.

'Good job I'm here then.' He unlooped his scarf a couple of turns though he could not possibly have been too hot, having been out in the wind and rain for so long. 'For I can take you there.'

'Yes please.' I closed the flaps, reaching over Cherry who was, apparently, unable to assist me.

'Ready when you are darlin'.'

'Who are you calling darling?' Cherry bristled.

'His horse,' I explained hastily.

'You,' Friendless explained unapologetically, and Cherry opened her mouth.

'We need him,' I whispered, and she closed it again.

234

I glanced back at Maccabee House. A light still glowed in the sitting room but there were no other signs of life.

What could the Brutons be doing? They had brutally murdered Cherry's parents and their maid. Were they chatting about it, comfortably in their armchairs? Would they be planning to wall Addie up with the Bights?

Friendless clicked his tongue. 'Ready when you are darlin',' he called to Old Queeny this time and off she plodded.

'I am sorry it is a late night for Old Queeny,' I said, for her movements were slow and weary.

'Not your fault,' he assured me magnanimously. 'God make nights late, not you.'

The gas lamps were few and far apart on the edges of town, but Old Queeny trod the roads unhesitatingly, even when we bumped over an inadequately filled trench.

I glanced at Cherry. Her face was expressionless and I wondered if she were truly cognisant of the night's events. I could recall shocks to which I had not really reacted at the time. Sometimes our brains refuse to fully acknowledge what has happened. It was three days before I cried after my younger sister, Xanthe, died and I do not know for how long I wept then. My whole family was too absorbed in its own misery for any of us to pay much attention to each other's grief.

Even Friendless, possibly aware of our sombre demeanours, was silent until we reached the end of town when he began to hum something, possibly Chopin's funeral march or 'Ta-ra-ra Boom-de-ay'. I had seen the latter performed by Lottie Collins at the Tivoli Theatre of Varieties, which I had disgracefully attended with my fiancé, Jack. We had told my parents that we were going to a harpsichord recital.

Pay attention, girl. Miss Kidd rapped my knee with a rule so sharply that I cried out.

'What is it?' Cherry asked.

'I am sorry.' I rubbed myself. 'It twinged.'

At length we turned into Cannon Street, the blue lamp over the police station door glowing through the misty drizzle.

'Will you wait for us?' I asked guiltily, for Friendless had been working all day. I would have let him go but it would be nigh on impossible finding another cab at that time of night and he would be deeply offended to find that I had sent him away only to use somebody else.

Friendless chewed a scarf tassel. 'I do,' he decided, 'but only 'til you come out again.'

'Thank you.'

He released the catch to open the flaps. 'Only dint tell him I int renewed my licence.'

'I was not aware that you had not.'

'Of course you int aware that I int renewed my licence, for I have.' Friendless turned his head skyward. 'So dint you goo tellin' him I int.'

'I shall not,' I promised, and followed Cherry onto the pavement. 'I hope you don't get too wet.'

'How wet is too wet?' he asked with interest, but I did not have an answer for that either.

24

ZEUS AND THE HALF-WIT

THERE WAS a cheerful fire burning in the grate in the foyer, but it was too far from the desk for Sergeant Webb or us to benefit from it. A family of eight ranging from a toothless baby to a toothless grandfather lay on the benches, some asleep, some staring at the ceiling. I had seen them before. They were not being questioned nor were they reporting a crime. The sergeant sometimes allowed them to stay out of pity. Alfred usually let them be but Inspector Goodman, failing to live up to his name in yet another way, invariably had them evicted.

'Dint say nothin',' a greasy-haired youth, sitting on the floor, advised. 'They write down your words.' He paused to add in awestruck tones. 'In a book.'

'Lady Vi'let.' Sergeant Webb put down his enamelled mug of tea. 'And Miss Bight. What brings you two here at this hour?' He eyed our tatterdemalion figures. 'Been havin' a fight? Who won?'

Before I could answer I heard a weary groan and the voice of Alfred Stanbury. 'Send them away, Webb but, if they won't go away, send them here.'

The sergeant viewed me quizzically. 'They wint go,' he decided without any consultation. 'Down the hall and third door…'

'On the right,' I broke in.

'We have tha' conversation afore.'

'We have,' I agreed as we tramped along the corridor.

Alfred was taking his feet off the desk but made no attempt to button his collar or retie his tie. He took one look at me, another at Cherry and groaned. 'What in the name of Zeus have you two been up to now?' His complexion was grey with exhaustion and he had a heavy midnight shadow.

'We got into Maccabee House.' I pulled out two chairs and we sat to face him.

'Got into?' His eyes narrowed. 'I trust you do not mean broke into.'

'We climbed in through a window,' Cherry told him as if that were the most natural thing in the world for two young ladies to do late at night.

Alfred pointed his cylindrical rule at my companion. 'I knew you were...' he searched for the apposite word, coming up with, 'unusual. But you...' the ruler swung towards me. 'I thought I told you to keep out of this.'

'I went to try to dissuade Miss Bight from her course of action but then I had to climb after her to avoid a rabid mastiff.'

His shoulders drooped. 'Of course you did.'

'Besides which,' I could hardly believe what I was about to reveal. It felt like an awful dream. 'We discovered three bodies in the cellar.'

Alfred leaned forward like a greyhound scenting a hare. 'Three?' he checked.

'My parents.' Cherry's voice was an odd monotone. 'And their maid, Addie.'

Alfred digested the information. 'Did you see the Brutons?'

'They were in their sitting room on the ground floor and, as far as we know, they did not stir.' I thought about my own statement. 'Which was odd because we made quite a lot of noise.'

'Well, you did,' Cherry said, and I decided to preserve an argument about which of us had shouted and knocked things over in the kitchen for another occasion.

'So what did you do?'

'Cherry locked the cellar door, and we climbed out of the window and padlocked the grid over it.'

Alfred waved the rule like the conductor of a lullaby. 'And you came straight here?'

'Friendless was waiting and we came as quickly as Old Queeny could go,' I affirmed.

'Poor old nag,' he said absently. 'Well, you were right to lock up. Is there any way they can get into the cellar?'

'No,' Cherry told him firmly. 'I left the key inside the door and took the only key for the grating.'

He nodded. 'How much light was there down there?'

'I had a lantern,' Cherry told him.

'And you are absolutely certain that you saw what you saw?' He addressed me. 'They were not mannequins this time?'

'No, I am absolutely certain,' I confirmed.

Alfred jumped to his feet. 'Right.' He buttoned his collar. 'Sergeant,' he roared so unexpectedly that we both jumped. 'Come here at once.' He knotted his tie hastily and untidily.

There was a barely audible muttering, the highly audible clumping of approaching boots on linoleum and Webb loomed up, blocking the doorframe with his own frame.

'Yes, 'spector?'

'Who else is here?'

'Just Cooper and Canning, but Bunleigh should be in soon to take over from me.' His expression was puzzled. 'But I can deal with these two if they are givin' you any trouble.'

Alfred ignored the offer. 'Tell Cooper to fetch the black maria. The ostler should be round the back in the mews. If he's asleep wake him up. Does Canning still live in the same lodgings as Westwood?'

'Yes sir.' Sergeant Webb was standing to attention.

'Tell him to fetch Westwood here immediately.' Alfred scribbled a note and folded it. He reached into his top waistcoat pocket for a few coppers. 'Tell that young lad out there – Eric, I think his name is – to take this to Inspector Goodman's house and make sure someone comes to the door.'

'How will you get home?' He took his creased ulster off a rickety coat stand in the corner.

'Friendless is waiting for us.'

'And I am still waiting for an apology,' Cherry announced, and he looked at her quizzically. Her face flushed, coloured deeper than I had seen before. 'If you had listened to me, my parents…'

Alfred paled. 'I know.' He looked her in the eye, but she turned her gaze from him. 'And I am truly sorry.'

Cherry clenched her fists. 'God alone knows what they were going through while you sat in your office smoking cigars and treating me as if I were a half-witted lunatic.'

'I can't imagine.' Alfred lowered his head. I had never seen him so chastened. 'For what it's worth I cannot tell you how much I regret not taking your claims seriously, but we will go now and retrieve the bodies and every officer in my force will do everything he can. No man will rest until we have detained their killers.'

'I'll tell you how to do that.' Cherry's voice was gelid. 'Knock on their damned front door, damn you. Damn you all.' Her shoulders shook and she bit her knuckles. Every fibre of her body must have been battling to stop her breaking down in tears.

I touched her arm and, this time, she did not pull away.

'Come to my house for the night,' I told her. 'Inspector Stanbury knows where I live when there is any news.'

Alfred ran a finger and thumb through his moustaches and pinched his philtrum. 'I will keep you informed,' he promised as Webb hurried in.

'Bunleigh has arrived, sir.'

'And the ostler?'

'Hitching up the waggon now. He'll be ready in five minutes.'

Alfred took his bowler off the mantlepiece and punched a dent out of it. It had been damaged while he was detaining a drunken corporal. 'The Sullivans will have to go outside, I'm afraid.' He donned his hat and the crown buckled.

Webb was hooking his police cape round his thick neck. ' 'Spector Goodman throw 'em out the minute he arrive.'

'Bless him,' Alfred murmured sardonically. 'Miss Bight.' He could hardly meet her eye. 'Might I trouble you for the padlock key?'

Cherry had the string around her neck and she fumbled to untie it.

'Take them.' She rammed the keys into Alfred's hand.

'Which one?' he asked automatically, and Cherry snorted.

'You're the detective, Inspector. You'll work it out.'

Alfred nodded and dropped them into a waistcoat pocket. 'I'll see you to the door.'

'Don't trouble.' Cherry strode out of the room and, for the first time, I noticed that she had been telling the truth about her knee and that she hobbled slightly on her left leg.

Leave observation to the professionals. Hefty scuttled away before I had a chance to retaliate.

'I shall wait to hear from you,' I told Alfred, picking up my gloves, and Cherry's, from his desk. 'However late it is.'

'Very well.' He slipped his arms into the sleeves of his ulster and, for the first time in all the years I'd known him, I found that Alfred could not meet my eyes either.

25

HORROR HORROR HORROR MOST SACRILEGIOUS MURDER

GERRUND DID NOT prepare my fountain that night. Drinking absinthe was a solitary pursuit in which I had begun to indulge after I was jilted. Agnust made us coffee and I poured Cherry and I a Courvoisier each.

'I dread to think what my parents would say if...' Cherry broke off and I held her hand.

'Are you unused to drinking spirits?' I had almost forgotten that she was only nineteen, but rightly or wrongly my parents had permitted – or, rather, encouraged – me to consume alcohol long before I was an adult.

Cherry sipped hers. 'I was more unused to my parents knowing about it,' she confessed. 'One of the reasons I used to sneak out of the house. They were a lovely couple but quite old-fashioned.'

We sat looking out over the square, the gas mantles turned low. If I had put the electric lights on, we would have been visible to anyone passing but unable to see out.

'It is very peaceful here,' Cherry commented.

I poured some milk into my coffee. 'It has not always been.' I pointed to our left. 'A friend and I were attacked by a panther on the pavement there.'

'A panther?' She echoed the word incredulously. 'Was there a circus in town?'

'It was stolen from my uncle's zoo.'

'For a prank?'

'I suppose you could call it that.' I picked up a sugar lump with the silver tongs and dropped it in.

'Was anybody hurt?'

'We were lucky to escape with cuts and bruises, but an unfortunate passer-by was killed.' I kept talking to distract her as much as I could from her recollections of the night. 'Luckily Gerrund had a revolver, and my friend shot it.'

'Ah yes.' Cherry took two lumps, presumably forgetting that she had done that twice already. 'I remember reading about that now. My father...' She stopped. 'What the blazes does it matter what my father thought?'

A few phrases came to mind, mainly about them being at peace now and not suffering any more, but I dismissed them all as banalities. They would only remind her that her parents must have suffered a great deal.

'If you would like a sleeping draught, I can offer you a bed.'

'Are you going to yours?' Cherry drank her coffee, seeming unaware of how syrupy it must have been.

'I doubt it.' I stirred mine but decided to stick with my cognac. I could and would blame Romulus for giving me a taste for that and I could not help but wish that he and Anthony were with us.

Who needs men? Ruby was applying a little Rouge Rosette Brune by Bourjois of Paris. *If you want protection get a Colt.*

Milady does not have a stable in Suffolk. Ignoring her explanation that she was referring to a Colt M1892, Hefty was peering down a microscope. *Fascinating.* He adjusted the focus. *The cross-sections of these hairs are completely different and yet they come from the same head.*

From the same wig. Ruby slipped a jar of Java Rice Powder into the secret drawer of my escritoire.

I jolted awake and was about to apologise to Cherry when I saw that she was slumped with her eyes closed. It was morning and somebody, presumably Gerrund, had laid tartan blankets over us up to our chins and made up the fire.

How could we, especially Cherry, possibly have slumbered for so long after the shocks and exertions that we had endured? I remembered reading how many a condemned man slept soundly on his last night. Perhaps our brains try to protect themselves by turning off, I hypothesised though, most nights, my mind was all too busy manufacturing bizarre and troublesome dreams.

The figure of a man was trudging across the square. Even at a distance and with his head down I recognised him at once.

'Cherry.' I lightly touched her shoulder and she shot up in shock.

'What is it?'

'Inspector Stanbury is coming.' He was nearing the front steps and would, in normal circumstances, have given me a wave, but this was no such occasion.

She rubbed her eyes. 'I see him.'

There was a light tap on the door and, by the time I reached the hall, my man was already there.

'I thought you might have gone to bed, Gerrund.'

'Not while you are still up, milady.' He opened the door and Alfred stepped in, a soggy sorry sight. Unsurprisingly his expression was grim.

'I'll pour you a Scotch,' I promised as he unbuttoned his coat. 'Come through when you are ready.'

'Allow me, Inspector.' Gerrund shook it through the open door.

'Thank you, Gerrund.' Alfred sounded distant.

Maybe you need an ear trumpet. Ruby primped Alfred's cravat, but it was still untidy when he came into my sitting room.

I motioned him into an armchair and sat with Cherry on the sofa facing him. He hardly seemed to notice when I put a glass into his hand.

'One of my men got into the cellar while I rang the front doorbell,' he began. 'There was no reply.'

'Please tell me they killed themselves in fear of capture.' Cherry interlocked her fingers as if in supplication.

'Another of my men climbed in through the kitchen window.' Alfred spoke in a monotone. 'You had not put the catch on, so it was easy. He opened the front door to admit us and the constable in the cellar unlocked that door. I kept a man at the front and another at the back of the house.' He put his tumbler down untouched. 'It was as you said, Miss Bight. The body of a maid was in the rocking chair and those of a man and a woman lay behind the false wall. I am truly very sorry.'

'And the Brutons?' She leaned forward. 'Have you arrested them?'

'We searched the house top to bottom but there was no sign of them.'

'You let them escape?' She wrenched at her hair incredulously.

Alfred scratched his lower jaw. 'They were not there when we arrived.'

'Did you search the stable?'

'And the greenhouse and potting shed and garden. They had already gone.'

'There is a secret door in my parents' bedroom so as not to spoil the wainscoting.' Cherry sipped her brandy. 'It leads into a dressing room.'

'We found it.' Alfred took his glass off the low table between us. 'And there was nobody in there.'

'They must have seen you coming.' She pointed at him accusingly. 'If you turn up in the middle of the night in a great rattling waggon half the town will be alerted.'

Alfred put his drink down again, still untasted. 'I have reason to believe that the Brutons left Maccabee House three days ago.'

'What reason?' Cherry's fingers blanched on her glass.

'First, the murders were committed a few days ago.'

'That doesn't mean that they fled immediately,' she challenged.

'Indeed.' He brought out his cigar case but slipped it back into his inside left breast pocket. I could not recall ever having seen him so rattled.

'What is your second reason?' I asked, for I knew him to be a methodical man and that he would not have said 'first' for no reason. By way of an answer, he reached into his inside right breast pocket to withdraw a folded sheet of paper.

'We found this note, but I fear you would find it too distressing.'

'Give it to me,' Cherry commanded.

Alfred made to return it to his pocket. 'It is a confession, but goes into horrific detail about their crimes.'

'Do not dismiss me again, Inspector.' Cherry's voice was as hard and cold as ice and, hesitatingly, he held it out.

'I really don't think this is a good idea.'

'I do not believe you would know a good idea nor that you have ever had one.' Cherry rose as if to spring and wrest it from him and it was obvious that Alfred, racked with guilt and shame at his failure to take her claims seriously, was cowed.

Cherry waved it towards me and I took it from Alfred. Did his hand tremble? I was not sure.

'I have broken my reading glasses,' she said.

The note was written on headed notepaper.

'Mr R Bruton, Maccabee House, Tannery Lane, Montford, Suffolk,' I read aloud.

Cherry looked over my shoulder. 'So they actually got that printed?' She screwed up her right fist. 'The utter callous presumptuousness of it.' She screwed up her left fist and banged the arm of the sofa furiously.

'Shall I continue?' She nodded, and so I did. The handwriting was spidery and smudged in places, but it was clear enough to discern the words. 'To whom it may concern…'

'Well it concerns me for a start.' Her fingertips dug into the claret floral fabric. Rommy once joked that, if ever I wanted to hide, I could lie down in my usual red attire and would never be found.

'I, Roger Bruton, of the above address…'

'He is NOT of that address and never has been.' Cherry clawed at the velvet.

'…wish to make a confession. My wife Joan and I murdered the owners of this house. We have long been fascinated by the black arts of witchcraft and necromancy and intended to ritually sacrifice them in the next full moon.'

'That would be in another eight days,' Alfred contributed. He told me once that his days as a constable on the beat had taught him to value moonlight.

'In the meantime we tortured them, for Lord Satan loves pain and we love him.'

'I knew it when you told me about those books.' Cherry threw out her arm, sending her glass flying across the room to bounce off the wall, spilling cognac down the William Morris trellis paper and over the hem of my curtain, but she paid no attention to it, and it seemed petty for me to do so.

'The first thing we did was to get Mr Bight to sign a contract. It was easy to bribe Mr Wink, the solicitor, to attest that it had been done in his presence.'

'I knew it.' Cherry brought the side of her fist down on the arm of the sofa but brought herself quickly under control. 'Please continue, Violet.'

Reluctantly, I did as she bade. 'Unfortunately, on the first night Jean Bight managed to loosen her gag and scream.'

'Good for you, Mummy.' Cherry jabbed the air in triumph.

'This aroused the suspicion of that impertinent maid Abbey.'

'Her name was Addie,' Cherry said sharply.

'It was obvious that she did not believe my quick-witted explanation that her mistress had seen a rat, but she only curtsied and said, *Very good, sir*. It was too risky to keep them alive any longer but at least I could punish them. We tied them in two wooden chairs facing each other...' I had used one of those chairs to climb out, never imagining what purpose it had served. 'And I set to work on him with the sledgehammer.' I folded the paper. 'Perhaps we should stop there.'

'No.' Cherry raked through her hair. 'I will find out at the inquest anyway.'

'The coroner does not always release information which may be too distressing for the deceased's families,' Alfred pointed out.

'I want to know,' Cherry insisted fiercely. 'I have the right.'

'Very well.' He rubbed his brow, and I read on in a horrible sort of near trance.

'His skull shattered on the first blow.' I swallowed. 'Are you sure you want to hear this, Cherry?'

'Read on, damn you.'

'And her face was splattered with his blood and brains and splinters of bone. Mrs Bight was stricken with terror when I turned to her. *Let me have a go please, dearest*, my darling sweet Joan begged, so I handed the hammer to her. *You shouldn't have screamed*, she explained to Jean, for my wife is a compassionate woman. But the hammer was too heavy for her and she lost her grip and bashed Jean in the face. It made a delightful squelchy noise, but the woman made such a fuss and started screaming again and thrashing about so I took the hammer off my wife and smashed Mrs Bight's head too.'

I looked towards Cherry. She was white with anguish and fury.

'Go on,' she said. 'It can't get any worse.'

'After that we took it in turns to hit them. Their heads were a mush by the time we finished, then my poor wife sprained her wrist so I had to stop to comfort her.' I turned the page. 'That night I built a wall to hide them until we decided how to dispose of their corpses, but that nosey maid grew suspicious and slipped past me into the cellar. I asked her what she thought she was up to, and she told me that she had told her friend that she thought we were up to no good, the impudent hussy. *Your wages are docked for a month*, I told her, and you will not credit what she said next. *I'm giving you my immediate notice*, she said, bold as brass.

'Well, I had a sacrificial knife that I had planned to use on the Bights, so I used it on her instead. I plunged it in her breast and through her presumptuous heart. She flapped like a stuck chicken and squawked like one too then fell back in the rocking chair dead.

'After that we knew the game was up, for we had no means of knowing who the friend was or who else she might have told. And so we must leave our beautiful home…'

'*Their* beautiful home,' Cherry breathed furiously.

'…and flee.' I hesitated to read the next word for, after all the horrors that Bruton had described, I was still shocked when he wrote, 'Again.'

'Again,' Cherry repeated. 'How many others have they slaughtered?'

Alfred shifted uneasily. 'I do not know.'

'It seems to me that you know very little about anything.'

Alfred rubbed his right temple. 'But I shall find out.'

'You had better,' she lectured. 'Before they select fresh victims.'

'I shall have a memorandum sent to every police force in the country. Unfortunately, we do not have any photographs of them.'

'Of course you don't,' she said scathingly. 'They are not the stupid ones.'

Alfred chewed his upper lip.

'It is signed in both names,' I concluded my reading. 'Your brother and sister in Beelzebub.' I refolded the paper. 'The devil will take them. You can be sure of that.'

'But will the police?'

'I shall do everything in my power to catch them.' Alfred took the letter back from me. 'One last thing.' He put the letter away. 'Normally we would need somebody to identify the bodies, but I doubt…' He drew a breath. 'That they are identifiable.'

'I will know them,' Cherry asserted.

'Rather than put you through that, Miss Bight. Do you have any close relatives who might be willing to view them?'

'Have you forgotten, Inspector, that I have already seen their condition?' Cherry swallowed. 'I should not want to expose anybody else to those sights.'

'If you are sure…'

'I am.'

'They are in the mortuary now and I shall leave instructions to admit you.'

'I have seen them as well,' I reminded him. 'I shall go with Cherry.'

'Thank you both.' He got wearily to his feet. 'I had better go.'

'Perhaps, if you get a spare minute, you could arrest the Wild Man who seems to be able to scatter body parts around the town without fear of detection,' Cherry told him acidly.

'We are doing every…' Alfred's voice tailed off.

'I shall see you to the door.' I rose.

'Please don't trouble,' Alfred almost pleaded, and it was clear that he was having great difficulty in controlling his emotions. I regained my seat. 'I shall keep you both informed,' he mumbled as he left the room. There were low voices in the hall, and a few moments later I heard a brief rise in the noise from the square and then the door shut.

I stood at the window watching him, hunched and, somehow, smaller.

'He is a good policeman,' I told Cherry, who was lighting a cigarette. It was not a habit that I cared for in my house, but I could hardly make a fuss on such an occasion about such a trivial matter.

'Is he?' She inhaled deeply and I found that I had nothing to say.

The hurdy-gurdy man was setting up his instrument outside my window. A baker's boy trotted past, a heavy wooden tray – the cover tied over his loaves – balanced on his head and held with one hand. A young couple, heads down against the light rain made worse by a gust of wind, hurried by arm-in-arm and I wondered if I would ever find true love.

I doubt it. Ruby poured a splash of maraschino into her Martinez cocktail. *You will never find anybody rich enough.*

Money isn't everything, Hefty told her.

Actually, Miss Kidd declared, *it is more than that.*

'I shall go back to my friend's house to change these clothes,' Cherry announced.

'Would you like me to come with you?'

'No.' She stood stiffly. 'Thank you, Violet. Shall I see you there at ten o'clock?'

'There is a small café next door,' I told her. 'I shall make sure to arrive early and wait for you there.'

We went into the hall and Gerrund came out of his kitchen.

'Miss Bight requires a cab,' I told him, 'for Gallows Lane.'

'Straight away, milady.' Gerrund went towards the front door, stopped beside Cherry, lowered his head and spoke to her so quietly I could not discern a word.

'Thank you Gerrund,' she said and, to my surprise, he took her in his arms and, while he held her close, Cherry's self-possession broke into helpless, hopeless sobbing.

Ruby had been about to say something, but she signalled to Hefty and they both dissolved away. Unlike many real people, my fictional characters knew when they were not wanted.

26

LAMENTATIONS AND THE END OF DEPRAVITY

I ARRIVED early, as promised, at Spanish Street and installed myself by the window in the ingeniously named The Café. The tablecloth was stained, I noticed, and the unidentifiable green-grey flower in a grubby vase wilted. A grumpy German waiter with skin pallid and pocked like unbleached tripe made no attempt to conceal his annoyance that I wanted a coffee.

He is spying for the Kaiser, Miss Kidd – in her half-day clothes – misinformed me. Everybody knew that Kaiser Wilhelm II was Queen Victoria's grandson and the Prince of Wales's cousin and links between the two royal houses had never been stronger.

The coffee came, lukewarm and fortified with a suspension of grounds. After sniffing the milk and deciding to forego it, I called the waiter. 'This cup is chipped.'

He came over, clipping a pince-nez to the bridge of his billhook nose. 'So it is,' he agreed. 'What of it?'

'I would like a fresh one.'

He made a noise of disgust in the back of his throat. 'Very well.' He went behind the counter and started sorting through the crockery with such violence it was a wonder that he had any left intact. 'Chipped. Chipped. Chipped. Chipped,' he recited in a monotonous litany. 'Chipped.' He held one up to the gas mantle. 'Chipped. Ah. I have two cups cracked, not chipped.'

The bell over the door tinkled with a merriness that was out of place in such a cheerless setting. I pushed my chair back and got up.

'Hello Cherry.' I kissed her cheek. It was cold. She had obviously washed and changed into fresh clothes but, if she had tried, she had not succeeded in looking smart. Her profuse red hair was already escaping from its clips, her clothes were crumpled and she had on a baggy brown cardigan. It was the same one, I thought, that she was wearing when I first met her, but if anything looked even worse, for she had buttoned it unevenly. This, however, was not an occasion to criticise her sartorial shortcomings.

I put a sixpence on the evacuated saucer, which was six pennies more than The Café deserved, and ushered her out. 'I do not think you would enjoy the fare.'

'But I went there in the summer and rather liked it,' she said. 'Especially that German waiter with his smouldering eyes.'

I had rather thought that, if his eyes did blaze, it was with contempt for his customers.

Only for you. Ruby was seated at what had been my table, cracking the claw of a lobster. I had not seen that on the menu.

'Are you sure that you are up to this?'

Cherry took my arm. 'Do I strike you as the kind of girl to have the vapours?'

'Most assuredly not.' I stepped over a puddle. The pavement was so cratered there was no telling how deep it might be. 'I know that you have seen them already, but

I wonder if seeing them again and in a good light might be too much for you.'

Cherry stopped suddenly so that my next effort to bestride a puddle was thwarted and I splashed into it, over the top of my boot.

'I have one ambition, Violet, which will dominate my every action until I achieve it – to see those two disgusting monsters in the dock while the judge puts a black cloth over his wig and sentences them to be hanged by their loathsome necks until they are dead.' She lowered her voice. 'And, if my identifying my parents can help expedite their arrest and convictions, nothing and nobody will dissuade me from doing so.' She gripped me tightly. 'You have told me that Stanbury is a good policeman.'

'He is.'

'A part of me understands why he was unwilling to believe my story, and I blame myself for not telling it more convincingly.'

'Cherry, you cannot reproach…'

Cherry spoke over me. 'Shall we get this over with?'

'If you are sure?'

We came to a nondescript single-storey flat-faced brick building, the windows shuttered and only a small plaque by the door to inform the passer-by that this was the Montford and District Mortuary. I had only been in there once before, to view a chimney sweep who I hardly knew but who had no family and no friends willing to identify him.

Cherry let go of my arm and went up the three steps to tug on the stirrup bellpull. Her call was answered within a minute by a young man whose cheery manner seemed at odds with the nature of his work but was all the more welcome for that. I had come across too many undertakers whose mawkish affectations of lamentation, while explaining why the deceased deserved a more expensive coffin, often grated. This man, presumably, had no financial incentive to feign sorrow.

'Good morning, ladies.' He beamed. 'How may I be of service?'

'I have come to identify my parents, Mr and Mrs Bight, and their maid Addie,' Cherry declared and, instantly, his face clouded.

'Oh dear.' He rubbed the back of his neck. 'That could be very difficult.'

'I have already seen their bodies,' she declared, 'so I know what to expect.'

He looked quizzically at me.

'I have seen them too.'

'If you are sure...'

Cherry hesitated and, for a moment, I believed that she was having second thoughts. She drew back a fraction and I half-turned in expectation of us leaving but she straightened her back. 'That is why I am here.'

'If you could give me a moment, I shall check that everything is in order.' He hurried down the corridor and into a right-hand room, leaving the door ajar. As we waited in the white-plastered entrance hall low voices came through the gap and the young man returned with a distinguished-looking gentleman in a well-tailored black suit and a monocle wedged over his left eye.

'Good morning.' His manner was much more funereal. 'I am Mr Trainer-Brown, the director. Which of you is Miss Bight?'

Cherry glanced at me as if in doubt as to how to answer.

'I am Lady Violet Thorn and this is Miss Bight.'

'My assistant tells me that you have already seen the bodies.' He brushed the backs of his fingers against his dundrearies. 'Was that not enough for you to identify them?'

'It was not,' she said firmly, and he screwed his monocle deeper into the groove in the side of his pointed nose.

'I wonder if a second viewing might overstretch your delicate feminine nervous systems.'

If either of us had any second thoughts, they were crushed by the well-intentioned insolence of his words.

Cherry jutted her chin, and I had a feeling that she was about to say what we were both thinking but in more abusive terms than might have been conducive to our gaining admittance.

'I assure you, Mr Brainer-Town…' My spoonerism was unintentional, but the young man struggled to control his lips. 'That we are neither delicate nor…' I nearly added *feminine* but changed it to, 'susceptible to the nervous disorders that I associate more with the weaker, i.e. masculine, sex.'

The young man's grin was ruthlessly assassinated as his superior looked over sharply.

'Very well,' the director said in an on-your-heads-be-it tone. 'Take them to room two, Mr Draper.'

We followed Mr Draper down a gaslit corridor, our leather soles clattering on the white-tiled floor in a way that felt unintentionally disrespectful to the nature of the building. Turning left at the end we came across a door on our right, which he opened for us.

Cherry took my hand. Hers was even more chilled than mine. There were three trolleys arranged parallel to the longer walls of the rectangular room and on them lay three bodies covered with green sheets.

'Shall I?' Draper took the top corners of the sheet covering the shorter form.

Cherry and I nodded, and he pulled the sheet down to just below the neck. It was unmistakably Addie. In repose she was even more childlike than she had been in life, though she had lost none of her weariness with her drained complexion and dark-rimmed eyes which stared, glazed and unseeing, at the ceiling. From a bulge in the sheet I judged that the knife was still in her breast.

'That is enough,' I said, for I knew at once who this was and, obviously, Cherry knew her a great deal better than I.

Cherry took a few deep breaths and Draper re-covered Addie's face. 'Do you wish to continue?'

She nodded and he pinched the bridge of his nose.

'Shall we look at the man first?'

'We shall.' Cherry's tones were hushed.

'I don't want to interfere,' he said hesitantly, 'but surely you must be aware that there is nothing to recognise him by.'

'There is his clothing.' I knew the fallacy of that statement even before I spoke the words, 'Though it does not prove that it was he who was wearing them.'

Cherry took a few deep breaths. 'Their hands.' She trained a fallen lock of hair back over her ear. 'I just need to see their hands, my father's right and my mother's left.'

The young man shuffled his feet. 'There's a problem with that.'

'Whatever it is.' I put a hand lightly on Cherry's back. She was starting to sway. 'Please show her.'

'Very well.' He puffed his cheeks and stepped alongside the middle table. 'I must warn you…'

'Kindly do not,' Cherry interrupted, yet still he hesitated. 'Show me.' She folded her arms and without a word he walked around the trolley. 'He has a very distinctive signet ring with his initials cut into the surface,' she told us.

'Well...' Draper raised the cloth and reached under it to reveal a hairy upper arm. 'Not now, I fear.' With a great show of reluctance, he pulled the man's arm out, holding it by the wrist, and Cherry emitted a short cry.

I viewed the mutilated hand in disgust. 'Is there no end to their depravity?' The ring finger had been crudely amputated.

'I'm sorry.' Draper made to put the arm back, but Cherry held out her hand in a halt sign.

'Let me have another look. Can you turn it round?' She indicated towards the ball of the thumb. 'See that scar?' There was a jagged white line. 'Years ago, he broke a glass and a shard cut deep into him. I thought it would never stop bleeding.' She closed her eyes briefly. 'That is my father's hand.'

Draper looked at her questioningly. She nodded and he put the arm away. 'And you just want to see the woman's hand?' he checked.

'The left.' Her voice was hardly audible.

We walked around the last trolley and he drew out the woman's arm.

'That is her.' Cherry said without hesitation. 'I would recognise that wedding ring anywhere – the pattern of fern leaves – that nick on the edge. I don't know how she did it, but I remember thinking what a shame it was.'

'It cannot have been slipped onto the finger recently,' I commented. 'The joint is too swollen.'

'So it must be her.' Cherry cleared her throat and then said what I was thinking but did not wish to articulate. 'But why did they not cut that off as well?'

'I have seen a few rings with that pattern.' I recalled. 'Perhaps they did not think it distinctive enough.'

'If it were not for the damage, I suppose it would not have been,' Cherry conceded.

Draper put the arm away.

'Perhaps we should go back into the hall,' he murmured. 'There is a waiting room and we have some sherry.'

Cherry pulled her collar open as if she were hot though the room was chilly. 'But...' She was swaying and I put a hand on her shoulder.

'I think that would be a good idea,' I said hastily. 'You need to sit down, Cherry.'

Draper hurried to her side. 'Come with me, miss,' he urged, and was just in time to catch her as she crumpled unconscious into his arms.

Draper scooped Cherry up and carried her back along the corridor and into a cosy lounge with a glowing coal fire and four easy chairs. He was just about to put her in one of those when I broke in.

'She needs to lie on the floor.'

'The chair is very comfortable,' he puzzled, 'and the floor is not.'

I had once attended a talk that Romulus had given on basic medical assistance procedures, he having been dismayed by the number of cases where those who sought to help in an emergency did more harm than good. One point that he was very keen to emphasise was the importance of ensuring a good blood supply to a fainting victim's brain. All too often bystanders would drag someone who had passed out to their feet and wonder why they took so long to recover.

'On the floor please.'

With a shrug he did as I requested.

'Put that footstool under her feet.' While he did so I looked through my bag. I had a blue bottle of sal volatile, but I had not had cause to use it for years and never required it personally. My youngest sister, Drusilla, used to find it amusing to wake me with the shock of it. Cherry had not stirred. I tipped my bag out on the linoleum and rummaged through. 'Where in the name of…'

'I have some smelling salts if that would help.' Draper held out a miniature flask.

'Thank you.' I unscrewed the cap and wafted it under Cherry's nose. She stirred and coughed and, opening her eyes, pushed my hand away.

'What are you doing?' She looked about her. 'Oh, did I swoon? How embarrassing.'

'Not in the least,' Draper reassured her. 'Sadly, we see a lot of these. The experience is too much for many people.' He allowed himself a fleeting smile. 'Policemen more often than not.'

Cherry exhaled heavily. 'There is a stain on your ceiling.'

'We had a leaking pipe,' Draper explained while she struggled up onto her elbows and slid her boots to the floor.

'Lay back a while longer,' I urged, but she was already in a sitting position.

Draper took her held-out hands and helped her to her feet.

'I must be filthy.' She patted her dress down.

'The floor is quite clean,' Draper assured her, letting go of her hands with regret, it appeared to me.

'Perhaps your hair needs a little,' I suggested, for it trailed down her back and dangled over her face like seaweed over a rock at low tide.

Fucus vulgaris rubicundus. Hefty was sealing my nail scissors into a brown envelope.

Cherry glanced in the mantle looking glass. 'No, that's all right.' She made a desultory attempt to rearrange it with her fingers.

'Would you like a sherry?' Draper produced a key, presumably to the cabinet standing in a corner, and I was opening my mouth to accept when Cherry said, 'No thank you.' And made for the door.

Pity. Ruby sampled the chestnut-coloured contents of an almost full schooner. *It's rather a fine Palo Cortado.*

27

RED HERRINGS AND LADIES OF THE NIGHT

ALFRED CAME, careworn and haggard, and settled into an armchair. Cherry and I occupied the sofa.

'You look exhausted,' Cherry sympathised.

'I am,' he admitted. 'I was up all the night before on another case.'

'Can you tell us about it?' I poured us each a coffee. 'Help yourselves to milk and sugar.'

'I do not think that you are easily shocked, Miss Bight.'

'Call me Cherry,' she invited, and his eyebrows ticked. 'And you are right. Like Violet, I do not pretend to be a delicate blossom.'

Alfred took his coffee black, presumably in an effort to keep himself alert. 'A young woman, known to be a prostitute, was attacked the night before last on her way home in Heretic Alley. A man came from behind, put a bag over her head and tried to carry her off. She fought back as best she could, kicking, throwing herself about and screaming and, luckily for her, her husband heard the noise, came out and cudgelled the attacker, who ran off in the direction of Market Square.'

'She is married?' I asked, though he had already told us as much.

'With three children.' He gulped his beverage, a sure sign that it was tepid. 'He sends her out to work so that he doesn't have to.'

'Was she hurt?' Cherry asked.

Alfred put his cup down and I refilled it. 'Not much, just shaken. She expects trouble in her profession, but nobody had tried to abduct her before.'

'Did you get a description?' I tested my coffee. It was probably tepid half an hour ago.

'Two.' He helped himself to a sugar lump. 'According to a bystander he was a slavering hunchback with claws for hands and flaming red eyes.' He added milk this time. 'But I think we will distribute the husband's description – a tall man in a long black cape.'

Isn't it always? Ruby felt the pot. *They might as well wear badges labelled 'Villain'.*

'I am glad you are taking it seriously.' Cherry leaned towards Alfred. 'From what I hear, the Metropolitan Police don't care what happens to those women. For all we know Jack the Ripper might have started in such a way, but if a victim complained she was more likely to find herself in a cell for plying her trade.'

'I fear you could be right.' Alfred leaned forward as well. 'And, to be honest, I have arrested a few ladies of the night myself, but only when they become a nuisance. Most of them are unfortunates who are bullied into the business or have no other way of keeping the wolf at bay.'

'No doubt the papers will attribute the crime to the Wild Man of Gorham,' I remarked, and he sniffed.

'*The Suffolk Whisperer* already has.' Alfred drained his cup again. 'I spoke to Mr Trainer-Brown, the mortuary manager.'

Cherry exhaled as if the conversation had, for a moment, distracted her from the reason for Alfred's visit.

'They are definitely my parents,' she said quietly.

'And Addie Hooper, the maid?'

'Her too.'

'I am very sorry.' Nobody could have doubted his sincerity.

Alfred went to put his cup and saucer down, and to my – and, clearly, his – surprise, Cherry reached out and touched his hand.

'I know you are, Inspector. I was very hard on you, and I should not have been.' Alfred shook his head and made to speak but she continued. 'I can see now how unlikely my story seemed, and at least you did make enquiries.'

'I wish to God I had made more.' Alfred's eyes glistened and Cherry squeezed his hand.

'You did your best.'

I observed her with astonishment. What on earth had so transformed her attitude towards him? I would have thought that seeing the bodies would have hardened her heart further.

She's in love with him, Ruby cooed. *Look at how she gazes into his toffee-coloured eyes... and those shaggy eyebrows. What woman could resist them?*

I could, and do.

I am talking about a real woman. She tickled the back of Alfred's neck and he shivered. *One who exists, as I do, within the pages of a book. Nobody has ever troubled to imagine you.*

I dragged myself back into what my characters regarded as my utterly inferior world.

'We have issued descriptions to all the ports,' Alfred was telling her. They were still holding hands and he was looking embarrassed but was, doubtless, preferring the overly amiable Cherry to the one who loathed him. 'But, as you know, we have by far the biggest merchant navy in the world, not to mention all the vessels from around the globe that sail to and from here.' He reached into his breast pocket. 'But, if they are still in the country, as I believe they are, we will track them down.'

'Why do you think they are still here?' I asked.

Cherry pouted. 'I think the inspector knows what he is doing, Violet.'

'They boast of having committed previous crimes and they did not flee the country after those.' He brought out his cigar case, and I nodded assent. 'Criminals are creatures of habit as a rule. Cherry mentioned Jack the Ripper, and we have no reason to believe that he turned into a strangler or a poisoner.' He pulled his hand free and Cherry smiled to herself. 'Besides, if they go to another country, they are more likely to draw attention to themselves.'

'Very true,' Cherry concurred.

There was a strange calmness about her now.

Shock. Ruby straightened Alfred's cuffs. He had pencilled some notes on the left one. *Sooner or later the full realisation of what has happened will hit her.*

Like a runaway train. Hefty had had to leap from one once just before it tumbled into a ravine.

Alfred struck a match to relight a quarter-smoked Havana, Ruby blowing simultaneously to extinguish the flame.

'I'm afraid you cannot enter Maccabee House at the moment. My men are still conducting a thorough search.' He puffed on his cigar.

'If you think that best.' She folded her hands primly on her lap. 'What do they hope to discover?'

'Anything that might help us find out where the Brutons – if, as seems unlikely, that is their real name – came from or may be going to – old train tickets for example. Criminals often flee to familiar territory. Most of those who escape from prison head straight for their own homes.' Alfred slid his feet under the table. 'It is possible there will be a diary or a notebook or a letter they forgot about, something with an address they may have gone to or of somebody who knows them.' He flicked the ash off his Havana, oblivious to Hefty scooping it into a test tube. 'The smallest clue might help.'

It is always the smallest clue that does help, Hefty propounded. *Large clues are invariably red herrings.*

'What will happen now?' Oddly Cherry was asking me.

'I assume they will get a doctor to examine the bodies.' I fiddled with the miniature penknife on my charm bracelet.

'I do realise that they will be dissected.' Cherry wrapped a tress around her hand.

'It's for the coroner to decide, but I would like Romulus to perform the post-mortems if he is free.' Alfred wafted with one hand to disperse a cloud of smoke.

'It may be difficult.' I twisted the cylinder that held a tiny flint. One was supposed to be able to light a fire with that, but I had never put it to the test. It was more the sort of thing that boys would like to do.

You would be surprised what boys like doing, Miss Kidd purred, but I knew more than I wanted to about her disgraceful behaviour at Thetbury Hall.

'Jane is not very well.' I swivelled the bracelet to find the compass.

Alfred rasped the stubble on his chin. 'As a matter of fact, she rang me and asked if I could lure him away. His solicitude is starting to make her uneasy.'

I laughed. 'I am sorry.' I addressed Cherry. 'Romulus is my second cousin and a doctor. He is one of the most benevolent men you will ever meet but Jane, his wife, told me years ago she wished he could be a tad cruel sometimes, just for the sake of variety.'

Cherry smiled. 'That has never been a problem with any man that I have met other than...' Her lips blanched and her eyes moistened. 'My darling papa.' Cherry stood up and went to the window. I made to join her, but Alfred was there first, putting his arms around her as she sobbed her heart out.

Hefty was taking a sample of milk from the jug, mindful of the case of the cow that was fed a poison harmless to it but deadly to humans. He cleared his throat, but Ruby put a finger to her lips and jerked her head to the door.

Police business to attend to, he said gruffly, shaking out a large white handkerchief. Ruby was dabbing her eyes and did not even pretend not to be upset as she stole from the room.

Stole what from the room? Hefty opened his notebook then, realising the foolishness of his question, hurried after his rival.

28

HIGHLY STRINGED, STRONG AND CLEVER

ALFRED LEFT soon afterwards, rather disconcerted by Cherry taking his hand and holding onto it again.

'I shall be in touch the moment I have any news.' Despite its shaking, his coat had dripped on the floor. 'Should you think of anything that may be helpful or if you need anything, I may be at the station. If not, you can always leave a message.'

'Thank you, Inspector.' Cherry stepped closer and gave him a kiss on the cheek, lingering longer than one would for a social peck. Alfred jumped and blushed. It was not like him to be quite so coy. Could she have aroused an interest in him other than professional?

I hardly think so. Ruby filed her fingerplate. *If he is immune to my charms he will most certainly not be entrapped by her lack of them.*

He cannot see you.

Daniel Devine was blind in The Disappearance of David Divine, but he still fell in love with me.

'Goodbye, Lady Violet.' Alfred stepped out and, as the door was closing, Cherry in a whisper that would have reached the gallery said, 'Pity he's married.'

I bit my tongue. She could not need me to remind her that less than two hours ago she had been identifying her parents and their maid in the mortuary.

She is trying to distract herself before she becomes distracted, Hefty explained with uncharacteristic sensitivity, and I remembered Sidney Grice saying, in one of the Gower Street adventures, that the human mind is not capable of comprehending or containing this world's agony or we should all go mad. I sometimes wondered if we had.

In the world of the mad the one-eyed man is half-blind, Hefty declared. Thereby demolishing my newfound respect for him in a single sentence.

'And happily married,' I struggled to retrieve the conversation.

'I am glad.' Cherry was feeling her wrist. 'He is a good man at heart.' She rolled up her left sleeve. 'Botheration.'

'What is the matter?'

'My watch is missing.'

'Perhaps you left it in Gallows Lane when you went back to change?'

'No.' She tugged on her earlobe. 'Now that I think of it I didn't have it on then, but I was too preoccupied to pay much attention.' She looked about. 'I know.' She clicked her fingers, an action for which Agnust would have scolded me, for to her mind it was almost as unladylike as crossing one's legs, splaying one's legs, smoking or spitting. 'I heard it drop on the gravel when we climbed out of the cellar.'

'Are you sure?'

'Positive.' She drew her lower lip briefly over her upper teeth. 'Botheration. It was a present from my mother on my birthday, the last one she ever gave me.'

'It should still be there,' I said, 'but the rain…'

'I must go and find it,' Cherry cried, turning to the door.

'Then I will come with you.'

'There is no need. I am not in any danger now.'

What if the murderers have built a second false wall and are hiding in a hidden room even now? Hefty theorised.

'Just to keep you company.' Even assuming Cherry was safe, I was concerned that she would find the experience of revisiting Maccabee House too distressing.

Gerrund came out of the kitchen. 'I could not help but overhear the conversation.' He wiped flour off his hands on a tea towel tucked into the waistband of his apron. 'Can I be of any assistance?'

'You could fetch me a cab,' Cherry replied, regardless of the convention that it was the employer's place to issue instructions.

'Certainly, miss.' Gerrund untied his apron and took it off.

'And tell him he must expect to wait for us.' I started to change my shoes. 'We do not want to be stranded on Tannery Lane.'

While Gerrund set off on his errand, Cherry put on her hat, viewing with apparent satisfaction its shapeless floppery – Miss Kidd drifted into view to question that word but, upon finding it in the *Thorn Dictionary of Modern English Usage*, she drifted away.

'I never thought of it as a place of desolation.' Cherry tied the belt of her coat around her waist.

'I did not intend to disparage the location.' I selected a plain burgundy hat. Floral arrangements did not, as a rule, withstand the wind and rain. 'As you know it is walkable from the railway station but rather far from here for a stroll, especially in this weather, and it could get worse.'

Gerrund's whistle came clearly through the closed door.

'Is that what you're wearing?' Cherry eyed my newish crimson coat.

'Yes.' I could not see any stains on it. 'Why?'

'Oh nothing,' she said doubtfully.

I viewed her assorted range of ill-fitting items in random shades of brown. Was that an example she expected me to emulate?

Gerrund returned. 'I could only find Jake,' he told us. 'But he has promised to wait.'

'Jake?' I took my gloves from a drawer under the table.

'The one with the odd sense of humour,' he reminded me, holding out a large black umbrella as we stepped into the rain. I took it from him, gripping the edge to stop it blowing inside out, and dashed with Cherry across the pavement, both of us nearly skidding on the wet slabs, to where our hansom awaited.

'Wild Man of Gorham ate my homework, schoolboy says,' the paperboy bawled. 'Read all 'bout it.'

Up I scrambled and turned to help Cherry off the running board. She had hardly got in before, with a great crack of his whip, we set off so suddenly that we were both flung back in our seats.

'Be careful,' I called, keeping my face down against the elements.

'No time for tha',' came from above and behind me.

I leaned forward to close the flaps. 'In that case I will not have time to tip you,' I said very quietly, for it would not do to let him know that in advance.

'Quite right,' Cherry shouted over the clattering of racing hooves on cobblestones. 'He doesn't deserve a tip for such behaviour.'

'Who dint?' our driver asked sharply.

'The crossing sweeper,' I improvised.

The flaps opened again, saturating us with the heavy spray flung up by the wheels from the flooded road. 'You have to hold it,' the driver explained as if we were clodhoppers who would not know that such an exercise was standard practice.

'Oh,' Cherry wiped her wet face with a wet sleeve. 'I thought you meant our driver.'

I turned my head and wondered if she were being obtuse or mischievous, but her expression was as inscrutable as something which is not such a cliché as the Sphinx. 'Most assuredly not.'

'When did we see the sweeper?' she asked.

Push her out, Hefty urged.

Please don't, Ruby – not usually the more compassionate of the pair – beseeched me. *Not until there is another cab in her path.*

'Never guess who I have in my cab last week,' the driver yelled over a squall.

'You are right,' I shouted.

'Tha's him,' he marvelled. 'Uriah Wright. How d'you know tha'?'

'He recommended you to us,' I lied, having no idea who the gentleman under discussion might be.

We swung violently to the left, out of the headwind, temporarily at least.

'When's tha'?' our driver asked with interest.

'Last Tuesday.' I repinned my hat.

'But we bury him last Monday.'

A live burial, Hefty shuddered. *How very Edgar Allan.*

Get out of that one, Thorn, Ruby taunted me, and not for the first time I wondered how I talked myself into having to make up strings of lies over something trivial.

'The last Tuesday that he was alive.'

Nicely done. Ruby treated me to a rare compliment.

My arm was getting cramped from holding the flap shut and the cold wet air was tunnelling up my sleeve.

We turned right, heading back into the wind, and I lowered my head again, sadly unable to hear any more of our driver's conversation or – more accurately – happily able to pretend to be unable to hear any more of our driver's conversation.

Such an inelegant sentence. Miss Kidd marched springily across my meninges. *No wonder you never passed any examinations.*

I never passed any examinations because I never sat any, I argued, and Cherry raised her head. *Did I say that aloud?*

Well I heard you, Hefty said, but Cherry only called, 'Stop here, driver.' And he hauled on his reins so violently that we came to a halt, hooves sliding along the road.

Gratefully, I let go of the flaps, which stayed closed.

'Dint have to hold 'em,' the driver told me. 'Just a joke.'

'How amusing.' I adopted my Lady Bracknell persona.

'Know you'd like it,' he sniggered, and pulled the cord to release us.

I had expected the long straight road to channel the wind towards us, but it had abated considerably. Perhaps the solid structure of the tannery had sheltered us to some extent. More likely it was the woods to either side of the road.

A police constable stood in his short cape outside Maccabee House, sheltering as best he could under the storm porch.

'When I say the word *electricity* walk smartly to your left and along the side of the house,' Cherry said between barely parted lips. 'And ignore his or my calls to return.'

'But why?'

'If he comes after you don't struggle or you may get arrested, but try to delay him.'

Having nothing more productive to say I repeated my question.

'Please.' So unused was I to hearing her articulate that word that it felt churlish to refuse.

'Very well.'

'Sorry ladies.' The policeman raised his hand, palm towards us. 'But the house is closed by orders of the chief constable.'

'But I live here,' Cherry argued.

'Sorry, miss, but I have orders nobody whosoever is to be admitted.'

'You look very cold and wet.' She walked up to him.

'That's for I am,' he explained.

'And how brave to stand there under that light.'

He pushed his helmet back a fraction to scratch his brow. 'Why is tha' dangersome?'

'All that water dripping from it could wash electricity down onto you.'

'Are you certain sure?'

I had already taken my cue and set off.

'Here,' he called. 'You can't goo there.'

'I think you'll find I am demonstrating that I can.' I rounded the corner to go along the side of the house, not at all sure why I was doing this.

'What on earth is she playing at?' Cherry asked loudly. 'Come back this instant, Violet. Don't worry, officer. I'll wait here.'

I hurried my step, passing the windows of the sitting room, but already I could hear heavy footfalls approaching fast.

'Gotcha.' A heavy hand landed on my shoulder.

'Oh my goodness,' I cried. 'Please take your hand away. You could be full of electricity for all you know.'

The constable released me and scrutinised his fingers. 'Daint think I am.'

'Perhaps not,' I conceded. 'But all that talk of it frightened me.'

The constable laughed avuncularly. 'Int no reason for you to fear, miss. 'lectricity int like gas. It daint smell and it daint go into explosions.'

'Are you sure?' I dithered.

'Sure as eggs is onions.'

'Thank heavens,' I sighed in relief. 'And thank you for reassuring me, Constable.'

'Tha's orrite, miss.' He reached out to pat my other shoulder, but I shied away. 'You female ladies are so highly stringed. Lucky you have us strong clever men to understand things for you.'

I could not imagine how Ruby would react to such condescension, but then I did not need to for she tipped a broken drainpipe to direct the flow down the back of his neck.

'Goff.' He shivered and stepped clear. 'Come along now, miss.'

'One moment.' I crouched to untie and retie a bootlace and, unable to think of any more delaying tactics, straightened up.

Swoon into his arms, Hefty advised.

If you do, Ruby threatened, *I shall outwit my adversary and solve all the crimes in chapter one.*

Cherry stood where I had left her. 'What on earth did you think you were up to?'

'She have a nervous episode,' the constable explained on my behalf.

'Oh Violet, you are such a silly goose.' Cherry linked her arm through mine. 'Come on dear. We had better get you home and to bed.'

'Thank you.' We reached the gate. 'Did you find it?'

'I did, and it is still working.'

'That was lucky.'

'Well done for not getting arrested.'

'It would not have been the first time.'

We reached the hansom.

'Nearly give up on you,' Jake informed us. 'When you say wait I dint know you mean for a whole few minutes.'

'Your impatience is an execrable example to us all,' I told him.

'Thank you very much.' He beamed and I clambered aboard but, when I turned to assist Cherry, she was starting to walk up the hill, bending forward against the rejuvenated wind and heavier rain.

'I need to go back to my friend's house.'

'But Gallows Lane is at least a mile away,' I objected.

'Not if I cut through the woods.'

'You will still get soaked.'

'I need to stretch my legs.' She crossed the road.

'Where are you staying?'

'At my friend's.'

'What number?'

She was getting a good pace up now and called something back, but I could not catch it.

'You wint get less fare for less passenger.' The cabby cracked his whip and we turned to face downhill, but at such a steep angle en route that it was a small wonder the hansom did not overturn. 'Never like her anyways,' he told me as we gathered speed. 'She was too – wha's the word?'

Other than Cherry's quizzing me on whether or not I would tip our driver, I could not remember her saying anything that might have caused offence. Perhaps he had an aversion to redheads. I waited.

'Too good for the likes of you and me.'

'You and me?'

'Tha's right.' He hawked noisily. 'Too hoity-toity grand for common folk like us.'

We rounded a corner and I glanced back at the tannery. In the rain it did not look such a good location for a story after all, I decided. It was not so much forbidding as a grimy eyesore.

29

THE FAKENHAM VISITOR *AND THE LAW OF FIVE*

I HAD not given a thought to lunch while I was out, but Gerrund had done more than think about it. He had made me a soup and presented it in my Émile Gallé tureen decorated in lilies and daisies and sinuously curling flowers of clematis. Beautiful and elegant in my eyes, the French called the style *Art Nouveau*. Agnust called it a *cat's breakfast*.

'Scotch broth, milady,' he replied to my enquiry. 'Mutton, carrots, onions, potatoes, turnips and…' Agnust entered bearing a platter of around a dozen assorted sandwiches. 'Ham, beef and egg,' he announced. 'And, if you're still hungry, we have some fruit pies, but I thought we might save those to go with the cakes and scones for your afternoon tea.'

Even the sight of so much food instantly satiated me.

'You do know that I am eating alone,' I told him in case he thought that Cherry had returned with half a dozen hungry friends.

'Indeed, milady, or I'd have baked some potatoes.'

The fourth post had been delivered – a circular from Messrs Cable and Fine, dental surgeons. 'Bored of having to clean your teeth? We can painlessly extract them all and provide you with a splendid vulcanite and porcelain set within the month.' To my mind this was not an especially attractive proposition.

Might be an improvement, Ruby suggested, though I had always believed that my natural teeth were one of my better features.

They are, Hefty assured me, *unfortunately.*

'More Realistic Than Your Own Teeth,' their slogan proclaimed. 'Ladies, save your husband from expensive dental bills. He might even buy you a new hat.'

If only I had a husband, I thought, I would be round to Cable and Fine's the very next morning. Appointments by appointment only, it ended, with half a dozen glowing endorsements of their skills from satisfied though edentate clients.

Disappointingly there was nothing from Anthony. He had written every day, sometimes twice, with reports of his travels across Norfolk, but I had not heard from him since the day before yesterday when he was performing in Wells-Next-The-Sea. Despite his positive reports I could not help but feel that his ebullience was forced. I had read a review in the *Fakenham Visitor* which was lukewarm, though Anthony did get an honourable mention.

From the backward slant of his Ks and the way his S's loop asymmetrically, Hefty deduced, *it is manifest that he has forgotten all about you.*

And embarked on a liaison with a chorus girl. Ruby was annotating her copy of Burke's Peerage.

It is not a musical, I told her.

He will find one somewhere.

Having finished a good-sized bowl of soup, I wrapped half the sandwiches in a napkin and put them under a silver dome on the sideboard to dispose of them secretly later.

Gerrund was in the hallway.

'That was delicious,' I told him.

'I can easily make a few more sandwiches, milady.'

'Thank you, but I am quite satiated.'

I should have gone upstairs to my study and rescued Hefty from the burning house or sent Ruby off on another adventure. She was pressing for Japan, not having been there yet, but I knew little of the country other than what I had gleaned from a spirited performance of *The Mikado* at the Theatre Royal Bury St Edmunds. In the end I decided that, though I had written the last two letters to Anthony, I would set about composing a third at my escritoire in the sitting room.

'Dear Anthony,' I wrote, but Ruby jogged my elbow and the ink splotted.

My Darling Anthony, she prompted.

'My Dear Anthony,' I wrote.

If you are thinking of being unfaithful to me, do not forget I carry a gun, Hefty dictated.

'We do not have an understanding,' I said aloud. 'So he cannot be unfaithful.'

And you claim that you live in the real world. Ruby stared at the tip of my nose so intently that I began to wonder if it had sprouted a hairy wart.

Not very hairy, Hefty reassured me.

Should I risk, 'My Dearest Anthony'? I screwed up the letter and started again, adding, 'I hope this finds you well.'

Future generations will peruse your missives with as much attention and fascination as scholars read Pepys today. Ruby glissaded away.

From the corner of my eye, I was conscious of movement outside my front door, but that was hardly an uncommon experience. There were several deliveries to the house every day, from post to food to clothes. Also, I lived in the corner of a busy square and passersby were always passing by.

The bell shrilled and Agnust grumbled her way along the hall. There were muffled voices which grew louder after the door closed so she must have admitted our caller.

Well deduced, Lady Violet. Hefty applauded. *Now, if you could turn your mind to my conundrum...* But Agnust was flinging open the door. 'Dint you greet your guests no more?' she scolded me. 'The poor man come all the way from somewhere else to visit, though I tell him you int worth it.'

'But I happen to know that you are worth a thousand journeys.' Anthony came in after her.

'Dint tell her tha',' Agnust chided gently. 'She'll only goo believe you.'

Anthony – splendid in shades of blue, green and yellow – was damp, as were most people who ventured out in those days, and his cheek was chill when I kissed it.

'Int you goo'in' to offer him a drink?' Agnust clucked. 'The poor man is half frozed and his other half is full frozed.'

'Whisky?' I was still holding onto him.

'Just a large one.' Anthony was still holding onto me.

'And we shall have coffee,' I said and, as my maid set about her onerous task without a word of complaint, Anthony kissed my cheek.

Reluctantly I parted from him.

'The play has folded,' he told me as I took the stopper off a decanter. 'Thank goodness. We had an audience of two on our last night in Cromer and that was one of the cast's sisters.'

'I am sorry.' I poured our drinks but, instead of taking them to the window, placed them on the table in front of the sofa.

She's a slow learner but she gets there in the end, Ruby approved.

'Yes, your letter does find me well, thank you.' Anthony settled next to me. 'Sorry, I couldn't help seeing it on your desk.' We clinked glasses. 'I will bore you into one of your daydreams with my theatrical anecdotes later,' he promised. 'And I got the gist of what was going on from your excellent written accounts. Now you must tell me everything.'

Over our malts and a pot of coffee, I summarised recent events.

Summarised? Ruby tried to snuggle between us, but I held firm. *The Decline and Fall of the Roman Empire was more succinct.*

'You didn't mention any of this in your letters.' Anthony drained his cup and replaced it on the saucer on his lap.

'I did not want to worry you.'

His deep brown eyes clouded. 'I like to think that there is something special about our friendship.'

'There is,' I assured him fervently.

'In that case will you…'

Say yes, Hefty urged.

I shall need a completely new outfit. Ruby rifled through my escritoire in search of my chequebook.

'Of course I will.' I took his hand.

'But I haven't asked you yet.'

'Sorry.' I turned to face him. 'Go ahead.'

'Will you do me...'

The honour, Hefty prompted.

'A favour,' Anthony was saying, 'and keep me informed of events? I worry far more when I know that you are hiding things from me.'

'I am sorry.' It was a good job that I never blushed, for I could feel my cheeks burning. 'I shall tell you everything in future.' I let go of his hand.

'Thank you.' Anthony sipped at his coffee, clearly unaware that his cup was empty. 'Is the fire too hot for you?'

'No. Why?' I had been thinking of adding a log.

'It's just that your face is flushed.' He leaned forward to put his cup back on the tray and leaned back with a quick smile. 'Rather attractively.'

'Now you must tell me everything,' I said stiffly.

'About your face?'

'About your tour. I read some very good reviews of your performance.'

'I cannot recall a production in which the prompt has been so frequently employed,' he quoted ruefully from the *Crimplesham Clarion*. 'Mr Anthony Appleton appeared to be the sole member of the company who had taken the trouble to learn his lines.'

'It was not your fault if the rest of the cast...'

The doorbell sounded stridently and we both jumped.

'Ever thought of replacing that?' Anthony touched his blue polka-dot cravat. It was still perfectly arranged.

'Many times.'

There were voices in the hall and a minute or so later Agnust burst in. She was always concerned that I, Jezebel that I was, might be leading poor Anthony astray.

'Inspector Stanbury,' she announced with a great deal more ceremony than was her habit.

'Alfred.' I rose to take his hand.

'Inspector.' Anthony rose and Alfred acknowledged him with a dip of his head.

'Will you take coffee or a whisky?'

'Neither, thank you.'

I signalled for him to sit in the armchair. 'Have you had some news?'

Alfred perched on the edge of his seat. 'We have identified that unfortunate man you came across.'

'The one we found near the monument?' Anthony checked and Alfred nodded.

'He had a secret pocket sewn into one trouser leg. It's often the way with people who travel for a living and have to sleep rough or in cheap lodgings or workhouses. There was a ten-shilling note and some coins and a letter addressed to a Mikah Cawn, care of Felixstowe post office, from a Mrs Thunberry of Bury St Edmunds. We checked with her and Mikah was her brother. He was a pedlar, and she hadn't heard from him in over a month.'

'So he had nothing to do with Dewbury Hall asylum?' Anthony straightened a crease in his trousers.

'I have already said as much.' Alfred found a half-smoked cheroot in his outer breast pocket.

'Have one of mine.' Anthony brought out his cigar case.

Alfred shook his head. 'I am happy with my own.' But it was split, and he let it fall into my ashtray.

'Do you think the Brutons could be involved in that murder too?' I suggested.

Alfred tugged an earlobe. 'Well, they would be the most obvious suspects. I have consulted a professor of anthropology at Cambridge who has an interest in the occult and is familiar with the gruesome reading matter you came across in their sitting room. He tells me that the removal of human skin plays a part in a number of pagan and satanic rituals.'

'How horrible.' Anthony put his case away.

'I sometimes think there are no depths of depravity to which some people will not sink.' Alfred's head flicked side to side as if trying to dispel the images that must have been foremost in his thoughts and, for a moment he looked lost. 'It haunts me,' he whispered, seemingly to himself.

'Which is why your profession is so vital,' I told him. 'Who else will protect us from such monsters?' But, if Alfred heard me, he gave no sign of having done so and we fell into an uncomfortable silence.

'Have you found anything else in Maccabee House, Inspector?' Anthony asked hesitantly and Alfred looked up as if surprised to see him there.

'Not much.' He grimaced. 'I have two men still searching but, so far, they have come up with nothing of significance other than the contents of the cellar.' He pulled his sleeve down to cover a sliver of exposed shirt whereas Anthony always liked to show an inch of his cuffs. 'Which reminds me, Violet, have you seen Miss Bight lately?'

'Not for a while now.' There was a flapping at the window, and I glanced round to see a pigeon strutting along the ledge.

Alfred tapped the arm of his chair. 'I have no urgent need to see her, but I would like to keep her apprised.'

'I know she is staying on Gallows Lane,' I told him, 'but I do not know which house.'

Alfred scratched his chin. 'I can't really send constables knocking on people's doors. She is not a criminal, and we have no reason to suspect that she is in any danger.'

'Anthony and I could try,' I offered.

'Could we?' Anthony asked without enthusiasm then, catching my eye, added, 'Yes, I suppose we could.'

Alfred stood, brushed his fringe back off his forehead, refastened a button on his waistcoat, pulled his rising sleeve down again and checked his watch. A silver key hung from the chain. It was a good luck charm, given to him by his wife on their wedding day.

In Lady Violet Thorn's excellent accounts of the investigations of the incomparable Havelock Hefty, Scotland Yard's premier detective declaimed from the hearth, *there is a law of five. So one of my colleague's actions must have been a vital clue.*

Everything is a vital clue in your eyes, I snapped.

'Oh, thank heavens,' Anthony said. 'I thought it was only in my company that you went off into daydreams.'

Alfred laughed. 'She has always done it.' For a moment he thawed towards my friend.

I saw our visitor to the door.

'Anthony is a good man really,' I whispered.

'About time he proved it,' Alfred said gruffly, and it was quite a while before I realised what he meant.

30

THE LONG LAST BREATH

OLD QUEENY looked tired before we had even boarded. I did not think that the weather helped. The day was so overcast that the gas lights were turned on high in many of the houses that we passed.

'She'll be all right,' Friendless responded to my enquiry. 'She have a bad night, tha's all. My woman friend tell me about a book she read called *Black Beauty* 'bout a horse called Black Beauty, who near goo blind from bein' in the dark.'

'Your woman friend?' I had never thought of our cabby as a romantic man.

'No, listen to wha' I say. She dint goo near blind. Black Beauty do.'

'Silly me.'

'Silly you.' Friendless clicked his tongue and Old Queeny began to heave.

'Do you think she might be better having a rest?' Anthony suggested.

'My woman friend?'

'No. Old Queeny.'

We were making such slow progress that a butcher's boy walking laden with a heavy basket was keeping up with us.

'I ask her, but she say wha' she do on a day off? She daint write letters.'

It struck me that Friendless probably only had a sketchy idea of how people occupied themselves on a day of leisure and I did not suppose that he had had very many in his life.

Old Queeny seemed to be perking up. She was gathering pace and tossing her head to survey her surroundings.

'I did not know you had a woman friend.' I pulled my collar up. There was a sharp breeze but at least it was not raining.

'Nor do I 'til last yisdee but she's a woman and she tell me she's my friend so she must be.'

'What is her name?' I asked, taking advantage of a gentle corner to slide against my companion.

Friendless rubbed his ear. 'Now as you mention it, I never do think to ask.'

'Where did you meet her?' Anthony reached out to embrace me, I thought, but he tucked a loose end of my scarf to fit more snuggly around my neck.

'She live next door.' Friendless wiped his wet face with his wet sleeve. 'And she tell me it's her birthday but not to ask her age for she int told none one tha' in all her fifty-eight year.'

I was about to laugh but, from what I could judge from his swathed face through the hatch, his expression was serious.

'What's she like?' Anthony squeezed my hand.

'Wellllll,' Friendless stretched the word until it snapped. 'She goh some of her own teeth and most of her sausage-colour hair. A fine big lumpy figure of a woman she is.'

We negotiated a parked pantechnicon, two removal men bumping an upright piano over the cobbles with as much care as a dustman might take with a can of ashes.

'And you should hear her sing.' Friendless steered us to the side again. 'Never hear anythin' so loud since the day afore I'm born. Fair burst my ears she do.'

'Does Old Queeny like her?' I asked.

'She do.' He grasped the handle of his whip as a gang of street slugs came out of Bishop's Alley, but they were more interested in upturning a battered tea chest in the hope of finding something to eat, sell or burn than in tormenting his horse.

As the houses thinned out, we came to a rise, barely discernible to me but sufficient to slow Old Queeny's already slow pace.

'If she did think of having a rest, Romulus will offer her a paddock.' I broached the topic tentatively, for if she retired it was more than likely that he would have to do so too.

'Daint think my woman friend want to live in a padlock.' Friendless snuffled in amusement.

'I meant Old Queeny.' I tipped my head towards Anthony's, not quite bold enough to rest it on his shoulder.

If you do not kiss him before this journey is over. Ruby had changed into the dress she wore to seduce the Duke of Saveloy. *I will.*

'And you could visit whenever you wanted to,' I continued. *If you dare to kiss him, I will give you whalebone dentures in your next story.*

'How I get there?' Friendless asked reasonably, and I did not dare suggest that he replaced his horse. Even if he wanted to do so, I doubted he could afford another.

'I'm sure we could work something out.' Anthony tipped his head until our hats brushed against each other.

This is pornographic filth. Hefty had turned a no-longer-fashionable shade of mauve.

If only it were. Ruby tugged one end of his cravat, but he clamped a hand over the bow to preserve it.

The road was steeper now. A year ago Old Queeny would have trotted up it with vigour, now she struggled to haul us up one step at a time and I was relieved when we turned left into a plane-tree-lined avenue.

'Gallows Lane,' Friendless announced loudly, as if he were a porter struggling to be heard over the whistling of a train.

'You can stop here,' I called up to save Old Queeny any further toil.

'I know I can,' our driver replied testily, 'but do you want me to?'

'Yes please.' Anthony sat straight, I followed suit and we came to what we had almost been at already, a halt.

The lane ran up through Jepson's Woods, and it occurred to me that Tannery Lane must run roughly parallel to it to our right. On the other side lay the town centre, but nothing was visible of either through the trees. A brook bubbled through a clearing to our left.

'Why don't you take Old Queeny in there?' I suggested when we had disembarked. 'She could have a drink and she'd be better sheltered from the wind.'

Usually Friendless would have asked me why I asked my question because that was exactly what he intended to do but today he rubbed his face in agitation and set about the manoeuvre.

'Would you like us to summon help?' Anthony offered. 'One of the houses may well have a telephone.'

Friendless nodded thoughtfully but said, 'She only need a rest.' His voice and manner lacked conviction, though, for we all knew that Old Queeny's working days were all but over. It was with sombre hearts that Anthony and I agreed to take opposite sides of the road.

Despite the warnings of the driver who had taken Cherry there from my house, Gallows Lane was not especially longly or wearisomish. There were about thirty houses in all, I estimated. Detached modern villas of individual designs.

The first door on which I knocked was opened by an elderly man, leaning on a beech cane with one hand and holding a brass ear trumpet with the other.

'Good afternoon,' I tried to speak loudly without shouting. 'I am looking for Miss Cherry Bight. Could you tell me if she resides here?'

'No.'

'Do you mean you cannot tell me or that she is not staying here?'

'The latter.' He slammed the door.

For no reason I could think of I looked up the road. Far from running parallel to Tannery Lane, as I had imagined, the two roads must have almost converged, which was why Cherry had been able to take a shortcut through the woods. At the brow of the hill to the right I could make out the tannery quite clearly and something caught my eye. Was that just a shadow in the windows? It looked more like the figure of a man moving along a long room or corridor before it disappeared?

Anthony was having a long discussion with a maid across the road. 'My half day is on Sunday,' she was telling him at such a volume that she might have thought that he was in need of a hearing aid. I could not catch Anthony's reply, but I trusted him to gently rebuff her.

Be very suspicious if he tells you he is attending vestas, Hefty cautioned, though I assumed that he meant *vespers*.

My next call was responded to by a burly maid with a stubbled chin.

'Can I help you, miss?' She gave me such a lovely smile that her face was instantly pretty.

How cruel to judge her by her looks, Ruby lectured me to my shame.

But you have always said that appearances are everything, Hefty argued.

I would never be so shallow. Ruby popped a jeweller's glass over her eye to examine a new moonstone ring. *What do a man's looks matter, if he has wealth and a title?*

I was aware that the maid was awaiting a reply.

'Does Miss Cherry Bight reside here at present?'

Her brow wrinkled. 'No, miss. There is only the master and the mistress and their nine children and cook and the master's valet and the kitchen maid, who doesn't live in, and the boot boy who sleeps in a cupboard but int called Cherry.'

'Thank you.' I continued up the road.

The next door was answered by a man as well. Was there a shortage of maids in the area? If so, I could lend him mine for an indefinite period.

This man was in his early to mid-thirties, I judged.

'Hello ikkle girl.' His tone was one that people who do not have children adopt to speak to other people's babies. 'What can I do for you?'

He had a roving eye, I decided.

So long as it is only his eye that wanders over you… Ruby put her hand on her hip.

'I am looking for a friend...' I began.

'Then your luck is in.' He grinned. It would have been a nice smile had I not known its portent. 'You won't find a better friend than me,' he informed me breathily.

'Cherry Bight...'

'Pleased to meet you, Cherry.'

'Is the lady I am seeking.'

'Why don't you come in and tell me all about her?' He beckoned. 'Is she young and pretty like you?'

'No.' I headed back up the drive.

'Well if you do find her, I hope she is more fun than you are,' he yelled after me.

Make a cutting remark, Hefty urged.

'Goodbye,' I called.

That will lacerate him into shreds. Ruby tossed a cigarette aside without bothering to stub it out.

By the time I had done all of the sixteen houses on my side, Anthony was still on his fourteenth and last one. The maids detained him longer than they did me for he was naturally a sociable man and quite good looking.

For 'quite' substitute 'exceedingly'. Ruby applied a second coat of lip rouge.

I crossed the road. 'No luck, I assume.' Anthony tugged his left sleeve down. It had risen half an inch when Ruby had linked her arm through his.

'None.'

'None of mine had even heard of her.'

'Nor mine, and servants usually know about any newcomers in their neighbourhoods.'

He's all yours. Ruby whisked away as Anthony took my arm. *I lied about our engagement so that you don't take him for granted.*

That maid was quite a stunner. Hefty plucked a carnation, strangely, for the time of year.

Anthony pulled up his collar. 'Rather late to ask you now…' We set off back down the lane and a fox ambled across the front lawn of a house opposite.

I knew you'd find a vixen here. Ruby's ivory shoes had not a speck of mud on them, though mine were as thickly coated as if I had taken a hike through the countryside.

'Hello.' Anthony waved a hand before my eyes.

'I am sorry.' I brushed away Hefty's floral offering, and he slid it into his buttonhole. 'What were you going to ask?'

'Why are we looking for Cherry at all?'

'I do not know.' I put a hand to my wind-tugged hat. 'But I am worried that she might be in danger herself. For all we know, the Brutons could still be in the area.' I tightened my grip on my collar. 'And I cannot help feeling that there is something one of those people was not telling me.'

If it's the square root of twenty-five, the answer is six and a half. Miss Kidd chalked up her calculation, and I realised why I had never excelled at mathematics.

'Oh no,' Anthony said, and for an absurd moment I thought that he was correcting her.

My mind went back to the light in the tannery. 'Did you see…' But, noticing that his attention was elsewhere, I followed his gaze. It was obvious at once that Old Queeny had been unhitched, for the roof of the hansom, just visible where it jutted over the pavement, was tipped down towards the front.

'Doesn't look like she'll be up to taking us home,' Anthony commented. 'Poor old thing.'

'There is a stud farm at East Kelham.' I released my collar and searched for a glove. 'If we can get a message to it, they will almost certainly have a horsebox.' Was it possible to put the glove on and hold onto my hat at the same time? As we hurried over the road, I found that it was not.

'The nearest telegram office is Vestry Street,' Anthony calculated as we approached the gate. 'I might be able to get a cab on Turner Street.'

I clutched his wrist. 'Oh please no.'

Only as we neared could we see Old Queeny lying on her side with Friendless kneeling beside her.

'Hang on darlin',' he was urging. 'Lady Vi'let come out soon. Remember how she get Dr Thorn to mend you when that rat bite you? She'll make him come out again. He'll give you a tonic and I'll tuck you up in bed and tell you stories and you'll be right as mustard pie.' Friendless gulped. 'Just see if you wint.' All the time he was unbuckling the rest of her harness and slipping the bit out of her gaping mouth.

With a great effort Old Queeny raised her head to look at us.

'I shall bring you a big juicy apple,' I promised. 'And a carrot.'

'And a mint?' Friendless checked.

'A whole bag of them.'

'All to herself?'

'Every one of them.'

'Hear that darlin'?' But even as Friendless stroked her muzzle, her head fell back again and she breathed a long sigh. We waited in the wind and drizzle but she was perfectly still. I knelt and lowered my ear, listening to her gaping mouth but in vain. Old Queeny was never to draw breath again.

'God rest your soul,' I said automatically as Friendless bent over to kiss her cheek.

'Do horses have souls?' he asked with interest.

'Old Queeny does,' I assured him and he lay in the road beside his horse and I could not tell if it was him or me who was sobbing the louder.

—

Anthony and I rang five doorbells before finding a house with a telephone and five more before finding a householder that would let us use his instrument and then only for five shillings.

The law of five, Hefty began but, realising that his presence was not required, slunk off into the woods muttering about suspicious patterns of lichen growth on an elm tree.

'Harrison's is the nearest knacker's,' he told us, but I was already asking for Suthy Hall. Junkins, the valet, answered my call. No other servants were permitted to touch the instrument since a maid had broken the mouthpiece by banging it on the wall in her attempt to hear through it.

'I can send a cart for her and a horse to take Friendless's hansom home.' Romulus sounded genuinely upset. 'We could bury her in the grounds here but poor Friendless would rarely be able to visit.' He clicked his tongue four times. 'What about the monastery gardens?'

'We would never get permission to bury her there.'

'You and I couldn't, but your father could.'

'Really?'

'Who do you think pays for the upkeep of the grounds?'

'The Thorns,' I presumed. 'That is very generous of us.'

'I think it goes back to a bequest made by the first earl.' Clearly Romulus knew more about our ancestors than I did. 'With your father's permission, I will arrange for a grave to be dug, and we can inter her first thing tomorrow morning.'

We both knew that you cannot delay in burying a horse. *The build-up of gasses,* Hefty explained to his sergeant.

'Rommy, you are a marvel.'

'Tell that to Jane,' he said ruefully. 'I tipped her breakfast tray all over her bed this morning.' I heard him clear his throat. 'I can't tell you how wonderful it was to find her with the energy to scold me, and at length.' His voice fractured. 'Leave it all to me, Violet. Just be there at nine o'clock tomorrow.'

Gerrund brought my fountain. Was that a look of reproach in his eye? I almost challenged him for his impertinence, but I knew that he was right. I had been trying to lose myself in my absinthe far too much lately. Perhaps I would put it aside that evening.

Come to me, the Green Fairy urged. *Just one little drink.* And, as always, I was seduced, enticed into her dreams. It took all my willpower to wait for the sugar lump to dissolve. Did my hand shake a little? Surely not?

The Green Fairy was in a sombre mood, matching my own as I sipped the sweetened bitterness.

In the past those reveries had always provided welcome escapes from reality, but recently they had become increasingly troubled. It was as if she was being transmogrified into a goblin, ugly and disturbing.

I am still me, she whispered, or had I said that?

I refilled my glass and lay supine on my sofa, propped up on two cushions against the arm, feeling the wormwood crawling, creeping through my brain.

The rain held off and I thanked God for that. The ground was muddy enough as it was without the hole being filled with water.

Old Queeny had been laid about eight feet down in a quiet corner of the grounds.

Rommy, Anthony, Gerrund, Agnust and I were already in attendance when Friendless turned up. We wore black but he was in his usual rabbit-skin coat, leather hat and patchworked scarf. I did not suppose that he owned any other clothes.

'We can plant a rose garden here,' Romulus proposed after he had expressed his sympathies.

'She do like eatin' people's rose bush.' Friendless stared into the pit. Apart from her head, Old Queeny had been covered in a flag emblazoned with the Thorn crest with its ram rampant azure on a maroon shield.

'No vicar?' he asked and we looked at each other and then him sheepishly. No cleric would agree to conduct a service despite my cousin's attempts to bribe or bully them.

'I do not tell many people,' Anthony announced, 'but, before I turned my hand to acting, I was a country parson.'

'Where?' Friendless enquired with interest.

'Tuddenham St Mary.'

'Tha' int a country.' Friendless appeared to be building up a spit but thought better of it. 'It's a village. Small wonder you never stick at it.'

'Would you like me to say a few words?' Anthony asked.

'You just sayed some.'

'For the funeral.'

Friendless nodded and my friend took a step to the graveside.

'Dear Old Queeny,' he said, 'you were the best horse I ever had the privilege to meet.'

'Amen,' Friendless said.

'Placid but brave,' Anthony continued.

'Amen,' Friendless repeated.

'Loyal and loving.'

'Amen.'

'Hard-working and uncomplaining.'

'Amen.'

'A good companion and true friend to Friendless.'

'Am... men,' Friendless managed. I reached out and took his hand. It was hard and calloused but hot, despite the cold air. 'She wint mind you doin' tha',' he assured me. 'She alway like you with your straculiar ways.' I squeezed his hand.

'Now you have gone to your well-earned rest.' Anthony swallowed. 'God bless you, dear Old Queeny. Rest in peace.'

'Amen,' we chorused except for Friendless, who had fallen to his knees and was fighting for breath, drowning in his emotions.

31

MOULDYWARP AND THE BLOOD OF CHILDREN

I INVITED Friendless to join us in my house for a drink, but he declined.

'If I have a drink today, I want a'nother and then a'nother and then a'nother and then I never stop and she wint like tha' for she know me to be a respectabled man.'

'Come in and have a cup of tea then,' I urged.

'Tha's the diff'rence 'tween people and the gentry,' he told me. 'You have a Chinese cup of foreign tea; I have a tin mug of slap. The likes on me dint belong in grand houses with your gold saucers and gas lights what use electricalicity.'

'You would be very welcome,' Anthony urged, but Agnust folded her arms.

'Leave him be.'

'What will you do now?' Romulus asked.

'You mean now this minute or amara and amara?'

Amara meant tomorrow in Suffolk. *Amara and amara* was for ever.

'For a living, I mean,' Romulus explained, too tactful to suggest that Old Queeny could be replaced.

'Nothin',' Friendless replied simply. 'I wint never get a-nother horse, even if I have the money, which I dint. I have enough put by to keep me for the worst part on a week. After tha' I goo to the workhouse and wait to die.'

'There must be other ways you can earn a living,' Gerrund said. 'You could be a groom.'

'Too old.' Friendless scratched his jaw. 'And those who have grooms want them to look shiny in uniforms. I wint be pretty whatever they dress me in.'

'Stable hand,' Gerrund persisted. 'You know horses.'

'I know 'bout two horse.' Friendless scraped his upper left, and only, canine with his fingerplate. 'First is Susan. He's a nasty horse and bite me nine or less time alway on my skin. Second horse we lie in the earth today.' And with those words, Friendless wandered off.

'He may well change his mind after a day or two,' Romulus suggested, 'and we can help him buy another animal.'

'I don't think he will.' Anthony came to my side, and I found myself forced to agree.

Agnust made us coffee.

'We should toast the departed,' Anthony said in his hitherto unsuspected clerical persona.

Gerrund poured four large whiskies and we raised our glasses, but Agnust refused to join us, even with a glass of water.

'The devil make toast,' she said, 'in the everlasting eternal forever flame on his pitchfork.'

'That is a different kind of toast,' I explained, but she shuffled her bosom side to side and said, 'Toast is toast and toast do wha' toast do and wha' toast do, Satan only know.'

I did not argue that I had toast for breakfast most mornings for it might inspire her to ban that too.

Gerrund handed out the glasses.

'To Old Queeny,' Romulus raised his tumbler and all, bar Agnust, followed suit.

'And Friendless,' Anthony proposed and the reprobates amongst us drank to that too.

I put my glass down. 'You never told me that you were a parson.'

'That is because I never lie to you.' Anthony dipped his head modestly. 'In fact I rarely lie at all, but this seemed to me to be a worthy cause.'

'A very worthy one.' I had a strong urge to kiss his cheek. 'Thank you.' But I resisted it.

If you find a dent in your wall it is because I have been banging my head on it. Ruby picked up my whisky and polished it off.

'I know you int a vicar.' Agnust, now that the demonic rituals were over, treated herself to a tumbler of water. 'You int wicked 'nough to be one.' According to the religious sect to which she belonged all clerics were evil for they preached the gospels of St Mark, which were written by Beelzebub in the blood of children.

'I must go.' Romulus finished his drink, and I walked him to the door.

'Can I visit you and Jane on Saturday?'

'Please do.' He took my hand. 'And you must stay the night. Bring Anthony, if he is free.'

'But Anthony and I are only acquaintances.' I helped him on with his coat and he smiled.

'I saw my optician last week.' He hung his scarf around his neck. 'He said that I needed stronger reading glasses, but he did not say that I was blind.' He bent over to give me a kiss. 'You were never much good at fishing.'

'I caught that carp,' I protested.

'Beginner's luck.' Romulus donned his homburg and lowered his head again as if to give me another kiss but instead he whispered in my ear. 'Get a strong keepnet and don't let this catch get away, Violet. You will never find his like again.' He opened the door.

'It is not like that,' I protested, and he tilted his head in askance.

'Goodbye, Violet.'

'Give my love to Jane.' I watched him for a while and closed the door. 'The nerve of the man,' I huffed and strove to be annoyed with him all the way back into my sitting room.

'Well,' Agnust put her hands on her hips. 'Those cobweb wint clear themself away.'

'Neither will she,' Gerrund mumbled. 'Thank you for the drink, milady. I must get back to my kitchen.'

Anthony did not ask if he could stay and I did not invite him to do so. We both assumed that he would and settled companionably by the window. The rain was still falling.

'You'd think the sky would have run out of water by now,' Anthony mused.

The Chronic had suggested that the earth might be flooded again but had to retract after charges of blasphemy because God had promised Noah that it would never happen.

A policeman walked past, his face ruddy and weather-beaten. A sweep was coming out of one of the houses laden with two sacks of soot. A donkey pulled a cart which was covered in tarpaulin.

Constable, stop that vehicle, Hefty barked. *It is carrying three corpses.* He wore a black armband.

'Can I ask you something?' Anthony fumbled in his jacket pocket.

If it's a ring, say 'yes', Ruby urged. *In fact, even if it isn't a ring, say 'yes'*. She was in half-mourning.

Tell him you can get a special licence today, Hefty counselled.

'Yes,' I said, and Ruby sighed. *You were supposed to wait for the question.*

'Remember you told me how Cherry gained access to Maccabee House?' Anthony crooked his finger.

'Of course.'

'Could somebody have got into this house in the same way? When they left the mannequin, I mean.'

'I do not think so. Gerrund checked all the windows afterwards. They were locked solidly. The only accessible back window is the one at the end of the hall. The others were screwed up by the previous owners after a burglary, and I have never troubled to have them unscrewed.'

'And there were no scratches on the paintwork?'

Exactly what I was about to ask. Hefty leaned back on the mantlepiece, his damp trousers steaming.

'Not that I noticed.'

You observe, but you do not see, Hefty propounded. *The distinction is translucent. There is no point in observing something if you do not know that you have seen it.*

Scotland Yard's premier windbag. Ruby yawned.

'Shall we take a look?' Anthony, confident of a positive response, was already rising.

'Why not?' I took his proffered hand to get to my feet and forgot to let go of it until we reached the window.

Anthony opened the catch. 'It's quite stiff so it would be difficult to slide back from outside.' Spurning Hefty's offer of a magnifying lens, he examined the paintwork. 'Not a mark on it.'

'He must have got in somehow,' I said stupidly.

Unless he was hiding in your attic, Hefty suggested. *Perhaps he has been there for years, which might explain who drinks all that absinthe.* I already had an explanation for that. *Perhaps he is still there.* He patted his coat to check that he was carrying his revolver.

'What happened to my key?' Anthony pointed to an empty hook.

'I was not aware that you kept any of your keys here.' I studied the rack and him in confusion.

'I mean the big one you lent me when I was playing the drunken porter in *Macbeth*.'

'Could it have fallen behind the chest?'

Anthony looked down the gap. 'I can't see it.' He went on his haunches. 'And there's not so much as a cobweb under here.'

'Gerrund cleaned it out after Agnust killed the eel.' I helped him up and this time he forgot to let go. 'There was quite an array of items under there, mostly from before I inherited the house.'

'What sort of things?' Anthony asked with more interest than I would have thought the subject merited. Had he been playing the part of a detective for too long?

So, Hefty hooked his thumbs into his waistcoat pockets, *he has been impersonating a police officer?*

And more convincingly than you. Ruby was indulging in an avant pre-sundowner.

'Just bits and bobs really.' I cast my mind back. 'A cotton bobbin, a button, a rusty penknife with a horn handle.' I waited for Hefty to tell me the latter was a murder weapon, but he was more interested in trying to summon a constable to handcuff my friend. 'I cannot help feeling that there was one thing to which, perhaps, I should have paid closer attention.'

Your coiffure, Ruby suggested.

How dare you, Hefty rallied to my defence. *Her ladyship does not have a coiffure.*

'I am not sure.' Something had flicked through my mind but whisked away before I could grasp it. 'Gerrund put it all in that pot for Agnust to throw away.'

'Another job she hasn't got round to,' Anthony observed, giving the pot a rattle.

'Who int got round to wha'?' Agnust materialised at my shoulder. 'Lor' but you're jumpier than a mouldywarp.'

A mouldywarp was a mole and I was not aware that they were especially nervous creatures. The head gardener at Thetbury Hall, who terrified me, never managed to frighten any of them away.

'I did not hear you approach.' I stilled my beating heart.

'Is that a new outfit, Agnust?' Anthony asked and Agnust blushed.

'Might may be,' she replied, though it was one of the three plain black that she had almost invariably worn for years.

'Well it looks very smart,' he assured her and an irrational twinge of jealousy flew through my mind.

Not irrational at all, Ruby assured but did not reassure me. *I told you not to trust those two together.*

Now you are being ridiculous, I told her, relieved that I had not spoken aloud.

'Who's bein' ridic'lous?' Agnust folded her arms, and I wondered if I should take the opportunity to flee.

'He is,' I floundered. 'You look very smart all the time.'

Agnust shuffled her shoulders. 'I do my best.' She looked to Anthony for affirmation, but he had tipped the contents of the pot out on top of the chest and was rummaging through them.

'And succeed,' he said absently and too late to fool me but in plenty of time to fool her. 'That's interesting.'

'What is?' I asked.

'There's a scrap of a postcard with a Llandudno postmark but, from what I can see of the picture, it came from Skegness.'

Eureka. Hefty punched the air in a very unHeftyishly flamboyant manner. *We have demolished the hitherto impregnable alibi of Colonel Armestices Quill.*

'I have an uncle never went to Skegness,' Agnust announced. 'Neither do anyone I know nor wish to know.'

Anthony scooped my treasure trove back into the pot and straightened up. 'Have you seen the big key that used to hang on that hook?' he asked Agnust, and she frowned, probably in part at the lack of interest he had displayed in her revelation and possibly at his question.

'Wellll.' She scratched her scalp so vigorously that I began to wonder if she had non-paying tenants in her hair. 'Course I do see it when it's there but course I dint when it's not. Why you want it anyways? It int pretty and it int safe in there.'

'In where?' Two voices spoke as one.

Agnust patted her chin, possibly checking that her furry mole had not absconded. 'Why scruffs ol' place, of course.'

'Scruffs?' Anthony and I were doing quite well as a chorus.

'The skin factory.' She clicked her tongue at our imbecility.

'Scroffs,' I realised. 'Scroff's Tannery.'

'Tha's wha' I say.' She stroked her mole. 'Though why Lady Strainge do keep the key for it, your guess int as good as mine and mine int good at all.'

'Of course,' I clicked my tongue at my imbecility. 'Great Aunt Herbena was Caractacus Scroff's niece and, I think, his sole heiress.'

Heiress you in the name of the law, Hefty guffawed, humour never having been his strong point.

I must apologise. Ruby blew smoke into his eyes. *I never knew that he had a point, let alone a strong one.*

'Gerrund,' I called. 'Could you fetch us a cab?'

'Us?' Agnust asked hopefully, for hansom rides were a rare treat for her and, given her size in a compact vehicle, an uncommon ordeal for me.

'Anthony and me,' I clarified.

'But where are we going?' Anthony put the pot down.

'Why Tannery Lane, of course.'

'Of course,' Anthony breathed, though there was no *of course* about it.

I tried to brush briskly past Agnust, rediscovering what happens when a resistible force meets an immovable object.

'Dint you goo gettin' him into scrapes,' she warned me, seemingly oblivious to an impact that sent me sprawling back against my Lincrusta wall covering.

'Why on earth would I do that?' Making a mental note to get the Byzantine pattern replaced with something more modern, I squeezed past, but she stepped readily aside for Anthony.

'Why on earth would you goo climb tha' chimney in your poor parents' house?'

'Peewick sent me up it to clear a bird's nest when I was three years old.' Peewick was the butler and my indignation was unassuaged in the quarter century that had elapsed since I, but not he, was punished for doing his bidding. 'And my parents are neither poor financially nor unfortunate.'

The latter point was not wholly true, for there had been a great number of misfortunes in their lives with the deaths and disappearance of so many of their children, including all my brothers, which was why Romulus would inherit the title when my father died.

'You get him in danger afore so he's near killed,' my maid reminded me. 'Twice times.'

'This is different,' I insisted as Anthony helped me on with my coat.

'Hummmm.' Agnust squinted at me so suspiciously that I wondered if it were.

'We are just going to Tannery Lane,' I explained, unsure, as always, why I was justifying my actions to my maid but unable, as always, to stand up to her.

'Do you goo into tha' house?' She sniffed like a dachshund on the scent of a badger.

'We will not,' I promised, even more unsure, etc.

'Then why you goo there?'

'Have you joined the secret police?' I straightened defiantly, unsure why I had not done so before now.

'Why?' Agnust rocked from side to side and back again. 'You think I should?'

God Forbid. Hefty paled. *It was bad enough when we allowed women cleaners into Scotland Yard. They tidied my desk.*

Did you lose much information? Ruby yawned.

Worse than that, he groaned. *We found much more than we could possibly deal with, including evidence that all the Ripper murders were really freakish accidents. Gentleman Jack*

Springheel, a witness to all the deaths, proved that beyond all doubt.

'Should what?' I struggled and failed to keep track of the conversation.

' 'nough said.' Agnust ran a finger under the window ledge, seemingly disappointed at the lack of dust that her action revealed. 'One nod is as good as another to a deaf goat.'

Gerrund came back in. 'I have summoned a cab from the Splendid.'

'Thank you.' Anthony handed me my scarf, and I wondered if thanking other people's servants for doing their bidding was a breach of etiquette but decided that it was not and, if it was, I did not care. I was, after all, the woman who had scandalised polite society by using a fish knife to spread butter on a bread roll.

'Don't worry,' Anthony reassured Agnust. 'Lady Violet will look after me.'

'Jus' like she look after tha' white glove on her first communion. There's still neither hide nor hairs of it.'

Hurry up. Ruby checked her watch. *Prince Olav and his regiment of Cossacks should be here in ten minutes and we are having a house-wrecking party.*

I shall summon reinforcements. Hefty hurried off and I could hear him clicking the telephone cradle up and down.

Good luck with that, Ruby laughed. *I've already cut the wires.*

32

BISCUITS, BUTTONS AND BONES

WE SAW little of our journey, keeping our heads down against the driving rain though Ruby, who was comfortably installed on the other side of Anthony, was unruffled and biscuit dry.

You appear to be confusing biscuits with bones. Miss Kidd had squeezed in on the other side of me. *Remind me to decline your invitation to afternoon tea.* I would sooner have invited Lucrezia Borgia than the governess who had bullied me and betrayed my trust.

As the hansom tipped backwards and our progress slowed, I peeked out sideways and saw, as I had suspected, that we were on Tannery Lane and, a moment later, passing Maccabee House. It looked much like any other property. There was nothing sinister about its outer aspect, no mysterious towers or forbidding turrets, only my knowledge of the almost unimaginable savagery of the previous occupants and the appalling fate of the Bights made it a house of horror in my eyes.

Anthony looked up too. 'I can't even see the tannery through this haze.'

Sheltering our faces as best we could with our hands, we screwed up our eyes.

How did they come unscrewed? Hefty gave his own eyeballs an experimental twist and winced.

'Whoa,' the driver called.

'But we aren't there yet,' Anthony complained.

'Tha's as far as I go.' The cabby leaned over the hatch. 'The road narrow from here and there int no room to turn. My horse dint like pushin' backward all tha' way.'

'Very well,' I sighed and a tin came down on a string. 'I will pay you when our journey is over.'

'You can pay me for this part.'

'Then how do we know you will wait?' Anthony argued.

'How do I know you dint run off?' He started to turn his cab.

I had had enough of this. 'You were hired to take us to the tannery, wait for us and take us home.'

'Pay me what you owe and I will.'

Anthony pushed on the flaps, but they were still bolted. 'Let us out,' he demanded.

'When you pay.' The cabby joggled his can.

'Very well.' Anthony counted a handful of coins into the can, which was hoisted up. The flaps clicked open and we scrambled out.

'If you do not wait...' but I was never to complete my threat for he had flicked his reins. 'Come back,' I yelled over the whining wind.

'We shall report you.' Anthony waved his cane, but the cab was already setting off back down the road.

'Report all you like,' the driver called back. 'Int my cab anyways.'

'Looks like we will have a long walk home,' I commented grimly as Anthony took my arm.

'Might as well take a look at the place,' he said, though it had not occurred to me to cancel our mission.

Heads down and hands on hats we struggled, buffeted as we were, up the hill.

'Remind me why we are doing this.' Anthony let go of my arm to redo the top button of my coat. I had not even noticed that it had come undone. He had a cord, which I had not noticed either, around his wrist, the other end looped around the cane, leaving both hands free to perform his task.

And I thought attentive men only existed in your stories. Ruby was hatless, her black hair suddenly long again after her Gibson Girl bob, streaming back like the heroine of a novel which, of course, she was.

'The tannery is supposed to be empty,' I said.

'Perhaps an impoverished family is seeking shelter there,' Anthony suggested.

'Perhaps.' I put my arm through his again. It felt natural now. 'But why did that key disappear from my house?'

'Do you think Cherry took it?'

'Yes.' I tried to click my fingers and rediscovered that one cannot do so with thick woollen gloves on. 'Her cardigan hung badly because she had lost a button.'

'The ivory one.' Anthony clicked his fingers. How on earth did he do that with even thicker woollen gloves on?

He didn't. Hefty was wearing rubber galoshes and I wished that I had had the foresight to wear mine. *You do have foresight, milady,* he told me kindly, *but only after the event.*

'It had three buttons in a straight line.'

'That's unusual.' Anthony plucked a leaf that had blown into his face. 'You would expect them to be in a triangle.'

He let the wind take the leaf away. 'I cannot think how I would sew such a button.'

I struggled to envisage Anthony bent over with a needle and thread. Would he also be darning socks by candlelight?

'But why would anyone want to get in? I cannot imagine there is anything worth stealing.' I stumbled over a loose cobble and he put an arm behind my shoulder to steady me, but withdrew it immediately to secure his felt hat. 'Unless one of the householders or maids was lying, Cherry does not live on Gallows Lane. When she told me she was cutting down the hill through the woods she could just as easily have gone up the hill. She has lived here most of her life so she must know the area.'

We pushed on in silence.

'Do you still see Daisy, your imaginary dog?' I wondered.

'I am surprised that you do not,' he replied, and there she was, a lovely red-golden cocker spaniel trotting loyally at his side, ears flying backwards but tail still wagging enthusiastically.

You will be happy to know that I have made enquiries, Hefty announced, *and there are still two vacancies at Dewbury Hall.*

'She has beautiful eyes,' Anthony said, though it seemed to me that he was telling his dog.

A branch perhaps three feet long sailed across the road.

'Fetch,' Anthony called, and Daisy galloped off in pursuit of it.

'Are we both mad?' I asked, and he laughed.

'If it is a contagious condition, I caught it from you.' He unlinked his free arm and slipped it around my shoulders. 'And I am not sure that I want to be cured.'

We came to the crest of the hill and, with only a sparse spinney to our left to break them, the gusts strengthened almost to a gale. I put an arm around Anthony's waist to steady myself.

Really? Ruby was completely unruffled now. *Do you really need a pretext to embrace him? Good heavens, Thorn. How can I be more worldly wise when I am so much younger than you?*

It seemed rather unfair that, while I had creaked to an ancient twenty-eight years of age, my creation had discovered the gift of eternal youth.

We came to a wrought iron boundary fence about ten feet tall and broken only by an even higher double gate wide enough for two waggons to pass each other. I imagined the scenes, one carrying the fresh bloodied skins of slaughtered cattle and the other piled high with their tanned hides.

A mossy path ran outside the fence in both directions.

The gate was bolted and secured with a bulky padlock so rusty that I could hardly make out the keyhole.

I looked up again. 'We'll never climb that.'

'I doubt anybody could,' Anthony said. 'So, if there have been people inside, there must be another entrance.'

The outside of Lady Violet Elizabeth Antoinette Cordelia Thorn was chilled, but the inside glowed for, unlike many men I had come across, Anthony could explain things without making me feel that he thought I was a silly girl. I glanced about.

'This way.' I pointed to our right and Anthony drew his eyebrows towards each other. 'How do you know?'

The moss, Hefty coached me.

'The moss has been displaced from some of the gaps between the cobbles.'

'Could have been a deer.' Anthony bent over for a closer look.

Scotland Yard's premier detective folded his arms. *Shall I tell him or will you?*

'A deer would have eaten it,' I reasoned, and Anthony drew his eyebrows apart.

'An observation worthy of Mr Sidney Grice himself.'

'Well actually...' I began but changed my mind.

Trust you to take all the credit, Havelock Hefty fumed, but we had set off on the trail.

Anthony paused. 'A broken twig.' He pointed.

The whole area is littered with them, Hefty sulked, but I said, 'Well spotted,' and we continued on our way, drawing each other's attention to crushed leaves and dents in the earth to the side of the path that might have been footprints.

They are not, Hefty seethed as we came to a side gate. *And neither of you noticed the albatross feather sharpened into a poisoned stiletto.*

'This looks more promising.' Anthony drew out his cane to indicate an arc scraped along the ground and I pushed on the gate. It was quite stiff but opened fully.

We were along the side of the tannery, and it was immediately clear that the fallen sycamore had not only damaged the roof but demolished a large section of the factory wall. Oddly there was a ditch about five feet wide coming out from a gap in the wall like an old river course down which the rain trickled but it was evident what had caused that, for behind the building was a long pile of rubble and an enormous iron cylinder.

'The water tower collapsed,' I stated, rather obviously. 'There must have been thousands of gallons in that tank. That would have been what washed away all this soil.'

Anthony eyed the ditch. 'Looks very muddy.'

'But only,' I said, 'because it is.' And he laughed.

'Hello. What's that?' Perhaps six feet upstream a plain wooden door had been laid across to form a makeshift bridge. Anthony stepped down onto it. 'Feels solid enough.' He held out a hand and I took it, slithering down the sloping bank. 'Got you.' Anthony took me by the waist though I had not been in much danger of falling and, for a moment, we gazed at each other. 'Are you sure you want to do this?'

'Do not worry,' I told him. 'I will look after you.'

Anthony smiled, 'I believe you will,' and led me by the hand across and up the other side onto the opposite bank to stand upon the fallen wall, scrambling over heaps of masonry and an iron girder into a cavernous hall.

The malodours of pures were still nauseating despite all the years of disuse, and I could not imagine how noxious it would have been in the tannery's heyday. We pulled our scarves over our mouths and noses, but the actions did little to abate the stench.

'What now?' Anthony asked in muffled tones.

'We look around.'

'For what?'

'Clues,' I said, which he seemed to accept, probably realising that I had no idea.

If you knew what clue you were looking for, Hefty expounded, *it would not be a clue.*

I was not sure if that pronouncement made any sense, but I felt certain that it was unhelpful.

More of the roof had collapsed than I had expected, with slates and rafters strewn over the floor. The gaping hole above us was partly filled by the trunk and branches of the fallen sycamore. A large section of the back wall had also been broken open, presumably by the force of the tumbled water tower and its contents.

'What a mess.' Anthony shunted some debris aside with his boot. 'Well, there doesn't seem to be anybody here. I can't imagine even a destitute family wanting to shelter in this place.'

'Somebody was here.' There was the sound of shattering, and I saw that I had trodden on a window frame, most of the glass already broken.

'Perhaps they came to see if there was anything worth salvaging,' my friend suggested, but I was not convinced.

'Surely scavengers would have cleared the timbers for firewood.'

'Perhaps they took what they could, intending to return.' Anthony sidestepped the maggot-riddled remains of a thrush. 'You would need a lot of waggons to clear this.'

'And yet not even one cartload has been taken.' I saw his puzzlement and explained. 'The path is too narrow to wheel a cart along and the ground has been soft for weeks now, but there was not a single rut in the verge on the way up.'

'Bloody hell!' Anthony jumped so I did too.

'What is it?'

'Sorry about my language.' He pointed with his cane to where a scrawny bedraggled rat was perched a few feet away. 'I hate the beasts.'

'It will not harm you.' I sought to reassure us both. I had attended a rat-baiting competition once and, much as I loathe the creatures, the scale of their slaughter by a terrier for sport was sickening.

'Probably not.' Anthony gripped my hand. 'But they give me the creeps.' He shivered to emphasise his words.

I scanned our surroundings. The hall was long and wide, rising high into the apex of the roof. The slates were uninsulated, some slipped or broken, creating openings to the sky hardly any less grey than the ceiling. Long rusted chains hung from pulleys fixed to the rafters. The walls were lined on three sides with shelves, presumably for storing the skins.

The door in the middle of the long internal wall was stiff but yielded to Anthony's shoulder and squeaked open about halfway before wedging on the concrete floor.

'Doesn't look like anyone has used it for years.' Anthony inspected the rusty hinges.

'I saw somebody,' I insisted.

'Could it have been the shadow of a tree blowing in the breeze?' he suggested.

'Not from the way it moved.' I raised my dress to step over a heap of debris and noticed Anthony looking at my shins, appreciatively, I hoped.

Do not be such a flibbertigibbet, I scolded myself in the absence of Ruby.

Here the stench was almost overpowering. We both fumbled for our handkerchiefs and clamped them over our faces. Remembering reading how Sidney Grice used camphor to mask the odours of decay, I found my sal volatile and, holding my breath as long as I could, took the glass stopper off and sprinkled a few grains to fold them inside my silly little feminine handkerchief. The vapours almost took my breath away but at least they relieved my nausea. I held out the bottle and Anthony tipped more than a few crystals into his neat voluminous masculine handkerchief, clamped it to his nose and mouth, reeling backwards on his first inhalation and shaking some of the contents away before reapplying it.

'Strong stuff,' he said, for I doubted that he had ever required it before.

Through my watering eyes I viewed our new location. This was a similar room to the previous though, bar a missing slate or two, the roof was intact. Six raised rectangular concrete tanks, each about fifteen by eight feet, occupied much of the floor, being built in two parallel lines. Being partially sunk into the floor, they were about three feet below ground and the same above. Five of them were empty, with large circular manhole covers sunk into the floors. There was a lever at the end of each tank. Anthony pulled on one and the cover began to rise but he returned it immediately. 'There must be thousands of rats under there.'

As we approached a tank in the middle of the row closer to us, we saw that it was filled with a foul brown slurry. It was from this that the stink arose. Bracing ourselves, we made our way to the side and peered in at the lumpy sludge.

'Ugghhh,' I said, slightly ahead of Anthony's even less articulated gagging, and hastily we retreated a dozen steps.

'Those are fresh pures,' I managed.

'I didn't know you had made a study of the subject.'

'You know as well as I that dog droppings rot away in a week or two.' I retched.

'I suppose so.' Anthony followed suit. 'There is nobody in here. Shall we go out?'

'We shall presently,' I agreed readily. 'But somebody has been here.'

'Let's try over there.' Anthony pointed his cane to another double door in the middle of the wall to our left. Unwilling to take any unnecessary breaths, I nodded assent and we headed towards it.

These doors opened easily and we found ourselves in another large room, this one furnished with rows of wooden racks.

'The drying room, I assume.' Anthony closed the doors behind us. The air here, while by no means fresh, was at least breathable without recourse to ammonia. 'No sign of life here either. Perhaps...'

I gripped his arm. 'Then how do you explain that?' The floor was carpeted in a gritty dust, and it did not require the services of the Gower Street Detective to observe that the surface had been disturbed. There were many scuff marks and some clear footprints and Anthony crouched to peer at a trail of them. Had the role of Jarvis De Hivernale gone to his head?

'Two people,' he announced, 'one smaller than the other. So, either a man and a woman or a man and a child, and one has...'

'A limp,' I broke in, for the left foot of the smaller prints was obviously dragged. Anthony pouted a fraction, for nobody likes their brilliant deductions to be exposed as obvious. 'And they are heading...' I allowed him to finish this time. 'Towards that single door. Probably...'

'An office,' I predicted hastily, for Anthony was not a big-head and I did not wish him to become one. 'Every factory has to be administrated.'

'Quite so,' Anthony agreed without rancour and stepped forward to open the door. 'Well obviously you were right about somebody being here.'

This room was smaller, probably about fifteen feet square, and better lit, with two large barred windows in the opposite wall. The wall to our right was completely curtained, but it was the furnishings that attracted our attention. An unmade bed had been set up against the wall to our right and in the middle was a pine table with two spindle-backed chairs. An unlit oil lamp stood on that table and there was a cupboard on the left-hand side.

'What was that?' I strained my ears.

'Sounded like a muffled cry.'

'The wardrobe,' we both said and, in confirmation of our suspicions, a drumming noise and a louder but still indistinct cry came from that direction.

Anthony sprang towards the sounds, taking hold of the right-hand knob and, not to be outsprung, I leapt to grasp the left and pulled. The doors swung open.

'Cherry!' I cried. She was sitting on the floor of the cupboard, a rope coiled around her and a rag stuffed into her mouth. We could not see her face but the mass of flaming hair enveloping it was unmistakable and the dull brown clothing reinforced my identification.

Anthony reached behind her head, fiddled for a moment and pulled the rag away.

'Oh thank God,' she said huskily. 'I thought he was going to kill me.'

'Who?' I asked, Anthony being occupied with untying a complex ligature that bound Cherry's ankles.

'Charon,' she gasped.

'Who is Charon?' Anthony directed his question at me though I was none the wiser than he was.

'May I help you over, little girl?' A man's voice came from behind.

33

THE DEVIL STALKS THE STRAND

I WHIRLED around. 'You cannot be him.'

'And yet I am.' The man's hand rose as if to tip the brim of an invisible bowler. 'I am going in that direction anyway.'

'What are you talking about?' Anthony asked.

'But I saw you drown.' I stared. I had not seen his face as he was wearing a balaclava at the time but tall and broad-shouldered, the newcomer was of a similar build to the man I had met on that awful night and the voice, though it was not raised over a gale now, was certainly very similar.

'You saw me submerge,' the man agreed before adding, 'May I help you over, little girl?'

'You cannot be him,' I insisted again, though with wavering conviction.

'I can only repeat myself. And yet I am.' The man gave me a quick smile. 'I have forded swollen rivers in Himalayan gorges.'

'Why are you telling Lady Violet that?' Anthony rose from his task.

'He is reminding me of his words that night.'

'You haven't finished untying me.' Cherry wriggled and twisted so that she was sitting upright with her feet on the ground, but Anthony was regarding the man warily.

'A man who could swim would doubtless have drowned in a futile effort to fight the current.' There were three bruises on Charon's face, the worst being around his right eye. 'I had no choice but to hold my breath and let the water take me where it would. The only thing I could do was to try to feel my way along the sides of the sewer. Another cover had come off downstream and there was an iron ladder embedded in the stonework. Just as I thought my lungs would burst, I managed to get hold of a rail and haul myself up the rungs and break through. I saw you being rescued by some ogress I took to be your servant. If the wind had been in the other direction, you would have heard my choking gasps for air as I collapsed against a telegraph pole, clinging onto it for dear life, but you were carried into your house without either of you glancing in my direction. You...'

'This man is a maniac,' Cherry broke in. 'He kidnapped me and kept me prisoner.'

'But why?' I looked from one to the other.

'Because he is a maniac,' she explained impatiently as Anthony crouched to finish releasing her. 'He kidnapped me.'

'No, he did not,' I said, aware that three pairs of eyes had become fixed upon me. 'Anthony's fingers did not blanch when he untied that rope.'

'The knots were very slack,' he agreed, 'and there were only two of them.'

'So that Cherry could untie herself if need be.'

'What are you talking about?' She got to her feet stiffly, holding the side of the wardrobe for support.

I had been fooled once before by somebody pretending to be held prisoner, but I had more than that experience to raise my suspicions.

'You are careless in your apparel,' I began, and her pale face flushed.

'You are not my damned father.'

'Damned?' I queried. How Agnust would have scolded me for such language. 'I thought you adored him.'

'I did,' she mumbled unconvincingly. 'What do my clothes have to do with anything?'

'I thought that your unevenly buttoned cardigan was just another example of that.' I stepped backwards, partly because I judged that Cherry was coiled to spring at me and partly to put my handbag on the table. 'Until I came across…' This was when I intended to take out my vital clue with a Heftyish flourish, but the ebony box in which I had stored it had submerged beneath all my accumulated paraphernalia.

'Across what?' Cherry demanded.

'Don't be so impatient,' Anthony scolded.

'And you sound like my damned mother.'

I brought out the box and hinged open the lid. 'This.' I held out my hand with an unHeftyish flourish and Cherry leaned over.

'A button.' She tisked dismissively.

'The one that is missing from your cardigan.'

'There must be thousands of buttons that look like that.'

'I do not think so.' I raised my hand for her to get a closer view. 'It has three holes.'

'Lots of buttons have three holes.'

'Yes, but usually they are in a triangular pattern. These are in a straight line.' I pointed. 'Like the rest of your buttons.'

She sniffed. 'Where did you find it?'

'On my hall floor.'

'So it fell off while I was there.' She made as if to pick it up between her thumb and forefinger, but I pulled away and closed my hand.

'I am sure that it did, but I found it at the back of the hall.'

'It must have rolled there.'

'Unlikely, since it is not a perfect circle.' I heard a click and saw that Charon was removing the key from the door, presumably having locked it.

'Give me that key.' Anthony advanced upon him, cane raised, but Charon only smiled. 'Think you can threaten me with that twig?'

'I certainly do.' Anthony scythed his cane towards the man's head, but Charon dipped, ducking agilely beneath the arc, the cane striking the wall behind him. His hand flashed out, grasping Anthony's wrist and twisting until the cane clattered to the floor.

'Damn it.' Anthony bent to retrieve his stick but he was too slow. Charon brought his knee up hard under my friend's chin, sending him reeling backwards.

'Darling.' The word slipped out unguarded as I stepped towards him. But I was stopped by a hard yank of my hair and I half-twisted towards Cherry, who had grasped a fistful of it, only to see that she was brandishing a long-bladed knife in her other hand.

'Sit down.' She hauled me towards one of the wooden chairs. 'You too.' She told Anthony, pressing the blade to my throat, and he obeyed so that we sat facing each other across the table. 'Tie them up.'

Charon too brought out a knife and used it to cut two lengths from the rope, tying Anthony's hands behind his back and around the spindles of the chair before approaching me.

'The police are on their way,' Anthony told them.

'Then why did you not come with them?' Cherry asked reasonably as her confederate wound the rope tight around my wrists.

'That hurts,' I complained.

'Good.' She put the knife on the window ledge. 'You lost the button when you went to steal the key to this place.'

Cherry's hair swung side to side. 'I didn't take the key. You might have noticed it was gone and realised it was me who took it. I unlocked the window. It was obvious from the sheet of cobwebs that it was never opened so I assumed that nobody would bother to check it was locked.' She tossed her head proudly. 'I even laid the cobweb back over it.'

'That was clever of you,' Anthony said, and we both looked to see if he meant that, but his face was such a portrait of innocence that I knew that he did not.

'It was.' Cherry smiled upon him.

Was this the time to tell her that an oversized rat was sniffing at her heels. I decided to let her find out for herself.

'And I relocked the window before I escaped through the back door.' Charon waited in vain for his share of the plaudits. 'And put the cobweb back again.'

Anthony did not even glance at the man. 'But...' He gazed at Cherry quizzically. 'How did you know about the key in the first place?'

I do not know if it was the angle of Cherry's face or something in her expression but, at that moment, I knew the answer to my friend's enquiry.

'You are Isabella, the horrid little girl who used to come to Break House to play with Dorissa.'

'How dare...' Charon began but Cherry shushed him and the rat slunk off into the shadows before she had even noticed it.

'That was me,' she confirmed. 'I called myself *Isabella* for a while after a character in a children's story, *The Magic Lantern*. My parents met Lady Strainge at a Picklemakers' Guild dinner they had been invited to by mistake. She was much taken with me and thought I would be company for her granddaughter, but you were right, dear Violet, I was a very horrid little girl indeed.'

'But how could you know the key would still be there?' I wondered and Cherry flopped her arms.

'I didn't but the chances were it would be. Who bothers to throw away one old key from a rack of them?' Her question was obviously rhetorical. 'And who throws away a whole rack of keys when they cannot know if one of them might be useful?'

'They could have been stored away,' Anthony reasoned.

'They could,' she agreed amicably, 'but, with no information that that was the case, it was worth the risk of breaking in.' Cherry smirked. 'And then I discovered a golden opportunity to get into your house to see for myself.'

Something else was troubling me. 'Oh sweet Jesus,' I whispered. 'Dorissa died whilst she was playing with you.'

'An apoplectic fit,' Cherry recalled cheerfully. 'Or choking on a stocking stuffed down her gullet. Who can say?'

'You are a monster.'

'I like to think so,' she agreed modestly.

'What about the mannequin?' Anthony asked and Cherry turned towards him.

'It was my idea for Charon to put it in her house.'

'But why?' I wondered and Cherry giggled in girlish delight.

'I knew it would confuse you. The plan was that Charon would get into your house while you were all at the royal visit.'

'Which was why I told you about FEAR,' Charon chipped in. 'To make certain that you all went out.'

'Even as you were drowning,' I marvelled.

'I had a part to play and I could not let my darling down.' He scratched his ear. 'I had never even heard of the Free East Anglian Revolutionaries and hoped you would think FEAR was some terrible dark society.' His mouth drooped. 'As it turned out, I was too debilitated by my experiences anyway to be able to play my part on the day of the ceremony.'

'You poor thing,' I said, and he looked at me uncertainly. 'But how did you manage to carry that thing through the town without attracting attention?'

'Ever heard of Gentleman Jim, the daring cracksman?' He jutted his jaw proudly.

'I think I might have,' I conceded, for I could hardly pretend that I had never read about that character. A year ago the papers were full of breathless reports of his audacious burglaries in broad daylight.

'Well, I am him.' Charon pouted in disappointment at the indifference that greeted his announcement. 'I carried the clothes and newspapers and the head in a valise and assembled the mannequin in your back garden. If you had searched at the time, you would have found the case in your shrubbery. I collected it later that day.'

'So that was why you suggested that Gerrund came to protect us,' I calculated. 'So that there would only be Agnust in the house.'

'There must have been simpler ways of creating a distraction,' Anthony objected, and Cherry flicked her hair back.

'Of course there were.'

'I wanted to set fire to your house,' Charon told me in tones that suggested I might sympathise with his deprivation.

'Bless you,' I murmured.

'But I wanted something more subtle, something that would puzzle you for the rest of your life.' She put her hands on her hips. 'You have no sense of the theatrical.'

The Chronic's critic had said as much after watching the first and final performance of *The Devil Stalks the Strand*.

'We knew that, if he was spotted breaking in, you would look about to see what had been taken, but if we added something to your house, you would not be clever enough to realise there had been a theft.'

'Lady Violet suspected as much from the very beginning,' Anthony lied staunchly.

'Actually...' I shifted in my chair from one uncomfortable position to an even more uncomfortable one. 'I suspected as much,' I said to sceptical glances, even from Anthony, though it was Havelock Hefty who had promulgated the theory. *A kipper of a crimson persuasion,* he had said. 'A red herring,' I translated aloud to my own satisfaction if nobody else's. 'And Mr Appleton spotted that the key had been taken,' I told them truthfully and proudly, 'and my maid knew what purpose the key served.'

'But how did you know,' Anthony gave his attention to Charon, 'that the key was still there and that you could get in?'

'That was simple,' Charon told him chattily. 'I kept a watch from the monastery gates. If Cherry stumbled it meant that the key was not there. If she carried her handbag in her left hand, the key was there but she had been unable to unlock the window. If she dropped it, the key was there and the window unlocked.'

'She could have just carried it in her right hand,' Anthony objected.

'I wanted a signal that could not be missed,' Cherry elucidated.

'I knew there was something odd about that incident,' I recalled before she had a chance to wallow in her smugness. 'You said *Oh, for heaven's sake* before you actually tripped.'

'Nonsense.' Cherry scowled. 'As it turned out,' she continued, 'the lock was too rusty to open, and it was only then that we discovered we could get in anyway. I thought it was just the roof that had been damaged by that tree.'

'An overly elaborate plot that served no purpose,' I gloated before recalling that those were the very words used by a reviewer of *The Tangled Sheet Murders*.

Cherry glowered. 'Well it fooled you.'

'There is no point in fooling people if there is no point in doing so,' Anthony pointed out.

'Nobody asked your opinion,' Charon snapped.

'I'm sorry.' Anthony shifted in his chair. 'Would you like me to leave?'

Cherry gave an empty laugh. 'You will quit this world before you quit this building.'

'If you hurt him...' My voice trailed off, for I knew that any threats I could make would be futile.

'I wouldn't worry too much about that,' Cherry assured me balefully. 'You will be joining him soon enough.'

Anthony blanched and cleared his throat. 'You are mad.'

'Perhaps,' she shrugged, and something almost physically lit up in my mind like a photographer's flash powder behind my eyes.

'Where are your parents?' I was almost as much surprised by my question as Anthony appeared to be.

Cherry closed her eyes briefly. 'My parents are mashed-up corpses in the mortuary. You have seen as much for yourself.'

I shook my head. The light had fizzled out as quickly as it had appeared, but the idea still glowed and I reached towards it. 'I saw the bodies of Mr and Mrs Bruton.'

Cherry stepped towards me. 'You cannot possibly know that.'

I did not know it at all but somehow it made sense.

'People would know that your father wore a signet ring engraved with his initials,' I extemporised. 'I expect it would not fit on Mr Bruton and so you amputated his finger. You did not need to do that with Mrs Bruton. All you had to do was pretend to recognise her less distinctive ring as belonging to your mother.'

'She's clever,' Charon remarked.

'She is,' Anthony concurred.

'So clever that she got you into this mess,' Cherry retorted with justification.

Anthony shivered and I saw that he was looking at another rat. Ruby Gibson had escaped capture once by smearing bacon fat on her bonds so that a rat chewed through them. I could think of at least two reasons why that would not work for me, one of them being that I neglected to bring any rashers with me.

'I have been trying to calculate what your motives are.' I tried but failed to rub my burning wrists behind the back of the chair. 'And, if your parents were complicit in your crimes, but I could not think what they hoped to gain from them or how they imagined they would evade justice.'

Anthony broke in. 'Greed,' he said. 'Simple as that. You not only would get the house back but the money that the Brutons paid for it. All you had to do was convince the police that they had murdered your parents. Then you could take possession of the house, sell it and buy another where nobody would know any of you and – who knows? – start the whole process all over again.'

'Enough.' Charon struck the wall with the flat of his hand.

'Just out of interest…' I had no plan other than to delay them as long as possible. 'When you pretended you had lost your watch, Cherry…'

'How can you know it was not true?'

'When you showed it to me it was telling the right time. You could not have had time to wind it up and reset the fingers. Also the strap was dry.'

Anthony pulled the corners of his lips down. 'An observation worthy of Inspector Havelock Hefty.' And, despite our predicament, I glowed at his praise.

'I dropped this,' Charon held out his hand, and I tilted my head for a better look. He was holding a dog whistle.

'So that hound that chased me through the window was yours.'

'Otherwise you would never have climbed in.' Cherry tied her hair back with a brown ribbon.

'Muffin is a highly trained animal,' Charon told me.

'Muffin?' Anthony repeated. 'That is not a very scary name.'

'I called him that because he is soft and sweet,' Charon told him conversationally. 'But you...' he turned to me, 'kicked him and hit him with a rolling pin. The poor creature is still sore.'

'He was trying to savage me.'

'He was playing with you.'

Clearly Muffin and I would never agree on what constituted a game.

'What was so special about the whistle that it had to be retrieved from under the nose of the police?' I asked, and he thrust it closer. 'Charon,' I read engraved on the barrel. 'That wasn't very clever of you.'

'Poor Muffin was so traumatised by your brutal assault that he ran away, bowling me over and sending the whistle flying out of my hand.'

'We couldn't risk the police searching the grounds and finding it,' Cherry explained, 'and it was easier for me to justify my presence at the house with my willing dupe to create a distraction.'

'I was trying to help you,' I muttered.

'You were a self-important interfering busybody.' Cherry wagged her knife. 'So grand with your title – *Oh, please call me Violet.*' She imitated me in a whine that I did not believe anyone would recognise as my voice. 'And your police inspector friend...' She waggled her head side to side. '*Oh, he is such a good policeman*,' she mimicked. 'Well I fooled him and you and everybody else.'

'If you fooled Lady Violet briefly it was because she is a kind person who thinks the best of people,' Anthony defended me, 'but it was she who deduced that you were here.'

'And, in doing so, lured you to your death.' Cherry stepped over to Anthony and ran the blade of her knife lightly across his throat. 'How handsome you will look in my trophy room.' Cherry licked her lips.

'Where are your parents?' I whispered, unsure that I wanted an answer, and she went to the curtain at the far end, drawing it open from left to right to reveal another space as large as the room that we were in. This area was darkened but, as my eyes accustomed themselves, I saw two hides laid on a rack, the heads still attached.

'Dear God.'

'What the devil?' Anthony craned his head around. 'Oh God.'

'Excuse them if they don't get up,' Cherry said in apparent sincerity. 'Mr Appleton, Lady Thorn, may I introduce you to my parents.'

'You have tanned them.' I stared in horrible fascination.

'And a lovely job we made of them too.' Cherry smirked. 'It is more difficult than you might think, flaying people without ripping their skins. We practised for weeks on commoners who didn't matter.'

'Everybody matters.' I dug my nails into the knot but it was too tight for me to loosen.

'A pretty thought,' Cherry sneered, 'but if you had lived in London, you would know that there are swarming masses of people who do not matter in the least, not to each other or even to themselves. Some of our experiments got washed away when the water tower collapsed.'

'Hence the body parts found in town,' Anthony surmised. 'What about Mikah Cawn? The scalped man we found in the woods?'

'Was that his name? We never knew.'

'Nor especially cared.' Cherry shrugged her shoulders. 'He was just a source of hide to us.'

'It was my fault.' Charon ran a foot to describe an arc in the dust. 'We had a strict procedure for moving our subjects. Two of us should always be present, with one of us armed. This Crawn fellow was so weak I didn't think he could possibly resist and I thought what a lovely surprise it would be for Cherry if she came in to find I had skinned him.'

'What did you use to anaesthetise him?' I asked, and Charon chuckled at my silly girlish ways.

'We never anaesthetised them.' He held up his hands. 'Please don't misunderstand me, we did not do it to be cruel. In fact we tried chloroform once, but our subject died.'

'But why did you want them alive?' Anthony wondered in undisguised disgust.

'What better way of keeping a specimen fresh?' Cherry asked reasonably.

'Anyway...' Charon waved irritably at these interruptions to his narrative. 'I untied him and started to lead him to the dissection table when he seized something and cracked me so hard over the head the next thing I knew was Cherry throwing a bucket of water over me and our specimen gone. We hunted of course but the next we heard of him was that you two had found him in the woods.'

'Is that how you got your black eye?' Anthony asked.

'No,' I answered. 'That was another example of his incompetence. He tried to kidnap a prostitute, but her husband came to the rescue.'

'At least he tried,' Cherry defended her partner as if his attempt to abduct an innocent woman for the purposes of mutilating and murdering her were a praiseworthy assignment.

'But surely your parents were already dead when you were practising on your other victims?' I pointed out. 'They were dead when I met you.'

'Oh Violet,' Cherry looked at me pityingly. 'How can somebody who writes detective stories be so naïve? Not everything everybody tells you is true.'

'But where were they?' Anthony tried but failed to stretch.

'Why here of course.' Charon paced between us.

'We kept my parents in a storage bay from which the racks had been removed. Some of them have iron gates. They make good cages.' Cherry smiled. 'Charon lured them here, telling them I had been injured.' She giggled in girlish delight. 'At first they thought it was just a silly prank. It was most amusing to hear them scold me. They threatened to cancel my allowance. Then they tried to reason with me then...' She laughed gleefully. 'They saw us bring in other people and w...' She almost chocked in mirth. 'W-what we did and I ex-explained that it was exactly what we planned to do to them. Oh Lucifer, you should have heard them beg and weep and tell me what good parents they had been and how much they loved me.' Cherry stopped, as if puzzled by something. 'And I suppose they did,' she mused and for a moment she looked lost. 'Oh well,' she forced a smile. 'Heigh ho.'

'And this is what you have to show for all those deaths and the agonies you inflicted.' Anthony stared appalled from Cherry to the remains of her parents.

'They will make lovely fireside rugs,' Cherry purred, her sadness dispersing as quickly as it had gathered. 'Think of the joy I shall experience walking all over them, just as they walked over me all my life.'

'You said you loved them,' I protested.

'Dear me.' Cherry fanned her face. 'Did Cherry tell another fib?' She slapped the back of her hand. I could have done that for her and much harder. 'Naughty naughty Cherry.' Her expression hardened. 'I detested them.'

'Small wonder they sold the house without telling you,' Anthony told her with loathing.

'Do you still believe that?' Cherry barked in laughter. 'Not only did they tell me, but they took me to see the house they intended to buy in Sackwater. It was a beautiful house with excellent sea views.'

'Then why...' I began.

'But it was not my home.' She stamped a foot petulantly. 'Maccabee House is my home and always has been. They tried to tell me that it would become my home, but that is like telling a child that she will have a new mama.'

'You killed them for wanting to move house?' Anthony shook his head in disbelief and Cherry laughed lightly.

'Then I decided that it might be a good idea to sell the house after all, knowing that I could get it back, and so I used my feminine... money to get Wink to add a clause. The Brutons could have Maccabee House for a much-reduced price if they agreed to keep the contents intact for a year.' She picked a long, frizzled hair off her tongue. 'That way I would regain my home as...'

'But why would you get it back?' Anthony queried and she raised her eyes.

'Because the signature was forged. I told Wink that my father was housebound with a contagious disease but that I would get him to sign the document.

An unusual stipulation, I remembered Wink telling me and Gerrund.

'So those books on black magic and the specimens in jars…'

'All mine,' Cherry confirmed.

'I understand why you spun all those stories,' I said, though I was not sure that I did. 'But how could you possibly arrange to be in the Tennyson at the same time as Mrs Greaves, and in a room so close to hers?'

'People always look for complicated explanations when the simple ones are usually the true ones,' Charon chipped in.

'I read in *The Suffolk Trumpet* that she had been taken there because the other hospitals were full of cholera cases and the Tennyson had converted their mad department to treating head injuries.'

Gone from treatin' crackle-heads to cracked heads, I remembered the porter telling me.

'And so you made up a story about the Brutons attacking you,' Anthony surmised, and Cherry smirked.

'But you did have a head injury,' I objected, and she snorted.

'I did that with an iron pan,' Charon declared proudly.

'And damned near broke my skull.' She glared at him.

Another objection occurred to me. 'So how did you ensure that the Brutons were there at the same time as I was?'

'People always look…' Charon started to say but Cherry gagged him with a glance.

'I went to see the Greaves woman and told her that she was at least entitled to an apology and that she should not wait for you to deign to visit but should insist that you attended at noon.'

'I sent the telegram for her,' Charon announced.

'Well done,' Anthony sarcasmed.

'Then I wrote to the Brutons apologising for letting myself into their home and making such a scene and asking them to visit me at the same time so that I could explain my actions and ask for their forgiveness in person. They were obliging people – or she was at any rate – and so they obliged. They were a bit early and you were a bit late, which turned out well in the event.' Cherry put her little finger through a buttonhole in her cardigan. It was a different world when I had first seen her do that. 'I spent the whole time telling them what monsters they were and how she had tried to kill me.' Cherry smirked. 'It worked even better than I had hoped when she was leaving and told him in exasperation that it was a pity that she hadn't actually killed me.'

'But how could you hate your parents so much?' Anthony wondered. 'Addie said they were kind to her.'

'They were kind to everyone.' Cherry sniffed. 'And they were so damned nice to me, so lovely and loving and attentive, they suffocated me, and so...' She giggled girlishly. 'I suffocated them.' For a moment her expression seemed regretful. 'I wanted to mash up their faces like I did with the Brutons but I needed to keep their carcasses intact. In fact I called the Brutons *Mummy* and *Daddy* as I smashed their skulls. It made it...' She shivered in pleasure. 'So very much more delectable.'

'And the consummation was exquisite,' Charon grinned, 'on the floor between them, our flesh united with their flesh destroyed.'

'Bathing our congress in their blood,' Cherry gloated.

'Just what I would suspect from a grubby perverted slut like you,' Anthony retorted.

'You'll pay for those words,' Charon raised his fist.

'Is that what satisfies you?' Anthony asked Cherry. 'Courtship with a craven worm?'

'What did you call me?'

'Is your memory so poor? I called you a craven worm.'

At that Charon lashed out, a cracking blow to the side of the face. Anthony toppled sideways, his chair rocking, shook his head and straightened up again.

'Which proves exactly what I was saying.' His lower lip was split and bleeding. 'Only a coward would have to tie a man up before he could pluck up the courage to strike him. If I was unfettered you would not dare to lay a finger on me.'

Charon laughed. 'Who overpowered you in the first place?'

'Only because I tripped on the edge of the rug.'

'No you did not.'

'He did,' I said with as much conviction as I could muster. 'You pretend to be a gentleman, but you kneed him in the face like a contemptible cad.'

'Cad?' he repeated indignantly.

'A vulgar cad,' I reasserted.

'In any fair fight you would have been disqualified.' Anthony's words sprayed blood.

Charon piffed dismissively. 'We were not fighting to Queensberry rules.'

'No you were not,' Anthony agreed. 'But I was.'

'You had a cane.'

'I brandished it as any gentleman would when faced with a vulgar thug.'

I was not sure what my friend hoped to gain by antagonising our enemy, but I could do nothing other than support him. 'Whereas you brawl like a street slug.'

Charon pulled his arm back ready to slap me with the back of his hand.

'Go on,' I taunted him though, looking at his face contorted in fury, I had a strong suspicion that he would. 'Strike a trussed-up lady.' I twisted my head to look at Cherry. 'You must be so proud of your cheap paramour.'

'Give me the knife.' Charon held out his hand, and I watched in alarm as Cherry handed it to him. 'Now we'll see what you are made of.' He strode back to Anthony and behind him and brought the knife down with a ruthless slash.

'No,' I cried aghast.

'I have only cut his bonds.'

Anthony brought his hands round to the front. 'He has,' he confirmed, rubbing his wrists.

'Pity,' Cherry sighed.

'Now we'll see which of us is the man.' Charon slammed the knife onto the mantlepiece and raised his fists as Anthony stood unsteadily, massaging his legs.

'We will,' he agreed, 'once I have regained the circulation in my limbs.' Anthony tottered a few steps sideways towards the middle of the room. 'Which may take a while.' He tottered back, steadying himself on the chair and leaning over it. 'If you could kindly…' His voice failed and he seemed about to swoon.

'Sit down, darling,' I called, that term of endearment coming naturally to me now, but Anthony shook his head and whispered something.

Charon stepped towards him. 'What?'

'I just…' Anthony grasped the arms of the chair and swung it in a wide arc, catching him with a loud thwack on the side of the head.

345

Charon staggered backwards but, as Anthony attempted to bring the chair back for another blow, his opponent snatched at a leg and wrenched it from him.

'Cad, am I?' He threw the chair backwards. 'I'll show you how a gentleman fights.' His left fist jabbed into Anthony's face and Anthony tottered sideways. A swinging right hook cracked under his jaw and he fell, unconscious before he landed heavily in a crumpled heap on the floor. 'So much for your big stuck-up talk now, you puny fob.' His foot lashed out and Anthony's head jerked back.

'Stop it,' Cherry shouted and, for one moment, I thought she was showing compassion until she added, 'we don't want him too damaged.'

I pulled uselessly at the rope that bound me. Anthony lay still though I could see from the blood frothing out of his nose and mouth that he was still breathing.

'And what of me? Will you batter me to the ground?'

Charon sneered but made no reply. He took the knife from the mantlepiece and handed it to Cherry. 'Cut the rope,' he said, suddenly the master after his pugilistic display, 'and we'll see how she likes a good slapping.' I felt the rope slacken and fall away and the blood rush burning into my numbed hands as he put the knife back.

I leaned forward but was checked by Cherry gripping the back of my dress. 'Why don't you show her what a real man is made of?'

'There is more to being a real man than behaving like a savage,' I retorted as Charon came close.

He was standing over me now, so close I could smell the sweat on him. It was an act of desperation and would almost certainly do nothing but antagonise him but, since he intended to defile and murder me anyway, what did

I have to lose? I had unhinged the knife on my charm bracelet, and if I could hurt him at least it might put him off one of his intentions. I unclipped the bracelet and grasped the knife. The silver blade was only about half an inch long and I was repelled by the idea but, if I could poke it into his eye... I jabbed upwards but he knocked my arm and I struck much lower than I had intended, the blade sinking into the side of his neck.

Charon winced and put a hand up as if he had been stung by a bee. There might be one more chance before they overpowered me. I pulled the knife out and was adjusting my grip when there was a fountain of dark red blood. It sagged but a moment later rose again, pumping between his fingers over his shoulder and into my face.

Cherry screamed, pulled her hands out and stepped backwards.

'What have you done?'

'His carotid artery.' The words came from me automatically. 'I didn't mean to.'

Charon looked at us both in horror. 'Do something.'

'Give me your handkerchief.'

He fumbled in his pocket and I snatched it from him to clamp over the wound, but the white cotton was instantly soaked and the blood flowed unabated.

'Sit down.'

He stumbled back to collapse into a chair.

'Find something else,' I commanded Cherry, but she stood staring in horrible fascination. 'Get me a cloth... anything. I cannot let go.'

In the slowing down of time that only occurs in nightmares, I looked towards Anthony. The bubbling of air through blood had stopped and his eyes were half open but staring unseeing towards me.

'Oh sweet Jesus, no.'

Cherry pulled off her baggy woollen cardigan and held it out dumbly. It would do no good, I knew, but I crushed it over the handkerchief. The blood was splattering in a pool on the floor and showing no sign of slowing.

Charon clawed at my wrist as if to pull my hand away, but his strength was ebbing fast. His lips moved and he gasped something inaudible before he slumped.

'You have killed him.' Cherry's words next were scarcely audible either, but she repeated them in a shriek. 'You filthy bitch.'

She rushed to the mantlepiece. In that instant I considered my options. I could not hope to get there before her and there was nothing I could do for my poor darling Anthony. I dropped the handkerchief, turned and fled.

'Got it,' Cherry cried triumphantly, and I had no doubt as to what she was referring.

Flinging open the door, I ran out into the drying room. There was nowhere to hide there and nothing that might serve as a shield or a weapon.

'Think you can get away, bitch?' I heard Cherry rushing up behind me as I squeezed through the doorway. I rammed my shoulder against the door in an attempt to slam it shut but it was wedged immovably. She was gaining fast when I glanced back to see her hurtling in my wake brandishing the knife at head level.

We were in the tanning hall. The stench made me cough and retch but there was nothing I could do about that. If I went outside she would be upon me, with her longer legs, before I had gone ten yards.

I stood behind the full tank, hoping the fumes would not overpower me, but, as I gasped for breath, I could feel my head starting to swim in the methane miasma. Cherry came up, on the other side of the tank.

'You killed my lover,' she panted, though she can hardly have thought that I would have forgotten.

'I am sorry.'

'Sorry? Sorry? Sorry?' she repeated the word with increasing incredulity, volume and pitch. 'Have you any idea how long it took me to seduce that man, entice him away from his loving wife and family, to convince him of the righteousness of my cause? It could take me ages to replace him.'

'It was an accident,' I tried to explain. 'I just meant to hurt him.'

'Well you did that all right,' she snarled. 'And I mean to hurt you too, but your death will not be an accident.' She took two strides along the side of the tank and I took three away, stumbling over a loose brick.

Odd how a simple trip saved the day, Anthony said in a different world a long time ago.

I stumbled again, deliberately this time, and fell to my hands and knees, crawling backwards as if trying to escape but feeling the floor blindly with my right hand.

Where is it? The floor was smooth. *Don't let it end like this.*

Cherry was almost upon me before I found the brick, but it was not as loose as I had imagined and I felt my fingers being crushed as I pushed them down into the gap on one side of it. For some reason I thought of Jane. She had gone through untold trials and never given up. Defying the pain, I forced my fingers down until I felt them gain purchase.

'Listen to my voice, bitch. It is the last you will ever hear.'

As Cherry bent to put the knife to my throat, my fingers closed around that brick, tugging it up and free, and I swung with all my strength, crashing it into her temple. She toppled onto me and, as I heaved with all my strength, fell away sideways.

Scrambling to my feet, I snatched up the knife and tossed it splashing into the tank. Cherry's eyes were open, and I hoped I had not killed her, but then decided that I did not care if I had. I was not callous by nature but, if she recovered, she would face the noose or a lifetime in an institution for the criminally insane and I was not sure which she deserved or which was worse.

I hurried back to the office. Anthony was on his feet staring perplexed at the gory soaked corpse of Charon.

'You are alive,' I cried. 'Oh, thank God.'

He looked towards me. 'Violet, my darling, what have they done to you?'

I saw myself in the mirror, clothes torn and hanging loose about me, hair wild, eyes wilder and all of me splattered.

'It is not my blood.'

'Thank heavens. But what happened?'

'I stabbed him with my charm bracelet.'

Anthony ran a hand over his brow. 'Are you all right?'

'A little bruised and battered but yes. And you?'

'The same.' His face was caked in blood and his left eye almost closed with swelling. 'What about Cherry?'

'I knocked her out cold and threw the knife away.'

'And, as usual, I did nothing.'

'I was not attracted to you for your pugilistic skills.'

Anthony smiled painfully with a split lower lip. 'So you are attracted to me then?'

I looped my arm around his. 'We need to get out of here, Mr Appleby.'

And, half-supporting each other, we stumbled out past the drying racks and into the tanning room.

'Where is she?' I looked at where I had left Cherry, and back at Anthony. There was a rustling, and it was only out of the corner of my eye that I saw Cherry rush towards us, a long-bladed knife in her hand.

'Look out,' I cried uselessly as she plunged it into Anthony's back.

Anthony looked at me in puzzlement and then, as he realised what had happened, aghast. 'She has killed me,' he cried, falling to one knee. 'Save yourself, Violet.' And he toppled, face-down on the floor.

'Anthony, my darling.' This was too cruel even by God's standards, to give Anthony back only to snatch him away again.

Cherry laughed and bent to retrieve her knife, but I lashed out with the back of my fist and caught her on the side of the face.

'Damn you.' Cherry wiped the corner of her mouth and looked at the red stain on her hand. 'That hurt.' Her hand shot out and snatched a fistful of my hair, hauling me to that one full tank. 'Haven't tried this before,' she cackled, 'tanning a living person, but don't worry...' She forced me to bend over it. 'You won't be alive very long.'

Dobbin her, a voice said.

I buckled at the knees and that gave me all the space I needed to rise again suddenly and flick my head backwards to smash it into her face.

Cherry gasped, let go of me and stepped back to clutch her nose. I grasped her hair and spun her around and, with both hands on her shoulders, pushed. She toppled backwards and, with a splash, into the tank.

Anthony was getting to his knees as I ran to him and the knife was still sticking out of his back. I had been told a hundred times by Romulus never to take a knife out of a victim but I could not bear to see Anthony like that and so I pulled. It was quite a job to get it out. The blade must have wedged in his shoulder bone and that, I imagined, was what saved him.

Anthony coughed. 'Thank you.' He got to his feet.

Cherry was wading across the tank towards us, covered in vile noxious slime. 'I will kill you both,' she vowed hoarsely, but the fumes must have overcome her for she stopped and swayed and splashed down into the vile sludge.

'We can't let her die,' I cried.

'I suppose not.' Anthony made his way to the far side of the tank and hauled, gasping with pain and the effort, on the lever. 'It's too stiff.'

'Let me help.'

Together we heaved and then, with a loud gurgle, the surface broke into a giant whirlpool. The contents drained much more quickly and violently than either of us had expected. Cherry raised her head and reached out to us imploringly and I would have clambered in had Anthony not stopped me. Cherry's head sank, only her hair still on the surface until, with a sucking sound, she disappeared, swirling down the drain.

'Oh dear God!' I watched in horror, but she was gone and there was nothing we could do.

Only as we were leaving did Anthony indicate a rack of knives, presumably intended for trimming hides, that was affixed to the wall. One knife was missing, doubtless the one that I had pulled out of my friend.

There was a full moon when we stepped outside and countless stars as we staggered away from that place and back down Tannery Lane, but I had forgotten that you cannot walk away from nightmares. They follow you like the hounds of hell and, sooner or later, they track you down and, if you do not turn to face them, they will destroy you.

34

THE RETURN OF THE DEAD

GERRUND WAS late with my fountain. 'Was there a problem?' I asked, and he cleared his throat but then appeared to change his mind.

Ignoring his disapproval, I measured my absinthe into a glass.

'Thank you, Gerrund. That will be all for this evening.'

Yet still he hovered. 'I know it is not my place, milady, but…'

'I know what you intend to say,' I broke in more sharply than I had intended. 'And you are correct. It is not your place.'

As the man who fetched my bottles from the cellar, Gerrund knew better than any how my consumption had increased recently.

'Very good, milady.'

For the first time in all the years I had known him I saw hurt in my man's eyes and I would have apologised but that was not my place either.

Damn your places, my brain fulminated.

'Before you go, Gerrund.' He was almost out of the room.

'Yes, milady?'

'I am sorry I was sharp with you.' For the first time I found myself unable to meet his gaze. 'I know you mean well.'

'Thank you, milady,' Gerrund said and, when I did raise my eyes, I saw hurt in his.

I knew without question that he was right, but the Green Fairy was waiting for me.

Just one more, she coaxed, *for old times' sake.*

I turned the tap and thought I heard a sigh as Gerrund left the room.

Usually I sipped slowly to savour the taste and the effects. That night I drank steadily.

And too quickly, Ruby censured me, and this from a woman who had been known to consume her absinthe straight from the bottle. *I have a head for alcohol.* She tossed a large vodka down her throat. *But you let her whisper regrets in your ears.*

I sniffed. *What is that terrible smell?*

Ruby shifted uneasily. *Must fly.* And she did, whisking away through the closed door.

'Good evening, Violet.' A voice spoke in my ear and I did not need to turn to recognise it.

'You are dead.'

'Am I?' There was a low chuckle. 'Clearly you do not learn from experience.' Her breath was cold on my cheek and foul in my nostrils. 'Seeing somebody submerging is not the same thing as witnessing their death.' A hand went to my shoulder. 'Why do you think they have not found my body?' The hand stroked my neck. Its flesh was moist and soft and I did not dare to look down at it.

'You are dead,' I insisted, and I knew that I could prove it to myself by looking up at our reflections in the mantle mirror, but I could only stare into the swirling green clouds.

'Perhaps I am.' Her stench was choking me. 'You think that is choking?' A hollow rasping laugh. 'Oh, Violet, you have so much to learn. This…' The fingers tightened. 'This is choking you.' And the other hand gripped my throat too. I was being throttled. I grasped the hands but mine sank deep into them and, when I tried to pull them away, I was left with gouts of fleshy slime.

The bones were digging in, and I could not breathe. I felt myself hot and dizzy and knew that I would pass out in a matter of seconds. I hurled the glass with all my might into the fire, the scarcely diluted spirit whooshing in the flaring flames.

'You are dead,' I shouted, flinging my arm to sweep my absinthe fountain off the table, sending it shattering to the floor.

I felt the grip loosen and rose to my feet. There was only one woman in that mirror. I spun around to find myself what I had been all too often, alone.

'Are you all right, milady?' Gerrund rushed into the room, taking the scene of destruction in at a glance.

'Oh, Gerrund, I am lost.'

'No, milady.' Gerrund took me in his arms and held me very gently.

'You do not understand.'

'I understand all too well.' The stink of decay had been replaced by the perfume of fresh coal tar soap. 'I was lost once.' Gerrund took my shoulders and held me at arms' length. 'And that is how I know…' He fixed my gaze with his. 'You have found your way and – if I might be so presumptuous – with the right man at your side, you will never lose it again.'

Romulus came with a horsebox and, with him driving, we rode together to the end of the mews, where we lowered the ramp to lead the horse out.

'You can cope with her now,' Romulus said. 'If I go with you he will know that I bought her.'

'God bless you, Rommy.' I kissed his cheek.

'We will see you tomorrow at Suthy Hall,' he said. 'Jane is looking forward enormously to seeing you.'

'And I her.' I gave him another kiss.

'And bring Anthony,' he said as he climbed back into the driver's seat.

'But we are not...'

Why in the name of Christendom are you not? Ruby and Hefty spoke like a Greek chorus.

'Bring him,' Romulus called and clicked his tongue.

'I'll think about it.'

I took the halter and led the horse along the cobbled lane. She walked with me placidly and watched trustingly as I tied her to an iron hoop in the wall before knocking.

'Go away,' I heard so, taking the hint, I opened the door.

Friendless was on his wooden chair, slumped over his table. 'You,' he said without enthusiasm.

'Hello Friendless.'

His face was gaunt and I wondered if he had been eating or even had anything that he could eat.

'I int gooin' to replace Old Queeny,' he told me.

'No horse ever could replace her.' I stepped in, leaving the door open wide. 'I want your advice.'

'What sort of advise?' he asked suspiciously.

'I have a horse, and I don't know what to do with her.' I clicked my tongue and, perfectly on cue, she poked her head around the doorway. 'The owner was going to take her to the slaughterhouse,' I said, shocked at the cruelty of this fictional man. 'But I bought her off him.'

'How much?'

'Hardly anything.'

He walked all around her. 'She's a fine-looking mare.' He patted her hindquarters. 'And good temprement. She make a not bad cab horse if I int retired but I am… retired.'

'I wondered if you could possibly look after her for the night.' I hesitated. 'I know that it was Old Queeny's stall.'

'She wint mind. She's very kind, is Old Queeny.'

'It is only two or three nights, until I find a new owner for her.'

'Might take a bit longer.' He ran a hand over her back and she nuzzled up to him.

'It might well.'

'Maybe I can try her in the shafts, just so she's ready when you sell her.'

'That is generous of you.'

'What's her name?'

'I do not think she has one. What would you suggest?'

Friendless plucked a stem of straw from a bale, chewed it up and swallowed the cud with apparent satisfaction. 'Princess,' he decided.

'That is an excellent name.' I started to move away but I do not believe that Friendless noticed. He was stroking her neck and murmuring, 'Dint you fret, Princess. You'll be safe here and I'll sing to you. Fancy a knob o' cheese, darlin'?'

Alfred came to tell me they had found Cherry's body in the sewage farm and, over a coffee, we spoke of her and how sceptical he had been of her story.

'And then I was racked by guilt when it appeared that she had been telling the truth.'

'She was all too plausible.' I stirred in another lump of sugar.

'Remember that incident in the hall?' Alfred coloured.

'How could I forget,' I teased. 'And I am still not sure who was kissing who.'

'You know perfectly well…'

I touched his arm. 'I am sorry, Alfred. That was in poor taste.'

'When she kissed me…' Alfred cleared his throat. 'She put a hand down there.' He indicated so vaguely it could have been his stomach or his knee, but I knew what part he meant.

'I saw you jump but I thought you were just taken by surprise at the kiss.'

'I put it down to her confused emotions.' He fiddled with his signet ring. 'Beats me what Charon saw in her, so straight and thin with all that flaming hair. She reminded me of a vespa just after it has been struck.'

'Now that I think of it,' I told Alfred, 'the young man at the mortuary jumped too.'

Alfred snorted. 'So I was not the sole object of her desire. I am cut to the quick.'

Use his cravat as a tourniquet, Hefty advised, but I was never sure whereabouts the quick could be found.

Anthony came often, sometimes several times a day and sometimes only once, but on those occasions he stayed all day long.

We were sitting side by side at my window one morning when he shifted uneasily. 'Violet.' He twiddled his thumbs. 'You know that I would never want to hurt you. So I hope you will not be upset about what I am going to say.'

I shifted even more uneasily. Would this be when he told me that he was bored with my company? I knew that he was friends with my friend Hettie Granger, and she had not been to see me for weeks, claiming to be working on a commission in Ipswich. Had they fallen in love? I could not blame either of them for they were both attractive, loveable people.

'I will try not to.' I steeled myself.

'I have been thinking about your problems with your writing,' he began tentatively. 'It seems to me that you are losing interest in your fictional characters because their adventures seem – and this is where I may unintentionally insult you – trifling.'

Trifling? Inspector Havelock Hefty, Scotland Yard's premier detective, slammed his fist on the table though not a cup rattled on its saucer. *Prancing about like a ninny on a stage, that is trifling.*

But Anthony was still talking. 'When such extraordinary things have happened to you in real life.'

Unaware until then that I had been holding my breath, I breathed again.

'It has occurred to me that their adventures are...'

Wonderful, Ruby urged.

'Trivial,' I concluded.

Trivial? For the first time since I had met her Ruby Gibson, extraordinary investigator and lady adventuress, was flustered.

'All those awful events connected with Martha Ryan for example,' Anthony continued.

'I cannot write about those.'

'Somebody should record what happened, and who better than you, who actually knows?'

'The newspapers got a great many of the details wrong,' I conceded. 'And there was that dreadful shilling shocker.'

'Quite so.' Anthony warmed to his theme. 'I have even thought of a name for it. How about *The Horror of Haglin House?*'

I mulled over the name, for he had found one of my many weak spots, my fondness for alliterative titles. 'I could have a go, I suppose.'

But what about us? Ruby and Hefty cried in unison.

I'm sure you will manage to get into it somehow, I reassured them and, clearly mollified, Hefty set about taking samples of soot from my chimney while Ruby popped open a magnum of Bollinger, pouring a glass for herself, me, Anthony and even Havelock Hefty.

'Think about it.' Unaware of her largesse with my champagne, Anthony drained his coffee and rose. 'Must be off. My aunt is threatening to cut my allowance if I don't visit her more often.'

'Will you come back tomorrow?'

'This evening, if I might.'

'That would be nice.'

Nice does not mean anything, Miss Kidd decreed.

It certainly does not mean you, I told her nicely.

As I accompanied him into the hall I noticed that my shoelace was undone and bobbed to retie it. Anthony put out a hand to help me up and, as I took it, I gazed into his beautiful Cadbury's chocolate eyes and found myself saying, 'Will you marry me?' I tried to make it sound like a joke so that, if he rejected me, we could still be friends, but Anthony gazed into my not quite as beautiful blue and green eyes and said, 'Violet, I am shocked.'

'That I proposed?' I lined up my lies in preparation.

'That it took you so long.' Anthony smiled. 'I was reluctant to propose in case everybody said I was a gold digger, though I know you would not have thought it. Of course I will marry you, Lady Violet Elizabeth Antoinette Cordelia Thorn.' He hauled me up and into his arms.

'Hearty congratulations to you both.' Gerrund materialised more unexpectedly than any of my characters could have managed and Agnust came heavily along the hallway.

'She'll make you a poor wife,' she assured Anthony, 'but he'll be the best husband you're ever likely to snare.'

'Thank you both,' I laughed.

'And you must all come to the wedding,' Anthony declared.

'All?' I puzzled, but I suspected that I already knew what he meant.

'Why Agnust, Gerrund, Miss Ruby Gibson and Inspector Havelock Hefty,' Anthony announced in all seriousness.

Hefty was blowing his nose.

I love a happy ending, Ruby sniffed.

But this is not a happy ending. Shamelessly, in front of the servants, the future Mrs Appleton kissed the present Mr Appleton and, as we held each other close, I had not a shadow of doubt when I told my characters, *It is a happy beginning.*